THE
ULTIMATE
EGOIST

Theodore Sturgeon, age eighteen
December 1936, aboard the Schoolship Annapolis

THE
ULTIMATE
EGOIST

Volume I:

The Complete Stories of

Theodore Sturgeon

Edited by
Paul Williams

Forewords by
Ray Bradbury, Arthur C. Clarke,
and Gene Wolfe

North Atlantic Books
Berkeley, California

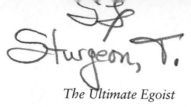

The Ultimate Egoist

Published by
North Atlantic Books
P.O. Box 12327
Berkeley, California 94712

Cover art: *Amok Harvest* © Jacek Yerka 1993
Cover and book design by Paula Morrison
Typeset by Catherine Campaigne

Printed in the United States of America by Malloy Lithographing

The Ultimate Egoist is sponsored by the Society for the Study of Native Arts and Sciences, a nonprofit educational corporation whose goals are to develop an educational and crosscultural perspective linking various scientific, social, and artistic fields; to nurture a holistic view of arts, sciences, humanities, and healing; and to publish and distribute literature on the relationship of mind, body, and nature.

Library of Congress Cataloging-in-Publication Data

Sturgeon, Theodore.
    The ultimate egoist : the complete stories of Theodore Sturgeon / edited by Paul Williams : forewords by Ray Bradbury, Arthur C. Clarke, and Gene Wolfe.
        p.   cm.
    Contents: v. 1.   1937–1940.
    ISBN 1-55643-182-1 (v. 1)
    I. Williams, Paul.   II. Title.
PS3569.T875U44   1994
S13',54—dc20

94-38047
CIP

2   3   4   5   6   7   8   9 / 98   97   96   95

EDITOR'S NOTE

THEODORE HAMILTON STURGEON was born February 26, 1918 on Staten Island in New York City, and died May 8, 1985 in Eugene, Oregon. This is the first of a series of volumes that will collect all of his short fiction of all types and all lengths shorter than a novel. The volumes and the stories within the volumes are organized chronologically by order of composition (insofar as it can be determined). This earliest volume contains stories written between the end of 1937 and the beginning of 1940. Some are being published here for the first time; many others are appearing for the first time in book form.

For invaluable assistance in the preparation of this volume, the editor would like to thank Noël Sturgeon and the Theodore Sturgeon Literary Trust, Marion Sturgeon, Jayne Sturgeon, Ralph Vicinanza, Lindy Hough, Richard Grossinger, Debbie Notkin, Tom Whitmore, Samuel R. Delany, Dixon Chandler, Marty Traynor, Stephen Pagel, Jeannie Trizzino, Ray Bradbury, Arthur C. Clarke, Gene Wolfe, David G. Hartwell, Jonathan Lethem, Charles N. Brown, Judith Merril, Eric Van, T. V. Reed, Cindy Lee Berryhill, Gordon Van Gelder, Sam Moskowitz, Robert Lichtman, Donna Nassar, Robert Silverberg, Russell Galen, John Clute, and all of you who have expressed your interest and support.

My thanks also to the staffs of North Atlantic Books and Publishers Group West for their enthusiasm and their efforts on behalf of this challenging project. Succeeding volumes in this series will be appearing regularly until the collection is completed.

CONTENTS

Three Forewords

by Ray Bradbury,

Arthur C. Clarke, and Gene Wolfe

ABOUT THEODORE STURGEON

by Ray Bradbury

PERHAPS THE BEST way I can tell you what I think of a Theodore Sturgeon story is to explain with what diligent interest, in the year 1940, I split every Sturgeon tale down the middle and fetched out its innards to see what made it function. At that time I had not sold one story, I was 20, I was feverish for the vast secrets of successful writers. I looked upon Sturgeon with a secret and gnawing jealousy. And jealousy, it must be admitted, is the most certain symptom a writer can know to tell him of another author's superiority. The worst thing you can say of a writer's style is that it bored you; the most complimentary thing I can think to say of Sturgeon is that I hated his damned, efficient, witty guts. And yet because he had the thing for which I was looking, originality (always rare in the pulps), I was forced, in an agony of jealousy, to return again and again to his stories, to dissect, to pull apart, to re-examine the bones. Whether or not I ever really discovered Sturgeon's secret is a moot question. It is pretty hard to dissect laughing gas with a scalpel. Wit and spontaneity are far too evasive, they are brilliant gaseous material all too soon exploded and vanished. You put your hand up, as to a pulsation of fireworks in a summer sky, cry "There!" and pull back, for even while you tried to touch the wonder it blew away.

Sturgeon has many of the attributes of a magnificent firecracker string, ending in a loud 12-incher. There are sparklers and wondrous snakes and Vesuvian cones of invention, humor and charm in his stories. And before essaying your journey through this book and its attendant wonders, it may well reward you to have your glands x-rayed. For it is evident that Mr. Sturgeon writes with his glands. And if you do not read with your glands functioning healthily, then this is no book for you.

Now, writing with the glands is a precarious occupation. Many a good writer has tripped over his gut, you might say, and plunged to a horrible death, vanishing in writhing messes of tripe, down within the maw of his black monstrously evil typewriter. This is not true of Sturgeon, for it is evident that his viscera, at midnight, cast a most incredible glow upon all nearby objects. In a world of mock-pomp and towering hypocrisy it is wonderful to find stories written not only with the large enwrinkled object above the eyes, but most particularly with the zestful ingredients of the peritoneal cavity.

Above all, Sturgeon seems to love writing, delighting in the swiftly paced and happy tale. True, some of the tales enclosed herein are not monuments of gaiety, but, perversely, are cold green edifices of fear. This book is to be recommended by those blackly unscrupulous physicians who wish to dispatch such violences of warmth and coldness to their patients that influenza is the inevitable result. The extremes of temperature herein are incredible. "It," a very serious tale, an unsmiling mask of a story, was evidently written in a black refrigerator at two in the morning. "Brat,"[1] on the other hand, was culled from a daisy field on a hot summer's day. "Shottle Bop"[1] and "The Ultimate Egoist" reside in some half-twilight, speckled here and there with flashes of sunshine, deepening into shadow at the last.

---

[1] These stories will be found in Volume Two. Mr. Bradbury, on being asked to write a foreword for this volume, said he felt he could not improve on the introduction he wrote for Theodore Sturgeon's first collection, *Without Sorcery* (1948), and suggested we reprint that essay here. We concur, and have done so.

I have never met Mr. Sturgeon, but his letters have been exploding in my mailbox for some time now, and from several days of theorizing, I see Mr. Sturgeon as a child run off from home on a spring day never to return, to take refuge and nourishment under a bridge, a bright small troll with whisking pen and ink and white paper, listening to the thunder of a timeless world overhead. And this incredulous troll, under his roaring bridge, unable to see the secret world rushing by above, has effected his own concepts of that hidden civilization. It might be 1928 up there, or 2432 or 1979, who knows? Part of his picture is drawn from a life he has guessed with hilarious accuracy from the sounds of the footfalls above, the clickings and talkings of people passing on the high paths; the rest is pure fantasy and invention, a giant carnival distorted but all the more real for its unreality. We see ourselves caught in grotesque gesture, in mid-act.

If you ask for the names of those stories most agreeable to me I would select "Poker Face,"[1] a tale with a nice, if coincidental, irony and some very humorous writing in it, "Microcosmic God"[1] for its fascinating generation on generation of Neoterics plus its unselfconscious hero, plus the Breather stories for their screwball antics. I also believe that "It," partaking of a locale all too often neglected by American writers, will be with us for a good number of years as one of the finest weird tales in the genre.

Some day I hope to meet Sturgeon. I shall take me a walking trip across the midwest and the east, down country roads and along sycamore lanes, stopping by every old stone bridge to listen and look and wait, and perhaps one summer afternoon, in the silence of which such days partake, I shall look down and beneath a shale arch I shall find Mr. Sturgeon busily writing away with pen and ink. It will be hard to find him. For I have not as yet figured out what sort of bridge he prefers, the tall metal soaring architectural bridges like those of Brooklyn and San Francisco, or the little, forgotten, moss-covered creek bridges in home town ravines where mosquitos sing and the silence is green. When I have figured the two halves of his split writing personality I shall start my trek. And if it is night when I come upon some lone bridge somewhere I shall recognize his hiding place by the pure shining glow of his viscera making a light you can see across the furthest night meadow and hill.

In the meantime, I compliment Mr. Sturgeon by concluding that I still hate him.

ABOUT THEODORE STURGEON

by Arthur C. Clarke

THOUGH I DON'T suppose I met Ted Sturgeon for more than a half dozen times, he is a person of whom I still have very warm memories. I was, of course, familiar with his work long before I made my first visit to the United States in 1952, and he was one of the authors I was most anxious to meet.

Our first encounter is still remarkably clear in my mind. It was at his own home, shared with his wife Marion and their beautiful little son Robin. I can still remember two of the stories he told me. The first is how his stepfather had discovered the precious hoard of science fiction magazines Ted had hidden in the attic, and had carefully reduced all of them to confetti. The job, Ted added, must have taken him hours...

The other incident is more heartwarming, and now that both Ted and Bob Heinlein are gone, I can safely report it. Once, when Ted was even more broke than usual, Bob sent him not only a cheque but something even more valuable—plots for a half dozen good stories. It would be interesting to know which of these Ted was able to use.

I have just realized, rather belatedly, another Sturgeon/Heinlein connection. Ted's original name was Edward Hamilton *Waldo*—and of course the word Waldo, for a remote-controller, was made famous by Heinlein. (I also wonder if Ted's amendment of his first two names was made to avoid confusion with the famous "Universe Saver" of the 1930s pulps.)

As I wander back through my memories, the titles of many of

Ted's stories are appearing in a kind of slow flashback. "Mewhu's Jet," though a minor piece, has long intrigued me as a kind of precursor to *E.T.* (For my own involvement in this tangled story, via Satyajit Ray's never-produced "The Alien," see the recent *Life & Death of Peter Sellers.*) "The Hurkle Is a Happy Beast" is also one of my favourites—even though I'm a dog- and not a cat-person.

Ted's stories have an emotional impact unmatched by almost any other writer (though two entirely different examples now come to my mind: Ray Bradbury and Harlan Ellison). "Thunder and Roses" is a classic example, and I've just realized, without the slightest embarrassment, that I used the same theme in "The Last Command." It must have taken some courage for an editor to publish so downbeat a story during the depths of the Cold War, and I'm sure it must have evoked protests from the "Better Dead than Red" brigade.

For such a gentle and sweet-natured person, Ted had a talent for provoking controversy. Just as "Thunder and Roses" must have infuriated pathological patriots, so "The World Well Lost" enraged incurable homophobes—who, he told me, mailed him lavender-scented letters. And I won't even mention "Affair with a Green Monkey" or *Some of Your Blood,* which I'm sure he wrote just to see what he could get away with...

Of all Ted's stories, "The Man Who Lost the Sea" is my favourite, and the one which had the greatest impact on me, for personal as well as literary reasons. I too lost the sea for many years, and only rediscovered it in later life. "Transit of Earth," which I consider my best story, owes much to Ted's, even though the treatment is completely different. I feel sure I had Ted's brilliantly-described skin-diving episode in mind when I incorporated a hair-raising incident from my own career.

"The Man Who Lost the Sea" is a complex, stream-of-consciousness story which may go over the heads of many readers. (Did Ted anticipate the New Wave?) But perseverance will be rewarded. This small masterpiece was anthologized as one of the best short stories of its year, in *any* category—not only science fiction. I can't even reread it without the skin crawling on the back of my neck.

One final comment: I have just discovered that though Ted's date of birth was a year after mine, I've already lived a decade longer than he did.

What might he have done. . .

ABOUT THEODORE STURGEON

by Gene Wolfe

THREE DAYS BEFORE my fortieth birthday, I was as sick as I have ever been in my life; and on my fortieth birthday Rosemary took me to the doctor, who told her to take me to a hospital. She did, and I was shoved into a wheelchair, wheeled rapidly into the Contagious Disease Ward, and ensconced in a small private room without a door. I had the mumps.

Doctors shot me full of antibiotics, and by the next day I had discovered myself in possession of a television set and a remote control. Ever since TV was a big black box with a tiny screen, I had been working forty-two and a half hours a week and cutting the grass and writing in my spare time; I had never watched daytime TV. That second day in the hospital I did, and it was marvelous. There were soaps and amusing game shows and a rerun of *The Dick Van Dyke Show* at twelve thirty—I still remember the time slot. On the third day I grabbed my remote full of happy anticipation and convalescent optimism.

And it was just the same, with the sole exception of Dick Van Dyke. They might have been rerunning the previous day's programs, and every ten minutes or so I thought they really were. Rosemary came to visit me, and I begged her to bring me something to read. Anything!

God, it is said, arranges everything for a purpose—and He's often real mad at us when He does. Rosemary brought me *Sturgeon Is Alive and Well . . .*, that wonderful, wonderful book.

My eyes have been deteriorating since the sixth grade. My right (good) eye is extremely nearsighted. My left (bad) eye is nearly blind.

When Rosemary had gone, I read Sturgeon until I could no longer see the print, and wept tears of eyestrain. I tried to watch daytime TV instead and wept again, knowing that there were stories of unexampled excellence waiting in the book I held, inaccessible. When I could read again, I read "To Here and the Easel," "Brownshoes," and "It's You!" I read "Jorry's Gap," a story I envied Sturgeon so much I felt like chopping him to bits at the end of it. I read "Take Care of Joey," "Crate," and "The Girl Who Knew What They Meant," and when I could read no longer, I calculated the number of words Sturgeon had required to tell "Slow Sculpture." I have the book before me, and the calculation is in the white space at the end of the story; nine thousand, nine hundred and seventy-five was my final estimate.

I wept, as I have said, and yelled at the crazy old man who wandered into my room every few hours carrying who knows what contagious disease, and tried to shoo away the beautiful little children who came hoping (I hope) that I would read them a story, carrying who knows what contagious diseases and in grave danger of catching mine.

I first met Sturgeon when I was in junior high school. I had fallen and hurt my leg, and for ten days or so my mother drove me to school, returning at three-thirty to bring me home. One afternoon there was a paperback book open on the car seat beside her, the book she had brought to read while she waited for school to let out. I'd seen Buck Rogers and Flash Gordon in the Sunday comics, and knew what the futuristic city on its cover portended; because I often got the mysteries my mother read in job lots when she was through with them, I asked her whether I could have this book—this science fiction book, though I did not know the words then—when she was finished. She told me she didn't like it much, so I could have it right away.

The first story I read was "Microcosmic God" by Theodore Sturgeon. It has sometimes occurred to me that it has all been downhill from there.

Later, after I discovered the pulps, I read "Killdozer!" three times, beginning each new reading as soon as I finished the previous one;

and though every story I read in those days might as well have carried the byline "A. Grownup," eventually I began to seek out stories by Sturgeon and few others.

Until at last, when I myself was a published author of science fiction and considered myself an important one, I had dinner with Theodore Sturgeon. You know how the rest of this goes, I'm sure; you know all that I wanted to say, and that I said none of it and pushed my chair back at the end of the meal wishing that someone would chop me to bits.

Still later (only last year, in fact) Joe Mayhew gave me the Sturgeon Project's pamphlet *Argyll,* containing Sturgeon's childhood memoir. Both are dead now, Edward Hamilton Waldo and William Dicky "Argyll" Sturgeon, the unhappy stepfather whom Edward Waldo so bitterly hated. Theodore Sturgeon, on the other hand, has only gone away, leaving for us the best part of himself: his love, his wisdom, his mastery of the written word, and his delight in it.

If we weep today, you and I, let it be because they are not ours.

THE
ULTIMATE
EGOIST

Heavy Insurance

"YOU AIN'T GOT much time to talk to him, you know," said my blue-uniformed guide.

"I know," I told him. "I'll cut it short." I followed him down a gloomy corridor into a room with a large grated window in one wall. In a few minutes Al appeared on the other side of the grating.

"Good grief, Phil," he said. "I never expected any visitors."

"Well," I said, "I'll never get over the shock of hearing that they had put you in here. Tell me about it."

"Sure. Remember the trouble I was in? Lola's hospital bill and the expense of Dad's funeral and the mortgage? I'd given up hope of ever paying off all my debts. I couldn't give Lola and the kid the things they should have. And such a little bit would have done it! But throwing luggage around in a baggage car doesn't pay enough to support a family and bad debts, too.

"When we left Miami with that insured shipment I was nearly batty from trying to figure out a way to get in the clear. And there I was, working in the middle of thousands of dollars' worth of fancy junk.

"The idea of pulling something never occurred to me, though, until I saw that package for Bernard. I can see that waybill yet: 'Emil Bernard, Jeweler, New York City. Weight, 11 pounds. Value, $30,000.' Thirty grand! And suppose it was bit stuff—rings and watches, etc.? To lift a couple of small items would cause plenty of trouble, but I might get by. The package was wrapped in heavy paper and glued with tape and tied with what looked like heavy fishing line. The cord was easy: a bowline at one end to make a loop, three turns around the package and a rolling hitch and two half hitches at the other end. The tape was a tricky proposition, but there was no ink anywhere near it. I wet my handkerchief, rolled it up to the same length as the tape, laid it on the floor and carefully put the package on it so that the water would soak through. Then I piled half a dozen shipments on top of it.

"I gave that tape time enough to soak, and when we pulled out of Jacksonville I had a look at it, and found it ready to peel. The coast was clear. Carefully I stripped the tape back until finally the edge of the paper appeared. I made short work of the cord and gently unfolded the wrapper.

"Inside were three layers of corrugated pasteboard. They covered a black leatherette case. It was locked. Nothing to do but wrap it up again. I picked up the first piece of pasteboard, to be stopped by a portable typewriter case, or whatever it was. Portable—holy smoke! I had a portable typewriter at home, and the key . . . I hunted feverishly through my pockets. I found it and stuck it in the keyhole of Bernard's shipment.

"With a tiny click it opened. I flung back the lid and wheeled as I heard a step behind me.

"'Hey, Al,' said Krantz, holding out a puzzle book, 'what's an eight letter word for—what the devil are you doing?' He stared into the case and whistled softly.

"'Pretty slick, eh, Al? You know you had no authority to open this package, no matter what the circumstances. Of course, I'll have to report this at Savannah. Trouble for you, boy, no matter how you look at it.'

"We were met in New York by two company big shots and an insurance man, as well as a city dick. I sure held the limelight for a while! We all went over to the express desk and waited. Pretty soon a little guy walked up and handed over a baggage slip. The clerk went over the carload that had just come in and found the package. The little guy picked it up and walked off, only to come back on the run.

"'It says on the waybill eleven pounds,' he said. 'This doesn't seem as heavy as that. Weigh it.'

"The clerk tossed it on the scales. 'Six pounds and three ounces,' he said.

"Bernard ripped the bundle open. He fished out a key and opened the case. It was empty. The plainclothes man looked at me and pulled out his handcuffs. 'Bring the manager!' Bernard squealed. 'I've been robbed.'

"The insurance man and the dick walked up to him. The former put a comforting hand on his shoulder while the other grabbed his wrists and slipped on the cuffs. 'You're under arrest, Mr. Bernard,' he said.

"'What do you mean?' Bernard yelled. 'I've been robbed and you arrest me? What is this?'

"'Fraud, Bernard,' said the insurance man. 'This messenger (he pointed at me) thought there was something fishy about that shipment and opened it. Luckily for us, the block of carbon ice you insured for thirty grand hadn't melted when he saw it.'

"Well," said Al, "that's about all. They gave me a reward, a bonus and this job—head shipping clerk for the district. The only thing I don't like about it is the building. It's more like a jail than an express office. Thanks for coming. And on your way out, tell that watchman who brought you in here that I want to see him, will you?"

The Heart

I DON'T LIKE to be poked repeatedly by a hard bony forefinger until I give my attention to its owner, particularly if said owner is a very persistent drunk who has been told to scram twice and still hasn't got the idea. But this drunk was a woman, and I couldn't bring myself to slug her, somehow.

"Please, mister," she droned. I pulled my sleeve out of her fingers. The movement was reflex, the involuntary recoil at the sight of a dead face.

She needed a drink; a fact that made little difference to me. So did I. But I had only enough change to take care of my own wants, and nobody ever had a chance to call me Sir Galahad. "What the hell do you want?"

She didn't like to be snapped at like that. She almost told me off; but the thought of a free drink made her change her mind. She had a bad case of the shakes. She said, "I want to talk to you, that's all."

"What about?"

"Somebody told me you write stuff. I got a story for you."

I sighed. Some day, maybe, I would be released from people who said a) "Where do you get your ideas?" and people who said b) "You want a story? My life would make the swellest—"

"Babe," I said, "I wouldn't put you on paper if you were Mata Hari. Go scare someone else with that phiz of yours, and leave me alone."

Her lips curled back wickedly from her teeth, and her eyes slitted; and then, with shocking suddenness, her face relaxed completely. She said, "I'd hate you if I wasn't afraid to hate anything ever again."

In that second I was deathly afraid of her, and that in itself was enough to get me interested. I caught her shoulder as she turned away, held up two fingers to the barkeep, and steered her to a table.

6

"That last crack of yours is worth a drink," I said.

She was grateful. "One drink," she said, "and I'm paid in full. In advance. You want the story?"

"No," I said, "But go ahead." She did.

I always kept pretty much to myself. I didn't have the looks that other women have, and to tell the truth, I got along fine without them. I had a fair enough job, slapping a typewriter for the county coroner, and I had a room big enough for me and a few thousand books. I ran to seed a little, I guess. Ah—never mind the buildup. There's a million like me, buried away in dusty little offices. We do our work and keep our mouths shut and nobody gives much of a damn about us, and we don't mind it.

Only something happened to me. I was coming out of the borough hall one afternoon when I ran into a man. He was thin and sallow, and when I bumped him he folded up, gasping like a fish. I caught him and held him up. He couldn't have weighed more than about ninety-four. He hung onto me for a minute and then he was all right. Grinned at me. Said, "Sorry, miss. I got used to a bad heart quite some time ago, but I wish it wouldn't get in other people's way."

I liked his attitude. A pump like that, and he wasn't crying any. "Keep your chin up that high and it won't get in anyone's way," I told him. He tipped his hat and went on, and I felt good about it all evening.

I met him a couple of days later, and we talked for a minute. His name was Bill Llanyn. Funny Welsh name. After a few weeks it didn't sound funny any more, I'd like to have had it for my own. Yes, it was that way. We had practically everything in common except that I have a constitution like a rhinoceros. Had then, anyway. He had a rotten little job as assistant curator in a two-for-a-nickel museum. Fed the snakes and tarantulas in the live-animal corner. He only got cigarette money out of it, but managed to eat on his wages because he couldn't smoke. I knocked together a supper one evening in my place. He went mad over my books. It was all I could do to pry him loose. Oh, the poor man! It used to take him ten minutes to get up

7

the one flight of stairs to my room. No, he was no Tarzan.

But I—loved that little man.

That was something I thought I didn't know how to do. I—well, I'm not going to talk about it. I'm telling you a story: right? Well, it's not a love story. Mind if I finish your drink, too? I—

Well, I wanted to marry him. You might think it would be a joke of a marriage. But God, all I wanted was to have him around, maybe even see him happy for once in his life. I knew I'd outlast him, but I didn't think about that. I wanted to marry him and be good to him and do things for him, and when he got his call, he wouldn't be all alone to face it.

It wasn't much to ask—oh yes—I had to do the asking. He wouldn't —but he wasn't having any. He sat on my armchair in front of the fire with an ivory-bound copy of Goethe in one hand, and held up his fingers one by one as he counted off his reasons why not. He wasn't making enough money to support both of us. He was liable to drop dead any second. He was too much of a wreck for any woman to call husband. He said he loved me, but he loved me too much to hang himself around my neck. Said I should find myself a real live man to get married to. Then he got up, put on his hat, said, "I'll get out now. I never loved anyone before. I'm glad I do now. You won't see me again. I haven't got much longer to be around; I'd just as soon you never knew just when I check out. That's the only thing left in the world that I can do for you." Then he came over to me and said some more, and be damned to you; that's for me to remember and for you to think about. But after he left I never saw him again.

I tried to get back into the old routine of typing and books, but it was rough. I did a lot of reading, trying to forget about it, trying to forget Bill Llanyn's wasted face. But everything I read seemed to be about him. Guess I picked the wrong stuff. Schopenhauer. Poe. Dante. Faulkner. My mind went round and round. I knew I'd feel better if I had something to hate.

Hate's a funny thing. I hope you don't ever know how—how *big* it can be. Use it right, and it's the most totally destructive thing in the universe. When I realized that, my mind stopped going round and round in those small circles, and it began to drive straight ahead.

I got it all clear in my mind. Listen now—let me tell you what happened when I got going.

I found something to hate. Bill Llanyn's heart—the ruined, inefficient organ that was keeping us apart. No one can ever know the crazy concentration I put into it. No one has ever lived to describe the *solidness* of hate when it begins to form into something real. I needed a miracle to make over Bill's heart, and in hate I had a power to work it. My hate reached a greatness that nothing could withstand. I knew it just as surely as a murderer knows what he has done when he feels his knife sink into his victim's flesh. But I was no murderer. Death wasn't my purpose. I wanted my hatred to reach into his heart, sear out what was bad and let him take care of the rest. I was doing what no one else has ever done—hating constructively. If I hadn't been so insanely anxious to put my idea to work, I would have remembered that hate can build nothing that is not evil, cause nothing that is not evil.

Yes, I failed. My boss came into the office one afternoon last week with a sheaf of morgue notes for me to type in triplicate and file away. Post mortems on stiffs that had been picked up during the last forty-eight hours. William Llanyn was there. Cause of death, heart failure. I stared at the notes for a long time. The coroner was standing looking out of the window. Noticed my typewriter stop without starting again, I guess. Without turning around, he said,

"If you're looking at those heart-failure notes, don't ask me if there isn't some more to it—pericarditis, mitral trouble, or anything. Just write 'heart failure.'"

I asked why. He said, "I'll tell you, but damned if I'll go on the record with a thing like that. The man didn't have any heart at all."

The woman got up and looked at the clock.

"Where you headed?" I asked.

"I'm catching a train out of here," she said. She went to the door. I said goodnight to her on the sidewalk. She went down toward the station. I headed uptown. When the police emergency wagon screamed by me a few minutes later I didn't have to go down to the tracks to see what had happened.

Cellmate

THEY SAY, "Ever been in jail?" and people laugh. People make jokes about jail. It's bad, being in jail. Particularly if you're in for something you didn't do. It's worse if you did do it; makes you feel like such a damn fool for getting caught. It's still worse if you have a cellmate like Crawley. Jail's a place for keeping cons out of the way a while. A guy isn't supposed to go nuts in one.

Crawley was his name and crawly he was. A middle-sized guy with a brown face. Spindly arms and legs. Stringy neck. But the biggest chest I ever did see on a man his size. I don't care what kind of a shirt they put on him. The bigger it was, the farther the cuffs hung past his hands and the tighter it was over his chest. I never seen anything like it. He was the kind of a lookin' thing that stops traffic wherever he goes. Sort of a humpback with the hump in front. I'm not in the cell two weeks when I get this freak for a jail buddy. I'm a lucky guy. I'm the kind of lug that slips and breaks his neck on the way up to collect a jackpot playing Screeno in the movies. I find hundred-dollar bills on the street and the man with the net scoops me up for passing counterfeits. I get human spiders like Crawley for cellmates.

He talked like a man having his toenails pulled out. He breathed all the time so you could hear it. He made you wish he'd stop it. He made you feel like stopping it. It whistled.

Two guards brought him in. One guard was enough for most cons, but I guess that chest scared them. No telling what a man built like that might be able to do. Matter of fact he was so weak he couldn't lift a bar of soap even. Hadn't, anyway, from the looks of him. A man couldn't get that crummy in a nice clean jail like ours without leaving soap alone right from the time they deloused him when they booked him in. So I said, "What'smatter, bull, I ain't lonely," and the guard said, "Shut the face. This thing's got his rent paid in advance an' a reservation here," and he pushed the freak into the cell. I said, "Upper bunk, friend," and turned my face to the wall. The guards went away and for a long time nothing happened.

After a while I heard him scratching himself. That was all right in itself but I never heard a man scratch himself before so it echoed. I mean inside him; it was as if that huge chest was a box and sounding board. I rolled over and looked at him. He'd stripped off the shirt and was burrowing his fingers into his chest. As soon as he caught my eye he stopped, and in spite of his swarthy skin, I could see him blush.

"What the hell are you doing?" I asked.

He grinned and shook his head. His teeth were very clean and strong. He looked very stupid. I said, "Cut it out, then."

It was about eight o'clock, and the radio in the area below the tiers of cell-blocks was blaring out a soap opera about a woman's trials and tribs with her second marriage. I didn't like it, but the guard did, so we heard it every night. You get used to things like that and after a week or so begin to follow them. So I rolled out of the bunk and went to the gratings to listen. Crawley was a hulk over in the corner; he'd been here about twenty minutes now and still had nothing to say, which was all right with me.

The radio play dragged on and wound up as usual with another crisis in the life the heroine, and who the hell really cared, but you'd tune in tomorrow night just to see if it would really be as dopey as you figured. Anyway, that was 8:45, and the lights would go out at nine. I moved back to my bunk, laid out a blanket, and began washing my face at the little sink by the door. At ten minutes to, I was ready to turn in, and Crawley still hadn't moved. I said:

"Figurin' to stay up all night?"

He started. "I—I—no, but I couldn't possibly get into that upper bunk."

I looked him over. His toothpick arms and legs looked too spindly to support a sparrow's weight, let alone the tremendous barrel of a chest. The chest looked powerful enough to push the rest of him through a twenty-foot wall. I just didn't know.

"You mean you can't climb up?"

He shook his head. So did I. I turned in. "What are you going to do? The guard'll look in in a minute. If you ain't in your bunk you'll get solitary. I been there, fella. You wouldn't like it. All by yourself. Dark. Stinks. No radio; no one to talk to; no nothin'. Better try to get into that bunk." I turned over.

A minute later he said, without moving, "No use trying. I couldn't make it anyway."

Nothing happened until three minutes to nine when the lights blinked. I said "Hell!" and swung into the upper bunk, being careful to put my lucky bone elephant under the mattress first. Without saying a word—and "thanks" was noticeably the word he didn't say—he got into the lower just as we heard footsteps of the guard coming along our deck. I went to sleep wondering why I ever did a thing like that for a homely looking thing like Crawley.

The bell in the morning didn't wake him; I had to. Sure, I should've let him sleep. What was he to me? Why not let the guard pitch icewater on him and massage his feet with a night-stick? Well, that's me. Sucker. I broke a man's cheekbone once for kicking a cur dog. The dog turned around and bit me afterwards. Anyway, I hopped out of my bunk—almost killed myself; forgot for a minute it was an upper—and, seeing Crawley lying there whistling away out of his lungs, I put out a hand to shake him. But the hand stopped cold. I saw something.

His chest was open a little. No, not cut. Open, like it was hinged— open like a clam in a fish market. Like a clam, too, it closed while I watched, a little more with each breath he took. I saw a man pulled out of the river one time in the fall. He'd drowned in the summer. That was awful. This was worse. I was shaking all over. I was sweating. I wiped my upper lip with my wrist and moved down and grabbed his feet and twisted them so he rolled off the bunk and fell on the floor. He squeaked and I said, "Hear that bell? That means you're through sleeping; remember?" Then I went and stuck my head under the faucet. That made me feel better. I saw I'd been afraid of this Crawley feller for a minute. I was just sore now. I just didn't like him.

He got up off the floor very slowly, working hard to get his feet under him. He always moved like that, like a man with nothing in his stomach and two hundred pounds on his back. He had to sort of coil his legs under him and then hand-over-hand up the bunk supports. He was weak as a duck. He wheezed for a minute and then sat down to put on his pants. A man has to be sick or lazy to do that. I stood drying my face and looking at him through the rag towel.

"You sick?" He looked up and said no.

"What's the matter with you?"

"Nothing. I told you that last night. What do you care, anyway?"

"Mind your mouth, cellmate. They used to call me Killer back home. I tore a guy's arm off one time and beat him over the head with the bloody end of it. He was a little freak like you. He didn't excuse himself when he walked in front of me."

Crawley took all this noise calmly enough. He just sat there looking up at me with muddy eyes and didn't say anything. It made me sore. I said, "I don't think I like you. See that crack on the floor? That one there. You stay on this side of it. Cross that line and I pop you. See?"

Now that was a dirty trick; the running water was on "my" side of the line, and so was the cell door, where he'd have to go to get his eats. So was the bunk. He got up off the bunk clumsy-like, and crossed over to the window and stood with his back to it, looking at me. He didn't look scared and he didn't look sore and he didn't look sorry. He just watched me, quiet, obedient like a hound dog, but all patience and hatred inside like a fat tabby cat. I snorted and turned my back to him, grasping the grating, waiting for chow. Prison rules were that if a man didn't want to eat he didn't have to. If he didn't want to eat he wouldn't show up at the grating when the mess wagon came along his deck. If he was sick, there was a sick call at ten o'clock. That was none of the trusty's business, the guy who pushed the wagon. He fed whoever was reaching through the bars with his square messkit and his tin cup and spoon.

So I hung out there, and Crawley was backed up against the other wall and I could feel his eyes on my back. My mind was clicking right along. Funny, though. Like—well, like this:

"I oughta get paid for having to bunk with a sideshow. By God I will get paid, too. I got two messkits, his and mine. *I can feel them eyes.* Here's one time I get four prunes and four pieces of bread and by golly enough prune juice to really sweeten that lousy coffee. Hot damn—tomorrow's Wednesday. Two eggs instead of one! I'll starve the—until he gets so weak an' sick they'll ship him out of here. Oh, boy—wait'll Sunday! Wait'll that misshapen cockroach has to watch me eatin' two lumps of ice cream! An' if he squeals I'll break his neck an' stuff it under his belt. *I can feel—two sets of eyes!*"

The wagon came. I stuck out one kit. A spoon of oatmeal and a dribble of watered, canned milk in one side; two prunes and juice in the other. Coffee in the cup. Two hunks of bread on the cup. I quickly stuck out the other kit. The trusty didn't even look. He filled up again and moved on. I backed away with a kit in each fist. I was afraid to turn around. There was one guy behind me and I could feel two pairs of eyes on my back. I spilled a couple of drops of coffee from my left hand and saw I was shaking. I stood there like a damn fool because I was afraid to turn around.

I said to myself, what the hell, he could not pull his finger out of a tub of lard and he's got you on the run. Put down the grub and walk on him. If you don't like his eyes, close 'em. Close all—I gulped—*four of them.*

Aw, this was silly. I went over to him and said, "Here," and gave him his messkit. I spooned a little oatmeal into his dish. I told him to go and sit on his bunk and eat. I showed him how to sweeten his coffee with prune juice. I don't know why I did it. I don't know why I never reminded him again about the line. He didn't say a damn thing. Not even thanks.

I ate and washed my kit before he was half through. He chewed enough for two people. I guess I knew from the start that there was more to him than just one guy. When he was done he sat there looking at me again. He put his kit on the floor beside him and then went and stood by the window. I was going to say something to him about it, but I figured I'd let him be.

It was raining, gloomy outside. That was lousy. On a clear day they let us in the yard for an hour in the afternoon. Rainy days we had a half-hour in the area under the cell-blocks. If you had money you could get candy and smokes and magazines. If you didn't have money you did without. I still had twenty cents. I was rolling my own, stretching it. Wasn't nobody going to bring me cash money. I was doing a little sixty-day stretch for something that doesn't matter very much, and if I watched it I could keep smoking until I was done here.

Well, anyway, on rainy days there's not much to do. You make your bunk. If you have a break, you can usually drag up something interesting to talk about with your cellmate. As long as your cell is halfway clean looking, it's okay, but they're all scrubbed bone-white and chrome-shiny because that's all there is to do. After I'd sat for an hour and a half smoking more than I could afford and trying to find something new to think about, I grabbed the bucket and brush and began to polish the floor. I made up my mind to do just half of it. That was a bright idea. When the guards came around inspecting for dirty cells at ten-thirty, one-half of this one would look crummy because the other half would be really scrubbed. That and Crawley's dirty messkit would get him into a nice jam. The guards knew by this time how I kept my cell.

Feeling almost happy at the idea, I turned to and began wearing out my knees and knuckles. I really bore down. When I came to the middle of the cell I went back and started over. I worked right up to Crawley's messkit. I stopped there. I picked it up and washed it and put it away. Crawley moved over to the clean half. I finished washing the floor. It certainly looked well-scrubbed. All over. Ah, don't ask me why.

I put the gear away and sat down for a while. I tried to kid myself that I felt good because I'd shown that lazy monstrosity up. Then I realized I didn't feel good at all. What was he doing; pushing me around? I looked up and glared at him. He didn't say anything. I went on sitting. Hell with him. This was the pay-off. Why, I wouldn't even talk to him. Let him sit there and rot, the worthless accident.

After a while I said, "What's the rap?"

He looked up at me inquiringly. "What are you in for?" I asked again.

"Vag."

"No visible means of support, or no address?"

"Visible."

"What'd the man in black soak you?"

"I ain't seen him. I don't know how much it's good for."

"Oh; waiting trial, huh?"

"Yeah. Friday noon. I got to get out of here before that."

I laughed. "Got a lawyer?"

He shook his head.

"Listen," I told him, "you're not in here on somebody's complaint, you know. The county put you here and the county'll prosecute. They won't retract the charge to spring you. What's your bail?"

"Three hundred."

"Have you got it?" I asked. He shook his head.

"Can you get it?"

"Not a chance."

"An' you 'got to get out of here'."

"I will."

"Not before Friday."

"Uh-huh. Before Friday. Tomorrow. Stick around; you'll see."

I looked at him, his toothpick arms and legs. "Nobody ever broke this jail and it's forty-two years old. I'm six foot three an' two-twenty soaking wet, an' I wouldn't try it. What chance you got?"

He said again, "Stick around."

I sat and thought about that for a while. I could hardly believe it. The man couldn't lift his own weight off the floor. He had no more punch than a bedbug, and a lot less courage. And he was going to break this jail, with its twelve-foot walls and its case-hardened steel bars! Sure, I'd stick around.

"You're as dumb as you look," I said. "In the first place, it's dumb to even dream about cracking this bastille. In the second place, it's dumb not to wait for your trial, take your rap—it won't be more than sixty—and then you get out of here clean."

"You're wrong," he said. There was an urgency about his strange, groaning voice. "I'm waiting trial. They haven't mugged me or printed me or given me an examination. If they convict me—and they will if I ever go to court—they'll give me a physical. Any doc—even a prison doc—would give his eyeteeth to X-ray me." He tapped his monstrous chest. "I'll never get away from them if they see the plates."

"What's your trouble?"

"It's no trouble. It's the way I am."

"How are you?"

"Fine. How are you?"

Okay, so it was none of my business. I shut up. But I was astonished at that long spiel of his. I didn't know he could talk that much.

Lunch came and went, and he got his share, in spite of myself, and a little more. Nothing much was said; Crawley just didn't seem to be interested in anything that went on around him. You'd think a guy whose trial is coming up would worry about it. You'd think a guy who was planning a jail-break would worry about it. Not Crawley. He just sat and waited for the time to come. Damn if I didn't do all his fretting for him!

At two o'clock the bolts shot back. I said, "Come on, Crawley. We got a chance to stretch our legs in the area. If you got any money you can buy something to read or smoke."

Crawley said, "I'm okay here. Besides, I got no money. They sell candy?"

"Yeah."

"You got money?"

"Yep. Twenty cents. Tobacco for me for another two weeks at the rate of two or three home-made cigarettes per day. There ain't one penny for anyone or anything else."

"Hell with that. Bring back four candy bars. Two marshmallow, one coconut, one fudge."

I laughed in his face and went out, thinking that here was one time when I'd have a story to tell the rest of the boys that would keep a lifer laughing. But somehow I never did get a chance to say anything to anybody about Crawley. I couldn't tell you how it happened. I started to talk to one fellow and the guard called him over. I said howdy to another and he told me to dry up, he had some blues he wanted to soak in. It just didn't work out. Once I really thought I had a start—one of the stoolies, this time; but just as I said, "Hey, you ought to get a load of my cellmate," the bell rang for us to get back in the cells. I just had time to get to the prison store before the shutter banged down over the counter. I went back up to my deck and into my cell. I pitched Crawley his candy bars. He took them without saying aye, yes, or no—or thanks.

Hardly a word passed between us until long after supper. He wanted to know how to fix one blanket so it felt like two. I showed him. Then I hopped into the upper bunk and said:

"Try sleepin' tonight."

He said, "What's the matter with you?"

"You was talking in your sleep last night."

"I wasn't talking to myself," he said defensively.

"You sure wasn't talking to me."

"I was talking to—my brother," said Crawley, and he laughed. My God, what a laugh that was. It was sort of dragged out of him, and it was grating and high-pitched and muffled and it went on and on. I looked over the edge of the bunk, thinking maybe he wasn't laughing, maybe he was having a fit. His face was strained, his eyes were screwed shut. All right, but his mouth was shut. His lips were clamped tight together. *His mouth was shut* and he went on laughing! He was laughing from inside somewhere, from his chest, some way I never even heard of before. I couldn't stand it. If that laughing didn't stop right away I'd have to stop breathing. My heart would stop breathing. My life was squirting out through my pores, turning to sweat. The laughter went higher and higher, just as loud, just as shrill, and I knew I could hear it and Crawley could, but no one else. It went up and up until I stopped hearing it, but even then I knew it was still going on and up, and though I couldn't hear it any more, I knew when it stopped. My back teeth ached from the way my jaws had driven them into the gums. I think I passed out, and then slept afterward. I don't remember the lights going out at nine, or the guards checking up.

I been slugged before, many a time, and I know what it's like to come to after being knocked out. But when I came out of this it was more like waking up, so I must have slept. Anyway, it wasn't morning. Must have been about three or four, before the sun came up. There was a weak moon hanging around outside the old walls, poking a gray finger in at us, me and Crawley. I didn't move for a few minutes, and I heard Crawley talking. And I heard someone else answering.

Crawley was saying something about money. "We got to get money, Bub. This is a hell of a jam. We thought we didn't need it. We could get anything we wanted without it. See what happened? Just because I'm no beauty winner a cop asks us questions. They stick us in here. Now we've got to break it. Oh, we can do it; but if we get some money it don't have to happen again. You can figure something, can't you, Bub?"

And then came the answering voice. It was the grating one that had been laughing before. That wasn't Crawley's voice! That belonged to somebody else. Aw, that was foolish. Two men to a cell. One man to a bunk. But here were two men talking, and I wasn't saying anything. I suddenly had a feeling my brains were bubbling like an egg frying in too much grease.

The voice shrilled, "Oh, sure. Money's no trouble to get. Not the way we work, Crawley. He, he!" They laughed together. My blood felt so cold I was afraid to move in case my veins broke. The voice went on. "About this break; you know just what we're going to do?"

"Yeah," said Crawley. "Gee, Bub, I'd sure be wuthless without you. Man, what a brain, what a brain!"

The voice said, "You don't have to do without me! Heh! Just you try and get rid of me!"

I took a deep, quiet breath and slowly raised up and hung my head over the edge of the bunk so I could see. I couldn't be scared any more. I couldn't be shocked any more. After seeing that, I was through. A guy lives all his life for a certain moment. Like that little old doc that delivered the quints. He never did anything like it before. He never did again. From then on he was through. Like a detective in a book solving a crime. It all leads up to one thing—who done it? When the dick finds that out, he's through. The book's finished. Like me; I was finished when I saw Crawley's brother. That was the high point.

Yeah, it was his brother. Crawley was twins. Like them Siamese twins, but one was big and the other was small. Like a baby. There was only the top part of him, and he was growing out of Crawley's chest. But that oversize chest was just built for the little one to hide in. It folded around the little one. It was hinged like I said before, something like a clamshell. My God!

I said it was like a baby. I meant just small like that. It wasn't baby stuff, aside from that. The head was shaggy, tight-curled. The face was long and lean with smooth, heavy eyebrows. The skin was very dark, and there was little crooked fangs on each side of the mouth, two up, two down. The ears were just a little pointed. That thing had sense of its own, and it was bad clear through. I mean really bad. That thing was all Crawley's crime-brains. Crawley was just a smart mule to that thing. He carried it around with him and he did what it wanted him to do. Crawley obeyed that brother of his—and so did *everybody else!* I did. My tobacco money; cleaning the cell; seeing that Crawley got fed—that was all the little twin's doing, all of it. It wasn't my fault. Nobody *ever* pushed me around like that before!

Then it saw me. It had thrown its hideous little head back to laugh, and it flung up a withered arm and piped, "You! Go to sleep! *Now!*" So—I did.

I don't know how it happened. If I'd slept all that time the bulls would have taken me to the ward. But so help me, from that time until two o'clock I don't know what happened. The Crawley twins kept me fogged, I guess. But I must have gotten dressed and washed; I must have eaten, and I'll guarantee that the Crawleys didn't wash no messkits. Anyhow, the next thing I remember is the bolt shooting back on the cell door. Crawley came up behind me as I stood there looking at it, and I felt his eyes on my back. Four eyes. He said:

"Go on. What are you waiting for?"

I said: "You've done something to me. What is it?"

He just said, "Get going."

We walked out together, out along the deck and down two long flights of iron stairs to the area. We took maybe fifteen, maybe twenty steps, and then Crawley whispered, *"Now!"*

I was loaded with H. E. I was primed and capped, and the firing pin of his voice stung me. I went off like that. There were two guards in front of me. I took them by their necks and cracked their heads together so powerfully that their skulls seemed soft. I screamed and turned and bounded up the stairs, laughing and shouting. Prisoners scattered. A guard grabbed at me on the first landing. I picked him up and threw him over my shoulder and ran upward. A gun blammed twice, and each bullet went *thuck!* as it bored into the body of the bull I carried. He snatched at the railing as I ran and I heard the bones in his wrist crackle. I pitched him over the rail and he landed on another guard down there in the area. The other guard was drawing a bead on me and when the body struck him his gun went off. The slug ricocheted from the steps and flew into the mouth of a prisoner on the second deck. I was screaming much louder than he was. I reached the third deck and ran around the cell-block chattering and giggling. I slid to a stop and threw my legs over the railing and sat there swinging my feet. Two cops opened fire on me. Their aim was lousy because only three out of the twelve bullets hit me. I stood on the lower rail and leaned my calves against the upper one and spread out my arms and shouted at them, cursing them with my mouth full of blood. The prisoners were being herded six and eight to a cell, down on the area level. The guards in the area suddenly stood aside, making way like courtiers for the royalty of a man with a submachine gun. The gun began singing to me. It was a serenade to a giant on a balcony, by a grizzled troubadour with a deep-toned instrument. I couldn't resist that music for more than a moment, so I came down to the area, turning over and over in the air, laughing and coughing and sobbing as I fell.

You watched me, didn't you, you flatfooted blockheads? You got out your guns and ran from the doors, from the series of searching rooms, booking rooms, desk rooms, bull pens? You left the doors open when you ran? Crawley's out in the street now. No hurry for

Crawley. Crawley gives the orders wherever he is. There'll be others—like me.

I've done work for Crawley. See me now? And—Crawley didn't even say, "Thanks."

Fluffy

RANSOME LAY IN the dark and smiled to himself, thinking about his hostess. Ransome was always in demand as a house guest, purely because of his phenomenal abilities as a raconteur. Said abilities were entirely due to his being so often a house guest, for it was the terse beauty of his word pictures of people and their opinions of people that made him the figure he was. And all those clipped ironies had to do with the people he had met last weekend. Staying a while at the Joneses, he could quietly insinuate the most scandalously hilarious things about the Joneses when he weekended with the Browns the following fortnight. You think Mr. and Mrs. Jones resented that? Ah, no. You should hear the dirt on the Browns! And so it went, a two-dimensional spiral on the social plane.

This wasn't the Joneses or the Browns, though. This was Mrs. Benedetto's ménage; and to Ransome's somewhat jaded sense of humor, the widow Benedetto was a godsend. She lived in a world of her own, which was apparently set about with quasi-important ancestors and relatives exactly as her living room was cluttered up with perfectly unmentionable examples of Victorian rococo.

Mrs. Benedetto did not live alone. Far from it. Her very life, to paraphrase the lady herself, was wound about, was caught up in, was owned by and dedicated to her baby. Her baby was her beloved, her little beauty, her too darling my dear, and—so help me—her boobly wutsi-wutsikins. In himself he was quite a character. He answered to the name of Bubbles, which was inaccurate and offended his dignity. He had been christened Fluffy, but you know how it is with nicknames. He was large and he was sleek, that paragon among animals, a chastened alley-rabbit.

Wonderful things, cats. A cat is the only animal which can live like a parasite and maintain to the utmost its ability to take care of itself. You've heard of little lost dogs, but you never heard of a lost cat. Cats don't get lost, because cats don't belong anywhere. You wouldn't get Mrs. Benedetto to believe that. Mrs. Benedetto never thought of putting Fluffy's devotion to the test by declaring a ten-day moratorium on the canned salmon. If she had, she would have uncovered a sense of honor comparable with that of a bedbug.

Knowing this—Ransome pardoned himself the pun—categorically, Ransome found himself vastly amused. Mrs. Benedetto's ministrations to the phlegmatic Fluffy were positively orgiastic. As he thought of it in detail, he began to feel that perhaps, after all, Fluffy was something of a feline phenomenon. A cat's ears are sensitive organs; any living being that could abide Mrs. Benedetto's constant flow of conversation from dawn till dark, and then hear it subside in sleep only to be replaced by a nightshift of resounding snores; well, that *was* phenomenal. And Fluffy had stood it for four years. Cats are not renowned for their patience. They have, however, a very fine sense of values. Fluffy was getting something out of it—worth considerably more to him than the discomforts he endured, too, for no cat likes to break even.

He lay still, marvelling at the carrying power of the widow's snores. He knew little of the late Mr. Benedetto, but he gathered now that he had been either a man of saintly patience, a masochist or a deaf-mute. A noise like that from just one stringy throat must be an impossibility, and yet, there it was. Ransome liked to imagine that the woman had calluses on her palate and tonsils, grown there from her conversation, and it was these rasping together that produced the curious dry-leather quality of her snores. He tucked the idea away for future reference. He might use it next weekend. The snores were hardly the gentlest of lullabies, but any sound is soothing if it is repeated often enough.

There is an old story about a lighthouse tender whose lighthouse was equipped with an automatic cannon which fired every fifteen minutes, day and night. One night, when the old man was asleep, the gun failed to go off. Three seconds after its stated time, the old fellow was out of his bed and flailing around the room, shouting, "What was that?" And so it was with Ransome.

He couldn't tell whether it was an hour after he had fallen asleep, or whether he had not fallen asleep at all. But he found himself sitting on the edge of the bed, wide awake, straining every nerve for the source of the—what was it?—sound?—that had awakened him. The old house was as quiet as a city morgue after closing time, and he could see nothing in the tall, dark guest room but the moon-silvered windows and the thick blacknesses that were drapes. Any old damn thing might be hiding behind those drapes, he thought comfortingly. He edged himself back on the bed and quickly snatched his feet off the floor. Not that anything was under the bed, but still—

A white object puffed along the floor, through the moonbeams, toward him. He made no sound, but tensed himself, ready to attack or defend, dodge or retreat. Ransome was by no means an admirable character, but he owed his reputation, and therefore his existence, to this particular trait, the ability to poise himself, invulnerable to surprise. Try arguing with a man like that sometime.

The white object paused to stare at him out of its yellow-green eyes. It was only Fluffy—Fluffy looking casual and easy-going and not at all in a mood to frighten people. In fact he looked up at Ransome's gradually relaxing bulk and raised a long-haired, quizzical eyebrow, as if he rather enjoyed the man's discomfiture.

Ransome withstood the cat's gaze with suavity, and stretched himself out on the bed with every bit of Fluffy's own easy grace. "Well," he said amusedly, "you gave me a jolt! Weren't you taught to knock before you entered a gentleman's boudoir?"

Fluffy raised a velvet paw and touched it pinkly with his tongue. "Do you take me for a barbarian?" he asked.

Ransome's lids seemed to get heavy, the only sign he ever gave of being taken aback. He didn't believe for a moment that the cat had really spoken, but there was something about the voice he had heard that was more than a little familiar. This was, of course, someone's idea of a joke.

Good God—it had to be a joke!

Well, he had to hear that voice again before he could place it. "You didn't say anything of course," he told the cat, "but if you did, what was it?"

"You heard me the first time," said the cat, and jumped up on the foot of his bed. Ransome inched back from the animal. "Yes," he said, "I—thought I did." Where on earth had he heard that voice before? "You know," he said, with an attempt at jocularity, "you should, under these circumstances, have written me a note before you knocked."

"I refuse to be burdened with the so-called social amenities," said Fluffy. His coat was spotlessly clean, and he looked like an advertising photograph for eiderdown, but he began to wash carefully. "I don't like you, Ransome."

"Thanks," chuckled Ransome, surprised. "I don't like you either."

"Why?" asked Fluffy.

Ransome told himself silently that he was damned. He had recognized the cat's voice, and it was a credit to his powers of observation that he had. It was his own voice. He held tight to a mind that would begin to reel on slight provocation, and, as usual when bemused, he flung out a smoke screen of his own variety of glib chatter.

"Reasons for not liking you," he said, "are legion. They are all included in the one phrase—'You are a cat!'"

"I have heard you say that at least twice before," said Fluffy, "except that you have now substituted 'cat' for 'woman.'"

"Your attitude is offensive. Is any given truth any the less true for having been uttered more than once?"

"No," said the cat with equanimity. "But it is just that much more clichéd."

Ransome laughed. "Quite aside from the fact that you can talk, I find you most refreshing. No one has ever criticized my particular variety of repartee before."

"No one was ever wise to you before," said the cat. "Why don't you like cats?"

A question like that was, to Ransome, the pressing of a button which released ordered phrases. "Cats," he said oratorically, "are without doubt the most self-centered, ungrateful, hypocritical creatures on this or any other earth. Spawned from a mésalliance between Lilith and Satan—"

Fluffy's eyes widened. "Ah! An antiquarian!" he whispered.

"—they have the worst traits of both. Their best qualities are their beauty of form and of motion, and even these breathe evil. Women are the ficklest of bipeds, but few women are as fickle as, by nature, any cat is. Cats are not true. They are impossibilities, as perfection is impossible. No other living creature moves with utterly perfect grace. Only the dead can so perfectly relax. And nothing— simply nothing at all—transcends a cat's incomparable insincerity."

Fluffy purred.

"Pussy! Sit-by-the-fire and sing!" spat Ransome. "Smiling up all toadying and yellow-eyed at the bearers of liver and salmon and cat- nip! Soft little puffball, bundle of joy, playing with a ball on a string; making children clap their soft hands to see you, while your mean little brain is viciously alight with the pictures your play calls up for you. Bite it to make it bleed; hold it till it all but throttles; lay it down and step about it daintily; prod it with a gentle silken paw until it moves again, and then pounce. Clasp it in your talons then, lift it, roll over with it, sink your cruel teeth into it while you pump out its guts with your hind feet. Ball on a string! Play-actor!"

Fluffy yawned. "To quote you, that is the prettiest piece of emotional claptrap that these old ears have ever heard. A triumph in studied spontaneity. A symphony in cynicism. A poem in perception. The unqualified—"

Ransome grunted.

He deeply resented this flamboyant theft of all his pet phrases, but his lip twitched nevertheless. The cat was indeed an observant animal.

"—epitome of understatement," Fluffy finished smoothly. "To listen to you, one would think that you would like to slaughter earth's felinity."

"I would," gritted Ransome.

"It would be a favor to us," said the cat. "We would keep our- selves vastly amused, eluding you and laughing at the effort it cost you. Humans lack imagination."

"Superior creature," said Ransome ironically, "why don't you do away with the human race, if you find us a bore?"

"You think we couldn't?" responded Fluffy. "We can outthink, outrun, and outbreed your kind. But why should we? As long as you act as you have for these last few thousand years, feeding us, sheltering us and asking nothing from us but our presence for purposes of admiration—why then, you may remain here."

Ransome guffawed. "Nice of you! But listen—stop your bland discussion of the abstract and tell me some things I want to know. How can you talk, and why did you pick me to talk to?"

Fluffy settled himself. "I shall answer the question socratically. Socrates was a Greek, and so I shall begin with your last questions. What do you do for a living?"

"Why I—I have some investments and a small capital, and the interest—" Ransome stopped, for the first time fumbling for words. Fluffy was nodding knowingly.

"All right, all right. Come clean. You can speak freely."

Ransome grinned. "Well, if you must know—and you seem to— I am a practically permanent house guest. I have a considerable fund of stories and a flair for telling them; I look presentable and act as if I were a gentleman. I negotiate, at times, small loans—"

"A loan," said Fluffy authoritatively, "is something one intends to repay."

"We'll call them loans," said Ransome airily. "Also, at one time and another, I exact a reasonable fee for certain services rendered—"

"Blackmail," said the cat.

"Don't be crude. All in all, I find life a comfortable and engrossing thing."

"Q.E.D.," said Fluffy triumphantly. "You make your living being scintillant, beautiful to look at. So do I. You help nobody but yourself; you help yourself to anything you want. So do I. No one likes you except those you bleed; everyone admires and envies you. So with me. Get the point?"

"I think so. Cat, you draw a mean parallel. In other words, you consider my behavior catlike."

"Precisely," said Fluffy through his whiskers. "And that is both why and how I can talk with you. You're so close to the feline in everything you do and think; your whole basic philosophy is that of a cat. You have a feline aura about you so intense that it contacts mine; hence we find each other intelligible."

"I don't understand that," said Ransome.

"Neither do I," returned Fluffy. "But there it is. Do you like Mrs. Benedetto?"

"No!" said Ransome immediately and with considerable emphasis. "She is absolutely insufferable. She bores me. She irritates me. She is the only woman in the world who can do both those things to me at the same time. She talks too much. She reads too little. She thinks not at all. Her mind is hysterically hidebound. She has a face like the cover of a book that no one has ever wanted to read. She is built like a pinch-type whiskey bottle that never had any whiskey in it. Her voice is monotonous and unmusical. Her education was insufficient. Her family background is mediocre, she can't cook, and she doesn't brush her teeth often enough."

"My, my," said the cat, raising both paws in surprise. "I detect a ring of sincerity in all that. It pleases me. That is exactly the way I have felt for some years. I have never found fault with her cooking, though; she buys special food for me. I am tired of it. I am tired of her. I am tired of her to an almost unbelievable extent. Almost as much as I hate you."

"Me?"

"Of course. You're an imitation. You're a phony. Your birth is against you, Ransome. No animal that sweats and shaves, that opens doors for women, that dresses itself in equally phony imitations of the skins of animals, can achieve the status of a cat. You are presumptuous."

"You're not?"

"I am different. I am a cat, and have a right to do as I please. I disliked you so intensely when I saw you this evening that I made up my mind to kill you."

"Why didn't you? Why—don't you?"

"I couldn't," said the cat coolly. "Not when you sleep like a cat ... no, I thought of something far more amusing."

"Oh?"

"Oh yes." Fluffy stretched out a foreleg, extended his claws. Ransome noticed subconsciously how long and strong they seemed. The moon had gone its way, and the room was filling with slate-gray light.

"What woke you," said the cat, leaping to the windowsill, "just before I came in?"

"I don't know," said Ransome. "Some little noise, I imagine."

"No indeed," said Fluffy, curling his tail and grinning through his whiskers. "It was the stopping of a noise. Notice how quiet it is?"

It was indeed. There wasn't a sound in the house—oh, yes, now he could hear the plodding footsteps of the maid on her way from the kitchen to Mrs. Benedetto's bedroom, and the soft clink of a teacup. But otherwise—suddenly he had it. "The old horse stopped snoring!"

"She did," said the cat. The door across the hall opened, there was the murmur of the maid's voice, a loud crash, the most horrible scream Ransome had ever heard, pounding footsteps rushing down the hall, a more distant scream, silence. Ransome bounced out of bed. "What the hell—"

"Just the maid," said Fluffy, washing between his toes, but keeping the corners of his eyes on Ransome. "She just found Mrs. Benedetto."

"Found—"

"Yes. I tore her throat out."

"Good—God! Why?"

Fluffy poised himself on the windowsill. "So you'd be blamed for it," he said, and laughing nastily, he leaped out and disappeared in the gray morning.

Alter Ego

ONCE UPON A TIME, when the world was younger than it will be, and a little more foolish, there appeared a Leader. He was, in his prime, the unquestioned master of his land, and the force of his mind and of the thousands of fools who served him stilled all murmurs of reprisal. He gained his power by suasion and held it by bloodshed, and he throttled his people and by doing so deified them. That they must believe; for that was the only justification they had, poor things, to tell themselves. . .

Now the Leader appeared before his people one day, to frighten and praise them, and a missile came from the crowd and killed one of his ministers. This happening frightened the Leader, and he began to think how terrible it would be for him to be killed. He was a great power in the world, this Leader, and the masses he controlled were also a great power. But the power of those masses sprang from him, and he knew that if he were dead, then the masses would not be as they were. Some other leader would come forward and destroy his work, and worse, his name and fame and memory. He gave deep thought to this matter, and decided that he must have a servant that resembled him in every way, so that at no time would anyone know whether it was the Leader that faced the people, or his substitute. It was a pleasing plan, and he instituted a great and secret search through the land for such a servant.

It was hard. The details of that vast and quiet search are one of the most monumental stories ever to write its dark lines on the pages of history. But in months the thing was done, and the man was presented to the Leader.

He was perfect. Nearly every line of his face, every tone of his voice, every gesture, was that of his Leader. He knew the Leader's ways, too, and the Leader's thought. The Leader himself taught him what details he lacked, in many secret conferences held in the Leader's rooms in the dead of night, with but one trusted sentry guarding the double doors.

There came a time when the Leader fell deathly sick from a malignance in his throat. He sent an urgent, secret message to the royal physician of a rival country's King, and the physician refused to come. For had the Leader died under the knife, the physician never would have left those rooms alive.

But the Leader did not die. One was found to cure him, an old wise man whose only thought was for gain, and it was done, and forgotten. He did not die, but while he was sick, something worse than death happened to the Leader. It was his man, his perfect prototype.

He was *too* perfect.

While the Leader lay abed, his great organization had gone on its way unchecked, unhampered by his illness. His man had stepped in to fill his place, and had done it so perfectly that no one knew—no one ever knew. There had been four momentous decisions then, too, and the man had handled them well, even as he would have. Too perfectly.

The Leader began to look askance at this man. Suppose he, the Leader, were to be killed now, tomorrow, quietly? He would be a nameless corpse, and thereafter the memories of man would record doings that were not his, but those of another. The Leader was a god. His people spoke of him as a god—because they must; yet they spoke of him so, and such speech was necessary to him, as worship is necessary to the perpetuation of any god...

And so it came about that a god knew the meaning of fear. Fear was hate, and hate was anger. The man must be killed.

The killing happened sooner than the Leader had expected. It was on a night shortly after the Leader had bloodlessly invaded a part of a neighboring land. He was, with his men's help, drawing up a promise to the world that he would take no more from that or any other neighbor.

And his man had the impertinence to disagree! It was the first time, and the Leader was frightened and filled with hate and anger towards him. The man said that there should be more such invasions, and more, and more, until the Leader's country not only had what territories she had lost to other lands in her stormy past, but had yet more and more, until she dominated a continent and then a world. The man gave reasons, too, and they were good. But in his stubborn anger, the Leader pretended to scoff, and the man caught the shifty glint of his eyes as he pawed a side-arm from his belt. The man, since he was dressed exactly like the Leader, also had a side-arm, and both weapons came up together. One man was a little faster.

The sentry outside heard a sound that meant death, and he flung open the double doors. He saw two men, identical in build, in garb, in hate-filled countenance. As he watched, one of the men slumped dead to the floor. The other shrugged, put away his weapon, and gave orders that the dead man was to be removed and disposed of, most secretly.

There followed a reign of terror and triumph, as the forces of the Leader swept south and east, taking country after country, land after land of their ancient possessions. Every nation was defied, every nation was cowed, and the land of the Leader stood in its prime, unconquerable, threatening.

Then there was the great fall. The trusted sentry betrayed his trust one day, and whispered a suspicion. His words became a murmur, a shout, and then a battle cry. The Leader is dead! *The Leader is dead!*

The man who called himself, then, the Leader, answered bloodily, and killed many of those that dared to use that battle cry. But for every one he killed, there were ten, a thousand, a million there to take it up. The government was overthrown, and starving people rejoiced, and nations that strained to attack drew back and watched the death of a régime.

And the man who had been the Leader? His was the most agonizing death, for they did not kill him. They laughed at his furious impotence, and they turned him loose in the streets, quietly, so that he would not be known and so would live to suffer.

Torture. The humiliation that man bore, walking the streets, hearing his name tossed about lightly, is beyond description. He had no friends, for he knew how to provoke no human emotion but fear and its child, hate.

He nearly starved, and then one day found a man who wanted gain, who saw in him a means for gain. It was the old wise man who had cured the Leader of his illness. The starving beggar found this man, and gave him certain proofs, and the address of the cellar where he skulked. The physician passed quietly about, here and there, in the right places, and said what was necessary. It took a very long time, and all the while, the beggar lay in his cellar. He began to think he had been forgotten, and the infrequent gibes that echoed down to him from the street began to drive him quite, quite mad.

At long last the day came when all was in readiness. The signal was given, and the country awoke one morning to find itself in the merciless grip of the old régime. The Leader lived! Found by his old physician, who knew him by the scars of his own knife, he lived beyond possibility of doubt. The Leader's men were in command, and the Leader was coming back!

They went to get him, their beggar-Leader, in his noisome cellar.

They were too late. Fearing him as they served him, they had never told him what they did, and so he had known himself neglected and forgotten—he, a god, a Leader! It was the final humiliation, and he had taken his own life. And so his government died a second death, even as he had—and they were both dead for evermore.

Mailed Through a Porthole

Mr. David Jones, Esq.
Forty Fathoms

Sept. 21, 1938

Dear Sir,

Just a little note to let you know what I think of you.

You're kicking up your heels a little, my friend. Since when were you a big shot? I've been going to sea for quite a while, you piker, and I've never had a sample of that far-famed strength of yours. A broken propeller once; but I have a hunch it had been brazed to save expense. Once a started seam; but that was in a thirty-year-old hulk that was headed for the boneyard anyway. Once you caught up with me when my ship was unballasted, threw a squall at her and rolled her over on her beam-ends, tossing me into the ice machines. Lucky punch. Otherwise you've muttered and mumbled by way of bragging.

And now it's a hurricane warning. Am I excited? Not on your life. You can't even get me seasick. Do your worst, half-pint. Maybe you have sunk a fisherman or two, but you'll never crack a new seven thousand ton tanker like this. Go ahead. Try it.

Listen to that Miami station, Jones. "The hurricane is now four hundred miles east-southeast of Miami, moving west-northwest at a speed of twenty to twenty-five miles per hour. Winds of hurricane velocity near storm center, approximately seventy-five miles in diameter. Small craft are urged to make port immediately. Residents of Miami and coastal environs, check on everything movable. The Board of Health suggests you sterilize your bathtubs and fill them with drinking water, as reservoirs may take sea water. Please take down all loose boarding. If you live in a wooden house, go at once to the nearest school, where accommodations are being made. If you have any sick or very old, have them removed to the hospital. When the wind rises, see that everyone is accounted for and is indoors. Be sure to leave one door open on the side away from the wind. . . " Make you feel good, Jones? Well, that's good enough for landlubbers. But you don't frighten me. Groundswell's a little heavier. . .

You're getting a kick out of the crew, aren't you? That Oklahoma bosun, for instance. He's sitting on the bitts by the galley. He's in a cold sweat. I'm wise to you, Davy; the kid on the 4 to 8 is wise; and the skipper is wise; but that bosun is fretting like an old maid with the shingles. Just because he had the roof blown away from over his head in the '34 blow. We are passing plenty of ships; it's the first time I've ever seen loaded tankers headed south. Every time one goes by the bosun starts moaning again, "Why doethn't the thkipper turn around? Don't he know there'th a hurricane coming?" and the kid and I sit and laugh at him. It's the kid's first trip; he's out to see the sights. Kick up a show for him, Jones. You don't want him to go back home and tell the truth about you, do you? Look at him. He's got his sea-legs now; he'll be a seaman before he gets his A.B. ticket. Look at him bracing easily against the roll of the ship, with the wind tearing at his hair. Seventeen years old, Davy, and you're as old as the earth, but that kid has you whipped.

Sept. 22, 1938

Well, small stuff, you've succeeded in getting in people's hair. Land-lubber stuff again. Special broadcasts all night; all the crew off-watch spent the night in the messroom listening to them. ". . . after the wind subsides special squads of police and deputies will cover the streets. If you need assistance wait at your home until one of the squads passes." Panic seed. You've got the bosun so worried that he knocks a man off when we are working on deck, to go back and get the hourly reports. We're carrying thirty-foot seas now, but we've got you fooled. I told you the skipper was wise to you. By the time the blow hits the coast we'll be a hundred miles north of it.

I can't figure O'Rourke. He was going to sea before my parents were born. He's been through three hurricanes on the coast here, and everything else, running foreign, from a typhoon to a williwaw. Yet when the kid said, "I hope it hits us. *Then* we'll see some fun!" O'Rourke clipped him. "Wait till ye know what ye're talking about," he growled, "before ye open yer young yap again." The kid stood there rubbing his cheek, pain and shock in his eyes. Then he turned and ran below. I can't figure it. O'Rourke knows what it's all about; if you could kill a big-ship sailor, which I doubt, as long as the ship is in good condition, O'Rourke's typhoons would have got him long ago. And he's alive, isn't he? So why should he clip the kid just because the kid has figured out in one trip what it took O'Rourke forty years to learn; that no hurricane is as strong as clean steel?

Sails Carmody is another one. He's a Boston Irishman, the kid's watchmate on the 4 to 8. Sails is at the radio for every report, but he never says anything. Each time he hears of another fifty miles less between us and the storm center he frowns more deeply. Yet I saw Sails take on two big Swedes at Evelyn Hardtime's and whip them both. I saw Sails run up the mast in oilskins in a heavy swell, to clear the signal halliard. He has no nerves. And yet this business has him worried. How can you buffalo a man like that, Jones?

So you decided to take me up on it, did you? That Miami station: "The storm center is reported 180 miles due east of Miami, moving approximately north-northwest. It will therefore not reach the Florida coast." Shifted north, hey? And will we meet? Let me figure this. If we hold course and speed, my ship and your little hurricane, we should meet a little to the north of Charleston, about 45 miles offshore. Hurry it up, old-timer, or we'll be there before you and safely north by the time you reach the spot.

Got to give you credit. You are putting on a show for the kid. When he's on watch at night he doesn't even go back aft for a smoke when Sails relieves him; just goes to the other wing of the bridge and leans there staring forward. They put the lookout on the bridge two nights ago; you're wetting down the foc'sle head nicely. The ship knows her way. She'll bury her nose and take two seas, spouting them up through the hawse-holes, tumbling the chains in the lockers under the windlass; then she'll shudder like a wrestler bunching his muscles, shoulder a streaming mantle of sea and spume back on to the foredeck, cut masses of water to ribbons with her bulwarks, and show her decks again. The engines are half-speed; you've got us there, old boy. The mill can take only so much; but the hull and those firm clean bulkheads are too much for you. That and the weight of 78,000 barrels of kerosene and furnace oil, and the tons of drums and crates in the fore and after holds.

Sept. 23, 1938

Davy Jones, I acknowledge your strength. It isn't all it's cracked up to be in the magazine stories. It couldn't be. But I have found out since early this morning when we hit the first seventy-five mile squall, that wind and sea can be strong enough to tear great strips of paint off the deck; that they can crumple sheet-steel steamguards like cardboard; that they can tear up the welded bases of the kingposts we use for raising tank tops, hurling them over the side. But the ship is tight and bone-dry inside, since we battened down the after hold, dogged the watertight doors, covered the ventilators. And I can still work my away around the poop if I hold to the rail. I can still get up on deck and tell you to your fish face that in me, and in the ship I ride, you have met your match.

You are a murderer.

The third squall passed and we labored like a panting ox reaching the crest of a long hill with his load. The kid and I opened a watertight door on the lee side and slipped out on deck, dogging it behind us. We worked our way to the rail at the break of the poop, stood watching her take every sea. She'd plunge, hiding her bulk. To port and starboard was ocean. At our feet was ocean. Seventy yards away the midship house was an island. Then more ocean. Then the foc'sle head. Behind us the after house was an island. Then she'd heave herself out again, and be a ship again instead of three islands.

Patchy clouds hurtled overhead like stones thrown. One was low, five miles away, broad on the port bow. The moaning in the stays rose an octave, then another as the fourth gale struck. The black cloud paused, whirling, looming up, then charged us, shouting. I yelled at the kid, "Look out! Come back!" but he never heard me. He stood there riding the deck as if he were a part of it. I vaulted the after cargo manifold, raced over the after hatch, and threw myself down behind the coaming, twisting my fingers around the batten. The rest happened in about three seconds, but it seemed to last forever ... the squall swept down and brought twilight with it, and blinding rain; swept past and took the ocean away from under the ship ... must have, for she dropped like a stone when the light left her. I saw that sea from where I lay, flat on my belly behind the hatch; saw its crest curling over the top of the foremast. And I saw the kid standing upright, both hands steadying him against the lashing wind, his face upturned to meet that wall of grey-green water. And I felt the ship jar as the midship house took the brunt of it, before I was covered by a great weight of strangling brine. Ages later it passed, and I breathed again, but the kid was gone. There was a white clot on the drum of the winch.

You dirty coward.

You win, Davy Jones. That sea stove in the midship house. Carried away the aerial. Smashed the lifeboats. Tore out the stack. Broke the ship's back.

There is kerosene and salt on my lips.

A Noose of Light

TERRY HAD BEAUTY and Florence had brains. Terry was all silk and brilliance, Florence was small and brown and neat. Terry sacrificed clarity to magnificence; Florence sacrificed nothing to cold logic. Therefore Terry was a very popular young lady, and Florence was not. But they were both happy, for they both had what they wanted from life. Popularity meant as little to Florence as did limited scientific recognition to Terry. For Florence was a research scientist, in spite of her mere twenty-odd years, and her paper on the comparative values of certain sub-visible radiations in the vicinity of ultra-violet had brought her wide acclaim in the small circle in which she moved.

They were sisters; and Florence's steady indifference to men and bright lights and sweet music was a source of constant exasperation to the younger girl. Terry was as analytical as her more serious sister; but to her, the ripples cast by a chance remark, the effect of a half-casual gesture, the reaction to slight nuances of tone and phrase—these were matters of profound interest. Being a woman, and an intensely feminine and beautiful woman at that, she simply could not understand Florence's passion for her work. When Florence made some new, small discovery, Terry shared her radiant happiness; but she could no more understand *why* Florence was happy than she could grasp the complex scientific phenomenon that had caused that happiness.

Terry's anxiety about Florence was not returned. In spite of her voluntary seclusion, Florence knew something about the human personality—knew that Terry was following the line for which she was best fitted. She translated the situation into scientific terms for herself, by likening Terry to a color; say, orange. Orange had a place in the spectrum; it occurred between red and yellow. It would be ridiculous to try to build a spectrum that would show orange between indigo and violet. It would be equally ridiculous to try to move Terry from her proper place in the world: it would not be logical. That last conclusion was all Florence ever needed to convince herself about anything. Logic ... in logic, Florence would say, is all the adventure, all the beauty, the glory, the poetry in the universe. Socrates once said that a well-ordered mind, given a single pertinent fact, and time for thought, could visualize the entire universe and all that it contained. It was that sort of mind that was Florence's ideal: her scientist's brain told her that her ideal was perfection, and therefore impossible; her realization of this impossibility gave her her brand of yearning, provocative happiness. The search for facts; the logical, symphonic regimentation of those facts into their predetermined patterns; the harmonization of these patterns with contrasting and correlative patterns to take their place in the rhythmic whole; this was her life and her reason for living.

Terry burst into their little apartment one afternoon to find Florence pacing worriedly about, the complete neatness of her bearing marred by a tiny annoyed frown between her eyes.

"Darling! Oh, it's good to be back! How are you? You've been working too hard. I wish you'd—how do I look? See—new shoes. Boa. Oh Florence, I met the most marvelous man! He's *just* your type. Look, we can arrange a little party. We'll get you a nice fluffy organdy. Powder-blue. He talks beautifully about the most amazing things. His name's Ben. Youngish, with a face like a very nice horse. Frightfully clever. Ph.D. and all that. Oh dear, your hair's all straggly. If only you'd let me set it—just once; you'd see how it would be—what have you been doing all this time?"

Florence smiled. Sometimes she almost envied Terry her bewildering personality, the vibrant dynamism with which she attacked life. Look at this; a weekend house party; three days of no doubt violent exercise; probably no little wear and tear on her emotional setup; yet she was as fresh and crisp-looking as a frozen lettuce leaf. "I've been trying the impossible and learning a great deal from it," she said. "I've a suspicion that the velocity of light is not, after all, a constant. I think that there are greater speeds in the deep ultraviolet. That's why I have this new gear-wheel light-interrupter; but it will take some close figuring. Any difference will be fractional— *very* small. I can't do a thing until I get that new rheostat. The one I've got is too clumsy; I haven't control enough. It's like the old gag about a drugstore sandwich: the first bite and you haven't reached the filling, the next bite and you're past it. When they get around to delivering the new 'stat—it's a micro-vernier, variable to three twenty-five thousandths of —"

Terry, listening vaguely, felt again that surge of impatience with her sister. Meeting Ben at the house party had filled her with plans. She was sure that if Florence and Ben ever met, they would hit it off beautifully. She was equally sure that it would take a stroke of genius—or a stick of dynamite—to pry Florence loose from her little laboratory long enough to spend a whole evening with him.

"Oh, Florrie!" she interrupted. "Don't you *ever* want to have any fun? Work all day and most of the night, puttering around with your beams and rays and colors; if you stopped for just a *little* while you'd see what I mean. . ."

Florence had a very lovely laugh. "Terry, look. I haven't been working all afternoon; can't, until I get my rheostat. And I'm all worn out fretting about it. When it gets here, *then* I'll have my fun. . . What would you like to eat?"

They both recognized that as the signal to drop the matter; and drop it they did. Florence, of course, promptly lost the subject in the maze of mathematics that constituted her own private dreamland; but Terry worried the problem tenaciously. This sort of thing had been going on too long. Why, Florrie was an old maid! Terry was frightened of that phrase. . .

In the next ten days Terry saw Ben Pastene four times. Each time she saw him she liked him better—for Florence, of course. Oh, of course. Ben's tall, serious, slightly stoop-shouldered self was a bit out of her field . . . but then he was awfully sweet. Oh, if only Florence—but no, Florence had refused point blank to come with her and meet him, had refused even to pretty up and let Terry bring him home. Some other time, perhaps; but this new stroboscopic effect . . . and the convention next month; she *had* to have her paper ready;

and oh, Terry darling, please don't be such a little schemer.

Terry's light, laughing efforts began to be just the slightest bit grim.

It came to a head one evening, with Terry standing near the foyer, instinctively choosing the one spot in the room where the lights would bring out to advantage her firm delicate profile. She had an innate dramatic sense; and in this last plea to her sister she played it for all it was worth. And the more she talked, the funnier it seemed to Florence. She had everything in the world she wanted—now that her micro-vernier rheostat had arrived!—and her beloved sister was trying to palm off one of her glamour-boys on her.

"You're wrong, Terry," she said steadily, when at last she could get a word in. "I *don't* live an unhealthy life, and I am *not* determined to be a spinster. Neither am I determined to marry. Can't you see that, you idiot? I've got more important things to think about!"

"Important?" shrilled her sister. "What could be more important that a husband, and a home, and—and the p-protection he could give you—" Terry was near the breaking point.

Florence's voice was very soft. "Sweetheart, I have a home. And I don't need protection. Now, please—"

Terry flung out of the room. "Sometimes, Florence, for a girl with so many brains, you can be un-ut-ter-ab-ly STUPID!" The door slammed, and Terry was gone for the evening. Florence shrugged. She hated scenes, but she knew that it was worth going through one every now and then: they cleared the air. Life would be peaceful for six or seven weeks, for two of which Terry would probably sulk. Ah, well. Now that Doppler effect with the interrupter at .065 ... and back she went into her laboratory.

Hours later the doorbell buzzed discreetly. Florence started, then sent her mind racing after the formula she had almost stumbled on. "N to the fifth power over this cosine, take the mantissa of the log of the denom— darn it!" she said with emphasis. She threw down her pencil and marched to the door, making up her mind that hereafter the buzzer would be choked with absorbent cotton. She threw the door open and found herself staring at a collar and tie—a very tasteful tie, she had to admit, and she knew something about color-value ... her gaze travelled up to a pointed chin with just the suggestion of a cleft on it, up to a well-shaped mouth, up past cheeks that were a bit too thin, up to a pair of friendly, green-flecked brown eyes. The eyes had it, she quipped to herself... "it"... "Oh," she said, feeling very silly.

"I do hope I haven't bothered you," he said in a voice that matched the eyes, for it was warm and friendly, too. "Your sister said you'd be working ... I'm Ben Pastene. She said you'd remember the name." He waited patiently. Florence let the silence build agonizingly before she collected wits enough to invite him in. She did, though; and they stood there in the middle of the room, staring at each other. He was very tall and gentle-looking, and she was very appealing in the tan lab smock, though she didn't know it. Ben Pastene had a sudden impulse to brush her soft-looking hair back from her face, and laughed at the thought. That broke the ice; she laughed too, and she did have a very lovely laugh.

She took his hat and coat, while he explained his errand. Terry was spending the night with a girlfriend, and her earring had broken, and since he would be passing this way, she had asked him to drop in and tell Florence not to expect her, and to leave the earring.

Florence was so furious at her sister's machinations that she laughed; and as soon as she had laughed she stopped being furious. But Terry would hear about this—oh yes indeed!

"Terry has talked and talked of you," Ben Pastene said. He offered her a cigarette, which she refused. She liked his hands and the way he handled them... "Terry is given to exaggeration," she said primly.

He looked at her so critically that she blushed. "By no means!" he said, and she knew he meant it. She thought it very foolish to be pleased, but she was—terribly. "And she has spoken of you too. She thinks you are quite a paragon. No vices. No objectionable characteristics besides that one. And a Ph.D."

He laughed. "She's more than generous... What is the work she says you bury yourself in, to the exclusion of all worthwhile things in life?"

"Oh, she's been talking that way, has she? Oh well—Terry lives in a different world from me. I'm no more fitted for the things she does and wants to do than she is for my particular sphere. I can't do the rumba—but then I can do wonders with the cube root of minus x."

He laughed again and she suddenly had the feeling that she would like to keep him laughing—it was such a pleasant sound... She wondered why she found it almost imperative to defend herself against Terry's influence with this man.

"You still haven't told me about your work, you know."

"Oh—I fool around with light that you can't see, trying to find out if it could be of any use to anybody... I'm afraid it wouldn't be very interesting. What's interesting to you?"

"Languages, mostly. I got my Ph.D. by making a left-hand stab at a thesis on the probable location of Atlantis, as shown by language trends ... but I'm interested in light too. Talk about it."

"Never mind that," she smiled. "I want to hear about Atlantis. It sank under the sea, didn't it?"

He gave in, for her interest was obviously genuine. As he talked he warmed to his subject, and so did she. He spoke of the dead civilizations of Atlantis and Mu; of the possibilities of a former great civilization in the heart of the Sahara, near the mountains called Atlas; of a sunken continent whose mountain peaks were the Azores; of a people of vast learning who taught the Maya and Incas of Yucatan and Peru how to pronounce the mystic word Atl; of the Greek legends of a land in the West, while west of Greece is the Mediterranean—the midst of the earth. Here were things that could not be seen nor felt, but which were real to those of us today, even as ultraviolet and infrared light ... she said as much, and then it was her turn. They went into the laboratory, and she spoke of heat and light and electromagnetic theory. She showed him how infrared rays can be focussed so that they can pass through a man's hand painlessly and set fire to a piece of paper at the other side. She showed him spectra of plain and polarized light, and initiated him into the mysteries of light that is violet and past violet, coming nearer and nearer to black which is not black, but invisible, vibrant light. In exchange for his stories of things once seen and now invisible, she showed him things once invisible but now seen.

It grew late, and he had to go. They stood together for a long minute, saying nothing. Florence felt as she had the night she discovered the new ratio of the invisible wavelengths to each other—joy of achievement, joy in adventure. But this was better. It was more—personal. He said, "I'll see you again soon, won't I?"

She nodded because suddenly she couldn't speak; he went to the door and slipped out. Three seconds later he was back. He pressed Terry's broken earring into her hand. "I didn't mean *that* soon," he joked. "But it was nice, wasn't it?"

"Goodnight, Ben," she said, using his name for the first time. "Goodnight. . ." and now he was really gone.

She stood there a long while, then laughed because she wanted to see if she still could. She went back to her desk in the laboratory and tried to go on with her knotty problem in solid trig. It was too much—not that she couldn't handle the math. It was only that tonight, somehow, she didn't give a hoot for her hypothetical light velocities. She went to bed.

She slept magnificently, waking very late. Terry was home, sitting in the bedroom easy chair, reading. As Florence opened her eyes Terry saw her, came and sat on the bed. She looked perturbed. Good old Terry! She was worried about her shrewd little plan! Well, let her stop worrying. It had worked. It had worked! Florence threw her arms about her sister, drew her close.

"You're terribly clever, darling, in spite of your pretty face," she whispered. "He's wonderful. I never knew a mere man could be so— so sweet. Oh, thank you, Terry. I'll never be able to thank you enough. . ."

"Did—did he like you, Florrie?"

"He wants to see me again—soon."

Florence lay holding Terry, looking up at a sunbeam, and smiling. She was afraid, and happy, and tremendously excited all at once. Suddenly, "Why—Terry! You're crying! Sweetheart! I haven't seen you cry since you lost that great big mama-doll when you were a kid! What is it? Oh, *please*, Terry!"

Terry wet Florence's cheek with her own. "Florence . . . I didn't want to. Really I didn't. I wanted him for you. I lay awake all last night, thinking about you and him here together . . . oh, why did he have to like you after all? Florrie, say you don't think I'm a pig. Please, dear..." she collapsed in a gale of sobs.

Dazed, puzzled, Florence repeated slowly, "Lay awake last ... didn't want to ... thinking about—Terry! Terry, tell me! You love Ben! Don't you? You—" Another storm of weeping was answer enough. "Terry! Snap out of it, child. Come on, imbecile; we have to talk this thing out. Good heavens; with all the men in the world, you have to pick on ... and me too ... oh, what a miserable, maudlin *mess!*"

Terry quieted after a bit; rose calmly and went to the dresser, where she stood with her back to the bed, skillfully applying a new complexion. Finished, she whirled and said suddenly with utter frigidity, "Florence, I love him and I mean to have him. I'm sorry, but I can't give him up, not even for you. I've *got* to do this!"

"Do you think you can?" Florence was desperately afraid, but tried not to show it.

Terry laughed and looked in the mirror, looked at Florence, and laughed again. "What do you think?" And she went out. She was as lovely as ever a woman could be, and they both knew it.

For weeks after that the two of them fought each other desperately. Florence was more than a little hurt at Terry's action; for Ben was truly Florence's first; it hit her harder because of that. Terry had hundreds of friends. She would get over it. If Florence didn't win this crazy battle, she'd never recover. Everything was at stake—her own peace of mind, her hopes of years of intensive work; all would be destroyed if her petulant sister got what she was after. Florence had two things on her side, however. One was a mental level on which she could meet Ben Pastene; the other was a philosophical sense of humor, which made things a bit easier for her. In spite of the agony she went through, she still found herself able to laugh at all three of them. If she thought in emotional headlines the way Terry did, she would no doubt term the conflict as one of science against beauty. An amusing thought ... true, though. Now, how catch a man with a noose of light?

Ben, poor fellow, hovered betwixt and between. True, his world was nearer that of Florence; but that was all the more reason why the brilliant, scintillating Terry appealed. After seeing either he could think of nothing else—until he saw the other. They both knew it, and both worked the harder.

The showdown came on a Thursday evening. Ben had two tickets to an opening night, and was to call for Terry. Terry took a good two hours dressing, and a beautiful job she did of it. Florence came to the door of the bedroom once to look. Terry had just slipped into a breathtaking gown—golden satin, with a great black sash. Terry's cornsilk hair artfully matched it, sweeping upward just enough to follow the clinging lines of the gown. Terry glanced up at Florence and said nastily, patting the smooth lines, "Point one for the common people." Florence made not a sound; she closed the door softly and went and stood in the middle of the living room, pulling her lower lip and thinking like mad. Then she slipped into her little laboratory, did some more thinking, and finally came back with an odd-shaped electric light bulb in her hand. She fitted it into a floor lamp, carried the lamp over to the daybed and adjusted it to throw its light left-center on the pillowed surface. Then she went to the closet and got a rich black velvet spread for the couch. When she had finished she changed the hall light for a pale blue globe, almost daylight. Then she went into her own bedroom, changed quickly into a very chic tailored tweed, and threw on a laboratory smock over it. A dab at face and lips, and she was ready.

The doorbell buzzed. Terry emerged from her room, uttered a gasp of delight at the way the stage was set. She could no more keep away from that bath of golden light on the daybed than could any other moth keep away from the flame ... the whole room shaped itself toward that artfully illuminated center stage. Terry sat just where the light would do the most good, arranged the rich fold of her dress, and called, "Open the door, there's a dear." Her voice was kinder than it had been in some time. How *sweet* of Florrie!

Florence slipped to the door. She leaned out and said softly in his ear, "Terry doesn't feel so well tonight, Ben ..." That was enough. He came in, was three steps across the room before he saw her.

"Terry—" he swallowed awkwardly and stared at her. "I—I'm so sorry. I had no idea, or I wouldn't have come. I'll c-come back again. Please take care of yourself . . . well, I—that is—well, goodn—"

"Ben," said Florence clearly, "You have the tickets already, haven't you? I'll go with you." She threw off her smock, tossed a coat over her arm. "I'm ready." She steered a bewildered Ben Pastene under the blue light. She looked sweet under its daylight rays, and she knew it. "Terry'll be happier by herself. Don't worry."

"If you say so. . ." The poor young man was badly shaken.

That's the end of the story. He proposed to Florence that night. On the borderline anyway, he needed very little persuasion. Florence never told him, of course, or Terry either, what had happened. The lamp was sodium vapor; its light is the cruelest in the spectrum. It illuminates every microscopic blemish, every inevitable wrinkle invisible in ordinary light. What choice had he, with that picture in his mind, the picture of a once-lovely Terry with black lips, dull hair, brown-rouged cheeks, blemished, lined skin, jaundiced flesh?

A shabby trick? Possibly. But all's fair—Terry would have tired of him; she only wanted what she couldn't have. She was enormously resilient. She was happy again very soon. Florence too. Florence is so happy with her husband today that she hasn't time for a hypothetical conscience. . .

Strangers on a Train

THE STEEL RAILS stretched back and back, closing steadily, following her like shears, great shining shears pursuing her. But they never closed on the train as they had closed on her life with Leo. Now that she could see it detachedly, she realized that the thread that bound them together had been doomed to be cut from the start. Funny . . .

A man stepped out on the observation platform and sat beside her. She resented it a little; she had been enjoying her sole possession of the cool retreat. Oh well—

She looked at him out of the corner of her eye. He was staring back at the flying roadbed, his face a little flushed as if he had been embarrassed. She smiled a little. Nice-looking guy, in his way, she thought objectively.

He said to her, out of the corner of his mouth, "The road from Reno. Hah." That "hah" can't really be spelt; it was just a sound, a wordless question, answer, excuse.

Well, why not talk to him? She could take care of herself. Meet a stranger on a train, talk to him, forget him. It was done every day. But she was still naive enough to get a little thrill of excitement out of it. What a world of hitherto unspoken things could be said by a stranger to a stranger!

"You, too?" Her tone was joking, but he looked at her understandingly. "Don't tell me you're sorry already!"

He joined her brief laugh. "No, not so you'd notice it." He looked at her quizzically. "You look happy yourself," he cracked.

"I'm not, particularly," she said gravely. "How can one be? I've got to undo what it took me years to build up. I don't think it will take me quite as long to do that as it did to build it all."

He said, with a shade of shyness in his voice, "You've got your divorce, haven't you? That's the finish, isn't it? What is there left to break down?

Her eyes stopped seeing the whizzing ties as she spoke, and her mind brought words out of the past. "There's lots left. I did what any woman does. I spent my teens growing up into the woman that would marry her man some day. Every minute of my life led upward and onward until the day I met him, and he went beside me along the same road. It went upward and onward too, until a few months ago. How silly!" she said suddenly. "I'm talking like a popular song!"

"Keep on singing." His face was turned away.

"Well, that's what I've got to tear down. The divorce means the end of those few months; that's all. But the years that we walked upward together ... well, I'll just have to walk back down them, alone, until I come back to the place where I met him. It will take a while, I imagine. But not as long as the last time I travelled it ... anyway, when I get there I suppose I'll turn around and start back. By myself."

He looked at her as if she were something strange. "You talk a mean talk, stranger."

She returned the look. "Bad habit. What's your story."

"Mine? ... Well, life'll go on, I guess. I've got a good job, that's something. I'll save money, invest it, get more, lose it. I'll keep myself busy, keep myself worried. Not so tough for me." He glanced at her again; her face was impassive. That face... In repose, it was like something carven. It was smooth, pastel-tinted, and her translucent eyelids were veils. One could imagine that face with its eyes wide open. There was an enchantment about her, a deep, provocatively mysterious quality. What a woman, he thought impulsively; *what a woman!*

"Oh, there'll be details," he supplemented. "I'll have to move—"

"Why?"

He flushed. "Oh, I don't know... I've got to shift gears. I'm not keyed to batching it." He paused, then tried again, seeing her slow smile. "It's just that I don't want to live in the same place where I—" He shrugged. "Let's put it this way; I'm not a sentimental person. Never was. And I don't want to give myself the opportunity to be. See?"

"Yes. I quite understand. . . I'm giving away everything I had—clothes, gifts, everything, and I'm getting new ones, for the same reason. Not because I hate the sight of them and what they represent, but because I'd rather not have them around. Tell me. How do you see your wife now?"

The question startled him a little. She thought he looked a little angry, too. "Well, really, I can't—I mean, you don't expect me to—I mean—"

"Don't be silly," she said firmly, quite taking his breath away. "I'm no relation to you; we're two strangers talking about this and that. When this train stops you and I will never see each other again, except as strangers. Besides—" and the little smile quivered wickedly about her lips "—it's your own doing. You've aroused my woman's curiosity. I wouldn't be surprised if you have never seen her straight until now that it's all over. Go ahead; I'd like to hear a man telling something like the truth about a woman."

He raised his eyebrows and smiled broadly at that. Then, laughing, "All right. You asked for it!"

He offered her a cigarette and lit one himself, watching her. She had leaned back, quite relaxed, her eyes apparently closed, though you never could tell about those eyes. . . It was almost a pity to have the stranger status forced on him by such a woman. Oh, well. Better that way.

"She was very lovely. When I married her she was the answer to all questions. We shared everything, and yet we both had our own lives and led them. She wasn't possessive or jealous; she had sense enough to realize that to give a sense of freedom is the best way to hold a man."

"Or a woman," she murmured.

His eyes flashed toward her, then away. "Yes," he said slowly. "I guess it is. . ." He was quiet for so long that she thought he had forgotten what he was saying—or that he had been saying anything at all. She overcame an impulse to make him go on, and sat waiting.

"Funny it had to be a stranger to tell me that," he said finally.

"What?"

"That business of freedom. She gave it to me so willingly that it never occurred to me that she might want some too. I guess I *was* a bit of a dictator. There were some pretty rotten scenes... I said once that if I ever tripped her up on one of her accounts of where she had been and what she had done there, that I would horsewhip her. I don't think she ever forgot that. She was very honest with herself and with me; so much so that I sometimes thought it was an act. It wasn't." He flicked his cigarette over the railing. It fell slowly until it hit the ties, and then was whisked out of sight.

"Well," he went on. "Life was pretty nice until she blew up one night. Soon afterward I met her in a nightclub, with a very good-looking youngster on her arm. That was the finish for me."

She told her story, then, quietly. "I married a man who shared everything with me—that he felt like sharing. But he cut me out of a great deal of his life. That hurt a little, although he never knew it. He had the old-fashioned double-standard; he could do as he pleased, but I couldn't. I didn't, either, for the two good years we were married. But in the last few months it got a little too much for me. He was never really unfaithful to me, just inconsiderate. He loved me, I think; but he had never suffered because of someone else, and he couldn't understand why I was hurt. It was my fault. I never let him know I *was* hurt until things had gone too far, and then it was too late to talk it over quietly. He couldn't understand me, so I found someone who could. It was a case of choosing between someone who I could love without understanding, and someone who could understand me without love. I chose. I made no effort to hide it from my husband, and of course he found out. He took it the hard way."

"The damn fool."

"No!" she cried, gripping his arm, speaking with a vehemence that almost frightened him. "He was right! I was wrong. It was wrong of me not to present myself to him, my true self, so that he could adjust himself to me, as I did to him! It was wrong of me not to tell him he was hurting me! It was wrong of me not to let him give me the understanding he would have, if I'd asked for it!"

Quite suddenly, she found his arms around her, and he found her clinging to him, sobbing madly against his rough coat. It was the first time he had ever seen her cry...

"Leona, Leona, why did we do it? Oh, my darling, why didn't you tell me? I've tried to be what I thought you wanted me to be... I love you! Believe me ... would I have followed you to Reno if I didn't? Would I have sat there in the courtroom, seeing them take you from me, if I didn't love you, want to give you what you wanted?"

"Courtroom ... Leo! Were you there? I saw you get on the train..."

"Try again, darling?"

Her kiss was her answer.

Accidentally on Porpoise

What a funny little bird a frog are ...
When he stand he sit ... when he walk he fly ...

WELL, A PORPOISE is like that. He isn't a fish, but he swim. He isn't a bird, but he flies. He lives for the hell of it and he's nobody's fool. Ask Whacker. He was a porpoise once. Still is, sometimes.

Whacker was 12 to 4 AB on the *Seabreeze*. There wasn't much of the average about Whacker. He could talk a blue streak when he wanted to, which wasn't often. Moody sort of man; well-read, well-schooled and as haywire as they come.

The *Seabreeze* was an old ship, but she was tight and she was clean. She was taking a load of casing-head from Texas City to Boston. Know what casing-head is? Aviation gas; plenty high-test. Throw a quart of it up in the air and nothing comes down. A bucket of it set on the deck will be empty in forty minutes. You can see the vapor rising out of the tank-vents like heat-haze off hot asphalt. You spray the decks to keep the temperature down, and you keep your cigarettes below. Low-flash, they call it, which means that it makes explosive vapors when the weather's hot enough to make you sweat. It isn't often carried in a gasoline-tanker like the *Seabreeze*. Casing-head ships have all the tank-vents enclosed and leading to an escape high up on the mast, while the *Seabreeze* had individual vents for her twenty-eight tanks. But it was a juicy contract for the company and they risked it.

She made it across the Gulf and through the Florida Straits, and then got away from the coast and slid up close to the Bahamas. Around Great Isaac light a heavy sea started running, with a fair wind. The smoke from the stack stood straight up, and it was stifling hot.

When she got out from the lee of the islands, the old hulk really started to go to town. You don't often see a sea like that; not much wind, but the sea like a running relief of the Rockies. Pitch? Why, she stood on her counter and wheeled slowly, as if she had eyes in her belly and was curious; then she'd bury her nose and put the sky back aft.

The smell of that vapor got into everything, because it wasn't blowing away. The crew ate it and slept with it. When she put her snout down that invisible mass of vapor swept aft and gagged them; when she came up again it would drift forward a little. That kept up for thirty-six hours.

The Maritime Commission, in its inquest, said the *Seabreeze* blew up because of mechanical failure; the cargo supposedly seeped through the seams of No. 9 tank into the fireroom. Hogwash. She exploded because of the carelessness of a man they called Tortugas.

He was on the 4 to 8 watch, and before he knocked off for chow at 5:00 he took some buckets down to the shelter deck. She was a well-decker, with a high poop and midship house, and an enclosed shelter deck under it. Pitching the way she was, taking seas the way any tanker will, the main deck was deeply awash. Tortugas threw the buckets in, swung the watertight door shut and ran back up the ladder to the flying bridge. He didn't take the trouble to force the dogs home on that door, because he didn't want to get wet. A very little thing, eh?

When they called Whacker that night at 11:40 he went up on deck to have a look at the weather. You know, a ship at sea is the loneliest thing in the universe. You don't need much imagination to feel that there is nothing on earth but you and the ship and the sea. That's why so many sailors are screwy, and Whacker was no exception.

He stood at the break of the poop feeling maudlin. He *was* alone in the world; the twenty-eight years of his life had deprived him of everything but his present trade and a startling number of memories . . . he'd been around. As he stood there in the still air, riding the deck and gaping at the moon, his mind drifted back over the years, pausing casually on impressions of a couple of years in college, a couple of years on the bum, flitting purposefully past memories of a home that was gone, and of five or nine ex one-and-onlys... The vagrant and persistent gas fumes didn't help any. Breathing too much of gas vapor affects you like eating canned heat.

There were no ships in sight from where he stood. Over on the port side, about five miles off, there was a little light that danced crazily in the swell, a forty-foot boat out of the yacht basin. Probably after tuna or sailfish, thought Whacker. No justice in the world. I'd like to be the guy that owns that tub. He hasn't got a thing in the world to worry about.

Whacker would have been surprised if he had been able to see the man standing by the wheel of the boat. She was the auxiliary sloop *Trigger,* and the most luxurious craft of her size afloat. She belonged to Steve Roupe, and Steve had come out that night to kill himself.

Bored. Terribly, morbidly bored. There was nothing that Steve Roupe hadn't done except work for a living, and nothing that he wanted to do except die. Last of a family of financiers, he had been humored and kow-towed to all his life. He was a moody, impulsive, childishly stubborn man, and for the last year or so he had been increasingly despondent. He had always been strangely popular, in spite of the fact that his dark bearing frightened people, yet he got no satisfaction out of his popularity. He disliked women because he was convinced that they were, one and all, after his money; yet he was bored with having money. He was overbearing because he was unsure of himself; he couldn't get rid of the idea that intrinsically he had nothing, and that he was only accepted, courted, and associated with because of his wealth. He hated his world and he hated himself, and the prospect of what he was about to do brought a great peace to him.

He left the wheel and dragged the anchor out of the tender. It weighed a hundred pounds and was hard to handle, but it would fill the bill. Laying it on the deck aft, he got a couple of fathoms of line out of the tackle locker, and then stopped the engine. Running back to the anchor, he set it on end, squatted beside it and let it rest against his chest. Passing the line around his body and through the shackle on the anchor, he made it fast to the shank; then, bracing his feet, he waited.

The *Trigger,* having lost weigh, began to come about. Her violent pitch changed to a roll as she took the seas on the quarter and then abeam. She took sea after sea, and Roupe felt his strength leaving him as he fought to keep upright, balanced on the six-inch rail. He was deathly calm. He stared off into the night and saw the lights of a tanker a few miles off. She seemed so strong and steady...

Suddenly, in between the mast-head lights of the tanker, a great yellow flame lifted, poking up and towards the moon. A great excitement filled Steve Roupe; here was something with a kick to it, something new and different. He snatched at the knot on the anchor-shank, and as he did so a huge sea swept aboard, slamming the little craft scuppers under. With a despairing cry, Stephen Roupe and his anchor disappeared over the side.

Aboard the *Seabreeze* Whacker was snapped out of his reverie by a jarring boom up 'midships on the port side. The shelter-deck door! Dogs adrift, it swung open and shut with each feverish dive of the ship; steel against steel as she came up, steel against packing as she plunged. Whacker started for the flying bridge at a dead run, but he hadn't taken two steps before she struck the inevitable spark.

A puff of transparent blue flame blossomed out, hung for seconds over the deck, and then vanished. There was a great coughing sound and a column of fire spouted out of the vent of No. 4 port main tank; rose higher and higher as the heat sucked the vapor out, vaporized more. The tip of the vent glowed red, and then she let go. No. 4 starboard went a half-second later. The midship house caved in on itself. Sparks staggered blindly from his room toward the radio shack that wasn't there any more, and then No. 3 and No. 5 blew out together. That was getting a little close to home, and Whacker raced aft, yelling down the ventilators.

They tumbled out, sleep-drugged, frightened. Some had their dungarees on, and some hadn't. Some were calm, but most of them were in a crawling panic. A big wiper was laying his fists right and left, trying to snap the panicky ones out of it. A few stood blinking at the flames. A few ran around in circles like trapped rats, too stupefied to make for the boats.

What Whacker wanted was a life jacket. He tried the hatch ladder, but turned back at the sight of Tortugas huddled on the steps, smashed to a pulp by hysterical feet. That's the way he paid. Whacker dropped down through a skylight into the alleyway, and burst into the sailors' fo'c'sle. As he snatched three preservers out of the rack the deck settled appreciably under his feet. After that he didn't mind climbing up over Tortugas.

Up on the boat deck there was a miniature riot. It's one thing to swing the boats out on an orderly weekly lifeboat drill; but it's something else again to fight weather and panic at the same time, with no one in charge but the bosun—if being in charge means yelling sensible orders at a bunch of raving maniacs. The three mates, the Old Man, Sparks, and two of the seamen on watch had all gone wherever the midship house went to.

The boilers popped off. Thank God for the safety valves.

Two more tanks exploded up forward, and the ship gave a crazy lurch and rolled over on her beam-ends. A great sea smashed the starboard boat, and the port boat swung inboard, useless.

The engines started to pound as she put her head down and the wheel began cutting air.

"... who art in heaven, hallowed be thy name ..." Who the hell was that?

"Come on in, boys, the water's fine."

Someone kept screaming like a horse with a broken leg.

The bosun ran past, leaning against the heel of the deck, yelling, "Someone give me a hand!" Whacker followed him blindly. He dropped onto the poop deck, started knocking the wedges off the after cargo-hatch battens. Whacker thrust his arms through the holes of a life jacket, threw the others at the bosun. They washed over the side. They got all the wedges off one end of the hatch, stripped the tarpaulin back, began throwing the hatch boards over the side. That bosun was a man. He'd thought of the only thing aboard that you could count on to float.

No. 7 and 8 went. The mainmast, with no decking under it, sagged, then speared through the bottom. The five-ton boom it carried crashed down on the poop deck, pinning the bosun's legs. He lay there with the water washing over him. Whacker set his shoulder to the boom and heaved until his muscles cracked, but it never shifted. The bosun grinned and shook his head. Whacker tore the pipe-vise loose from the pumpman's bench and brought it over. The bosun grinned again and nodded. Whacker let him have it . . .

There was burning gasoline for seventy yards around the ship, except back aft. Whacker ran drunkenly to the taffrail, feverishly knotting the tapes on his jacket. He wondered vaguely as he dove whether that jacket would drown him or starve him. Then he was in the water. A sea carried him high and pitched him sickeningly downward. Something smashed him cruelly in the face and he felt the skin shredding and tearing away; then the lights went out.

It was daylight when he opened his eyes. They burned agonizingly. The sea was still running high. His patent life-preserver had turned him over on his back as he floated unconscious. He took a few feeble strokes and looked around him. It was a small world. On a ship there's eleven miles on each side of you; here there was hardly eleven yards.

The ocean is a soft bed and the Gulf Stream is not cold. But his head ached in great throbs and the salt bit into his tattered face. He tried to cough, and when he did he couldn't stop. He coughed until he passed out.

Hours later he came to the second time. He was going to ask the 8 to 12 man if it was one bell yet but his tongue was so thick he couldn't talk. He had to ask because if he didn't he might oversleep and miss a watch. He tried hard and made a horrible cackling sound that frightened him. He was sick, that's what it was. Better tell the steward. When do we dock, steward? You don't dock, you rock. Up. Down. The steward's dead. The steward's red. No, Red's dead too. He heard that cackling sound again, and thought it was laughter.

There's a light in my eyes, he thought. I'm sick, mother. Mother sat beside me for four days and nights because I had rheumatic fever. Mother drank coffee and smoked and never moved for four days and nights, because I couldn't breathe and my joints hurt. But don't hit me! Hey!

He was jolted into almost complete awareness by a heavy bump in the ribs. A dark fin whipped by him, a great streamlined shape leaped glistening into the sun. As it hit the water another gave him a crushing blow in the back. Two more curvetted gaily to one side, and another appeared beside the first. The leader turned and rushed again and Whacker tried feebly to escape. His hands splashed clumsily and one of the porpoises made a noise like a baby crying, and he was suddenly alone again. A porpoise won't touch a live man but he'll roll a dead one for miles. Hah! That showed 'em!

Nobody's fool... We know, don't we, porpoise?

You are a porpoise, a voice in Whacker's brain told him. You are beautiful and strange, and you live for the hell of it. You are fearless and strong and swift. You run before a ship's cutwater, tantalizing the menace of its bruising steel. There are never sharks in your neighborhood. Arch your back strongly, porpoise, and drift clear of the water.

In that moment Whacker, able seaman, sole survivor of the tankship *Seabreeze,* ceased to exist, and became transmuted.

As yet he could not leap, but it was easy to make a noise like a baby crying, and he did it many times.

The seas grew larger. A seam on the shoulder-piece of his jacket ripped, grew slowly wider. And then he sensed the presence of another object plunging about his little turbulent world. It was a boat with no hand at the tiller, a trim little sloop that danced and dived and shouldered valiantly up through masses of water. Closer and closer it came, until a sea picked Whacker up and slammed him against the white side. The wrenching blow tore the jacket off his right shoulder, dipped him deep. The pain of the strangling brine brought his last reflexes to life. As the next sea lifted him he grabbed for the low rail and was swept up and over. For minutes he lay there with his sodden hand cramped on the bulwark, and then the strangeness of this new element pressed to his shining porpoise's body penetrated his consciousness. He started groggily up and tumbled into the cockpit, freeing himself of the rags that were once a life-preserver. Working forward, he fell up against the sliding door of the cabin, jerked it open just as the sloop hurled herself into a half-loop. He tottered wildly and then crashed to the deck below, full on his broken face.

And the *Trigger* of Miami danced and danced, carrying her strange cargo huddled at the foot of the ladder below; carrying a man that had been a porpoise, a porpoise that did not know he had been a man.

The man in the white bed heard music, and it was the music of a voice. It was soft and cool. The whole world was soft and cool. He opened his eyes. . .

She was glorious. Her hair was auburn and her eyes were green, and the cleft in her chin was a dimple and her teeth twinkled. She said, "You silly, salty, pseudo-sophisticated son of a sea-going Swede!"

He closed his eyes quickly, startled at things he could not understand. Then with exaggerated slyness he opened them again. She was still there. He opened his mouth to speak, and a light weight closed on his face. Raising a three-hundred-pound hand to his cheek, he found that his head was swaddled in bandages, tight and close as an eye-splice parcelling. "What the hell—"

"Easy, boy!" said the vision that was real. She put her hand gently on his shoulder and pressed him back. "Don't say anything. You've been through the mill."

He lay there, relaxed and wondering. "What—"

The soft hand touched gently on the bandages over his lips. "No, Steve. Take it easy, will you?" She moved her chair closer and took his hand. "Doctor's orders; no talking. But you can listen. And I'll let you say Yes and No. But no more. Agreed?"

"Yes," he said. "But—"

"One more but out of you and I won't talk to you," she said sternly, yet smiling.

"Yeah."

"Steve, it's a miracle that you're alive. You've been here three weeks and this is the first time that you've heard me. You've been lying there with your eyes open, and the only sound you've made until today was a noise like a baby with the croup. Good Lord! We thought you'd lost your mind! You *can* hear me, Steve?"

"Yes."

"That's the ol' fight. Well, what do you want to know—I mean, do you know where you are, and what happened, and all that?"

"No."

"You *did* take a beating! Well, you took one of your spur-of-the-moment runs on the *Trigger*, all by yourself. I guess we'll never know where you were bound unless you can remember it sometime. My guess is that you went out there to be morbid." She laughed a little. "Chances are that you saw the *Seabreeze* and went over to investigate. But before you could get near enough to help, you fell down the hatch and knocked yourself out. How you could have been messed up like that is a mystery to me."

"*Seabreeze?*" he said.

"Hey! Is that a yes-or-no? The *Seabreeze* was a tanker that exploded right near where they picked you up. A terrible thing; killed every soul aboard. They were looking for survivors when they found you."

He raised his hand to his face again.

"Oh, the damage? Lucky break you're living in the twentieth century, Steve. Besides a strained shoulder and a couple of broken ribs, your face ... but don't worry about it. This is Dr. Dubois's clinic. He's rebuilding your face from photographs. He says that a year from now no one will ever even guess that he's been working on you. It's costing you plenty, Steve, but you always did say that you had too much money. Anything else?"

"Yes."

"Let's see ... I think I've covered everything..."

"Who are you?"

A great amazement turned swiftly to hurt in her clear eyes. "Steve ... you don't know me? Remember Orlando, Steve, and what Winchell called our 'whirlwind courtship'? Remember the fight we had, Steve, when you told me I bored you, and you went off in a paddy?" Anger suddenly flared. She was beautiful that way. "Steve, if you're putting this on ... don't play games with me!"

"No! No!" he cried.

"It's true then?" She leaned back in her chair, overcome. Then, "Permit me to introduce myself. Mr. Roupe, meet Miss Perry. Sandra to you. Chawmed, I'm sure."

"Roupe?" he said weakly.

"Steve! Even your own— Don't you remember anything?"

"No!" he cried, agonized. "No!"

"Oh, Steve, I've tired you out. I'm a fool. Don't worry about it darling. Please. It will be all right." She leaned over and lightly kissed his bandages. Suddenly she was all intentness. "Listen to me, Steve. No one must know of this. There are too many people that would welcome this as a godsend. You are a very rich man. If it could be proved in court that you had completely lost your memory, ways might be found to put you in a sanitarium, so that your money could be handled by someone else. I think we can do it. You've always been a peculiar, uncommunicative sort of man. Keep that up, only more so. We'll brave this thing through, you and I."

"Sandra, I—"

"Shhhh. Leave it to me. You'll be on your feet before long and we can—"

"Time, Miss Perry," said a voice at the door. A tall, gaunt man with exquisite hands came in and stood looking down at them.

"Doctor, he's really awake!" Sandra said joyfully. "He knows me!"

"Great stuff!" said Dubois. "You'll be your old self again in no time!" The old bromide.

And with a wink and a grin, Sandra was gone. They put Steve Roupe on a wheeled table and took him in to his third operation.

Eight months later Steve and Sandra went to their first party since the accident. It had been a hectic time for both of them, those months. A thousand and one details had been painstakingly taken care of. Every day there was some strange new development in the rebuilding of the man called Roupe.

There was the handwriting, for instance. In going over hundreds of documents, they had found that his old signature differed entirely from his new one. And Steve had spent two hours a day, every day, in painstakingly learning his old hand.

Then there were people. When he returned to his huge home near Boca Raton, Steve was deluged with invitations and visits. The servants were instructed to let no one see Mr. Roupe without being announced and made to wait. Sandra was usually within shouting distance, and when she wasn't she left a phone number. By the time the visitor saw Steve, Steve was well primed on all available essentials. He could call the visitor by name, gloss lightly over "memories" they shared, and cut the visit short. He learned a bushel of tricks. "About that business proposition, Mr. Roupe; could you give me an answer today?" Steve would say, "I'd like the details again, Smith; you see, since my accident I've been able to do nothing, and I'm way behind the times." This with a charming smile quite new to the traditionally solemn Mr. Roupe. And when he had the details, "All right, I'll think it over and let you know." Then he'd talk it over with Sandra.

Some things that they ran up against were astonishing and unaccountable. When Steve tried on some of his clothes, they fitted him perfectly; except shoes. The shoes that he bought now were a half-size smaller than those he had. And many of his tastes differed. Sandra found out one evening that he could dance, and remarkably well; he had never, as far as she knew, danced before. Most amazing of all was that he had forgotten how to play the piano but had mysteriously learned the guitar.

For seven of those months Steve was covered to the eyes by bandages, and during the eighth he had strips of adhesive on his cheekbones and across the bridge of his nose. He used to stand before the cheval glass in his room, staring at the outlines of this new face, memorizing it even as he had memorized his old habits and acquaintances. It was a dark face with a pointed chin and deepset, luminous eyes. He liked it.

Sandra had become his life, even as he was hers. In more ways than one, his life had begun that day he opened his eyes and saw her by the white bed.

She came on him in the garden one day, strumming on his guitar and singing, most mournfully, the "St. James Infirmary Blues." She knew by this that he was happy.

"Steve," she said softly.

He looked up at her and smiled, tossing the melody about with his long fingers, ending it with a bewildering arpeggio. She took the guitar from him and laid it on the grass and sat on his lap, putting her head on his shoulder. "Funny egg. I'd still like to know who taught you to play like that."

"King Neptune," he grinned

"He's been a wonderful teacher. You have no idea how different you are, Steve. Nicer. I've learned things about you. . . Tell you something, I never suspected that you'd have the strength to pull through this. You always were so wishy-washy. But you've worked like a Trojan on the biggest job any man was ever given to do, and you've won. No one knows about your memory but me; and the only difference anyone has seen in you is that you're ten times the person you were. I think you're wonderful, don't we?"

"All I've been is a good boy, darling, who has done what he's told. Anyone could do what I've done if he had you to lead him around by the hand." He pressed his shapely new nose into her little ear, catching the fragrance of her red-gold hair. She laughed.

"I didn't come out here to join the mutual admiration society. I came out here to tell you that Babs Fresner is throwing a party for you. How on earth she found out that you would be unveiled next week is beyond me, but she did. Her idea of a lark. Everybody is going to be dressed like Frankenstein's monster, in your honor."

"Nice girl. How do we duck this one?"

"We don't, beloved. Don't you think it's time we moved around a little?"

"Think we can do it?"

"We can if you'll keep out of dark corners with people!"

"Jealous?" he whispered.

"Terribly," she said. . .

Babs was the living prototype of the screwball deb of the movies, all sheer silk and studied spontaneity. She was built like a Coca-Cola bottle, Steve thought as he and Sandra made their entrance.

Babs was dressed in a modish grave-shroud and had grey circles painted around her eyes. She took Steve by both hands and gazed soulfully at him. The effect was astonishing.

"Babs!" Steve grinned at her. "You're marvellous. You're quite the most hideous woman I've ever seen."

66

"Continental as ever, aren't you? Hello, Sandra. You're not so bad yourself."

"Check!"

"Oh!" said Babs. "I had an idea that's the way it was. Come and meet people."

They went. Sandra stayed close to his elbow like a President's secretary, whispering names, thumbnail sketches, and comebacks; nudging, covering up, and ordering retreats. Time and again she subtly changed the subject; time and again Steve grew conveniently deaf. They carried it off well.

Wherever Steve went he was surrounded by an admiring mob. Dubois's surgery was unparalleled. He was asked a thousand and one questions about it, and congratulated a thousand times. It was in just such a group that he sensed a malignant and unpleasant stare. Turning, he looked at the man beside him.

He was quite the slimiest-looking individual Steve Roupe had ever seen. He had small eyes and a mouth oddly pointed at the corners. He was wall-eyed and flat-faced, and his dark skin shone liquidly. He had too many pointed little teeth.

Steve squeezed Sandra's arm, and she followed his eyes. They broke away from the group.

"Who's the greasy gentleman?"

"Goyaz. Your private enemy number one."

"Oh? What seems to be his trouble?"

Sandra giggled. "Last year you called him a _____." She whispered it in his ear. "He sued you for defamation of character and you proved that it was true."

Steve looked over his shoulder at Goyaz. "Come to think of it, I wouldn't be surprised if he were... Sandra, he makes me feel—oh, I don't know."

Alarmed by the sudden flare in his eyes, Sandra asked, "Steve! Steve, what is it?"

His brain began to rock. Up. Down. There was a light in his eyes... "Shark..."

She shook his arm. "Steve! Darling! Snap out of it!"

His face was white and she knew he didn't hear.

"Let's get out of here." She piloted him to the door, where they bumped into Babs. "My god!" she shrilled. "You're not going? You can't do this to me!" And before Sandra could stop her, "Hey, everybody! Steve's running out on us!"

"Shut up!" hissed Sandra, too late. "He's sick!"

They crowded over, Goyaz with them. As he approached Steve left the floor in a great arc. Never had any of them seen a leap like that. He hit Goyaz before he hit the floor, and Goyaz skittered across the room on his back. Steve lay where he had fallen, flopping, flopping, making a noise like a baby crying...

They took him home, those shaken, frightened people, and left him alone with Sandra.

For two weeks he lay like a log, unmoving, silent. Sandra and a trained nurse cared for him, fed him, bathed him. And gradually he regained his senses. He was Stephen Roupe again, but he was a frightened, trembling travesty of himself. But under Sandra's care he slowly returned to normal, with but occasional attacks of weakness.

They were married soon after that, and they sailed on the *Trigger* for a leisurely coastwise trip, casually exploring Florida's thousand and one lovely inlets. Sea and sun and quiet completed the cure, and that could be the happy ending.

But there was one thing more. One afternoon they outran a tanker, heading south in ballast.

She was old, but she was clean. She was a well-decker, with a high poop and midship house. The gang on deck were chipping; they could hear the roar of her pneumatic hammers. As they drew abreast, a deep-toned bell rang twice, calling the 4 to 8 watch to relieve the 12 to 4. Its sound echoed and re-echoed in his brain, and the mental reflex of years of training made him look over his shoulder to look for his relief. But instead of a stretch of steel deck, and the flying bridge, and the skeleton outline of the ladders to the poop, a vision in blue slacks and a red bandanna halter sprawled on a polished teak deck met his eyes... It was with an astonishing calm that he met the fact that he did not know where or who he was...

Whacker.

Roupe.

He clutched at one, and then the other identity. And then the little pieces of his personalities began to fit together, and bit by bit he knew the truth.

"Hey!" cried Mrs. Roupe. "Off course! — Steve! What is it?"

She came into the cockpit and he reached out an arm and gathered her close. "Look over there," he said.

"What; the ship?"

"Do you see what I see under the bow?"

"Yes. Porpoises; a whole school of them. But—"

"A porpoise is a wonderful creature, Sandra. He isn't a fish, but he swims. He isn't a bird, but he flies. A porpoise won't harm a live man, but he'll roll a dead one for miles... Sharks can't live where there are porpoises. He does things for the hell of it and he's nobody's fool."

The Right Line

EVERY MAN A Casanova? Sure. Every man can be, if he has the right line. A little experience, and you get to know just what line to use for each of them. Nine times out of ten, you land. What happens the tenth time is a tossup. Like Gay, for instance.

I saw Gay first as she walked into the Blue Anchor and spoke to the Syrian. I don't know what she said to him, but she got the job. He always hires assured-looking girls. He didn't see what I saw through the showcase as I knelt there cracking ice for the seafood display; her white, damp hands twisting and pulling at her handkerchief.

Her hair swept her slim shoulders, and her almond-shaped green eyes were deeply shadowed. She had a way of tilting her pointed chin as she spoke, parting her lips as if her teeth were a joyful secret.

The Syrian told the chef to feed her, and she walked across the dance floor and sank into a booth. I brought her dinner over, and she scarcely saw me as I put it before her. She was very hungry.

She had what it takes, and far be it from me to pass anything up. "Congratulations," I said.

Startled, her great eyes flashed at me like heat lightning, radiant but undirected. "I mean the job," I went on. "There's plenty in it if you want it."

"Oh—yes. Yes. The job. Thank you." Her voice was small, pinched like her cheeks. Deep, though. A voice that could sing.

I liked her. She ate hungrily, but she broke her bread before she buttered it, and she cut her meat into very tiny pieces. Her fingernails were coral, not scarlet or crimson like the rest of the come-on girls at the Anchor. I glanced at the short-order counter where the chef was absent-mindedly greasing the hot plate. No orders, then. I slid into the booth opposite her. I think she saw me for the first time.

"Like it?" I asked, indicating the food.

Again that quick, impersonal glance. "Yes. He's a good cook, isn't he?"

I thought, now we're getting somewhere. "Say, you're not a Southerner."

"How on earth did you find that out?"

Watch my smoke, says I to me. I have *just* the right line.

"Meet me," I spouted. "Name's Leo. Besides being the best combination bouncer and sandwich man on the Gulf Coast, I'm a master philologist. No Southerner cuts off his words or speaks as precisely as you do. Speak me a hundred words and I'll name your origin within two hundred square miles. I'll tell you more, too. You don't want this job and you don't like it, because you are not the type for it. You don't need the job or you wouldn't be wearing clothes like that. But you'll go through with it because you have to, and you have to because something's bothering you and this is the way to clear it up. See," I wound up, just to prove how clever I was, "It's written all over you!"

She smiled charmingly, but there was a gleam in her eye. "I know about you, too. You're not a Southerner either. Yet you don't cut off your words." The smile disappeared. "That *is* a pity."

Right on the chin. "Listen, sister—"

She slid her empty plate across the table to me. "Take that back where you got it, and see if you can't find something besides me to keep you busy." She wasn't kidding.

And before I knew what I was doing I was toting that plate back to the counter. Retreat in disorder. Me!

They can't do that to me.

The evening dragged along, and the crews started straggling in. As I whipped into my work, turning out hamburgers and Westerns, I burned. First, because I was sore. But after a while I began to wonder why I was sore, and that's when I started to be surprised.

I watched her. A honky-tonk in a Southern oil-seaport is no bed of roses. She was green, but she caught on fast. Soon she was wheedling nickels from drunken sailors to feed the hungry maw of the phonograph, dancing with two-legged wolves, drinking numberless glasses of cracked ice with three drops of cheap wine in it at two bits a throw on somebody else, coaxing trayfuls of water-cut kidney-killer down their thirsty throats—doing all this, and doing it like an old timer. She had grit, and it did things to me. I'm no lily of the valley. Five years of being a truck driver, tanker sailor, hash-slinger, had, until she came along, cured me of being impressionable and idealistic. But something about Gay cracked that veneer of tough living, tough thinking, tough acting. When I saw a flash of disgust, quickly concealed, on her pale face, or a flash of shock at some particularly flowery bit of profanity, it hit me somewhere deep, in a place I thought was dead. Because she had shown me up, I couldn't bring myself to say a word to her. But I watched her. It seemed as if I had spent my whole life getting ready for a chance to watch her. . .

And I *had* to find the right line.

About eleven o'clock she was fooling around the second pumpman off the *Swansea Queen*. He'd stopped spending and the Syrian caught Gay's eye and motioned her over to a two-table party of jabbering squareheads. But when she tried to break away the pumpman took two round turns and a half-hitch around her waist with his sweaty arms and seemed to be there for the night. I vaulted over the oyster bar, slipped into the next booth, and leaning over the pair of them brought the edges of my hands scissorwise, and with everything I had, down on the back of his neck. He stayed where he was, and Gay and I went back to work. But not before I grabbed her arm and whispered, "How'm I doin'?"

"Fine," she said. "As a bouncer."

Point two.

So not even rough stuff, that old standby, would do it. Well, I wasn't at the end of my rope. By this time I'd stopped fooling around.

When we broke up for the night I left the odds and ends to the cook, who saw I was on the make and that it would do no good to keep me, and slipped out early, crossed the street and stood in the shadows of a store. Soon Gay came out and started up Flimson Street. I gave her a block, and then followed, catching her just as she crossed Sixth. Coming up from behind I confidently took her arm. She started, pulled away violently, and looked into my face. Then, "Oh," she said, without enthusiasm, "it's you."

"Looking out for you, as usual," I said breezily. "Youngster like you has no business parading around town this time of the morning alone."

"Good grief!" she cried in exasperation. "Don't I have enough trouble getting away from the customers without having to fight the help too?"

"Help"! How do you like that? "Listen, sub-deb," I said roughly, "if you can't see an honest gesture when your nose is rubbed in it, you can live happily ever after without it."

"Swell!" she said, and as I started off, called, "Leo! Did you mean that?"

"Yeah." And suddenly, I did!

"Come on," she said briefly.

It was a heavy night, and the sky was luminous from the reflection of one of the occasional "flashes" at the refinery, where a heater had got out of control and lighted up a few hundred barrels of crude. By the soft glare Gay seemed strange, other-worldly. I was trying to find a name for the precise shade of her green eyes under neon, and having a hard time of it; but as long as puzzling over it made me keep my mouth shut she seemed content to have me along. Imagine getting on the right side of a cool cookie like her without a line!

Suddenly she gasped and clutched my arm. A drunk was lying sprawled out on the sidewalk almost under our feet. His arms were stretched out and his head was back. A thin trickle of blood ran from the corner of his mouth and he had a nasty knot on his forehead. He was moaning quietly.

I bent down, took him under the armpits and set him on his feet, but he seemed to have no control over his legs. I put him in a doorway out of the way, and came back to Gay. She was hysterical, sobbing in painful little shrieks.

"What's the matter?" She stood there, sobbing crazily, openly, her hands at her sides. God! No woman should cry like that. I slapped her, hard, but it seemed only to add me to the legion of terrors that plagued her. I started to bawl her out. I called her things . . . but none of it did any good until I snapped, "It's nobody's fault but your own. You *would* come to this God-forsaken hole. When you came here, you were looking for just what you're getting. It's your own damned fault!"

"It isn't!" she wailed; then pushed me away and started walking. I was beside her as soon as I could make it, but she said no more.

"Why isn't it?" I prompted gently.

Irrelevantly, she asked, "Why did he have to be there just as we passed?"

"Who; that rumdum? Gay! Don't tell me that's what's bothering you? Holy smoke! Didn't you ever see a drunk before?"

"Not like that," she said brokenly. "Oh, I'm sorry, Leo. But I hate it so here, and seeing him just topped it off." And she began crying again.

"Gay, how long have you been here?"

"Four days."

"Tonight's Thursday," I said conversationally. "Monday night a woman shot her husband in front of the Evergreen Tavern. Saturday two men were killed: one right there in the Anchor, the other across the street in front of the beer distributor's. It averages three a week. No one keeps track of what happens over there across the tracks. An oil town isn't Park Avenue. What did you come here for, a vacation?"

She shuddered. "How can you be so matter-of-fact about it?"

"You've got to be. You get to be. If you don't, you might as well go back where you came from. That last goes for you too; go back where you came from. This is no place for people like you."

"You're like me," she said softly, quite taking my breath away.

"I do, Gay, I do; and maybe I was once. But I'm not."

She was quiet a while, figuring that out. Then, "But I *can't* go back—yet."

We had come to the Franklin, the four-a-week joint where she was staying, but she walked right past it and sank onto the shadowed steps of the next house. I stood before her feeling—what was it?—humble, by golly! Me! She glanced up, then moved over almost imperceptibly. I took the hint and sat down.

"Who are you?" she asked quietly.

"I told you. Leo. Hash-slinger, able seaman, midget Lothario." I saw, out of the corner of my eye, her eyebrow go up three thirty-seconds of an inch, and added, "Blowhard, hey?"

"You fool." But she didn't mean it.

"Changee for changee."

"What? Oh. Who, me? Just somebody looking for someone."

I got up. Maybe if I acted like a gentleman—

"Gay," I said, "I'd like to know about it. But I'm not asking for anything you don't want to give. Shall I beat it?"

"Sit down again, Leo."

I did, and she sat for a moment with her chin in her hands. Then,

"I'm down here looking for a boy on one of the ships that loads here."

"Which one?" I asked, immediately interested.

"It's called *S.W. Wanderford.*"

"Midderland Oil? Coastwise? Loads here for Bayonne, Norfolk, and Revere, Massachusetts?"

"Yes! Have you ever been on her?"

"Yeah. Two years ago. I went wiper and then ordinary seaman. Got fired in the shipyards at Brooklyn for being careless about throwing my fists around."

"Then you knew Billy—Bill Atherton?"

"Atherton? No; I was only on her two months. What is he?"

A glow came into her voice. "He's a fireman. He was a wiper for only six months and then got a fireman's papers!" I didn't say anything about the legal qualifications for fireman, which are six months wiping time. "He works terribly hard; twelve hours a day, sometimes more, and the heat is terrible. The meals are very bad, and he told me that he is sometimes so sick he can hardly stand; but he goes right on stoking those fires."

This Billy is a pip, I thought to myself. I'd seen his kind before. Ride one of the ships for a month or two, and then get salty; tell the little woman all about the hardships of life at sea. Holy pumps! If four hours on and eight off comes to twelve hours work a day, and if the Midderland tankers are hungry, and if the *Wanderford,* which is a motorship, has anyone but the chief wiper "stoking" her oil-burning donkey-boiler, then I'm a Chinese Indian.

I said, "And how does the gentleman rate having you chase some two thousand miles for him?"

"It was all a misunderstanding," she said miserably. "You see, I had know him for years; I was in school with him. And we had planned to—to get married when he had a good job—" she gulped, and then went on, "And then when he went to sea he used to write and tell me when he'd be in next, and I'd plan all sorts of things for us to do. Well, about a year ago he docked in Bayonne and took the train home, and hired a car and we rode all around the city. And when it got dark we went into the park and sat there talking, and— well, I hadn't seen him for so long, and—" She stopped, confused.

"All right," I said. "You don't have to draw me any pictures."

"Please, Leo," she said angrily. ". . . well, then he just stopped writing. I couldn't understand it, but all the time I knew it wasn't his fault. Something must have happened to him. Mother said that he had run out, but she didn't know Billy. And Father—he was rotten about it. He had a suspicion of what had happened, and actually took out a court order against poor Billy!"

"Poor Billy," I said under my breath.

"It took me a long time, but I found out through the company that he was still on the ship. I saved all I could of my allowance until I had enough to come down here. I couldn't meet him anywhere up North because Father would have found out about it, and had Billy put in jail."

"Tsk tsk."

Luckily she was too deep in her story to hear. "So here I am, and when Billy comes in, we'll be married and I can stay here and see him every trip."

Just like that, eh? "Gay, did you buy a round trip ticket from up North?"

"Of course not. Why should I?"

"Never mind," I said. "Does he know you're here?"

"No. Won't he be surprised? One of his shipmates once told me that he 'hangs out at the Blue Anchor' when he's in here. You *must* have seen him."

"No, lady. Not that I can remember. I came here with the cook only about two weeks ago. If I have seen him I don't remember it."

"Well," she said, "you will. He docks here on Saturday."

Afraid so, I thought.

Well, that was the setup. I can fight anything I can see, or anything I can understand. If I'm on the make for some gal who's carrying the torch for someone else, I know what to do if he's halfway normal; simply use his own line better than he does. But here was Gay, dead gone on a phony, playing God knows what sort of game. They say love is blind, and no one can understand women, and so forth; but until I met Gay those things were just collections of words. And talk about youth and innocence...!

I got up to go. "I hope things work out the way you want them to, Gay," I said. "But if they don't, remember I'm standing by. If I can ever do anything—"

"Oh, thanks, Leo. But you'll never have to. You don't know Billy."

"No," I said, "I don't."

She opened the door of the Franklin, and then turned to look at me. "You're such a comfortable person to be with, Leo."

That wasn't exactly what I wanted, but it would have to do. I left in a rosy haze.

And I mean just that. Remember how it was the first time you went for a girl? I don't mean an attraction; I mean something big. I mean wanting a girl so badly that you're afraid to touch her. I mean something that fills you and yet leaves a hollow inside. What the hell. You know what I mean.

Poor Billy, my starboard elbow!

Saturday really was busy. The Syrian circulated around the floor rubbing his hands and beaming, and the cook and I were mobbed. I wasn't too rushed, though, to watch out for how the boys were treating Gay. She had learned quickly. Her artificial smile was brighter and she stopped freezing when the men she was dancing with held her too closely. She was doing all right.

About nine, the crew of the *Wanderford* began to struggle in. I saw two or three of my old shipmates, among them a little Swede who had been my particular sidekick. He was the only one who had thrown in with me in that ruckus in the Brooklyn shipyards.

"Ho!" I cried when I saw him.

"What ho?" he bellowed, in the old formula.

"Tallyho!" and then the usual handshaking and free beer.

And as any two seamen will, we starting gossiping about old shipmates. Blackie got left in Revere; the mate pulled a gun on a limejuicer in port here last trip; the Feds got Murphy for an old forgery charge through the fingerprints on his papers.

"But you ought to be on the old can now," Swede wound up. "I'd like you to see Steamboat."

"Steamboat?"

"Yeah. A wiper we picked up in Bayonne when Didon got fired. Believes anything you tell him. One night we were running through a heavy swell and we told him he better pack his suitcase. We says we'll have to take to the boats during the night. By golly, he did! Not only that, but he turned in with his life-preserver on, and got one of the boys to lash him in his bunk! Yeah!" Swede took a pull at his beer.

"Another time the first assistant spent two hours explaining the burners on the donkey boiler to him, and when we got in he left the kid in the fireroom. Fifteen minutes later she popped off, and the first runs in and finds the water shut down and the oil wide open in all three fires. He finally found the kid in the messroom playing five hundred. He'd gone up for a drink of water, he said, and forgot he was on watch!"

"Holy smoke!" I said. "What's his name?"

"*I* don't know," said Swede. "We call him Steamboat."

"How long has he been on there?"

"About a year."

"A year? How the hell does he last?"

The Swede's face sobered. "The chief." And he held up two fingers very close together. "The kid uses words a mile long and three miles deep, and reads the weirdest damn books. It started when the chief found him reading a book called *Jurgen* by a guy called Cable. You remember the chief. He's a peculiar duck himself. Well, they got to talking about that damn book. From then on the kid got away with murder. Always running to the chief with some pome or something, and knocking off work at 4:15. Boy, he don't work for a living. He cruises."

"Nice guy," I said. "I know about three dozen damn good wipers on the beach here without a slug."

The Swede picked up his beer and then put it down again. "Speak of the devil—"

A kid was weaving toward us across the dance floor. He was drunk, but not half as drunk as he thought he was. He was dressed up in a lapelled vest, a purple shirt, pants with about five pleats on each side, and square-toed shoes. Under his ear, which was dirty, was the fruitiest-looking yellow necktie in the South.

"Hiyah, Swedey, ol' boy ol' boy," he squeaked. "Have a beer?"

Swede winked at me and had two beers set up. The kid wandered over to the phonograph and stood there looking over the selections until the Swede paid for the beer. Then he was back and guzzling.

Swede winked again and said, "Hey, Steamboat, show us that dogcatcher."

The kid got out on the floor, barking like a dog and swinging an imaginary net. It wasn't funny; but everybody laughed because he was making such a damn fool of himself. It was derisive, cruel laughter, but Steamboat didn't seem to know that. If he did, he didn't care. An A-1 grandstander.

Someone yelled, "Be a quartermaster!" Steamboat grabbed an invisible wheel and put an imaginary ship thirty degrees off course. The whole ginmill howled, booed, and bellowed. "Oiler!" "Streetcar conductor!" "Hey, Steamboat," Swede roared, "Give us 'Bellbottom Trousers'"!

He did. It wasn't a funny song, and it wasn't dirty. Just crummy. It was well received. After it was over he came back to the oyster bar, regaining his stagger on the way. But the wolves had found prey; it was open season on twerps. Steamboat was dragged away and plied with beer until he encored.

It was then that I noticed Gay. She was standing with her back to the bar, staring with wonder and unbelief and something like disgust on her face. I went up behind the bar, leaned over and put a hand on her shoulder. "Quite a show, isn't it?"

"Leo, what's the matter with him? What's happened to him? Is he drunk? He looks sick. Why are they making him do that?"

"It's all right, Gay," I said. She didn't look at me as I spoke, just kept staring at Steamboat. "He's gundecking; he isn't drunk. But he soon will be. They're doing that to him because he's a twerp, that's all. Gay!" I said sharply, an awful fear clutching me. "Gay! What's it to you?"

She didn't answer but suddenly ran to the crowd around Steamboat, shoved and elbowed people aside. Steamboat was on the third verse of "Bell-bottom Trousers" when she burst through, screaming, "Billy! Billy! Stop it, Billy!"

"Oh my God," I groaned.

Steamboat stopped singing and stared at her, shook his head and stared again. "Gay..."

Gay had forgotten the Anchor, the job, Leo ... everything but that her Billy was acting like a twerp. She started on him in a low voice, in the dead silence that had fallen in the place. A phonograph shrilling "Bewdyful, bewdyful Tex-us" suddenly lost pitch and grated to a stop as someone jerked out the plug. Gay had a perfect stage voice; every syllable rang clear.

And I don't remember what she said. Not to repeat it, anyway. They say Lincoln once made a speech so moving, so eloquent, that no one remembered a word afterwards. Gay did too. I don't remember her words, but I remember the hush in the town's noisiest beer joint; I remember the smiles on the faces of sailors and come-on girls, barkeeps and refinery workers, fading, growing, fading again, dying. I remember there being something about a promise, something about a pedestal, something about waiting ... but most of all I remember Gay, how she half crouched as she spoke, how her eyes were slitted with anger, wet with tears, and how her mouth writhed with her contempt.

When she stopped speaking she turned her back on him, marched proudly through the aisle that was made for her in the crowd and up to the Syrian. He shook his head and waved his arms at what she told him, but she turned from him almost as she had from Steamboat, and disappeared into the dressing room.

The crowd melted away from Steamboat, leaving him with his bowed head and shocked eyes and his shame . . . and things got noisy again. "Sizzle one!" cried the barkeep to the chef. "Four beers!" Somebody laughed drunkenly. "Where the bewdyful blue-bonnets grow" moaned the phonograph. The door of the dressing room slammed violently, Gay came out and straight to me.

"Leo, I'm quitting."

"I know," I said. "Good. What are you going to do?" Over her shoulder I noticed the crowd gathering around Steamboat again.

"I'm going home—up North. But Leo," and she flushed painfully, "I haven't very much money. . . "

Steamboat's voice rose, half saying, half singing something. Gay's eyes strayed from mine for a second, and when they came back there was something new there. "Leo, could you lend me a little? I'll pay you back as soon as I get home. Really I will."

I began to hear what Steamboat was saying, there in the midst of the crowd that hid him from us.

> ". . . A flowery band to bind us to the earth,
> Spite of despondence . . ."

"What the hell is that?" I asked her.

"Keats," she said. "'Endymion' . . . we used to read it together."

> ". . . of the gloomy days,
> Of all the unhealthy and o'er-darkened ways
> Made for our searching . . ."

Gay had turned slowly from me, leaned back against the bar. That high, kiddish voice pounded at us. Someone in the crowd saw Gay, nudged his neighbor, who also stared. The movement spread, the crowd broke and we saw Steamboat. He was on his knees, with his arms outstretched, his head up, and tears in his eyes. He was a striking and ridiculous picture as he knelt there, intoning his poetry. . . Keats in a honky-tonk! His gaze slowly fell until it rested on us.

"... Such the sun, the moon,
   Trees old, and young, sprouting a shady boon ..."

Out of place, but from the heart. Laughable, yet agonized. Gay was like a drugged thing, answering a call. She stood there, absolutely spellbound, while that drunken child took her away from me ... what could I do? For the spell was there.

"... the mid-forest brake,
   Rich with a—"

He stopped, repeated himself, stopped again. Gay's eyes widened a little, and it was as if she had forgotten to breathe and was just starting again. And Leo?

With a great rush, the hard veneer around me splintered and was gone, and an old Leo, a Leo that I thought was dead, a Leo who loved beauty and beautiful things, leaned over her shoulder and spoke into her ear.

"Rich with a sprinkling of fair musk-rose blooms:
   And such too is the grandeur of the dooms
   We have imagined for the mighty dead."

And the spell was there again, and it was my spell, and I wound it round and about Gay, and she responded, for a great light dawned in those green eyes, a light that threw its glow over us two, and shut out the world.

That's how I won her. Billy forgot, and, you see, I had the right line.

Golden Day

I SAW A painted pastoral come to life...

There were two small figures on a country lane. He was dressed in sturdy blue denims, and her hair shone brightly in the late sunlight. His face was smooth and rosy, and he was masterful and strong for his age. They walked hand in hand. I heard them speak...

"It's better than the city, Tommy."

"Sure it is. How does anyone ever sleep in the city, Sue?"

"Oh, I don't know... Tommy, there's a bull!"

The bull was a little red Jersey cow, belly-deep in sweet timothy. She stared at them with great tender eyes, her head moving perceptibly with the steady champing of her jaw.

Tommy laughed. "Don't be afraid of her, Sue. That's just an ol' cow! Gee, you *are* a city slicker! Watch." He walked over to the cow and put out his hand, but she jerked her head away and stood watching him out of the corner of her eye. Tommy was startled, but he caught his lower lip in his teeth, advanced, and laid his hand on the smooth red neck.

Sue stood in the middle of the lane with her hands clasped, scarcely breathing until Tommy came back to her, swaggering a little. "My goodness! Aren't you afraid of *anything*?" she asked, her eyes wide.

"You know me," he said, and suddenly began to whistle loudly and out of tune, because he was so happy.

She looked up at him as they walked (he was ever so little taller than she) and took his hand and pressed it. He smiled at her, and then snatched the hand away and thrust it deep into his pocket. It came out with a huge jackknife.

"My," she said, looking at it with awe. "That's an awful thing to carry around with you."

"Everybody around here has one of these," he said. He opened the bright blade, and you could see he was very proud of it. "It's real sharp, too." He crossed the ditch and cut a switch, and then came back to her side, whittling busily.

Her hands were clasped again. "Don't cut yourself, Tommy."

He laughed at her and ran his thumb confidently over the blade. He did cut himself.

"Oh, Tommy, I knew it! Won't you *ever* grow up?" she scolded. "Here. Let me see it. Oh, what a cut!" She took the injured hand gently, clucking softly over the tiny slit.

Tommy said, through slightly puckered lips, "It doesn't hurt much. I've been cut lots of times."

"We'll have to bind it or it will get infested." She used that word as if she loved it. Pulling a handkerchief out of a little pocket in her spotless blue-and-white checked dress, she folded it precisely and wrapped it around the wound. The softness of her hands belied her age. Before she tied it she asked anxiously, "Is it too tight, Tommy?"

"No," he said bravely. When she had finished he stared at the bandage. "You sure know how to take care of a man, Sue," he said. His cheeks glowed.

"Silly." But she was terribly pleased.

They walked on until they came to a little brook where a bridge carried the lane from one grassy bank to the other. They stood at the rail for a while, Sue watching Tommy, Tommy tossing pebbles at the minnows that slowly fanned in the clear water. Once they saw a little turtle, and once a frog splashed noisily and frightened them.

Then they went on up the hill, and just before they reached the top, Tommy said, "You'll be able to see it from here."

Sue was all eyes as they crossed the brow of the hill, and saw before them a clump of Norway poplars shading a little white house. It was nearly covered with trumpet vines and morning glory, and it had a little white picket fence. There were roses in the garden, and hollyhocks at the corners of the house.

They walked up to the gate and, ceremoniously, Tommy held it open for her. She stared at him, and at the house, and at him again. "Is this your house?" she asked wonderingly.

He did not answer immediately, and so she went in. Together

they walked up the crooked flagstone path to the shadowed porch that half hid the green door.

Tommy opened it, then turned to her. "This is *our* house," he said.

And then the little old man in the blue denims picked up his little old wife and carried her over the threshold of the green doorway.

It was his present to her on this, their golden wedding day.

Permit Me My Gesture

SHE PULLED ACE'S five-dollar bill from her pocketbook and handed it and the telegraph blank to the clerk. The bill was clean and fresh, and it crackled inaudibly in her fingers as she handed it to him—it and the message that would bring Ace back.

Bring him back! Not to her feet again, but to her side. It would all be different this time, she thought, wincing again at the memory of his hurt brown face and the sudden flare in his eyes and his voice when he said, "When you send that wire, Margot, you'll know what you've done—to both of us."

It seemed so unjust, she thought, anger flooding against the penitence that filled her, that a woman as beautiful as she should be denied the power of it because the exercise of her power was his pain—not that she had ever denied herself that. And now she was calling him back; now she was caught in her own bright net. Where was her pride? she thought, suddenly panicky, suddenly tempted to snatch his five-dollar bill from the clerk and run from the office. No—too late now. She needed him desperately. How could she have been so cool and self-assured when she sent him away? She'd gone too far!

The clerk took the message (imperious surrender! "NOW I KNOW ACE MY DEAR YOU MAY COME BACK") and the bill slipped out of her fingers with the same soft swish as it had made coming out of his wallet. What a funny, dramatic thing for him to do! She remembered every word he had said that night, every expression on his taut dark face when she told him so coldly to go away.

"I knew it was coming," he said roughly. He lit a cigarette, and she remembered the little thrill that shot through her when she saw how his hand shook. "You've known you could walk on me, throw me down, pick me up again . . ." his voice trailed away, and she smiled

86

gently, to herself, she thought. But he saw her, and burst out furiously:

"Don't you know that the day when a woman can throw her glove into the lion's den for the brave to retrieve is past? Don't you know that you can go too far with that fair demoiselle performance? I've got your out-of-season strawberries for you; I've given you the star sapphire you demanded but won't wear; time and again I upset my days and nights for your whims, barging out to the middle of a Connecticut nowhere because you called me, only to find that you were here in New York gloating over your power. Canceling my vacation and rushing back to the city because you said you needed me, only to find you out of town; going to places I don't like to, visiting people I don't care to know because of your desire to make me bohemian, religious, radical, or whatever you think I should be at the moment—and now you tell me to go in that holier-than-thou tone; now you are Victoria saying, 'We are not amused.'"

His voice turned suddenly low, intense. "Now you want me to beg you to keep me. Here—" he flung a card on the table. "That address will always find me. And now allow me *my* gesture." He took out his wallet, leafed carefully through it and slipped a five out. He looked at it closely, then laid it on the card.

"When you want me back, Margot, wire me. Use that particular bill—call it sentiment or a dose of your own whimsy, but use that bill and *no other.* When you send that wire—oh, you will, Margot, you will!—you'll know what you've done. To both of us. Remember that, Margot."

He had stalked to the door, turned to look at her standing there wearing her best half tender, half amused smile, said, "I wish I could brand your forehead, Margot, as a warning to the next poor devil." And suddenly he was gone.

At first she had laughed delightedly. It was just such a scene as she reveled in, and he had done it so beautifully! She had laughed delightedly, crossed the room with a swift, approving glance at the mirror as she passed, carefully put the card and money away in a separate pigeonhole in her desk.

But she had not laughed delightedly the next morning when she awoke, when the full realization that he was gone struck her, when she began to regret. At first she thought that it was because her toy had been taken away from her, but when days went by and she caught herself shaping a new way in which to torment him, and when weeks went by and every time she closed her grey eyes and saw, so startlingly clear, the fire deep in his blue ones, she felt a new loneliness; and when months went by and she could think of nothing but his dear, dark face, then she knew that he was more to her than a trained animal. And now she had learned her lesson, and she and Ace would—what was the man at the desk saying?

"I'm sorry, lady. This bill is counterfeit."

Watch My Smoke

I WAS TAKING No. 14 back to the base when it happened. The figures painted on her gray fuselage didn't mean that we had fourteen planes. It was one of four crates—and I mean crates—that comprised our charter service. In the six years we had been operating, we had bought and rebuilt seventeen wrecks and seen the end of thirteen of them. One more just at this time would finish us. We couldn't stay in business with less than four planes, what with the sudden influx of mining machinery into the north and the competition of two more airlines on our lake. And here I was about to wash out the biplane.

I smelled smoke. Try it for a thrill sometime. Sit in an old plane, closed in by a homemade cellulose cowling, with 8,000 feet between you and an uninhabited stretch of tangled forest called northern Quebec. Yeah, and with pontoons on your ship, and not a lake within miles.

Not much at first: just a little curl of it poking its filmy head up in between me and the crash pad, and bringing with it the unforgettable smell of smoldering fabric. Old 14 was built like a kitchen match, so far as inflammability goes.

A flier, according to Hollywood, is a man of steel quite impervious to nerves and hysteria. Hogwash. Flying is a job just like any other, and the men who fly are human. Speaking for myself, I can say that in that moment and those that followed I was in what the jolly old Limies call a blue funk. It was then I peered down through the floor ports and saw the tarpaper shacks that were called, collectively, Pont-aux-Trois-Rivières. ("Privvers" to you.)

There was my chance. The pit was rapidly filling with smoke, the fire was somewhere in there with me and I didn't dare open the cowl for fear of starting a draft. But if I circled toward the base, the odds were that I'd crash miles from nowhere in the middle of the woods. Reason told me to jump. Everything else, from instinct to sentiment, told me to sit tight. That was foolish, too, because there wasn't one chance in a thousand that I'd be able to save the ship. That's the point I want to make: that it wasn't bravery made me do what I did—just out and out foolishness. So I held my course, with the straps of my parachute hanging on their pullaway hooks at my shoulders.

The smoke was filtering around my legs now. I figured it came from somewhere back in the fuselage. I took down my extinguisher, held the stick steady with my knees, poked the nozzle of the gun as far back as it would go and wet down the whole inside of the empennage.

Then I began to cough. My eyes filled with tears, and what with tearing my throat out with explosive, racking wheezes and trying to see the instruments through tear-filled eyes and the thickening cloud of smoke, it was no wonder I went so far off course.

That's what happened. On a hunch, I bent close to the floor port and peered through. In the second between one watery blink and the next, I saw Corkscrew Point. Which placed me about 67 miles off course and speeding merrily in the wrong direction. Nice work.

I had a fair-sized puddle underneath me now, if I could stay conscious long enough to sit down. The lake was deep enough, I remembered from studying the maps of the area, but it was long and narrow, with a flirtatious twist in the middle.

I circled down, trying to do the thing right, trying to ignore the fact that it was getting insufferably hot in the pit. And I was praying at the top of my cracked voice that the wind would be right.

It wasn't. It blew straight across the lake, not along it. I'd have to crab, fishtail and pancake at practically the same time, to sit down in that little cupful of water.

Those last 200 feet are a blur to me now. The only thing that stands out clearly is the coldly logical fact that came to me then: that I should have bailed out over Privvers, saving the chute and my stupid hide, and leaving the plane and the business to end themselves without my cooperation. I'd have been a hero in Privvers, dropping down out of the sky that way. I knew a swell little French girl there, too. And still I hadn't jumped. What a dope!

I skimmed over the trees that lined the south end of the lake and threw her nose up, gunning down. As she lost speed and height I shoveled on all the coal she would take so she wouldn't wing over, and when I had flying speed again, started crabbing. With about ten feet of altitude I straightened out, threw her nose up, cut the gun and waited. She settled to the water like a tired duck, and every strut and stay in her groaned. Almost before she had her scallops under I had thrown the cowl back, leaped out on the step and dragged a now flaming mass out from the pit. And as I dropped it into the quenching drink, I breathed 10,000,000 thanks to the Providence that watches over fools. Know what had been burning, probably from some airport bum's cigarette?

My parachute.

The Other Cheek

NOW THIS GUY Drew—that's the kind of man I mean when I say that any number of perfectly O.K. people have a funny twist. Well-to-do, happy, has a swell wife and two swell kids. A man that'll go out of his way any time to help out someone else. You'd never think that he spent twelve years of his life planning revenge for a little thing like the theft of a pair of cuff links, would you?

Sure, they were good cuff links. Solid platinum, with a big diamond in each. A woman had given them to him, and that woman meant everything in the world to him. She'd thrown him over, and it hit him pretty hard.

O.K. So all he had to show for it was this pair of links. He made a sort of symbol of them. Carried them with him all the time. He traveled a lot on business, and he used to keep 'em under his pillow wherever he slept. In the daytime they were in his side pocket, underneath his wallet.

Well, he took a trip to Philly one time. Had to see a wholesaler down on the waterfront. He was coming down 2nd Street in his honey of a car—six grand, they say it cost him—and he got into a right-of-way argument with a coal truck. Nothing serious: crumpled a fender and broke one of his windows. But it was quite a jolt. Shook him up a little. He climbed out and went over to the truck driver, who looked a little green. Drew walked up to him, pulled out his wallet, made the guy take down his number and make out a report, and then said, "Don't worry about this, buddy. We'll say it was my fault. I'll settle with the company." The driver all but cried on his shoulder. Yeah, it might have been Drew's fault. But more likely it was the other guy's. One of those things: a tossup.

So he got back into that jeweled wagon of his and went on about his business. The links? You guessed it. Dropped them when he hauled his wallet out. There was a crowd around, naturally. Water-front bums. So when he went back to look for them, of course they weren't there.

Maybe you still think that was a little thing? Well, it wasn't to him. I tell you, they'd taken the place of something in his life. Having those links for his own was the next best thing to having the girl who gave them to him. For two years they had been to him what the girl was before that. It was like losing her all over again.

That's when he began planning what to do to the guy who'd lifted them. Sure, it was swipe. Whoever picked those up had seen him drop them and waited until he was out of the way. Drew, after he spent so many sleepless nights over them that he almost dropped, used to dream about it. Always the same dream—sometimes twice a night. He'd see the links in his hand. Then they'd drop. Then someone would come and pick them up, and he'd stand there without moving because he'd be paralyzed. Then suddenly he'd be able to move and he'd take after the crook and whip the daylights out of him and search him. But he'd never find the links, not even in the dream. Then he'd look up, and he'd see the girl standing there, crying. Then he'd wake up in a cold sweat.

Well, he went on about the same. Worked harder, though, and made plenty. Still the same guy, a prince all around. Helping everybody, hating no one—except the guy who swiped the links. Anyhow, he got one break. He met the girl again and they're married now. That's the swell wife I mentioned. But she cried when she heard about the links. And he kept on dreaming.

One night last year he stopped at a roadside diner for a snack and got talking to the kid who ran the joint. It was a swell place, clean as a whistle, all chromium and black marble. Drew asked about it. The kid said he owned it and two others like it. Drew slapped him on the back. He always admired people who could build from scratch. So the guy told Drew that years ago, when he was in his early teens, he was broke and hungry and cold. One day there was a smashup—a truck and a car—and the driver of the car dropped a pair of links. He never even looked at the man, just stared at those links. He grabbed them when he got the chance, faded out and hocked them for twelve bucks. Bought a basketful of candy and laces, saved his pennies, got in on a restaurant proposition—worked hard, and here he was.

Old Drew froze up like an iceberg. Suddenly he got up and went out. Left his car and hurried down the highway, walking that poison out of his heart. He hoofed it twelve miles like a blind man . . . well, he had gone out feeling a murderer. But he came back a big man, the only kind of a man he could be. Told the guy this story.

So that's how he came to back me in this outfit—these restaurants all over the country. And that's why we call the chain the Diamond Link system. Yeah, I'm the guy that stole a pair of cuff links.

Extraordinary Seaman

CHIN ON HAND, Joye leaned on the rail, her eyes fixed on the horizon. It was one of those nights when one should be glad that there is a sea, so that there may be nights like this. There was a full moon, and smooth little waves yearned weakly toward it, bearing their bright black shadows behind them. An impulsive breeze smelling of Florida and clean salt snatched now and then at the fine hair that rebelled against Joye's confining bandanna. They went well together, the night and Joye. Both were lovely in their soft, warm way, and both hid their untold strength in a moonlight mood.

A porpoise leaped near the ship's side, almost below her, and startled her with its wheeze and its great splash.

"Beat it, son," she told the porpoise softly. "This hulk may be a plaything to you, but it's a jail to me. Why anyone would want to be around a dirty old tanker when there is an out, is beyond me. Beat it, boy."

"Oh, I don't know," said a quiet voice at her side. "If you'd been soaking in salt water for nineteen years you'd be pretty crusty yourself."

She started violently and gasped, "How—who—what do you mean by sneaking up on me like that?"

"What do you mean by monopolizing my wailing wall?"

"For your information, shellback," she said to the seaman, "I was taking advantage of a much needed solitude, which seems to have been rudely snatched from me." She looked him over coolly. He had the face of a slender man and the arms of a wrestler. The rest of him was lithe and tall, and not the least bit bulky. "Satisfied?"

"Not at all," he said politely. "This is not a passenger ship, and never will be. She's a gasoline carrier. Yet every time someone pulls a few gold-plated wires and ships a Jonah aboard us, said Jonah immediately assumes all privileges formerly reserved for licensed men and the crew off watch."

"And you are—?"

"The 12 to 4 ordinary seaman, at your service within limits."

"Do tell me all about it," she said in the gentle voice that meant she was losing her temper.

"With pleasure," he said, and added modestly, "the pleasure, you understand, lasts as long as I am the subject of the conversation."

"I quite understand," she said through tight lips. Little flecks of fire danced in her dark eyes, and she trembled slightly with the effort of keeping herself under control. That violent temper of hers had done her no good; wasn't it responsible for her being here with this insufferable person, on this disreputable old ship?

"At twenty minutes to twelve every night," the insufferable person went on suavely, "my friend the 8 to 12 A.B. wakes me with the words, 'One bell, lug.' I slide into my dungarees, grab my watch cap and come up 'midships, up here on the boat deck, where for fifteen minutes I smell the wind and say to myself, 'Charming—'"

"Charming?"

"Yes, aren't I? Charming, my dear lady—" he clicked the heels of his fabric-soled tanker man's shoes—"is my humble name. 'Charming,' I say to myself, 'it will rain tonight.' Or, 'It will not rain tonight.' I am always right, and I say to myself, 'Charming, you are an admirable fellow.' Then I review my past and find it satisfactory."

"What *is* this?" she burst out furiously. She was completely snowed under; and that was a new experience for her. There was lots more violence crowding up her slim throat, tumbling over her tongue, but it was stopped by his gesture; one long finger touched his lips and he leered at her. She subsided, and moved some two inches away from him. He moved toward her a good four. She was a little uncomfortable.

"Tonight," he continued in his deep, quiet voice, "I came up here as usual, expecting it to be as usual. The rest—" he threw an arm up dramatically "—you know. The spell was broken. No more can I say to myself, 'Charming, that is a fine girl. She is very pretty, and she stays out of my life.' It will rain tonight."

"Stop it," she gasped. "I can't stand any more. Go away!"

"I shall go," he told her firmly, "because it is my duty. I must relieve the 8 to 12 ordinary, and for that reason only I shall leave you. Good night, Joye."

"Good night," she said before she could stop herself.

"My first name is, of course, Prince," he said, and disappeared down the ladder forward.

Prince Charming!

She leaned weakly against a davit and tried to pull herself together. The moon was darkened suddenly by a ragged shred of cloud, and a quiet moaning began in the stays. "It will rain tonight." She went below and turned in.

That was all, though. Turning in was simple enough, but sleep was something else again. After half an hour of restless listening to the increasing whine of the wind and the quickened slap of the waves against the rusty hull, she gave it up, turned on her bunk light and thought about things.

What things? Well, this awful trip, for one. It was Aunt Hagar's wild idea, of course. Her anger, never quite quenched since that impossible ordinary seaman left her, turned to the memory of her frozen-faced aunt. It had happened this way:

Joye's father had been one of those legendary figures of humble beginnings who had, by the sweat of his brow and the astuteness of his business sense, made a considerable fortune. When, at Joye's birth, his wife died, he buried his grief in work, and the result of that work was wealth in six figures. But in throwing himself into his affairs he had had little time for his baby daughter, and had turned her over to his sister Hagar with instructions that Joye was to be given the best private education, with particular emphasis on controlling her temper.

For Joye had a terrible temper. The father she had seen only four or five times before his death three years ago when she was in college knew all about that temper, for she had inherited it from him. And the upbringing she had had under Aunt Hagar and her bevy of tutors had been carefully calculated to submerge that temper in a flood of rules and regulations. Well, it just hadn't worked. The temper was still there, all the more violent for being suppressed so long.

She had exploded when Aunt Hagar told her about this trip. "It was your father's last wish, my dear, that you should be placed in some utterly new and different environment, where any vestige of that temperament which he feared for in you might be removed." Aunt Hagar always talked that way—like the Harvard Classics.

"I *have* no temperament!" Joye said violently.

"Do not interrupt," Aunt Hagar said primly. "I have found just the right thing for you. You will board the *S.S. Nueva* at noon tomorrow, and will sail to Port Arthur, Texas. I shall go by land and meet you there."

"Oh! a ship? A cruise ship?"

"She is a seven-thousand-ton tanker, Joye, and I have gone to considerable trouble to get you aboard her. It was a special concession given me through a friend of your father's."

That was when Joye had exploded. A filthy old tanker! Her aunt had sat passively watching her while she stormed and stamped. She had said only:

"That settles it, Joye. Your father said in his will that I was to have the choice of this finishing touch to your education. If you accepted my judgment in the matter, no more was to be said. But if you objected, you were to be forced to obey me. Get ready, Joye."

That was the last straw. But further defiance was useless; that was something she had learned through many painful scenes. Once Aunt Hagar made up her mind, nothing could move her. And on this occasion Joye found it physically impossible to avoid the trip. She was watched every second by firm and gentle servants, and by the eagle eye of Hagar herself. But what sort of a crazy game *was* this?

And when she had come aboard (she'd have dodged ashore again at the last minute had it not been for the presence of Aunt Hagar's huge limousine at the dock, and Aunt Hagar's chauffeur on the pier to see the lines cast off) she had found it very pleasant. She hated to admit it, but she was fundamentally honest and had to. Captain Avery and the chief engineer, with whom she dined, made everything as pleasant as they could. In about three days she had calmed down a little, and by the fourth she was almost normal. And then she had to meet this disgustingly conceited seaman and be upset again! She wondered if she should tell the Captain about it, and then decided not to. She'd ignore him. That was good for conceited people. She told her pillow, "You're Prince Charming." Then she punched it with all her might, and fell asleep.

The next day she was up early, full of her plans to ignore him. She would cut him dead. She would insult him by her lack of interest. She would—but somehow nothing seemed to work out right. All morning she watched for him in vain. She'd have given anything to be able to stroll aft to the crew's quarters and poke around to see where he was hiding. But Captain Avery had put that one injunction on her; she was to stay 'midships.

By eleven o'clock she couldn't stand it any longer. She wandered up into the wheelhouse and asked the quartermaster what the 12 to 4 watch did in the morning. "Sleep," he told her gruffly and returned to his steering.

Which made her feel very, very foolish.

She saw him after lunch, painting busily on the pump room hatch. She idled along the flying bridge and stood over him, staring. He said nothing. She scraped a bit of the peeling paint off the catwalk with her toe, and kicked it casually onto the back of his neck. He glanced up at her and then went on with his painting. She felt her anger choke her again. "Hello," she said sweetly.

"Beat it," he said. "Do you want to get me fired?"

"Yes," she said, and strode back to her room. The colossal nerve of him! The—there were no words. She'd never speak to him again!

Which, considering that she was up on the midship boat deck at exactly 11:40 that night, was a peculiar resolve. It was calm again, though overcast, and very dark. Over on the port side the light on Tortugas winked steadily. A slight fair wind, tailing the ship, made the air aboard still and resonant, so that she heard his firm steps plainly by the time he was halfway over the catwalk. She waited rather breathlessly until his shadow loomed toward her from the ladder, and then she turned her back.

He began talking to himself. She caught the words. "Yes, Ivan, you were right. She is here again, that stupid girl, to spoil your evening. But bear up, Ivan, my fine fellow, bear up. In two days we dock at Galveston and then she will be out of your life."

"Ivan?" she said, her curiosity overcoming her anger for the moment. She moved closer and looked up into his face. Yes, it was the same bronzed countenance, with the same annoying smile. "I thought you said you were Prince Charming."

"You don't think so? Well, then, I am no longer Prince Charming. I am Ivan. I am also the center of the universe, Ugly."

"Are you calling me Ugly?" she asked, aghast.

"Certainly. I have been thinking about you. I believe that you have been called everything imaginable but Ugly. We must be original, you know. So, to avoid being like anyone else, I call you Ugly."

She felt her cheeks flame, and was glad of the dark. What he said was perfectly true, and could be called a tribute of sorts. She realized suddenly that he was laughing at himself too, and that was quite a revelation. Womanlike, she began to hate him less the more he harmlessly insulted her.

"So you're the one who makes the world go round," she said conversationally. "Do tell me about it."

"It will not rain tonight," he said irrelevantly. "You are a spoiled brat with an ungovernable temper. You are very inconsiderate of other people's feeling. You are snobbish and narrow-minded and generally unproductive. Besides—"

The calm, even tone of his voice was broken by the small hand that lashed across his lips. He did not step back nor exclaim; simply reached over, took her by the scruff of the neck and slapped her cheek smartly.

They stood there in the blackness, staring at each other in silence—she with her eyes smarting with angry tears, he quite impassive but for his raised eyebrows and the tiniest quiver at the corner of his mouth.

"I am very fond of this tea-time talk," he said after a tense moment, "but I must deprive you of myself for four hours. Good night, Joye."

Trembling a little she said, "Good night, Mr. —er—"

"Hoe," he said from the ladder, and was gone.

Ivan Hoe!

She leaned on the rail staring down at the rushing water, listening to the hiss of millions of bursting bubbles along the ship's side. A flying fish popped out of the water with a brilliant phosphorescent flash, and she could see the little path of bluish light made by its drooping tail as it kicked itself over the crest of a swell. Ivan—she felt like swearing and laughed instead. She cried a little too. Then she went below and climbed wearily into her bunk.

Ivan—Prince—his names and his lips and his eyes ran a crazy merry-go-round in her bewildered brain. Never in her life had she met a franker and more inhuman and charming person—Charming...

It must have been two hours later when she suddenly sat bolt upright in bed. What was that he had said? Something about, "I must deprive you of myself for four hours." And he was off watch in four hours! And that was his way of telling her to be there waiting for him when he came off the fo'c'sle head.

"Giving me orders," she muttered indignantly as she slid out of the bunk. "Expects me to—" she pulled on some clothes "—be at his beck and call!" And she threw a sweater over a slender arm. "Who does he think he is?" She slipped softly out on deck and made her way to the boat deck, fuming. "Ordering me to meet him at four in the morning!"

She was early, though. Seven bells struck, and she sat down on the tub that held the boatfall. A half hour to wait.

Suddenly she asked herself, "For what?" Well, nothing. Nothing at all. It wasn't really important to either of them to see each other again. No, this was foolish. Ridiculous. The thing to do was to go below and get some sleep. That was logic. Cold, clear logic.

So she stayed where she was, waiting for him.

After an age, one bell rang. Twenty minutes to go. She heard the A.B. on watch walking aft in the still damp air. She shuddered, looking at the moon. It was like a ghost suffocating in grey moss...

She may have dozed; eight bells frightened her. She jumped up and into the arms of the 12 to 4 ordinary, who had appeared at the sound of the bells as if he were Aladdin's djinn. He held her and kissed her very gently. He had been quite right. He was the center of the universe.

Quite without warning he released her and shoved her against the tub, on which she sat with an ungraceful thump. "Listen, Ugly," he said flatly, "listen well and shut please the mouth." She did, surprisingly.

"First place," he began without flourishes, "I'm seventy kinds of a heel. I've led you astray on I don't know how many counts. I've ganged up on you more than you deserve—not much more, though, come to think of it—and I even took a poke at you tonight without apologizing for it, even if I was justified."

"Oh, Ivan—"

"Will that decorative oral orifice of yours remain closed, or must I close it? As I was saying before I was so rudely interrupted, I've been a heel. Now I'm going to tell you why.

"Your Aunt Hagar is a friend of mine and was a friend of my dad's before he died. She is a very astute business woman in spite of the Model T silks she wears. I don't know if you ever appreciated that in her, but you can thank her for more than that too. She has— Lord knows why—a great affection for you. It's up to you to live up to it. I'll help you."

"Oh, you will!" Joye said icily, the glow of his kiss suddenly leaving her. "And who are you?"

For the first time surprise entered his voice. "Why, I'm Vince Randall. I'm the guy who's going to marry you." Ignoring her gasp he went right on with his speech. "Well, the part of your father's will that you don't know about states that when you were thrown into an environment in which it would make no difference what you broke or how furious you got—this is it, you see—then someone was to be appointed temporary guardian angel. That's where I come in. My orders from your aunt were to keep you as furious as possible until you realized what a dope you were. The first three days you did quite well by yourself; I could tell that by looking at you. When you started enjoying yourself I stepped in and spoiled it all."

She put a hand on his arm. "Why are you telling me all this?"

"Because I couldn't carry it through. I fell in love with you," he said matter-of-factly. "It was my fault, the whole thing. I shipped on here last month to get a vacation. I told Hagar about the ship. I promised to look after you for the trip. Now I promise to look after you forever. What say?"

"Oh, you *are* asking me, after all? Why you conceited, over-bearing, cold-blooded reptile! You—you—oh, darling, of course I will! I don't care what Aunt Hagar says."

"She says it's swell. She says it pleases her sense of the ridiculous. I radioed her yesterday. Let's go down and wake up the Old Man and have him marry us."

"Captain Avery ... but will he? I mean, won't he be furious?"

"Why should he be? He works for me. I own this company."

So they woke up the Old Man and the mate.

One Sick Kid

GUESS YOU'VE ALL read about the radio service of the United States public health bureau. Let me tell you, it's a great thing to feel that Uncle Sam is backing us that way. When you make a living riding one of the freighters or tankers that swarm around our coasts it sure eases your mind to have a thing like that to bank on.

See, most merchant ships under 15,000 tons don't carry doctors unless they are passenger jobs. That means that every time a tanker, for instance, sails, she has thirty-five or forty men aboard who can have no medical attention besides the first aid that the skipper or steward can handle. Suppose someone gets really sick? Well, then, Sparks sends the letters MEDICO out on the radio until one of the government stations picks him up. Every other ship shuts up on that call, same as on S.O.S. Then the sick man's condition is described, and the government doctor replies with treatment. Captains have even operated for appendicitis, guided by that radio voice. But if the man's condition is bad they send a cutter or a plane out to get him.

Like that time Cotter got sick on the tankship *S.W. Wonderford*. Cotter was the ordinary seaman on my watch. Swell kid. He made a pier-head jump, catching the ship just as we threw the lines off in Baytown, Tex. Never been to sea before. Green but willing to learn. He was tall and very thin. Been out of work a long time, he told us. Hadn't been eating much.

Well, he was all right till we got about as far as Dry Tortugas, not far from the Florida straits. Took us about three days; the Gulf was acting friendly. No wind, no waves. But around Tortugas she began kicking up a little. Not too much, but it floored the kid. We all laughed at him same as we always do about seasickness. Sometimes you can kid a man right out of it. But not this one. We wandered into the tail end of a Caribbean hurricane off Old Isaac light

104

in the Bahamas, and the old can began standing on her nose.

It couldn't have been seasickness. Anyone could see that. The kid just passed out cold in his bunk one morning. Couldn't get him to stay on his feet. The steward brought him around all right with ammonia, but he went under again. The Old Man was told; he came aft and looked Cotter over for a second, then had Sparks call MEDICO. Messages went like this:

"Medico O.K. Give symptoms, condition."

"Seaman periodically unconscious, hard to rouse. Spirits of ammonia not very effective. What shall I do?"

"Feverish?"

"Yes, 103."

"Apply cold pack to head, keep us advised."

It didn't do much good. Yeah, Cotter came to after a bit. But that was worse.

"Medico. Man conscious, complains of acute internal pain. Not localized. Advise."

"Are symptoms those of appendicitis as per manual?"

"No. Pain not localized. Fever now 104. Advise."

The Old Man was frantic by this time. That was one sick-looking kid.

"Continue cold pack treatment. Give position. Dispatching coast guard cutter to take man off."

The Old Man gave the position and we changed course a bit inshore to meet the cutter halfway. It was blowing hard; we had a job on our hands. How to get him aboard the cutter in that sea? Now and then I'd look in on Cotter. Poor kid. Very low.

Well, in about five hours we saw the lights of the cutter. She was boiling along under forced draft, rolling like a spruce log. She came up under our port bow broad on and kicked alongside as near as she could get without sinking both of us. She shot a line over us, and we hauled a cable aboard. She had an automatic tension engine aboard her that worked like a miracle, taking the slack out of that cable no matter how we tossed and rolled. Never saw anything like it.

Next we hauled a breeches buoy across the cable, put the kid in, lashed him, and they snatched him back. I timed the whole thing.

Just under eighteen minutes from the second they shot their line aboard, the cutter was headed for her base. We gave her three blasts and the crew cheered like maniacs. I tell you, at that moment we were proud of the old man with the whiskers and the striped pants.

So you see why a seaman will like as not take a poke at the guy who says the government is lying down on the job. Radio, trained doctors and a half million dollar cutter at the disposal of one sick kid.

Oh, the kid? Sure he got well. That was almost a joke. Not one man in a million will get it as bad as he did. Yeah, just a very bad case of seasickness. Darndest thing I ever saw.

His Good Angel

GENE WILLIS WAS slipping. It was the sort of thing that no one could have foreseen and yet, when it happened, everyone was wise. They all said, "What can you expect when you put a leg-man into a spot like that?" and "How could a youngster like that, with only a year's experience in the newspaper business behind him, handle that sort of an assignment?" and "Willis turned out too many wows. He's played out."

They didn't know, of course, what Gene had been through—what he was going through. How could he fill that column, day in and day out, with the stupid answers that stupid people gave to the stupid questions he asked them as the *Evening Sunburst*'s Inquiring Reporter, when his heart was heavy and his steps dragged and his whole being cried out for someone who didn't want him? Betty Riordan ... she'd been impatient when he asked her to set their wedding date a year ahead so that he could save for it. She'd been jealous and accused him of wanting time to play around with someone else. She'd said she never wanted to see him again. Unfair? Certainly, but he loved her. He loved her! And what did it matter what people answered when he asked them, "Who'll win the pennant this year?" or, "What do you think of the Third Term movement?" or "How did you propose to your husband?"

At first, when the assignment was given to him, he brought the "Inquiring Reporter" column to life. He had the knack of pointing up the comments of the man on the street without misquoting. Each and every one of those comments, as it appeared in print, was brilliant, original, amusing, and intensely interesting. And now? He did his job. That is, he asked enough people the daily question received in the mail, wrote enough words to fill his column, and submitted it. But the rawest cub could have turned out the kind of work he was doing since Betty Riordan and he had quarreled. Gene Willis was a discouraged man—a man on the way out.

And today's question! Why did the Features Editor have to pick a thing like that? "How would you tell an ex-sweetheart you wanted him back?" The prospect of hearing little stenogs and waitresses tell him their answers was the most refined torture. Well, he'd go through with it . . . he always did. "Here goes," he said to himself.

"Beg pardon, miss. I'm the Inquiring Reporter. Would you care to answer today's question? Fine! Name? Occupation? Now, the question. How would you tell an ex—" How would Betty Riordan tell him?— "You would? Very well, Miss Rand." *Would* Betty Riordan tell him she wanted him back? "You'll see it in tomorrow's *Sunburst*. Thank you. Beg pardon, miss, I'm the Inquiring Reporter. Would you—"

On and on and on through the afternoon. Out of fifty interviews, he'd use the five best. And submit them. And have the editor tell him they lacked punch. And he'd go out the next day and do worse. And who cared?

The thirty-fifth interview was with a plump lady who insisted that once she had put a man out of her life she would keep him out. She was rather vociferous about it, and a tittering crowd had gathered. Well, that saved work. There were always a half a dozen idiots ready to push forward with their two cents' worth. "Thank you very much, Miss Robertson. You'll see it in tomorrow's *Sunburst*," he said automatically. "Is there anyone else who might like to—"

The crowd surged lightly and another girl stood before him. Without looking up from his notebook he said, "Your name?"

"Betty Riordan," said that soft, familiar voice.

The last straw! But he wouldn't give her the satisfaction of knowing how terribly he was hurt by having to ask her that question. The shaking of his voice was almost unnoticeable as he asked, for the thirty-sixth time that day, "How would you tell an ex-sweetheart that you wanted him back?"

She said, "I'd tell him that I was a fool for ever having quarreled. . . I'd say that I couldn't live without him. . . I'd tell him that he was right and I was, oh, *so* wrong. I'd—oh, Gene! Gene darling! I've followed you ever since you left the *Sunburst* office, hoping you'd see me. You were too proud to call, and I was too proud to write, and—oh, Gene, take me back! Take me back."

The crowed roared as two young people held each other close and kissed lingeringly...

"How do you like that!" bellowed the Features Editor, as he hurled Gene's manuscript at the copy boy. "Here we are, ready to fire Gene Willis because he's lying down on the job, and he submits a minor masterpiece. Tell the cashier to take the pink slip out of Willis' pay envelope. By the way, who was it sent in today's question?"

"Someone named—" the boy studied the front page of manuscript "—Betty Riordan. Why?"

"Just wondered. She was sure Gene Willis' good angel!"

Some People Forget

BUTCH WAS A card. He was a wild Indian, a jitterbug, and in the words of a harassed high school principal, a troublemaker. There was never a dull moment with Butch around. There was no real harm in him, his aunt used to say. He was just a lively young man who got his fun by annoying people. He lived with his aunt—had, ever since his father died in 1922. That left him an orphan; his mother had died when he was born, and his aunt never could do much with him. She stopped trying when he was in his teens.

He was two years out of high school and had an office boy job somewhere or other. He still lived with his aunt, and shot his salary on clothes and the nerve-wracking things he called fun.

One warm afternoon, Butch and three of his sidekicks were loafing out in front of Murphy's place. No one seemed to have any good ideas for killing the evening, and all four of them were tired of holding down that corner. But there was no other place to go, so they stayed there. After a while even small talk petered out. Butch began scuffing the side of his shoe on the curbstone. Those who knew him always welcomed that little sign, because it meant that Butch was bored, and when Butch was bored things happened.

And just at that moment Harry Jack peered up the street and saw Pushover Britt coming along. The situation was made to order. Britt had been in the neighborhood about two weeks, which was about as long as it took Butch to find out that the guy was quiet and harmless and would just as soon avoid trouble.

"Hey, Butch!" said Harry. "Get a load of this!"

Butch looked. "Well, strike me pink!" he said. "Pushover Britt himself, and—by golly, he's got an armload of posies!"

"I'd like to know who the gal is that would give him a tumble," said Al Schultz.

"Anyone could get a tumble with that many flowers," said Mario Petri. "Musta cost his whole pay day."

Harry started toward Britt, but Butch caught his arm. "Wait a second. Let's follow him. I'd like to have a look at the girl who rates all that shrubbery, myself. Maybe we can get to know her."

So they let Britt pass them without a word and gave him half a block lead. "Now who in blazes can he be going to see?" Mario asked no one in particular. "I thought I knew every skirt in the neighborhood. Let's see..."

The same thought was running through all four minds as they followed Britt. For a while they were sure it was Sue Reale, but Britt passed her street without a glance. Aggie's house was just around the corner from it, but he ignored that, too.

"I've got it!" said Al suddenly. "Little Marion Kennedy who lives opposite the cemetery!"

"You got something there," said Butch. "This is going to be good!"

It seemed as if Al Schultz was right. Britt turned toward the churchyard. Butch began planning his campaign. It was going to be one spoiled evening for Pushover Britt. They were so sure of themselves, those four, that when Britt turned into the burying ground they stopped short, open-mouthed.

"Come on!" said Mario. "He's wise to us—or he's going to meet her inside. That's a laugh!"

"Nuts," said Butch. "Leave him be. I don't like that place. I'm going back."

Harry hooted. "Scared of ghosts, Butch?" He ducked as Butch swung at him. Then the four of them went after Britt.

They saw him just as they poured through the gate. He was walking slowly down one of the paths, reading the headstones as he went. "How do you like that?" breathed Mario. "Come on!"

As they reached Britt he was leaning over a low railing, placing his flowers on one of the graves. The rest of them made way for Butch; he always started the fun. But this time it didn't look like fun. Butch's face was paper white and working crazily. He came up behind Britt and whirled him around.

"What's the idea, mug?" he snarled.

Britt looked very much surprised, but not at all frightened. "Why," he said coolly. "I always do this on Memorial Day. Look." He pointed to the headstone.

JOHN ROLFE HARRISON
1890–1922
He died at home but gave his life to his country.

"I guess he was a war vet who died of his wounds. There's no flowers on the grave, and there should be today. Some people forget. It's up to you and me to remember."

"Yes," said Butch. His voice was choked. "Some ... people ... forget ..."

Britt said to the others, "Let's go, boys. I think your friend wants to be by himself for a while." He turned to Butch, put a hand on his shoulder. "I didn't know—"

Butch brushed the hand off. "Okay, Okay."

So they left him there, Britt and the three flashily-dressed youths; left him standing with bowed head, gazing through what might have been tears at the flowers on his father's grave.

A God in a Garden

KENNETH COURTNEY, ANYONE could see, was plenty sore. No man works so hard and viciously digging his own lily pond on his own time unless he has a man-size gripe against someone. In Kenneth's case it was a wife who allowed herself to be annoyed by trifles. The fact that in her arguments she presented a good case made Kenneth all the angrier because it made him sore at himself too. Suppose he *had* come in at 4 A.M.? And suppose he *had* told Marjorie that he was working late? A lie like that was nothing—much. The only trouble with lies was that people—especially wives and bosses—can make such a damn fool out of a man when they catch him in one. All right; so it was a poker game, and he had lost a few bucks.

Marjorie, as usual, got all the details out of him; but she didn't stop there. She cited instance after instance when he had done the same thing. Her kick, it developed, was not so much the poker, but the fact that he had lied to her about it. Well, and why should a man brag to his wife about losing twenty-four bucks? If only she'd take his simple little explanations without all those fireworks, life would be more worth living. At least he wouldn't have to retreat into the garden and take out his fury on a pick and shovel.

He had reached about this stage in his mental monologue when his shovel rang dully against old Rakna.

Of course, he didn't know then that it was Rakna. He might well have stopped digging altogether if he had known. And then again, he might not. It didn't work out so badly in the end.

At any rate, all he knew was that there was an unyielding mass, and a large one, in his way, and he couldn't finish digging the little lily pool until he moved it. That *would* have to happen now, he thought bitterly. Everything's going wrong today.

He threw down his shovel and stamped up the garden path toward the house. Sore as he was, he still found room in his sulking mind to admire that garden. It began at the house, almost as if it were part of it, and led downward into a little gully. Kenneth had, by ranking trees and shrubs carefully, built a small lot up to look like something twenty times as big.

The sunken rockery, well out of sight, was the hidden theme of the whole; you stumbled on it, that rock garden; and yet because of the subtle placing of the trees and plants around it, you knew that it had been there all the time. There was a miniature bridge, and a huge pottery teapot—all the fixings. And once you were in the rock garden, you and your eye were led to the shrinelike niche by the lily pool.

For months Kenneth had been searching for an old idol ugly enough for that niche; he wanted it there so that it would frighten people. Something nice and hideous, to be a perfect and jarring foil for the quiet and beautiful effect of all that surrounded it. Kenneth determined to leave that niche empty until he found a stone face ugly enough to turn an average stomach—not wrench it, exactly; Kenneth was not altogether fiendish in his humorous moments!—but plumb ugly.

He went into the back kitchen—it served as a tool shed as well—and took down a crowbar. His wife came to the door when she heard him.

"How's it going?" she asked in the dutifully interested tone of a wife whose most recent words to her husband were violent ones.

"Swell," he said, his casualness equally forced.

"See?" she cried in feminine triumph. "You even lie to me about a little thing like that. If everything was swell down there, you wouldn't need a crowbar to dig with. This ground isn't rocky. Why can't you tell the truth just *once*?" Then she fled into her own territory, to be alone with her indignation.

Kenneth shrugged. Fight all morning with your wife, and you're up against things like that. He hesitated. She was probably crying, after that blowup. That's a woman for you. Fire and water all at once. Oh, well. He shrugged again and started back with his crowbar. The tears would wait, he reflected callously. There were more where they came from.

His conscience bothered him a little, though. Maybe she had something there. It did seem as if he couldn't tell her—or anyone— the absolute truth. It was just a conversational habit, that lying; but it did make trouble. But what could a man do? Maybe he'd be a little more careful in future—but, damn it, why did she have to be so picky?

As usual, he took it out in work, picking and prying and heaving. Well, this lump of brownstone or whatever it was, was something worthwhile working on. Not like digging in the soft earth around it. He began to forget about Marge and her annoyances in the task on hand.

Slipping the bar well under the brown mass, he heaved strongly and lifted it a few inches at the corner. Kicking a rock under it, he stepped back for a look at the thing, and was confronted by quite the most hideous imaginable face. He stared, shook his head, stared again.

"Well, I'll be . . . here's my idol, right where I need it. Now where the devil did that thing come from?" he asked no one in particular.

Yes, it was an idol, that brown mass in the half-finished lily pool. And what a face! Hideous—and yet, was it? There was a certain tongue-in-cheek quality about it, a grim and likable humor. The planes of that face were craggy and aristocratic, and there was that about the curve of the nostril and the heavily lidded eyes that told Kenneth that he was looking at a realistic conception of a superiority complex. And yet—again; was it? Those heavy eyelids—each, it seemed, had been closed in the middle of a sly wink at some huge and subtle joke. And the deep lines around the mouth were the lines of authority, but also the lines of laughter. It was the face of a very old little boy caught stealing jam, and it was also the face of a being who might have the power to stop the sun.

"Or a clock," thought Kenneth. He shook himself from his apathy—the thing nearly hypnotized by its ugliness—and walked around it, knocking off clods of dirt with his hands.

The face was lying on its side. Yes, he discovered, it was more than a face. A body, about half the size of the head, was curled up behind it. Kenneth shuddered. The body looked like an unborn fetus he had seen at the Fair, floating in alcohol. The limbs were shriveled, and the trunk was big-bellied with an atrophied chest, jammed up against the back of that enormous head. The whole thing was, maybe, five feet high and three wide, and weighed a good ton.

Kenneth went back to the house shrugging off an emotional hangover, and called up Joe Mancinelli. Joe had a two-ton hoist at his "Auto Fixery" that would do the trick.

"Joe," he said when he got his connection, "I want you to come right over with your truck and the two-ton lift. And listen. What I've got to lift will knock your eye out. Don't let it scare you."

"Hokay, Kan," said Mancinelli. "I feex. I no scare. You know me, boy!"

Kenneth had his doubts.

"Who are you calling, dear?" Marjorie called.

"Joe Mancinelli. I've got to have help. I ran across a . . . a big rock in the lily pool." There it was again. Now, why did he have to say that?

Marjorie came across the room and put her hands on his shoulders. "That's so much better, sweetheart. It isn't terribly hard to tell the truth, now, is it?"

Her eyes were a little red, and she looked very sweet. He kissed her. "I . . . I'll try, kiddo. You're right, I guess." He turned and went out to the shed, muttering to himself.

"Can you beat that? Tell her a lie and she raises hell. Tell her another and everything's all right. You can't win."

He rigged a set of shear poles so that the chain hoist would have some kind of a purchase, and dragged them down to the rock garden. The sight of the half-buried idol gave him another fascinated shock. He looked at it more closely. It seemed old as time itself and carved—was it carved? Its execution made him think that if nature had carved rock into idols, then this was a natural work. And yet, it was so flawless! What human artist could do such macabre sculpture? Kenneth had seen the *striges* on the carved galleries on Notre Dame cathedral in Paris, and had thought that they were tops in *outré* art. But this— He shrugged and went back to the shed for a wire strap to slip under the thing, meeting Joe halfway to the house. Joe was staggering under the coils of chain over his shoulders.

"Hi, keed! Ware you got heem, thees beeg theeng?"

"Down at the bottom of the garden, Joe. What made you come over here so fast?"

"I like to see thees theeng make scare Joe Mancinelli," wheezed Joe.

"Well, look it over for yourself. It's half buried. I've got shear poles rigged. Be with you in a jiffy."

As he reached the shed, Kenneth smiled at the roar of polylingual profanity which issued from the rock garden. Joe was evidently impressed. Coming to the door with the wire strap in his hand, Kenneth called: "Scared, Joe?"

The answer came back hollowly: "I no scare. I sorry I come. But I no scare!"

Kenneth laughed and started down. He had taken about five steps when he heard a sound like a giant champagne cork, and Joe Mancinelli came hurtling up the path as if he were being chased by one of the devil's altar boys.

"Hey! Whoa there!" Kenneth called, laughing. "What happened? Hey!"

He surged forward and tackled the Italian low. They slid to a stop in a cloud of dust. "Easy, now, boy. Easy."

"The 'oist is down dere. You do you work, calla me, I come back, get heem. I don' *never* touch that theeng."

"All right, all right. But what happened?"

"You don' tell nobody?"

"No, Joe. Course not."

"So I see thees face. Thees not so gooda face. Maybe I scare, maybe no. I tell this face, 'I no lika you. So. I speet on you. So. *Ptui.*'" Joe turned white at the recollection, and swallowed hard. "Thees thing shake all over like wan piece jelly, is make the mouth like dees"—Joe pursed his lips—"an' . . . *ptow!* Is speet on me. So. Now, I go."

"You dreamed it," Kenneth said unconvincingly.

"So, I dream. But I tella you, boy, I go now to church. I take wan bat' in holy water. I light wan dozen candles. An I bring you tomorra plenty dynamite for feex that thing."

Kenneth laughed. "Forget it, Joe," he said. "I'll take care of old funnyface down there. Without dynamite."

Joe snorted and went back to his truck, starting it with a violence that set its gears' teeth on edge. Kenneth grinned and picked up the wire strap. "I no scare," he said, and laughed again.

He was not, evidently, the only one who was amused by the episode. Old funnyface, as Ken had called the idol, really seemed to have deepened the humorous lines around his tight-lipped, aristocratic mouth. A trick of the light, of course. "You know," said Kenneth conversationally, "if you *were* alive you'd be a rather likable dog."

He burrowed under the idol and pushed the end of the strap as far under as he could reach. He was flat on his stomach, reaching out and down, with his shoulder against the mass of the thing, when he felt it settle slightly. He pulled his arm out and rolled clear, to see old funnyface settling steadily back into the hole.

"You old devil!" he said. "You almost had me that time. Bet you did that on purpose."

The idol's face seemed to have taken on a definite smirk.

"—is speet on me," Joe had said. Well, he was no better than Joe. He picked up a clod of earth, held it poised, and expectorated explosively, following up by ramming the clod into the sardonic lips of the idol. There was a small but powerful explosion and Kenneth found himself flat on his back six feet away.

Now Kenneth Courtney was no storybook hero. He was just an ordinary driver for an ordinary trucking firm. But in his unbrilliant but satisfying past, he had found that the best thing to do when he had this cold, crawling feeling at the pit of his stomach was to smile at his antagonist. Nine times out of ten, said antagonist was floored by it. So he reared up on his elbow and smiled engagingly at the idol.

The smile faded quickly; one glance at the idol's mouth took care of that. The lower lip was quivering, like an angry child's, or like a railroad bull about to take a poke at a tramp. Suddenly it snapped shut. The jaws bulged and contracted, and little bits of earth fell into the hole around its cheeks.

More than a little shaken, Kenneth got his feet under him and walked over to the idol. "I'd bury you where you are, tough guy, but you're in my lily pool. Come up out of there!"

He went furiously to work, rigging the hoist over the idol. In a remarkably short time he had the ends of the strap hooked into the chain-fall, and was heaving merrily. To his surprise, he found that the idol came up easily—there could not have been more than three or four hundred pounds' load on the hoist. He stopped hauling and stood off a bit.

"Why, you son of gun!" he exclaimed. "So you've decided to cooperate, hey?"

It was true. The idol's emaciated legs and arms straddled the pit, and were lifting the massive head steadily. Even as he watched, the chain-fall began to slacken as the weight came off it. By this time Kenneth was almost beyond surprise at anything.

"O.K., buddy," he cried, and heaved away. Higher and higher rose the idol, until the shear poles creaked and their bases began to sink deeper into the soft earth. Finally it swung clear. Gauging the distance nicely, Kenneth toppled the shear poles and the idol swung face forward into the niche, landing with a rubbery thump. Kenneth grinned.

"Stay that way, old boy," he told the idol. "You're no uglier behind than you are face-outward." He threw the strap over his shoulder, lifted the shear poles at the lashing and dragged them back up to the shed.

When he came back with a spouting garden hose, the idol was facing outward.

"On second thought," said Kenneth conversationally, as he busily sluiced down that hideous humorous face, "I don't blame you. You are a little more presentable stern-foremost; but then you're a damnsite more likable this way." Kenneth was scared stiff, but he wouldn't show it, not even to an old graven image.

"That's much better," said the idol, blinking the mud out of its eyes. Kenneth sat down weakly on the nozzle of the hose. This was the payoff.

"Don't sit there looking so stupid!" said the idol irritably. "Besides, you'll catch cold, holding down that hose."

Kenneth's breath came out in a rush. "This is too much," he gasped. He was more than a little hysterical. "I ... I ... in just a minute I'll wake up and smell coffee and bacon. I don't believe there *is* a crusty old idol, or that it talked, or that—"

"Get off that hose," said the idol, and added meaningly, "and dry up."

Kenneth rose and absently began wringing his clothes. "What sort of a critter are you?"

"I'm a god," said the idol. "Name's Rakna. What's yours?"

"K-Kenneth Courtney."

"Stop stammering, man! I'm not going to hurt you. What's the matter; didn't you ever see a god before?"

"No," said Kenneth, a little relieved. "You don't seem like ... I mean—" Suddenly something about the god, something in his incredibly deep eyes, made it very easy to talk. "I thought gods lived up in the clouds, sort of. And anything I ever read about it said that gods come to earth in fire, or lightning, or in the shape of some kind of animal, or—"

"Nuts," said the god.

Kenneth was startled. "Well, gods don't talk like that ... uh ... do they?"

"You heard me, didn't you?" asked Rakna. "Think I'm a liar?" The piercing gaze made Kenneth wince. "Like you? No, you dope; I was created by common people, who thought common thoughts and spoke in a common way. Not in this language, of course, or in this time. But people are pretty much the same, by and large. Think the same way, y'know."

"Well, what people were you the god of?"

"Oh, you wouldn't know if I told you. They disappeared quite a while back. Used to be one of them buried near me. Had his thigh bone poking into my ... well, never mind. Anyhow, he faded out. There's not a trace of those people left anywhere. This earth has been here quite a while, you know. They come and they go."

"How come you can speak English, then?"

"Because I know everything you know, which isn't much, by the way, and considerable besides. Every time a thought passes in that gab factory of yours I know what it is. You drive a truck. Your wife's named Marjorie. She's very capable; knows all about budgets and calories and such. She thinks you're a liar."

"If you're a god," Kenneth said quickly, to change the subject, "why couldn't you dig yourself out?"

"Listen, lamebrain, who said I wanted to dig myself out? Can't a god grab forty winks once in a while?"

"Forty winks? How long were you asleep?"

"*I* don't know. Couple of hundred million years, maybe. I'll tell you when I get a chance to look at the stars."

"But there wasn't any earth that long ago!"

Rakna leered at him. "Vas you dere?"

Kenneth sat down again, this time on dry ground. Standing was too much of a strain.

"Hm-m-m . . . I see steam's back again. Electricity? Yes. You're getting along, you people. Atomic power? Oh, well, it won't be long now. Levitation? Trans—"

Kenneth had the uncomfortable feeling that he was being read like a newspaper—a back number at that. He was a little annoyed, and besides, those waves of beneficence still flowed from Rakna's eyes. Kenneth's fear departed completely, and he rose to his feet and said:

"Listen. All this is a little too strong for me. As far as I'm concerned, you're somebody's half-ton Charlie McCarthy. Or maybe you're wired for sound."

Rakna chuckled deep in his jowls. "Aha!" he rumbled. "A skeptic, no less! Know what happens to little mortals who get cocky? They suffer for it. In lots of ways. For instance, I can increase the density of your bones so that your own skeleton will crush you to death. Like *this!*"

The deep eyes turned on Kenneth, and he fell to the ground, crushed there by an insupportable and increasing weight.

"Or I can put your eyes on your fingertips so that you have to see with your hands."

Kenneth found himself on his feet again. He was staring at the ground, although his head was up. He saw the world reel about him as he clapped his seeing hands to his face. He cried out in an ecstasy of terror.

"Or," continued the god conversationally, "I can finish your lily pool for you and drown you in it."

Kenneth was hurled forward into shallow water, where no water had been before. He bumped his head stunningly on a solid concrete surface and lay there, immersed and strangling. Suddenly he found himself before the idol again. His clothes were dry; his eyes were in place; everything was quite, quite normal. Except that damned idol, and the brand-new lily pool. It had all taken possibly eight seconds.

"Or—" said the idol.

"O.K., O.K.," said Kenneth weakly. "You win."

"That's better," smirked Rakna. "Now listen to me. I don't want you to think I intend any harm! I don't. But unfortunately for my character I was created in more or less a man's image. The only faults I have are human ones, and even though I have improved considerably, I still possess those faults. One of them is vanity. I don't like to be called a weakling any more than you do. You'll take a poke at someone who calls you a pansy; all right, so will I. Savvy?"

Kenneth nodded.

"Right. All I want from you is a little consideration. Keep your mouth shut about me; I don't mind being admired, but I don't want to be a museum piece." Amused pity suddenly manifested itself on those craggy features. "Look, Kenneth, I've been a little hard on you. After all, you did give me a comfortable place to sit. Anything I could do for you?" Again those fear-erasing waves of friendliness. Kenneth stopped trembling.

"Why ... I don't know. I've got a good job, and about everything I want."

"How about your wife? Are you altogether happy?"

"Why, sure I am. Well ... that is—"

"Never mind the details. I know all about it. She calls you a liar and she's right, and you wish something could be done about it. Want me to make you incapable of telling a lie? I can do it."

"You mean—"

"I mean that every time anyone asks you a question you'll be able to tell them only the truth. How much money you have, what you did that night in Denver"—Kenneth quailed at that—"what you honestly think of your boss—"

"Oh, no!" said Kenneth. "That doesn't sound so hot."

Rakna grinned. "All right. Let's do it this way. Everything you say will be the truth. If you say black is white, it will be white. If you tell your wife you were working late instead of playing poker, then it will be true. See what I mean?"

Kenneth couldn't see anything wrong in that. "By golly, Rakna, you've got something there. Can you do it?"

"I've done it," said Rakna. "Look. See that chain hoist you hauled me up with?"

Kenneth glanced at it. "Yeah."

"Now tell me it's not lying here, but it's in the shed."

"It's in the shed," said Kenneth obediently.

The hoist vanished. A clinking of chain drifted down the garden path. Rakna grinned.

"Hot cha!" exclaimed Kenneth. "Nothing but the truth. Thanks a million, Rakna. You're an ace!"

"Skip it," said the god. "Now beat it. I want to think."

Kenneth started up the path, his surliness quite gone and a new spring in his step. Rakna gazed after him and chuckled deeply.

"Cocky little devil," he said. "This ought to be good." He relaxed and let his mind dwell casually on profound matters.

As he came to the turn in the path and out of the range of old Rakna's quizzical gaze, Kenneth's steps suddenly slowed and he began to wonder a little at all this. Surely a thing like this couldn't be true! He found himself in a very precarious mental state. He could go back again and see if there really was a god in his garden, or he could blindly believe everything that had happened, or he could go on as usual and try to forget the whole thing. The worst part of it all was that if it all was a dream, he was probably nuts. If it wasn't a dream, who was nuts? He shrugged. Once you got used to the idea of having a god in your back yard you could get a kick out of it. But how did the old sourpuss think he could prove his power by making Kenneth speak the absolute truth? Not, of course, that there was anything in it.

Marjorie heard him coming into the house.

"Hurry and wash up, darling," she called briskly. "Supper's on!"

"Be right with you, kid!" He scrubbed up, put on a clean shirt and came down to the dining room. In one of the steaming dishes on the table was turnips. He frowned. His wife noticed, and said forlornly:

"Oh, dear, I forgot. You don't like turnips!"

"Don't be silly," he lied gallantly. "I love 'em."

No sooner had he said the words than the lowly turnips seemed to take on a glamour, a gustatory perfection. His mouth watered for them, his being cried out for them—turnips were the most delicious, the most nourishing and delightful food ever to be set on a man's table. He loved 'em.

A little startled, he sat down and began to eat—turnips more than anything else. "Most delicious meal I ever had," he told a gratified Marjorie. No sooner said than done. It *was*. And as a matter of fact, it was strictly a budget meal—one of those meals that good little managers like Marjorie Courtney throw together to make up for yesterday's spring chicken. She was vastly flattered.

"You must have worked terribly hard to fix up a meal like this," Kenneth said with mouth full. "You must be tired."

She was, suddenly, a little. Kenneth laid down his fork. "You *look* tired, dear." Lines appeared on her fresh little face. "Darling!" he said anxiously, "You're terribly tired!"

"I don't know what's the matter," she said haggardly.

"Marjorie, sweet, you're sick! What is it?"

"I don't know," she said faintly. "All of a sudden I feel—" Her head dropped on the table. He caught her in his arms.

"Buck up, kid. I'll carry you upstairs. Hang on, now. I'll get you settled and call a doctor." He crossed the room and started up the stairs.

"I'm too heavy—" she murmured.

"Nonsense!" he scoffed. "You're as light as a feather!"

Her body seemed to lift out of his arms. He was halfway up the stairs by this time, poised on one leg, about to take another step. The sudden lightening of her body had the effect, on him, of a kick on the chin. Down he went, head over heels, to the bottom of the stairs.

It was a nasty jolt, and for the moment he couldn't see anything but stars. "Marge!" he muttered. "You all right? Say you're all right!"

A whimpering cry cleared his head. Marjorie was settling gently down toward him, bumping each step lightly—lightly, like a floating feather.

He reached out dazedly and took her hand. She came drifting down toward him as he sprawled there, until their bodies rested together.

"Oh, God," moaned Kenneth. "What am I going to do?"

He rose and tried to help her up. His gentle pull on her arm sent her flying up over his head. She was crying weakly, hysterically. He walked into the living room, his wife literally streaming out behind him, and held her poised over the day bed until she rested on it. Then he ran for the telephone.

But as the singsong "Operator!" came over the wire he laid down the receiver, struck with a thought. Bit by insane bit he pieced the thing together: Rakna's promise; the power that he now had over the truth—the whole crazy affair. In the last few hectic minutes he had all but forgotten. Well, if he could do it, he could undo it.

He went back to his wife, drew a deep breath, and said:

"You're not sick. You weigh one hundred and fourteen."

Marjorie bounced up out of the day bed, shook her head dizzily, and advanced toward him. Kenneth sensed thunder in the air.

"What sort of a joke was that?" she demanded, her voice trembling. Kenneth thought a little faster this time. "Why, darling! Nothing has happened to you!"

Marjorie's face cleared. She stopped, then went on into the dining room, saying: "What on earth made us wander out here when we should be eating?"

"Nothing," said Kenneth; and that seemed to tie up all the threads. He felt a little weak; this power of his was a little too big to be comfortable. He noticed another thing, too; he could make his wife forget anything that happened, but he still knew about it. Lord! He'd have to be careful. He had a splitting headache, as always when he was excited, and that didn't help any. Marjorie noticed it.

"Is something the matter, Kenny?" she asked. "Have you a headache?"

"No," he said automatically; and as he said it, it was true! For the first time he grinned at the idea of his power. Not bad! No more toothache, stomach ache, business worries—business—Holy smoke! He was rich! Watch.

"Marge," he said as she put two lumps in his coffee, "we have twenty thousand dollars in the bank."

"Yes. I know. Isn't it nice? Cream?"

"You know? How did you know?"

"Silly! I've always known. You told me, didn't you? Anyway, I've known about it quite a while, it seems to me. Why?"

"Why?" Kenneth was floored. Then he shrugged. The truth was like that, he guessed. If a thing was true, it required no explanation; it just *was*. He finished his coffee and pushed back his chair. "Let's go to a show, kiddo."

"That would be nice," she said. "Just as soon as I get the dishes done."

"Oh," he said airily. "They're done."

She turned astonished eyes to him. It occurred to him then that if he persisted in this sort of thing he might make her doubt her sanity. A bank account was one thing; but the dishes—

"I mean," he explained. "We did them."

"Oh ... of course. I ... well, let's go."

He mind up his mind to go a little easy thereafter.

That was the beginning of a hectic three weeks for Kenneth Courtney. Hectic, but fun, by golly. Everything came his way; everything he said was true, and if everything he did wasn't quite right, it could be fixed. Like the time he was driving his big twelve-speed Diesel tractor-trailer job through the mountains one night, and a light sedan whipped around a hairpin turn and steered right between his headlights.

"Look out!" he called to Johnny Green, his helper, who was in the bunk over the seat. "We're going to smash!"

And as the car approached, as their bumpers practically kissed, Kenneth remembered his powers. "We missed him!" he bellowed.

Miss him they did. The car vanished, and a second later its careening tail light appeared in the rear-view mirror. It just wasn't possible—but it was true.

He did learn to be careful, though. There was the time when he casually remarked that it was raining cats and dogs. That mistake cost him half an hour of running madly around telling people that it wasn't really raining cats and dogs, you know, just raining hard. The thing would have made quite a sensation if he had not thought of declaring that it had not rained at all that day.

His influence was far-reaching. One night he happened to tune into a radio soprano who was mutilating Italian opera to such an extent that Kenneth inadvertently remarked: "She's lousy!" Thirty seconds later the loudspeaker gave vent to a series of squeaks and squalls which had no conceivable connection with Italian opera.

He had to watch his language. No author or orator was ever so careful about avoiding clichés and catch-phrases as was Kenneth Courtney in the weeks in which he enjoyed his powers. A friend once remarked that he had been working all day; "I'm dead!" he said. Kenneth turned pale and solemnly swore he would never use *that* expression again. He began to notice things about the way we speak: "I'm starved." "You're crazy." "You look like a ghost." "I hate you." "You're a half-wit," or "idiot" or "imbecile." "You never grew up."

At first Kenneth was a good man to have around the house. From his easy chair he did the housework, made the beds, cooked a delicious series of meals, redecorated the living room, and renewed every article of clothing and linen in the house. Pretty soft. But he found that the wear and tear of the thing was too much for his wife.

Though Marjorie had every evidence that the work was done, still she had no memory of doing it—unless, of course, she remarked on it to Kenneth. In that case she would be told, and truthfully, that she had done the work herself. But she began to worry a little about her memory; at times she thought she was losing it altogether. You don't cook a six-course dinner without remembering anything about it except the fact that you cooked it; and Marjorie even had to be told about that. So Kenneth, after a while, left the house to its appointed boss, and amused himself elsewhere.

And Kenneth never told her—or anyone—about Rakna and what he had done. Why? Because the conviction that matter-of-fact, efficient little Marjorie Courtney wouldn't believe such a farfetched tale was so deep-rooted that it never occurred to him to use his power on her. She had, in the past, called him a liar so many times with justice that he felt subconsciously that she would do it again. That, incidentally, *might* have been Rakna's doing.

Well, for three weeks this went on. Kenneth had money to burn, all the leisure time he wanted—he worked now for the fun of it—and life was a song—in swingtime, of course, but still a song. He had been so busy experimenting and amusing himself that he hadn't thought of really celebrating. And on one memorable Saturday night he went downtown and threw a whingding that made history.

Only an old sailor or an ex-soldier or a man with Kenneth's powers can throw that sort of a binge. He was not a heavy drinker; but every time that sickly, cloying feeling came over him he'd say, like every other swiller: "*I'm* not drunk. I may be tight, but I'm not drunk." And then he could start over. Never mind the details; but let this suffice: the next morning, stocks on liquor jumped two points, and on the various hangover remedies, six to ten points. Not a sober man went out of a barroom anywhere in town that night. Kenneth painted the town bright, bright red; and he and all the tipplers he could possibly find—and everything was possible to Kenneth!—literally drank the town dry.

He reeled home about six in the morning. He had poured some two hundred gallons of the best down his throat, and his breath would fell a strong man at thirty yards. Yet he was only delightfully high; he even remembered to eradicate the breath as he came in the door, by remarking that it was sweet as a baby's.

Marjorie was up when he entered rockily, flinging his hat to the right, his coat to the left, and himself on the carpet. She said nothing, which was bad; just walked daintily around him and upstairs. He called her, but she kept on going.

"Oh, oh!" he said. He started after her, found the stairs a little too much for him, and so declared himself on the second floor. Once there, he stumbled in on Marjorie. She was packing.

"What goes on?" he wanted to know.

"I'm going to stay with mother for a while," she said tiredly. "Till you sober up."

"Sober up?" he repeated. "Why, I'm perfectly sober!" It was true, of course; but that made no difference. Just because a thing is basically, unalterably true doesn't mean that a woman and a wife is going to believe it. She kept packing.

"Now wait a minute, darling. Haven't I been good to you? What do you want me to do? Marjorie!" This was the first time she had pulled anything like this. He was flabbergasted.

She turned toward him. "Kenneth, I'm sorry, but I've got to go away from you for a while. Maybe forever," she added forlornly. "You see, something's happened to me ... to us ... in the last few weeks. I don't know what it is, but I think sometimes that I'm losing my mind. I forget things ... and you, Kenneth! I can't understand what you're up to, with all your running around at all hours of the night, and the strange things that are happening. The other day I was in living room and just happened to be looking at Aunt Myrtle's vase when it disappeared ... vanished, just like that." She snapped her fingers.

Kenneth swore under his breath. That was a slip. He had hated that eyesore, and happened to think of it one day when he was on the road. He had stated that it no longer existed, forgetting that his wife might be in the room at the time.

"So you see I need a rest, Kenneth." She began to cry, but turned to her packing all the same. Kenneth tried to put his arms around her, but she pushed him away.

Now Kenneth had learned during his year or so of marriage that the only way to stop one of these bickerings was to tell the truth, take his medicine like a man, and then be forgiven. Well, he reasoned, the truth wouldn't be so hard to tell this time. Again, it never occurred to him to tell her that nothing was the matter, that she wasn't angry and frightened. No, the only thing he could think of that would fill the bill was to share his secret about the god in the garden. That was the cause of it all, so it might be the cure.

"Marjorie ... I can explain everything."

"Oh, yes," she said bitterly. "You always can."

He swallowed that and tried again. "Listen, darling, please. I was digging our lily pool, and—"

As the story unfolded she stopped her packing and sank down on the edge of the bed. His words carried a peculiar conviction, and he thrilled to the dawning belief in her face.

"—and so last night I thought of celebrating it. It would do no harm that couldn't be set right. See? So don't go, sweetheart. There's no need—"

The remark brought her engrossed mind back to the fact that she had been in the midst of leaving his bed and board when he had interrupted with this story, this—yes—preposterous story. She remembered that she was angry at him, and that fact was quite sufficient. He was so horribly smug, so terribly in the right about everything. Marjorie Courtney was by no means the first woman who, incensed, refused to believe the absolute truth simply because that truth put her in the wrong.

"I don't believe any of it!" she said firmly. Suddenly she drew back a little. "Kenneth . . . I do believe that it's *you* who are losing your mind, not I . . . Ohhh—"

Kenneth realized then that if she kept that up any longer she'd have herself convinced. That wouldn't do. He took her by the arm, hurried her out and down the stairs. "Come on," he said grimly. "You're about to be introduced to a god. That'll show you who's crazy."

She struggled a little, but allowed herself to be forced out into the yard and down the garden path. She wouldn't believe it! She wouldn't!

As they reached the pool she looked up at Kenneth's face. It was grimly determined; she was frightened. She did not see old Rakna grin and raise his carven eyebrows.

"Rakna!" called Kenneth. "My wife won't believe in you. What can I do to convince her?"

Marjorie said brokenly: "It's just an old statue . . . I know . . . I saw the hideous thing last week . . . it can't talk . . . It's stone—"

Rakna said: "I *am* stone, to her. I told you I didn't want anybody but you knowing anything about me."

"But . . . she's my wife!" cried Kenneth.

Marjorie said: "What?"

"You see," said Rakna, "she can't hear me. She thinks you're talking to a piece of stone." The god laughed richly. "I don't blame her for thinking you're nuts!"

"Skip that," Kenneth said angrily. "She's going to leave me if I can't convince her I'm sane. She just won't believe me. I thought you said I would always speak the absolute truth? Why won't she believe me?"

"Kenneth!" gasped Marjorie hysterically. "Stop it! Stop talking to that awful statue! Please, Kenneth!"

Rakna laughed again. "Look, dope, don't you know that truth, as such, does not exist to an angry woman, unless she happens to agree with it? As for my doing anything about this, that's up to you. You got yourself into this. I found it most amusing, too. Now get yourself out. That ought to be funnier."

"Why you old. . . Listen, Rakna, give me a break, will you?" said Kenneth desperately.

Rakna just chuckled.

Suddenly Marjorie fell on her knees beside Kenneth. She looked up at him with tear-filled, imploring eyes. She was incredibly lovely, lovely and pitiful, as she knelt there.

"Kenneth," she moaned. "Oh, darling, I love you . . . I always will, no matter what happens to you, no matter—" She drew a great shuddering sigh, and Kenneth's heart and soul went out to her. "Tell me you're all right, Kenneth. Tell me this is all a dream. Oh, God . . . Kenneth! I'm your wife, and I'm crying for you! You're out of your mind! This idol . . . its power over you—"

Kenneth dropped beside her and held her close. Rakna chuckled again—his last chuckle.

Kenneth whispered in Marjorie's ear: "Darling, it's all right! I'm quite sane, truly I am. Just forget everything. There is no Rakna . . . you're right. Just a brownstone idol. Rakna has no power over me. I have no powers that he gave me—" Anything to comfort her. He murmured on and on.

They crouched there, those two young people, at the foot of an incredibly old brownstone idol, who was once Rakna, a god with the power of a god. The stone idol had no power over Kenneth Courtney, for Kenneth had spoken the truth when he said those words.

They lived, of course, happily ever after. And if you visit them, Kenneth may take you into the rock garden and show you his ugly old idol. It has a craggy, aristocratic face, with an expression on it of rueful humor. He was a good sport, that Rakna. Kenneth, by the way, still lies to his wife.

Fit for a King

SWEEPING AND POLISHING; the moan of high-powered vacuum cleaners and the chatter of chambermaids; sharp orders, hurrying feet, and the half eager, half resentful scurrying of employees; and over it all, the suave efficiency of Percy Gregg, the hotel's dictatorial little manager. This was an epoch-making spring cleaning, for this was an epoch-making spring; the spring that was to bring a King-Emperor and his Queen to our shores. And they were to honor this great hotel with their august presences.

Bill Foxx, the bell captain, took it all with a grin. It was almost funny to see Mr. Percy Gregg driving himself and his employees to distraction; to see the hustle and bustle centering around the impending visit of, after all, two mere human beings. That he could take it all with a grin did Bill Foxx credit, because Bill was held responsible for every unshined button on each impeccable uniform, and for every false move in the elaborate dress rehearsal of the carefully planned entrance. Sometimes, too, Mr. Gregg's near psychopathic efficiency was a little hard to take. The man was inhuman on occasions, and his cold anger was feared by every desk clerk, bellhop and pot-walloper in the hotel. His rigid discipline and unbending manner toward all who worked for him were the qualities that made him one of the best, and certainly the least liked, hotel managers in the country.

It made no difference how old and trusted an employee might be, one tiny slip and he was out. Percy Gregg prided himself on never giving anyone a second chance. Bill Foxx had made it his business to avoid making such little slips. His was a good job, and he *had* to keep it. Bill Foxx was saving up to marry, and when a man feels that way about a girl, he will bear anything—anything at all—to achieve his aim.

133

As the days dragged on in a heartbreaking succession of drills and speed-up routines, there was more than one occasion when Bill almost forgot to grin. But he kept the vision of the girl he was to marry in his overworked mind. Like any human unjustly treated, the thought formed with greater and greater intensity, "Some day I'll tell old man Gregg where to head in!" But he didn't—not quite. Almost, though, time and again.

It was on the day that Their majesties arrived that the last straw was piled on Bill's uncomplaining back. Gregg's anger was particularly uncalled for, because everything had been executed without a hitch; the grand entrance, with the lines of scrubbed and pressed and polished bellhops on each side of the door while the King's National Anthem was played, and the ceremonial registering of royalty in the hotel books—all were performed with the greatest precision. And Gregg went out of his way to catch Bill Foxx, who had not made a mistake in four faithful years, in a most trifling error in etiquette. He could have glossed it over—but he wouldn't. Not Percy Gregg.

It happened this way. As Gregg was showing the royal couple into their suite, Bill appeared with ice water. He stood waiting until his entrance would be unnoticed, then crossed the room swiftly and set down his burden. Just as swiftly and quietly he turned and walked to the door, passing Gregg who, mouthing obsequious phrases, was backing from the room. Bill had seen this sort of thing in the movies, but had the impression that it was a little out of date. If Gregg wanted to make a fool of himself that way—

"Foxx!" Gregg's icy little voice cracked at him like a whip. He turned back. Gregg was standing at the door, closing it, and his smooth face was distorted with fury. Bill turned back.

"You *walked* out of that suite," Gregg said, his voice trembling. "You stupid, useless, blundering idiot! Don't you know enough to keep your face toward a king when you leave his rooms? Get your money. You're through!"

Bill drew himself up and grinned, trying to check the torrent of words that swirled inside him. But why? He was through. He'd have his say, he decided. He began quietly, but his voice carried well, and it rose steadily as he said, "With pleasure. But I want to tell you this, you slave driver. I am an American, and I happen to be proud of it. I have treated these people with the respect and consideration due any guest. But I'm not paid to kowtow to any man or woman, and as an American I never learned to do it. I—" He stopped suddenly as the door was flung open and the King stepped out. In that tense moment Bill admired the man; he was a king, and he looked like a king.

Gregg was frantically bowing and scraping, saying: "Your Majesty, I had no idea—a thousand pard—it is unthinkable that—"

The King looked at him coldly, and Gregg subsided, trembling. Then the King came toward Bill and said, "I heard this unfortunate argument, and feel that I must speak to the first American who has acted as I understood all Americans act. I shall be honored to shake your hand in the American way." And he did.

No, Gregg did not fire his bell captain after that. For once he did not dare.

Ex-Bachelor Extract

A BUNCH OF us were there, former bachelors all. Now a former bachelor is ever so subtly different from the ordinary run-of-the-mill married man. A former bachelor is essentially a reformed person, whereas the average married man never reformed. Not so you'd notice it. He just steps into marriage as he stepped into school when he was a kid, or as he stepped into his first job. A casual, necessary thing. But a former bachelor is uprooted, reorganized; never a natural fit in the new order, but an artificially adjusted person.

And when a bunch of former bachelors—yes, they flock together!—indulge in a bull session, sooner or later the talk will drift around to the reasons that this one and that one had for abandoning the blissfully independent single state. These yarns are always worth hearing, because it takes plenty to lead a natural born bachelor to the altar. A former bachelor will get married for some of the doggonedest reasons, but quite the most superlatively doggonedest was the way little Louise Brett caught Carl Hansen.

Carl met Louise at a cocktail party and they really took to each other. Carl's a hard worker, interested in his job, and he likes to talk about it. Louise is intelligent, and made a very interested audience. Before they knew it they had chatted the party away, so of course he had to take her to dinner. And then a show. And then a supper-dance. It must have been at about that point that Louise made up her mind to lasso the lad.

Now I've said she was intelligent. She could see Carl for what he was—an up and coming youngster with a taste for the finer things of life. She could see that he was perceptive and discriminating and fastidious. But above all she realized that he was a bachelor to the core, and she was going to have a hard time making him pop the question without frightening him away.

How she found the answer I don't know. But she found it all right.

The third time they were out together he noticed her perfume. It grew on him during the evening, and at first he didn't even realize that Louise owed her increased attractiveness to a scent, so subtle was it. There was something about her, though, something that stirred deep within him. She made him think of a succession of clean and sweet and pleasing things. Little pictures and impressions flickered through his mind as he talked to her and danced with her—mental photographs of the whiteness of washed enamel and the warm smell of home-cooked meals; blue checked aprons and bright curtains; fire glow and soft cushions. Louise exuded a magic all her own, completely original and completely devastating. She made Carl think of his mother—and when a woman achieves that, she has tied the binding knot, and needs only to pull it tight.

After he left her in the wee small hours that morning, Carl drifted homeward in a rosy fog. This had never happened to him before, this hot-cold shivery feeling. The scientist calls it "emotional involvement" and the poet calls it "beatitude" and the swingster calls it "ickey." But it's love in any language—except a bachelor's. Poor guy, he doesn't know what to make of it.

When he had a little time to relive that unforgettable evening, he reasoned and analyzed and discarded until he had isolated the fact that it was her perfume which had done the trick. But its name escaped him. It was a familiar odor, but it was familiar in a way that cloaked it. Like your front stairs. How many steps do you climb when you come home? You climb them each night, and yet you can't name the number of them. Louise's perfume was like that; everyday and indefinable. But it seemed like the essence of all the good things in the universe, and gave Louise the status of No. 1 woman in Carl's life. And when he saw her again, so haunted and enchanted was he by that scent that he demanded in the same breath as his "Hello, darling,

"What kind of perfume is that?"

She looked up at him and smiled a warm mysterious smile. "Guess," she said, "But it's my secret."

He took her by the shoulders and inhaled the telling whiff of her sorcery. "I'll find out what it is," he said softly, "if I have to marry you to do it."

"Oh, Carl!" Soft arms around his neck, soft lips inches from his own... Oh, well—they were married in due time.

She stuck to her word. It wasn't until they were on their honeymoon that she showed him the bottle of vanilla extract. And they call women the weaker sex!

East Is East

LAURA WAS DELIGHTED. She had come here in a spirit of adventurous defiance, and the one thing that could possibly have spoiled the evening would have been loneliness in this noisy crowd. Rebelling at her mother's insistence that she kowtow to the conventions, that she confine her dancing to the Greek interpretative, that she learn the gracious arts of being hostess and mistress of ceremonies at afternoon teas, and that she express her youthful exuberance in masterly playing of Chopin on her mother's concert grand, she had flown in the face of fate, flung herself into the great unknown. She had come to the Jitterclub on East Beaufort Street, which club should have been dignified by the term "joint."

Well, that's East Beaufort Street for you. At one end, on the west side of town, it is lined by great mansions and exclusive apartment houses. These grade down in quality until West Beaufort Street, in the business section, undergoes its transition to East Beaufort Street. From that point on it descends the social scale. Its windup is a waterfront—a colorful, noisy, malodorous waterfront. And the center of the odors—hemp, copra, fish, stagnant water; and the noise—trucks and drays and a spur line of the central R.R.; and the color—shawled immigrant women, turbaned lascars from Limey ships and the ships themselves—in the center of all this, then, was the Jitterclub.

Some joints are loud and some funny, but the "Jitter" was by all counts the loudest and funniest. And Laura had fled to it. She was supposed to be at a meeting of the Cultural Society for Poetry and Orphan Dogs, and the prospect had been too deadly. It was simply a choice between breaking up a meeting of the CSPOD with violence, or letting off steam with equal violence where it would not be noticed. The way she felt, the Jitterclub was the only place that would do.

And here she was, with jam and jive washing over her in great waves; and now she was delighted, because she wanted someone to talk to, and this incredibly handsome young man was saying, "Look, sister, I'm lonely too."

Knowing the value of protective coloration (as long as she acted like an habitué, she felt safe) she carefully popped her huge cud of chewing gum at him before she said (*very* East Side!), "That makes two of us, all right. Somp'n' oughta be done."

Somp'n' *was* done—plenty. He *was* delightful. He acted just as a flashy East Sider should act. She knew. Hadn't she been to the movies? His name was Sam Reynolds but he said, "Call me Sooky."

He could dance. She giggled as she thought of the hours spent in Mme. Kokkinakski's studio—"Ant-a-wan, ant-a-two, ant-a-t'ree, ant-a-vour, naow, you air a wave. You move like a swan—so!" Sooky whirled and shagged and hopped; carried her into a land far away, a land made of sharps and flats and blue crescendos and crazy heart-beat syncopation.

He knew the lingo, and he knew the gags and comebacks. He called her "Toots" and she liked it. Why not? Tomorrow she'd be back in her right little, tight little luxurious boring world; but now—the music's playing, let's dance.

Later they went to Antonio's Spaghetti Emporium and ate *tagliatelli* and *costoletti* and it was delicious. They talked, and they sang to each other the lyrics of the popular songs that poured out of the brass throat of Antonio's radio. They laughed a great deal—and it was in the middle of a peal of laughter that Laura suddenly stopped, put her hand to her mouth and stared with frightened eyes at Sam (Sooky) Reynolds.

"'S'matter, Laura?"

She couldn't tell him. She wanted to—oh, yes! She wanted to tell him that, as if a light had been turned on, she realized that she didn't want to say good-bye to this beautiful, vulgar young man. Not ever. "Nothing," she said tiredly. Nothing? This filled up, choked feeling? This wild beating of her heart?

Antonio twisted the dial of the radio, and music poured forth—rich, glorious, emotional symphonic music. It was too much. Laura cried. Sooky came around the table, put his arm around her, thrust a spotless handkerchief in her hands. "Take it easy, kid," he said softly. "I know how it is . . . Brahms' Fourth Symphony gets me that way too."

Laura sniffed and sat up stiffly. "Brahms' Fourth? What would a jitterbug know about Brahms' Fourth? Besides, it's Tchaikovsky's Fourth."

"Brahms!" he said sharply to get her angry, make her forget her tears.

"Tchaikovsky!" she insisted. "I know. I have to listen to it almost every day."

"You—how come?"

She laid her cards on the table. "I'm not what you think, Sooky. I'm terribly sorry. I live on the west side. I wanted fun. I've had fun. I . . . I'd better go." She was crying again.

"Fun," he said. "I had fun too. I'll go with you, Laura. It's the same with me. I live next door to you. I followed you here tonight. Something might have happened to you. I had a chance—my mother went to the meeting of the CSPOD." Laura sank back in her chair. He thought she was laughing, and then that she was crying. Then he saw that she was doing both.

The announcer said that they had been listening to Tchaikovsky's Fifth Symphony. They weren't interested.

Three People

THEY WERE SCARED, those three. Mrs. Mulligan, as magnificently poised as ever, stood between Benny and Betsy, with a firm and inexorable grip on the back of each moist neck. George stood in front of them, his grubby face revealing the conflict between loyalty and self-preservation going on within him. They were caught red-handed, those three. It had been George's idea, of course. All of his ideas were good, and most of them wound up this way. Set a couple of cannon crackers in front of Mrs. Mulligan's door, light the fuses, ring the bell and beat it. Why Mrs. Mulligan? Because she was the terror of every child on the block. Not, certainly, because she ever did anything to anyone. But she was so mysterious. She never spoke to anyone, and she always dressed in black. An ignorant mother had once told her disobedient son that if he were not good, Mrs. Mulligan would get him. This little story had spread and grown with the telling. Mrs. Mulligan ate little boys and girls. She hid in dark corners and jumped out atcha. She—well, now she had neatly caught Benny and Betsy and George. They had set their cannon crackers and had rung the bell. They had stampeded around the corner of the house—right into the capable arms of Mrs. Mulligan. Like lightning, and yet with no apparent effort, she had captured the napes of Benny and Betsy, and fixed George with a baleful eye.

They held the tableau for a long painful moment. George could have fled, but the enemy had the two younger children in her power. And it was George's fault. George stayed where he was, with his mouth open alarmingly.

"Come with me," Mrs. Mulligan said quietly. Three scared pairs of eyes searched her face and found it inscrutable. And as she turned and went up the steps, three small pairs of legs followed obediently, without enthusiasm. And so they passed through that fearsome portal, into the unknown beyond.

But it wasn't so fearsome, after all. There were bright chintz curtains and neatly contrasting upholsteries. There were deep rugs, and there was a canary and a big aquarium. Mrs. Mulligan lined the three up in front of a huge divan and pushed them gently but firmly onto it. They were so frightened that they stayed where they were put, like dolls. Mrs. Mulligan laughed and went out of the room.

Betsy said, "I'm scared, George."

"I'm not," Benny quavered. George flashed a look around the room. "Let's make a break for it!"

"No!" said Benny. "My father said if a bee flies around you and you don't move, he'll go away."

"Snakes, too," whispered Betsy absently. Mrs. Mulligan came back bearing a huge tray. She set it in front of them. It was loaded down with ice cream and cake and mints and chocolates. Three pairs of eyes tore themselves from the sight and looked again at that soft, quizzical face. It was smiling now, and suddenly they were not afraid any more, just very, very puzzled. Betsy sobbed twice, and tears came, and then she smiled at Mrs. Mulligan. "Go ahead," said Mrs. Mulligan. "The cream will get soft."

They needed no second invitation. And as they stuffed themselves Mrs. Mulligan sat opposite in a big chair and looked at them and laughed softly. It sounded like cool water running down a flight of thin glass steps. Benny suddenly looked up at her with his mouth crammed, and laughed with her, spraying crumbs on the carpet. Betsy and George laughed too, and after that they were all friends.

Their rather frantic munching began to slow, and all at once they realized that their hostess was telling them a story. It dawned on them slowly, like music in the background that gradually fills a room. It was a story, beautifully and simply told, about boys and girls, and how they sometimes do things without knowing why. "Why are you shooting off firecrackers today?" she asked. Benny said promptly, "It's the Fourth. Everybody does." "Why?" and they looked at each other and at her.

Then she asked them their names, and they told her. She thought a minute, and then told them three stories.

One was about a girl named Betsy. Betsy was very clever with her hands, and she loved her country. If she had been a man, she would have been a soldier. But she thought and thought, and finally decided that the best thing she could do would be to make a flag for her country.

And one was about a boy named Benny—Benjamin. When he grew up he was a very great man. He was a scientist, and he discovered that lightning was electricity. He was a great statesman and a diplomat. That's what he did for his country.

And then she turned to George and told a story about a boy named George who grew up to be a general—the kind of general who would fight like a private and suffer with his men when they suffered. Valley Forge—Trenton—and a man named Cornwallis.

Three stories about three people—patriotism, brains, and force. Three stories about a country and a Day of Independence, and what it meant.

And then she led them out into the back garden. There were piles of punk and torpedoes and crackers there, and big tin cans to make them loud. The three ran out laughing, and Mrs. Mulligan stayed at the door and laughed too. She may not live in your neighborhood, or in yours. But remember, on the Fourth, what she told those three. So many never think...

Eyes of Blue

SHE WAS A deb and he was a taxi driver and they met in the big city where things like this happen.

She was Estelle Rudd and she had seven million dollars and some odd cents in her own name and a dollar or two coming to her, which would be in two years now, so you can see that she was only nineteen. And because she was only nineteen, and in spite of her gilt edge pedigree a very normal girl, she was doing something crazy. She was riding in a taxicab and the taxicab was going downtown, farther and farther away from the deluxe suburb where she had been incarcerated in Mrs. Van Kurp's Finishing School. She figured she was finished but not what Mrs. Van Kurp meant by "finished." Estelle was finished with being finished, if you see what I mean, which is that she was rebelling because she did not like it out there.

She had thrown her thesies and thosies into a suitcase and had dropped silently out her window. She had $300 and lots of mistaken ideas about making a career for herself and laughing in the faces of her relatives, who really knew what was best for her. She was going to do the kind of disappearing act known as a blackout, which was very selfish of her. But she had cried and pleaded because she did not like Mrs. Van Kurp's Finishing School, and nobody had paid any attention and so she was convinced that nobody loved her, which was not true, but which gave her a good excuse to do something violent.

So, here she was, bumping comfortably toward her newer and freer life in a great big taxicab, feeling very small and brave and admirable because she was nineteen and thought she was very clever. But after a half hour of that she began to feel lonesome. She needed someone to tell her that she was small and brave and admirable, and there was no one around but the taxi driver. She began to talk to him.

He was used to it, because he didn't do anything but grunt. She thought that a man who could only grunt could not have very much intelligence, so she began to expand her tale. She lay back in the cab and talked and talked and did not watch where the cab was going. The more she talked the prouder she grew, and before she knew it she had told him who she was and exactly what she was doing. She made it all very involved, and because he did not say anything she wound up asking, "And what do you think of me now?" She was a little hysterical.

The cab stopped and the driver got out and took her bag and opened the door. "I think you're a headstrong little brat," he told her, and pulled her forcibly out of his cab. She was so astonished that she did not notice anything for a while except that the driver was young and had the bluest eyes on earth, and that the eyes were amused and a little angry but not at all disgusted, which was something.

And then, as she caught her breath, she realized that the cab was standing beneath the pillared marquee of Mrs. Van Kurp's Finishing School. Estelle was very angry, of course, but what good did it do her? The cab driver smiled a very nice smile and demanded his fare, which was a large one because Estelle had been talking a long time before the young man began listening and decided to take matters into his own hands. Estelle thrust a bill at him and hurried into the building without waiting for her change. The driver laughed and drove off, and Estelle went to bed where she should have been in the first place. She was surprised to find that she was glad to be back.

Now I will jump two years in my story, because nothing much happened for two years except that Estelle was graduated and became a very wise and popular young lady. This was because she was tempted to do many foolish things, and every time she was tempted she would say to herself, "I think you're a headstrong little brat," and she would imagine the bluest eyes in the world smiling angrily down at her; and then she would not do what she was tempted to. It may seem odd, but it is true.

Well, one night at a party two years later, she was standing at the window alone for the first time that evening, looking out the window at the boulevard and the taxicabs, and thinking. And all of a sudden she was swung around by a strong hand and there were the blue eyes again, just like that. Only this time the taxi driver was in a white tie and tails, and he was no waiter, either.

"Hey," he said, which is no way to talk to a lady, "I want to talk to you." She was quite cold to him but he didn't mind. He took her out on the floor and danced, and he danced beautifully. She did not say anything because her heart was beating so wildly. Then he said, "This belongs to you." He took something out of his pocket and pressed it into her hand. It was a quarter. "Your change," he explained. She laughed and then blushed very prettily.

And so they were married. Not right away, but after they had been around some time together. The taxi driver? That was Raoul Bettered, the one the columnists call "the social author." He had been driving a taxicab for local color—and boy, did he get it!

Ether Breather

IT WAS "The Seashell." It *would* have to be "The Seashell." I wrote it first as a short story, and it was turned down. Then I made a novelette out of it, and then a novel. Then a short short. Then a three-line gag. And it still wouldn't sell. It got to be a fetish with me, rewriting that "Seashell." After a while editors got so used to it that they turned it down on sight. I had enough rejection slips from that number alone to paper every room in the house of tomorrow. So when it sold— well, it was like the death of a friend. It hit me. I hated to see it go.

It was a play by that time, but I hadn't changed it much. Still the same pastel, froo-froo old "Seashell" story, about two children who grew up and met each other only three times as the years went on, and a little seashell that changed hands each time they met. The plot, if any, doesn't matter. The dialogue was—well, pastel. Naive. Unsophisticated. Very pretty, and practically salesproof. But it just happened to ring the bell with an earnest young reader for Associated Television, Inc., who was looking for something about that length that could be dubbed "artistic"; something that would not require too much cerebration on the part of an audience, so that said audience could relax and appreciate the new polychrome technique of television transmission. You know: pastel.

As I leaned back in my old relic of an armchair that night, and watched the streamlined version of my slow-moving brainchild, I had to admire the way they put it over. In spots it was almost good, that "Seashell." Well suited for the occasion, too. It was a full-hour program given free to a perfume house by Associated, to try out the new color transmission as an advertising medium. I liked the first two acts, if I do say so as shouldn't. It was at the half hour mark that I got my first kick on the chin. It was a two-minute skit for the advertising plug.

148

A tall and elegant couple were seen standing on marble steps in an elaborate theater lobby. Says she to he:

"And how do you like the play, Mr. Robinson?"

Says he to she: "It stinks."

Just like that. Like any radio-television listener, I was used to paying little, if any, attention to a plug. That certainly snapped me up in my chair. After all, it was my play, even if it was "The Seashell." They couldn't do that to me.

But the girl smiling archly out of my television set didn't seem to mind. She said sweetly, "I think so, too."

He was looking slushily down into her eyes. He said: "That goes for you, too, my dear. What *is* that perfume you are using?"

"Berbelot's *Doux Rêves*. What do you think of it?"

He said, "You heard what I said about the play."

I didn't wait for the rest of the plug, the station identification, and act three. I headed for my visiphone and dialed Associated. I was burning up. When their pert-faced switchboard girl flashed on my screen I snapped: "Get me Griff. Snap it up!"

"Mr. Griff's line is busy, Mr. Hamilton," she sang to me. "Will you hold the wire, or shall I call you back?"

"None of that, Dorothe," I roared. Dorothe and I had gone to high school together; as a matter of fact I had got her the job with Griff, who was Associated's head script man. "I don't care who's talking to Griff. Cut him off and put me through. He can't do that to me. I'll sue, that's what I'll do. I'll break the company. I'll—"

"Take it easy, Ted," she said. "What's the matter with everyone all of a sudden, anyway? If you must know, the man gabbing with Griff now is old Berbelot himself. Seems he wants to sue Associated, too. What's up?"

By this time I was practically incoherent. "Berbelot, hey? I'll sue him, too. The rat! The dirty— What are you laughing at?"

"He wants to sue you!" she giggled. "And I'll bet Griff will, too, to shut Berbelot up. You know, this might turn out to be really funny!" Before I could swallow that she switched me over to Griff.

As he answered he was wiping his heavy jowls with a handkerchief. "Well?" he asked in a shaken voice.

"What are you, a wise guy?" I bellowed. "What kind of a stunt is that you pulled on the commercial plug on my play? Whose idea was that, anyway? Berbelot's? What the—"

"Now, Hamilton," Griff said easily, "don't excite yourself this way." I could see his hands trembling—evidently old Berbelot had laid it on thick. "Nothing untoward has occurred. You must be mistaken. I assure you—"

"You pompous old," I growled, waiving a swell two-dollar word on him, "don't call me a liar. I've been listening to that program and I know what I heard. I'm going to sue you. And Berbelot. And if you try to pass the buck onto the actors in that plug skit, I'll sue them, too. And if you make any more cracks about me being mistaken, I'm going to come up there and feed you your teeth. Then I'll sue you personally as well as Associated."

I dialed out and went back to my television set, fuming. The program was going on as if nothing had happened. As I cooled—and I cool slowly—I began to see that the last half of "The Seashell" was even better than the first. You know, it's poison for a writer to fall in love with his own stuff; but, by golly, sometimes you turn out a piece that really has something. You try to be critical, and you can't be. The Ponta Delgada sequence in "The Seashell" was like that.

The girl was on a cruise and the boy was on a training ship. They met in the Azores Islands. Very touching. The last time they saw each other was before they were in their teens, but in the meantime they had had their dreams. Get the idea of the thing? Very pastel. And they did do it nicely. The shots of Ponta Delgada and the scenery of the Azores were swell. Came the moment, after four minutes of icky dialogue, when he gazed at her, the light of true, mature love dawning on his young face.

She said shyly, "Well—"

Now, his lines, as written—and I should know!—went:

"Rosalind ... it *is* you, then, isn't it? Oh, I'm afraid"—he grasps her shoulders—"afraid that it can't be real. So many times I've seen someone who might be you, and it has never been ... Rosalind, Rosalind, guardian angel, reason for living, beloved ... beloved—"

Clinch.

Now, as I say, it went off as written, up to and including the clinch. But then came the payoff. He took his lips from hers, buried his face in her hair and said clearly: "I hate your _____ guts." And that "_____" was the most perfectly enunciated present participle of a four-letter verb I have ever heard.

Just what happened after that I couldn't tell you. I went haywire, I guess. I scattered two hundred and twenty dollars' worth of television set over all three rooms of my apartment. Next thing I knew I was in a 'press tube, hurtling toward the three-hundred-story skyscraper that housed Associated Television. Never have I seen one of those 'press cars, forced by compressed air through tubes under the city, move so slowly, but it might have been my imagination. If I had anything to do with it, there was going to be one dead script boss up there.

And whom should I run into on the 229th floor but old Berbelot himself? The perfume king had blood in his eye. Through the haze of anger that surrounded me, I began to realize that things were about to be very tough on Griff. And I was quite ready to help out all I could.

Berbelot saw me at the same instant, and seemed to read my thought. "Come on," he said briefly, and together we ran the gantlet of secretaries and assistants and burst into Griff's office.

Griff rose to his feet and tried to look dignified, with little success. I leaped over his glass desk and pulled the wings of his stylish open-necked collar together until he began squeaking.

Berbelot seemed to be enjoying it. "Don't kill him, Hamilton," he said after a bit. "I want to."

I let the script man go. He sank down to the floor, gasping. He was like a scared kid, in more ways than one. It was funny.

We let him get his breath. He climbed to his feet, sat down at his desk, and reached out toward a battery of push buttons. Berbelot snatched up a Dow-metal knife and hacked viciously at the chubby hand. It retreated.

"Might I ask," said Griff heavily, "the reason for this unprovoked rowdiness?"

Berbelot cocked an eye at me. "Might he?"

"He might tell us what this monkey business is all about," I said.

Griff cleared his throat painfully. "I told both you ... er ... gentlemen over the phone that, as far as I know, there was nothing amiss in our interpretation of your play, Mr. Hamilton, nor in the commercial section of the broadcast, Mr. Berbelot. After your protests over the wire, I made it a point to see the second half of the broadcast myself. Nothing was wrong. And as this is the first commercial color broadcast, it has been recorded. If you are not satisfied with my statements, you are welcome to see the recording yourselves, immediately."

What else could we want? It occurred to both of us that Griff was really up a tree; that he was telling the truth as far as he knew it, and that he thought we were both screwy. I began to think so myself.

Berbelot said, "Griff, didn't you hear that dialogue near the end, when those two kids were by that sea wall?"

Griff nodded.

"Think back now," Berbelot went on. "What did the boy say to the girl when he put his muzzle into her hair?"

"'I love you,'" said Griff self-consciously, and blushed. "He said it twice."

Berbelot and I looked at each other. "Let's see that recording," I said.

Well, we did, in Griff's luxurious private projection room. I hope I never have to live through an hour like that again. If it weren't for the fact that Berbelot was seeing the same thing I saw, and feeling the same way about it, I'd have reported to an alienist. Because that program came off Griff's projector positively shimmering with innocuousness. My script was A-1; Berbelot's plugs were right. On that plug that had started everything, where the man and the girl were gabbing in the theater lobby, the dialogue went like this:

"And how do you like the play, Mr. Robinson?"

"Utterly charming ... and that goes for you, too, my dear. What *is* that perfume you are using?"

"Berbelot's *Doux Rêves*. What do you think of it?"

"You heard what I said about the play."

Well there you are. And, by the recording, Griff had been right about the repetitious three little words in the Azores sequence. I was floored.

After it was over, Berbelot said to Griff: "I think I can speak for Mr. Hamilton when I say that if this is an actual recording, we owe you an apology; also when I say that we do not accept your evidence until we have compiled our own. I recorded that program as it came over my set, as I have recorded all my advertising. We will see you tomorrow, and we will bring that sound film. Coming, Hamilton?"

I nodded and we left, leaving Griff to chew his lip.

I'd like to skip briefly over the last chapter of that evening's nightmare. Berbelot picked up a camera expert on the way, and we had the films developed within an hour after we arrived at the fantastic "house that perfume built." And if I was crazy, so was Berbelot; and if he was, then so was the camera. So help me, that blasted program came out on Berbelot's screen exactly as it had on my set and his. If anyone ever took a long distance cussing-out, it was Griff that night. We figured, of course, that he had planted a phony recording on us, so that we wouldn't sue. He'd do the same thing in court, too. I told Berbelot so. He shook his head.

"No, Hamilton, we can't take it to court. Associated gave me that broadcast, the first color commercial, on condition that I sign away their responsibility for 'incomplete, or inadequate, or otherwise unsatisfactory performance.' They didn't quite trust that new apparatus, you know."

"Well, I'll sue for both of us, then." I said.

"Did they buy all rights?" he asked.

"Yes . . . damn! They got me, too! They have a legal right to do anything they want." I threw my cigarette into the electric fire, and snapped on Berbelot's big television set, tuning it to Associated's XZB.

Nothing happened.

"Hey! Your set's on the bum!" I said. Berbelot got up and began fiddling with the dial. I was wrong. There was nothing the matter with the set. It was Associated. All of their stations were off the air—

all four of them. We looked at each other.

"Get XZW," said Berbelot. "It's an Associated affiliate, under cover. Maybe we can—"

XZW blared out at us as I spun the dial. A dance program, the new five-beat stuff. Suddenly the announcer stuck his face into the transmitter.

"A bulletin from Iconoscope News Service," he said conversationally. "FCC has clamped down on Associated Television and its stations. They are off the air. The reasons were not given, but it is surmised that it has to do with a little strong language used on the world premiere of Associated's new color transmission. That is all."

"I expected that," smiled Berbelot. "Wonder how Griff'll alibi himself out of that? If he tries to use that recording of his, I'll most cheerfully turn mine over to the government, and we'll have him for perjury."

"Sorta tough on Associated, isn't it?" I said.

"Not particularly. You know these big corporations. Associated gets millions out of their four networks, but those millions are just a drop in the bucket compared with the other pies they've got their fingers in. That color technique, for instance. Now that they can't use it for a while, how many other outfits will miss the chance of bidding for the method and equipment? They lose some advertising contracts, and they save by not operating. They won't even feel it. I'll bet you'll see color transmission within forty-eight hours over a rival network."

He was right. Two days later Cineradio had a color broadcast scheduled, and all hell broke loose. What they'd done to the Berbelot hour and my "Seashell" was really tame.

The program was sponsored by one of the antigravity industries—I forget which. They'd hired Raouls Stavisk, the composer, to play one of the ancient Gallic operas he'd exhumed. It was a piece called "Carmen" and had been practically forgotten for two centuries. News of it had created quite a stir among music lovers, although, personally, I don't go for it. It's too barbaric for me. Too hard to listen to, when you've been hearing five-beat all your life. And those old-timers had never heard of a quarter tone.

Anyway, it was a big affair, televised right from the huge Citizens' Auditorium. It was more than half full—there were about 130,000 people there. Practically all of the select highbrow music fans from that section of the city. Yes, 130,000 pairs of eyes saw that show in the flesh, and countless millions saw it on their own sets; remember that.

Those that saw it at the Auditorium got their money's worth, from what I hear. They saw the complete opera; saw it go off as scheduled. The coloratura, Maria Jeff, was in perfect voice, and Stavisk's orchestra rendered the ancient tones perfectly. So what?

So, those that saw it at home saw the first half of the program the same as broadcast—of course. But—and get this —they saw Maria Jeff, on a close-up, in the middle of an aria, throw back her head, stop singing, and shout raucously: "The hell with this! Whip it up, boys!"

They heard the orchestra break out of that old two-four music— "Habañera," I think they called it—and slide into a wicked old-time five-beat song about "alco-pill Alice," the girl who didn't believe in eugenics. They saw her step lightly about the stage, shedding her costume—not that I blame her for that; it was supposed to be authentic, and must have been warm. But there was a certain something about the way she did it.

I've never seen or heard of anything like it. First, I thought that it was part of the opera, because from what I learned in school I gather that the ancient people used to go in for things like that. I wouldn't know. But I knew it wasn't opera when old Stavisk himself jumped up on the stage and started dancing with the prima donna. The televisors flashed around to the audience, and there they were, every one of them, dancing in the aisles. And I mean dancing. Wow!

Well, you can imagine the trouble that that caused. Cineradio, Inc., was flabbergasted when they were shut down by FCC like Associated. So were 130,000 people who had seen the opera and thought it was good. Every last one of them denied dancing in the aisles. No one had seen Stavisk jump on the stage. It just didn't make sense.

Cineradio, of course, had a recording. So, it turned out, did FCC.

Each recording proved the point of its respective group. That of Cineradio, taken by a sound camera right there in the auditorium, showed a musical program. FCC's, photographed right off a government standard receiver, showed the riot that I and millions of others had seen over the air. It was too much for me. I went out to see Berbelot. The old boy had a lot of sense, and he'd seen the beginning of this crazy business.

He looked pleased when I saw his face on his house televisor. "Hamilton!" he exclaimed. "Come on in! I've been phoning all over the five downtown boroughs for you!" He pressed a button and the foyer door behind me closed. I was whisked up into his rooms. That combination foyer and elevator of his is a nice gadget.

"I guess I don't have to ask you why you came," he said as we shook hands. "Cineradio certainly pulled a boner, hey?"

"Yes and no," I said. "I'm beginning to think that Griff was right when he said that, as far as he knew, the program was on the up and up. But if he was right, what's it all about? How can a program reach the transmitters in perfect shape, and come out of every receiver in the nation like a practical joker's idea of paradise?"

"It can't," said Berbelot. He stroked his chin thoughtfully. "But it did. Three times."

"Three— When—"

"Just now, before you got in. The secretary of state was making a speech over XZM, Consolidated Atomic, you know. XZM grabbed the color equipment from Cineradio as soon as they were blacked out by FCC. Well, the honorable secretary droned on as usual for just twelve and a half minutes. Suddenly he stopped, grinned into the transmitter, and said, 'Say, have you heard the one about the traveling farmer and the salesman's daughter?'"

"I have," I said. "My gosh, don't tell me he spieled it?"

"Right," said Berbelot. "In detail, over the unsullied airwaves. I called up right away, but couldn't get through. XZM's trunk lines were jammed. A very worried-looking switchboard girl hooked up I don't know how many lines together and announced into them: 'If you people are calling up about the secretary's speech, there is nothing wrong with it. Now please get off the lines!'"

"Well," I said, "let's see what we've got. First, the broadcasts leave the studios as scheduled and as written. Shall we accept that?"

"Yes," said Berbelot. "Then, since so far no black-and-white broadcasts have been affected, we'll consider that this strange behavior is limited to the polychrome technique."

"How about the recordings at the studios? They were in polychrome, and they weren't affected."

Berbelot pressed a button, and an automatic serving table rolled out of its niche and stopped in front of each of us. We helped ourselves to smokes and drinks, and the table returned to its place.

"Cineradio's wasn't a television recording, Hamilton. It was a sound camera. As for Associated's ... I've got it! Griff's recording was transmitted to his recording machines by wire, from the studios! It didn't go out on the air at all!"

"You're right. Then we can assume that the only programs affected are those in polychrome, actually aired. Fine, but where does that get us?"

"Nowhere," admitted Berbelot. "But maybe we can find out. Come with me."

We stepped into an elevator and dropped three floors. "I don't know if you've heard that I'm a television bug," said my host. "Here's my lab. I flatter myself that a more complete one does not exist anywhere."

I wouldn't doubt it. I never in my life saw a layout like that. It was part museum and part workshop. It had in it a copy or a genuine relic of each and every phase of television down through the years, right from the old original scanning disk sets to the latest three-dimensional atomic jobs. Over in the corner was an extraordinarily complicated mass of apparatus which I recognized as a polychrome transmitter.

"Nice job, isn't it?" said Berbelot. "It was developed in here, you know, by one of the lads who won the Berbelot scholarship." I hadn't known. I began to have real respect for this astonishing man.

"Just how does it work?" I asked him.

"Hamilton," he said testily, "we have work to do. I would be talking all night if I told you. But the general idea is that the vibrations sent out by this transmitter are all out of phase with each other. Tinting in the receiver is achieved by certain blendings of these out of phase vibrations as they leave this rig. The effect is a sort of irregular vibration—a vibration in the electromagnetic waves themselves, resulting in a totally new type of wave which is still receivable in a standard set."

"I see," I lied. "Well, what do you plan to do?"

"I'm going to broadcast from here to my country place up north. It's eight hundred miles away from here, which ought to be sufficient. My signals will be received there and automatically returned to us by wire." He indicated a receiver standing close by. "If there is any difference between what we send and what we get, we can possibly find out just what the trouble is."

"How about FCC?" I asked. "Suppose—it sounds funny to say it—but just suppose that we get the kind of strong talk that came over the air during my 'Seashell' number?"

Berbelot snorted. "That's taken care of. The broadcast will be directional. No receiver can get it but mine."

What a man! He thought of everything. "O.K.," I said. "Let's go."

Berbelot threw a couple of master switches and we sat down in front of the receiver. Lights blazed on, and through a bank of push buttons at his elbow, Berbelot maneuvered the transmitting cells to a point above and behind the receiver, so that we could see and be seen without turning our heads. At a nod from Berbelot I leaned forward and switched on the receiver.

Berbelot glanced at his watch. "If things work out right, it will be between ten and thirty minutes before we get any interference." His voice sounded a little metallic. I realized that it was coming from the receiver as he spoke.

The images cleared on the view screen as the set warmed up. It gave me an odd sensation. I saw Berbelot and myself sitting side by side—just as if we were sitting in front of a mirror, except that the images were not reversed. I thumbed my nose at myself, and my image returned the compliment.

Berbelot said: "Go easy, boy. If we get the same kind of interference the others got, your image will make something out of that."

He chuckled.

"Damn right," said the receiver.

Berbelot and I stared at each other, and back at the screen. Berbelot's face was the same, but mine had a vicious sneer on it. Berbelot calmly checked with his watch. "Eight forty-six," he said. "Less time each broadcast. Pretty soon the interference will start with the broadcast, if this keeps up."

"Not unless you start broadcasting on a regular schedule," said Berbelot's image.

It had apparently dissociated itself completely from Berbelot himself. I was floored.

Berbelot sat beside me, his face frozen. "You see?" he whispered to me. "It takes a minute to catch up with itself. Till it does, it is my image."

"What does it all mean?" I gasped.

"Search me," said the perfume king.

We sat and watched. And so help me, so did our images. They were watching *us*!

Berbelot tried a direct question. "Who are you?" he asked.

"Who do we look like?" said my image; and both laughed uproariously.

Berbelot's image nudged mine. "We've got 'em on the run, hey, pal?" it chortled.

"Stop your nonsense!" said Berbelot sharply. Surprisingly, the merriment died.

"Aw," said my image plaintively. "We don't mean anything by it. Don't get sore. Let's all have fun. *I'm* having fun."

"Why, they're like kids!" I said.

"I think you're right," said Berbelot.

"Look," he said to the images, which sat there expectantly, pouting. "Before we have any fun, I want you to tell me who you are, and how you are coming through the receiver, and how you messed up the three broadcasts before this."

"Did we do wrong?" asked my image innocently. The other one giggled.

"High-spirited sons o' guns, aren't they?" said Berbelot.

"Well, are you going to answer my questions, or *do I turn the transmitter off?*" he asked the images.

They chorused frantically: "We'll tell! We'll tell! Please don't turn it off!"

"What made you think of that?" I whispered to Berbelot.

"A stab in the dark," he returned. "Evidently they like coming through like this and can't do it any other way but on the polychrome wave."

"What do you want to know?" asked Berbelot's image, its lip quivering.

"Who are you?"

"Us? We're ... I don't know. You don't have a name for us, so how can I tell you?"

"Where are you?"

"Oh, everywhere. We get around."

Berbelot moved his hand impatiently toward the switch.

The images squealed: "Don't! Oh, please don't! This is fun!"

"Fun, is it?" I growled. "Come on, give us the story, or we'll black you out!"

My image said pleadingly: "Please believe us. It's the truth. We're everywhere."

"What do you look like?" I asked. "Show yourselves as you are!"

"We can't," said the other image, "because we don't 'look' like anything. We just ... are, that's all."

"We don't reflect light," supplemented my image.

Berbelot and I exchanged a puzzled glance. Berbelot said, "Either somebody is taking us for a ride or we've stumbled on something utterly new and unheard-of."

"You certainly have," said Berbelot's image earnestly. "We've known about you for a long time—as you count time—"

"Yes," the other continued. "We knew about you some two hundred of your years ago. We had felt your vibrations for a long time before that, but we never knew just who you were until then."

"Two hundred years—" mused Berbelot. "That was about the time of the first atomic-powered television sets."

"That's right!" said my image eagerly. "It touched our brain currents and we could see and hear. We never could get through to you until recently, though, when you sent us that stupid thing about a seashell."

"None of that, now," I said angrily, while Berbelot chuckled.

"How many of you are there?" he asked them.

"One, and many. We are finite and infinite. We have no size or shape as you know it. We just ... are."

We just swallowed that without comment. It was a bit big.

"How did you change the programs? How are you changing this one?" Berbelot asked.

"These broadcasts pass directly through our brain currents. Our thoughts change them as they pass. It was impossible before; we were aware, but we could not be heard. This new wave has let us be heard. Its convolutions are in phase with our being."

"How did you happen to pick that particular way of breaking through?" I asked. "I mean all that wisecracking business."

For the first time one of the images—Berbelot's—looked abashed. "We wanted to be liked. We wanted to come through to you and find you laughing. We knew how. Two hundred years of listening to every single broadcast, public and private, has taught us your language and your emotions and your ways of thought. Did we really do wrong?"

"Looks as if we have walked into a cosmic sense of humor," remarked Berbelot to me.

To his image: "Yes, in a way, you did. You lost three huge companies their broadcasting licenses. You embarrassed exceedingly a man named Griff and a secretary of state. You"—he chuckled—"made my friend here very, very angry. That wasn't quite the right thing to do, was it?"

"No," said my image. It actually blushed. "We won't do it any more. We were wrong. We are sorry."

"Aw, skip it," I said. I was embarrassed myself. "Everybody makes mistakes."

"That *is* good of you," said my image on the television screen. "We'd like to do something for you. And you, too, Mr—"

"Berbelot," said Berbelot. Imagine introducing yourself to a television set!

"You can't do anything for us," I said, "except to stop messing up color televising."

"You really want us to stop, then?" My image turned to Berbelot's. "We have done wrong. We have hurt their feelings and made them angry."

To us: "We will not bother you again. Good-by!"

"Wait a minute!" I yelped, but I was too late. The viewscreen showed the same two figures, but they had lost their peculiar life. They were Berbelot and me. Period.

"Now look what you've done," snapped Berbelot.

He began droning into the transmitter: "Calling interrupter on polychrome wave! Can you hear me? Can you hear me? Calling—"

He broke and looked at me disgustedly. "You dope," he said quietly, and I felt like going off into a corner and bursting into tears.

Well, that's all. The FCC trials reached a "person or persons unknown" verdict, and color broadcasting became a universal reality. The world has never learned, until now, the real story of that screwy business. Berbelot spent every night for three months trying to contact that ether intelligence, without success. Can you beat it? It waited two hundred years for a chance to come through to us, and then got its feelings hurt and withdrew!

My fault, of course. That admission doesn't help any. I wish I could do something. . .

Her Choice

IT WAS BAD enough to have the three of them owning the car. But when they all got a yen for the same girl, the theory of cooperative proprietorship couldn't stand up under the strain. Tom, George and Sam had roomed together at college, and after graduation had suddenly bumped into each other in town. Well, of course, they must room together again! It would be just like old times!

Then they bought the car. They made rigorous rules, of course, as to who was to have the car and which nights, and for how long.

It worked pretty well—until they met Judy. Then everything went haywire. She liked them all—she was quite impartial. So much so, they soon found out, that if one of them put something over on the other two, Judy would be quite content to be monopolized for an evening by that one. What bothered them was that it didn't matter to Judy who monopolized her. Not a bit.

They went to all lengths to achieve the unsurpassable combination of the car, Judy, and a summer evening. Tom would, for instance, gallantly switch his turn with George for the car. George would be so delighted that the evening was half gone before he realized that Tom had given him the privilege of taking Judy to a mere movie, whereas Tom's turn would now fall on the date of the country club dance. And so it went.

The showdown came on a hot summer day. By then the question of whose turn was whose had become a supercomplicated question of extradimensional proportions. No one knew exactly who was going to take Judy for an all-day outing, and all three had excellent reasons for being the lucky one. After coming to blows about it, the three ardent swains agreed to submit it to the lady in question. Judy promptly chose the one thing that was sure to make the day a frost.

"Well," she said, "if you can't decide which one of you is going to take me, then you'll all take me." And there was no budging her from her enviable strategic position. Had they known it, Judy was tired of all this nonsense. She welcomed the occasion. If all three went out with her, one of them was bound to show up best. One of them had to! A girl can't go on being impartial all her life.

The great day arrived. At the strident honking of the boys' jalopy, Judy hurried out. George was driving, and Tom sat beside him. "Why, where's Sam?" asked Judy.

They grinned. Cooperation at last, but only to narrow the field. "We lost him. He just wasn't around when it was time to start." One down!

Judy squeezed in between them. Thank heaven she didn't have to choose with whom to ride! She would have, if Sam had come. How funny that he wasn't there! To make conversation, she asked, "What's it going to be? I see a picnic basket back there."

George took a corner on two wheels and headed for the country. "An idea of Tom's," he said. "He doesn't realize we're going to roller skate at the Highway Rinks."

"That's what you think," said Tom. Tom was a rank amateur on skates, and George was an expert. "We'll picnic. No sense in—"

"We tossed a coin, mug, to see who'd drive. I won. We'll go where I want to take us. Savvy?"

"Now, boys, please—" said Judy—but just then the engine sputtered and stalled. They coasted to a stop. "We picnic," said Tom smugly. "Out of gas."

George looked around. It wasn't a bad spot for a picnic. But it would be a technical defeat for him. A nasty suspicion about that gas crossed his mind. Then the fireworks started. It went on for quite a while, until Judy got sore.

"I'm sick and tired of all this bickering!" she snapped. "One of you go back down the road for more gas."

"Yeah," said George. "I go, and when I get back, you and the car and Tom are gone. Not on your life! There's too much chance of your getting a gallon from some motorist."

Impasse. "Then both of you go," decided Judy. "I'll be all right here. Hurry, though."

As the two glum young men rounded the bend in the road there came a thumping and bumping from the back of the car.

"Hi, Judy!" said Sam, as he climbed out of the trunk.

Judy was floored. "W—what—"

"Simple," said Sam, pouring gasoline into the tank from a five-gallon can he had with him. "I suggested to Tom that he pack a basket and then drain out most of the gas, so we'd have to stop by the roadside and picnic. Then I lent my half dollar to George so he could win the toss for who drove. It has tails on both sides. I knew this would happen! It was hard riding, though, in the baggage trunk, with that gasoline can." He screwed the top back on the tank.

Judy was laughing now, because she couldn't help it. "Three was a crowd, at that," she giggled, as they climbed in and started.

"Yeah," cracked Sam. "But it's a great day for the fourth!"

Cajun Providence

FIRST I THOUGHT the old man was kidding and then that he was crazy. I've seen many a farmer, these last few years, standing at the edge of his fields, scratching his head and wondering if he'd get enough out of them for the planting next spring. But not old Veillon. There were lines on his ancient face, but they were all lines of good humor. He stood there, looking out over his scratchy rice paddy, rubbed his hands and chortled, while the Louisiana sun beat down and cooked his shiny pate to the color of a well-done frankfurter.

You who say, "See America first," let me chime in, will you? But, don't mind if I am quiet while you chant of Yosemite and Manhattan, Pike's Peak, Grand Canyon and the Golden Gate. When you have quite finished, I will start. I will tell you about a great tract of moccasins and mud, moss and miasma. Of a climate of unbelievable gentleness supporting a wilderness of incredible viciousness. They call it Louisiana; but Louisiana is not New Orleans and Baton Rouge and the wonderful new bridges and highways upstate. Louisiana is the Cajun who lives in the steaming back bayous, whose bicycle is a canoe and whose ice cream is Louisiana rice. By comparison and contrast, Louisiana is one of the most astonishing, most awe inspiring and most delightful states in the Union. Nowhere else would you find a person like old Veillon—or a reason for his being that way.

Day after day I looked out of my cabin door and saw the old man squatting on his heels, watching the tender green rice shoots poking their yielding heads out of the water. Rice to the Cajun is what wheat is to the western farmer. I did a great deal of poetical reflection about Veillon. Out there under the sun, close to the earth, nurturing his little wet acres, he was a symbol.

I went out to the paddy one day to speak to Veillon. He did not, somehow, make me welcome. I squatted beside him and he waited for me to speak. He had all day.

"Good rice crop this year," I remarked.

"Non," he said nasally, in his unspellable argot. A little surprised, I pursued the subject, knowing from experience that if I did not we could sit there all afternoon like a couple of clods, for all of him.

"No?" I therefore returned. "Well, it looks good to me."

For the first time he deemed it worthwhile to look me over. "W'at you know about rice?" he inquired, not at all pugnaciously.

"Why, not very much," I said, fidgeting under his calm appraisal. "It just—well—looks good to me." I discovered long ago that a Cajun takes fiendish pleasure in making a defenseless urbanite feel like a fool. He can do it, too. Wonderful people.

He shifted his cud of 'baccy—the "long black" that only a pepper-cured Louisiana gullet can bear—and at last offered a piece of information. "Ain' goin' tak' no rice heah," he said. "Come July time, ain' go' be no mo' rice heah." He chuckled.

I saw the swift disappearance of a symbol. "My gosh!" I expostulated. "That's terrible. What are you laughing at? If you don't get a good crop out of here, what are you going to eat when winter comes?"

"Ain' no wintuh heah, Yaink," he said evenly.

I got up and stormed back to my shack. If the old idiot wanted to sit there and laugh while he faced starvation, it was none of my affair. For the next three weeks I stuck to that. But I couldn't forget old Veillon. In the back of my scornful mind, a real admiration was born for a man who could laugh that way at the contemplated failure of his crop. One evening, after he had gone home, I went down there to look at it.

The paddy was definitely patchy. There were great spaces of open water where there should have been thick rows of spiky green. A slight motion caught my eye. One of the nearby shoots, a new and very tender one, staggered and suddenly disappeared under the surface. There was a tiny swirl, and the shoot stayed down. Curious, I reached under and felt around where the root should have been. My hand closed on a violently wriggling horny mass. I lifted out a monster crawfish, all of seven inches long, and was severely nipped for my pains. I didn't hold on! So that was it. Veillon had known all along that these fresh water scavengers had been eating his shoots. Yet he had sat there and chuckled and done nothing. It was too much for me.

About a month later I was on Royal Street in New Orleans when my attention was drawn to a striking procession. It was old Veillon all right; he and his descendants, even unto the third and fourth generation, so far as I could see. I walked up to him. "Hey, Veillon," I said. "No rice this year and here you are in N'Orleans, the whole bunch of you in store clothes. Did you strike oil?"

Veillon shook his baked head, laughing. "Non, Yaink. Wan man pay me savan hondre' sixty dollar for my crawfeesh." His grin all but flapped his ears together.

How do you like that? Crawfish are a Louisiana delicacy, not a pest! I'll bet they're a delicacy because they eat rice shoots, too. Pity the Egyptians didn't think of that when they had their plague of locusts!

Strike Three

SON, YOU CAME to the right man for advice. A question like that requires deep thought, and a true insight into the feminine mind. Yes indeed, my boy, I'm your man.

You want to know just what to do when you have been spending alternate periods of spare time with two sweet young things, and a third pulls her lovely self over your horizon. You want to know if it would be wise to get Miss A and Miss B together somewhere so that they will scratch each other's eyes out while you disport yourself with Miss C, hey?

Well, my lad, I must go back many years to get you a good example. Let's see . . . yes, the case of Miss Celia Blank will do fine.

It was back in the days when I was also young and charming in my own way. I was a mere schoolboy like you, my boy. Life was a dream, and a kiss was a conquest. I made the mistake of rather fancying myself a Lothario—a bad business at best, particularly at that age. Heh! Ah well. Those were the days!

Now in this case my misses A and B were (most conveniently) named Anna and Betty. Anna was small and dark, with huge eyes and a predisposition for people of my type. I was stringing along with her because she thought I was wonderful. I was, of course. In common justice I must say that I was not as wonderful as she led me to believe, but at the time that fact was unimportant.

In the course of time I began to feel a growing necessity to justify Anna's lofty opinion of me, in some small way. She thought so much of one particular trait—my facility with words—that I decided a bit of poesy would be in order.

My English course was just then covering the technique of the sonnet. It fascinated me. The rhythmic beat of iambic pentameter, the cunningly interwoven rhyme scheme, and the prestige to be had by wresting these things about so that they would work my will—these things determined me. I wrote a sonnet. Don't worry, lad. I'm not going to quote it. It wasn't very good, but I thought it was expressive. I called it "Anna" and gave it to the lady with something of a flourish. Voila; I got my kiss and my conquest.

It so happened that just about this time I became conscious of Betty's presence on this green earth. Betty was tall and as dark as Anna. But Betty's hair was long, and she braided it and wore it like a crown on her magnificent head. She had a little turned-up nose that went well with her dignified mien, and I met her in the library at school, reading Mrs. Browning's *Sonnets*. We found that we had many interests in common. By that I mean that she like my attitude toward life, the clever little way I had of saying things, and the magnetic effect that I obviously had on her. Oh, I was a pip in those days. Heh!

Yes, I felt that faint flutter in my young breast which signified that Betty and I were about to fall into each other's traps. But I saw no reason at the time for denying myself the pleasure of Anna's company. Betty was the more decorative of the two, but I didn't feel that she appreciated me as much as Anna. She didn't say she did, at least, nearly as often as Anna.

Things went on in this way for several weeks, and Dame Fortune was with me. It was a big school, and my classes were fortuitously so arranged that one girl was always in class at such times as I found it convenient to associate with the other. I was, of course, deprived of the privilege of escorting either home from school.

Betty, having high aspirations, was a member of the debating club, which I steadfastly refused to join because they would only let a member speak for seven minutes at a time, which cramped my style. I used to wait for her, then, once a week after school—Anna would be out of the way by that time. While I was waiting I did my best to compose another sonnet to give to Betty; but apparently the first had drained me dry. What to do? Well, I recopied the work, titled it "Betty" and gave it to her as an original. It may have been unethical, but the effect was marvelous. Again I got my osculative victory.

Now it was about this time that Celia swam into my ken. Unfortunately she was in a splendid position to watch developments with Anna and Betty, since she spent two periods a day with the former and three with the latter. Celia appealed to me because of her eyebrow. Yes. She had an eyebrow with which she could, by a minuscule lifting motion, upset the most carefully presented line. Also the ego that presented it. It was fascinating.

Well, I had to do something. And I hit on this plan. One bright Tuesday I said to Anna, "Will you meet me in the music room after school? There will be just you and me. . ." Then I went to Betty and said the same thing. And after school I escorted Celia home, with much inner merriment as to the effect of the tactic.

The following day I encountered Celia in the hall and with great ceremony presented her with a copy of my sonnet, this time called "Celia." She took it with a sweet smile, and as she read it the smile broadened and stopped being sweet. She took two pieces of paper out of her handbag and gave them to me, saying, "It's a beautiful sonnet—every bit as good as these." "These" were a sonnet to "Anna" and one to "Betty" ... somewhat aghast, I looked up to see the three of them walking arm in arm down the corridor, expressing great merriment over something.

How does that help you, lad? Not at all? Ah well. It only goes to show you—we must each find out for ourselves!

Contact!

"IT DIDN'T WORK!" Peggy wailed, burying her face in Mrs. Mulligan's capable shoulder. Mrs. Mulligan sighed and reflected bitterly on the stupidity of males in general and Roy Bell in particular. Mrs. Mulligan was a fixture in the office—no one knew just how long she had been there. She knew everyone's business, not because she was nosey, but simply because she had that kind of a face. It was all right, because she could be trusted with any confidence.

"But what happened?" she asked the girl softly, stroking her blue black hair. "Everything seemed to be all right. He fell in love with you—I'm sure he did—the instant you walked into the office without your glasses on. I told you it would happen that way. 'Guys don't make passes at gals that wear glasses.' You haven't worn them around him again, have you?"

"No," she sobbed. "I'll never have to wear them again. Roy was so sweet to me for about three days. Oh, Mrs. Mulligan, I did think you were right. I was beginning to hope . . . anyway, it's all over now. Roy hardly speaks to me any more. And just three days ago he took me out and we had the most wonderful evening together . . . and he—he kissed me good night, and he made me promise to have lunch with him the next day. . ." She burst into renewed sobs.

Mrs. Mulligan waited until the outbreak was spent. "Well?" she asked kindly. "Did something happen at lunch?"

"No. That is, I can't understand it; but he took me to lunch as if he were only doing it because he'd promised. I noticed it even before we left the office. He was—changed. He kept looking at me so strangely, with the oddest expression on his face. And he hardly ate anything. Just sat there staring at me, and when I'd look up suddenly he'd try to pretend he was looking over my shoulder, or at the ceiling or . . . oh, dear . . . and he couldn't talk! He'd forget what he was saying when he was half through, and just sit staring! And today at lunch time I was eating alone at Tony's, and Roy came in. He saw me there, and turned right around and walked out. He crossed the street to the hot dog stand. Oh, Mrs. Mulligan, what's the matter with me? You'll tell me, won't you? Won't you?"

"There's nothing, darlin'," said Mrs. Mulligan. "You're lovely. I'll find out what's bothering that idiot. Go home now, child, and try to forget about it. I'll fix Roy Bell myself."

The next morning Mrs. Mulligan stopped beside Roy's desk. "You'll have lunch with me," she said, and passed on without waiting for an answer. There was that about Mrs. Mulligan which left no room for argument when she spoke that way. Roy was curious.

At lunch time Peggy was already at Tony's when Roy and Mrs. Mulligan came in. They sat in a booth across the restaurant, ordered, and then Mrs. Mulligan began talking rapidly. Roy seemed embarrassed, and Peggy could see that the old lady was enjoying herself. Peggy strained to catch a word, but could not. She was tempted to cross over and find out what it was all about, but by sheer will power forced herself to sit still.

Suddenly Mrs. Mulligan's hearty laughter rang through the room. Roy made an impulsive move toward the door, but was detained by Mrs. Mulligan's firm hand on his wrist. When her merriment subsided she rose and virtually dragged the protesting, beet red young man to Peggy's booth. She pushed him down beside the girl and sat opposite, retaining her grip on Roy, who, from the look of him, would most certainly have bolted otherwise.

"This idiot," Mrs. Mulligan told the startled Peggy, "is more stupid than I thought he was. Didn't think it was possible."

"Peggy, do you know what happened the day this creature acted so strangely to you for the first time? He was sitting at his desk watching you, mooning over you. I told you he was in love with you. Stop squirming, man! Anyway, you, Peggy, were sitting staring off into space, thinking about him, I'll bet. You were fooling around with a pencil. You hit the desk with it, tapped your typewriter, your cheek, and then rapped your eye with it. Of course, there was a sharp little click! And this fool here felt his stomach miss a beat, the moron."

She laughed uproariously. The faces of the young people defied description. "Peggy," she said, wiping the tears from her eyes, "Roy thinks you have a glass eye!"

Peggy gasped, and Roy looked as if he would be happier dead. "Show the fool your new glasses, Peggy. And then forgive him if you can. I wouldn't."

With shaking fingers Peggy drew a little stick tipped with a rubber suction cup from her handbag, moistened it in her water glass, and set it gently against her eye. She blinked, and out came a little glass disk which had fitted closely against her eyeball. It was Roy's turn to gasp.

"Contact lenses," Peggy explained breathlessly. "Mrs. Mulligan's idea. She thought that you'd like me better if my glasses were out of sight. And you thought—oh-h-h!"

Five minutes later Mrs. Mulligan left them, kissing and making up. The old lady was still hilarious.

The Call

No, I'M NOT arguing with you. All I said was that you've been talking about telepathy for a half hour, and still haven't given me a good example of it. Now I'll give you one.

It happened to Bert Colley. He and Selma had been married only about six weeks then. It was the first morning after Bert had come back from his vacation honeymoon, and they had been driving all night. Bert had heard duty call with the brass voice of an alarm clock, and he rolled out. He'd have given anything to be able to sleep late. Selma could—Selma was! And they say it's the woman who pays. He looked at her and grinned. She even looked cute with a headache. The acid test!

Bert slid into his clothes and stepped aboard the ornate little elevator with its chrome, ivory and indirect lighting, and dropped swiftly to the ground floor. This was the right kind of place for a bride, he thought proudly. He flashed a glance at himself in the huge lobby mirror as he sprinted out and into a taxi.

When her husband left, Selma opened one eye at the discreet slam of the door. Then she rolled over and closed the eye sleepily, smiling a little. Good old Bert. It had been glorious, last night ... they were so wrapped up in each other that they had even forgotten to eat. Eat ... she toyed drowsily with the word. She couldn't quite figure out whether she was more sleepy or hungry. But the hours without food told; she rocked up out of bed and half felt her way to the stove. She put an egg and some water in a pan, set them on the stove, turned on the gas and punched the pilot button. Then she went back to bed "just for a minute." And in a minute she was fast asleep again. She'd been careless about the way she lit the gas. As a matter of fact, it wasn't lit at all.

Bert sat on the edge of his seat in the taxi, coaxing the driver with

$5 notes and trying to change the traffic lights by will power. He was the boss, but he liked to get to the office at the same time as everyone else. He thought of Selma, lying so safely asleep in the apartment, and smiled. It had been her idea, that apartment. He had wanted a huge place with 80 rooms and 20 baths and swarms of servants; but Selma, who had budgeted all her life, had insisted on "just a couple of rooms and a kitchenette somewhere." Well, she had them ... but what rooms! Bert combed the town for the most elaborate and expensive little place that money could buy. He'd got it, too. "Come on, buddy, step it up," he urged the driver.

And in the apartment, Selma stirred in her sleep, coughed violently, gasped once or twice and settled down into a still deeper sleep.

Bert was going over the day's business, trying to get his mind attuned to it. But something seemed to be in the way, like a haunting tune he couldn't quite remember; like a face casually seen which plagues one all day. He tried to put the impression out of his mind, and couldn't. Something was wrong ... something—

(In the apartment, escaping gas hissed on and on...)

"Go back ... go back ... go back..." Bert shook his head sharply. He could have sworn he heard a voice.

"Bert! Bert! Oh, Bert..." It beat inside his brain, clear and tiny— Selma's voice! He leaned forward, tapping the driver on the shoulder. "Did you hear something, Buddy?"

"No—what?"

"Turn around," snapped Bert. "Back to the Winfred—and hurry!"

Tires screamed as the cab took the U-turn on two wheels, scuttled back up the avenue. Bert almost told the man to head downtown again, and then leaned back in his seat. He didn't know whether to curse himself for a fool or to begin thinking about nervous breakdowns. Only one thing was clear—he had to get back to the Winfred, and he had to get there in a hurry.

(Selma was there. She lay very quiet...)

The cab stopped for a light. "Take a chance on it," Bert gritted. "If you get a ticket I'll make good." The driver did not hesitate. Never, in all his years of hurrying frantic people from one place to another around the city, had he met such urgency, such hysterical haste, in a fare. This one looked as if he could pay—what could the driver lose? He ground into gear, hurled the cab across traffic.

Cutting in and out, blasting trucks and cars out of the way with horn and vocal cords, the driver did his utmost to push the accelerator through the floor. Bert, white, tense, sat on the edge of his seat, his eyes straining ahead. Why, he would never know, but he was frightened. He noticed the voice again, not because he heard it but because he suddenly stopped hearing it.

The cab hooted up to the Winfred's marquee and Bert was out and up the steps before it stopped, leaving the cabby gloating over a nice, crisp twenty. Bert threw himself into the elevator and cursed it roundly as it crawled interminably to the twelfth floor. Gasping with effort and nervous tension, he finally reached his door, fumbled for his key, fumbled for the keyhole, flung the door open. Gas!

He ran to the stove, turned it off. Now; there's your example. I know those folks; it's a true story. What? Selma? Why, sure she was all right. Why shouldn't she be? That ritzy little place was air-conditioned; she could have slept there all day with all the jets on and lived through it. I'm talking about telepathy, not gas!

Helix the Cat

DID YOU SEE this in the papers?

BURGLAR IS CAT

Patrolman and Watchman
Shoot "Safe-cracker"

It was a strange tale that George Murphy, night watchman for a brokerage firm, and Patrolman Pat Riley had to tell this morning.

Their report states that the policeman was called from his beat by Murphy, who excitedly told him that someone was opening the safe in the inner office. Riley followed him into the building, and they tiptoed upstairs to the offices.

"Hear him?" Murphy asked the policeman. The officer swears that he heard the click of the tumblers on the old safe. As they gained the doorway there was a scrambling sound, and a voice called out of the darkness, "Stand where you are or I plug you!"

The policeman drew his gun and fired six shots in the direction of the voice. There was a loud feline yowl and more scrambling, and then the watchman found the light switch. All they saw was a big black cat thrashing around—two of Riley's bullets had caught him. Of the safe-cracker there was no sign. How he escaped will probably always remain a mystery. There was no way out of the office save the door from which Riley fired.

The report is under investigation at police headquarters.

I can clear up that mystery.

It started well over a year ago, when I was developing my new flexible glass. It would have made me rich, but—well, I'd rather be poor and happy.

That glass was really something. I'd hit on it when I was fooling with a certain mineral salt—never mind the name of it. I wouldn't want anyone to start fooling with it and get himself into the same kind of jam that I did. But the idea was that if a certain complex sulphide of silicon is combined with this salt at a certain temperature, and the product is carefully annealed, you get that glass. Inexpensive, acid-proof, and highly flexible. Nice. But one of its properties—wait till I tell you about that.

The day it all started, I had just finished my first bottle. It was standing on the annealer—a rig of my own design; a turntable, shielded, over a ring of Bunsen burners—cooling slowly while I was turning a stopper from the same material on my lathe. I had to step the lathe up to twenty-two thousand before I could cut the stuff, and Helix was fascinated by the whine of it. He always like to watch me work, anyway. He was my cat, and more. He was my friend. I had no secrets from Helix.

Ah, he was a cat. A big black tom, with a white throat and white mittens, and a tail twice as long as that of an ordinary cat. He carried it in a graceful spiral—three complete turns—and hence his name. He could sit on one end of that tail and take two turns around his head with the other. Ah, he was a cat.

I took the stopper off the lathe and lifted the top of the annealer to drop it into the mouth of the bottle. And as I did so—*whht!*

Ever hear a bullet ricochet past your ear? It was like that. I heard it, and then the stopper, which I held poised over the rotating bottle, was whipped out of my hand and jammed fast on the bottle mouth. And all the flames went out—*blown* out! I stood there staring at Helix, and noticed one thing more:

He hadn't moved!

Now you know and I know that a cat—any cat—can't resist that short, whistling noise. Try it, if you have a cat. When Helix should have been on all fours, big yellow eyes wide, trying to find out where the sound came from, he was sitting sphinxlike, with his eyes closed, his whiskers twitching slightly, and his front paws turned under his forelegs. It didn't make sense. Helix's senses were unbelievably acute—I knew. I'd tested them. Then—

Either I had heard that noise with some sense that Helix didn't possess, or I hadn't heard it at all. If I hadn't, then I was crazy. No one likes to think he is crazy. So you can't blame me for trying to convince myself that it was a sixth sense.

Helix roused me by sneezing. I took his cue and turned off the gas.

"Helix, old fellow," I said when I could think straight, "what do you make of this? Hey?"

Helix made an inquiring sound and came over to rub his head on my sleeve. "Got you stopped too, has it?" I scratched him behind the ear, and the end of his tail curled ecstatically around my wrist. "Let's see. I hear a funny noise. You don't. Something snatches the stopper out of my hand, and a wind comes from where it's impossible for any wind to be, and blows out the burners. Does that make sense?" Helix yawned. "I don't think so either. Tell me, Helix, what shall we do about this? Hey?"

Helix made no suggestion. I imagine he was quite ready to forget about it. Now, I wish I had.

I shrugged my shoulders and went back to work. First I slipped a canvas glove on and lifted the bottle off the turntable. Helix slid under my arm and made as if to smell the curved, flexible surface. I made a wild grab to keep him from burning his nose, ran my bare hand up against the bottle, and then had to make another grab to keep it off the floor. I missed with the second grab—the bottle struck dully, bounced, and—landed right back on the bench? Not only on it, but in the exact spot from which I had knocked it!

And—get this, now—when I looked at my hand to see how big my hypothetical seared spot might be, it wasn't there! That bottle was *cold*—and it should have been hot for hours yet! My new glass was a very poor conductor. I almost laughed. I should have realized that Helix had more sense than to put his pink nose against the bottle if it were hot.

Helix and I got out of there. We went into my room, closed the door on that screwy bottle, and flopped down on the bed. It was too much for us. We would have wept aloud purely for self-expression, if we hadn't forgotten how, years ago, Helix and I.

After my nerves had quieted a bit, I peeped into the laboratory. "Come on in here, you dope. I want to talk to you."

Who said that? I look suspiciously at Helix, who, in all innocence, returned my puzzled gaze. Well, I hadn't said it. Helix hadn't. I began to be suspicious as hell of that bottle.

"Well?"

The tone was drawling and not a little pugnacious. I looked at Helix. Helix was washing daintily. But—Helix was the best watchdog of a cat that ever existed. If there had been anyone else—if he had *heard* anyone else—in the lab, he'd have let me know. Then he hadn't heard. And I had. "Helix," I breathed—and he looked right up at me, so there was nothing wrong with his hearing—"we're both crazy."

"No, you're not," said the voice. "Sit down before you fall down. I'm in your bottle, and I'm in to stay. You'll kill me if you take me out—but just between you and me I don't think you can get me out. Anyway please don't try ... what's the matter with you? Stop popping your eyes, man!"

"Oh," I said hysterically, "there's nothing the matter with me. No, no, no. I'm nuts, that's all. Stark, totally, and completely nuts, balmy, mentally unbalanced, and otherwise the victim of a psychic loss of equilibrium. Me, I'm a raving lunatic. I hear voices. What does that make me, Joan of Arc? Hey, Helix. Look at me. I'm Joan of Arc. You must be Beucephalus, or Pegasus, or the great god Pasht. First I have an empty bottle, and next thing I know it's full of djinn. Hey, Helix, have a lil drink of djinn..." I sat down on the floor and Helix sat beside me. I think he was sorry for me. I know I was—very.

"Very funny," said the bottle—or rather, the voice that claimed it was from the bottle. "If you'll only give me a chance to explain, now—"

"Look," I said, "maybe there is a voice. I don't trust anything any more—except you, Helix. I know. If you can hear him, then I'm sane. If not, I'm crazy. Hey, Voice!"

"Well?"

"Look, do me a favor. Holler 'Helix' a couple of times. If the cat hears you, I'm sane."

"All right," the voice said wearily. "Helix! Here, Helix!"

Helix sat there and looked at me. Not by the flicker of a whisker did he show that he had heard. I drew a deep breath and said softly, "Helix! Here, Helix!"

Helix jumped up on my chest, put one paw on each shoulder, and tickled my nose with his curving tail. I got up carefully, holding Helix. "Pal," I said, "I guess this is the end of you and me. I'm nuts, pal. Better go phone the police."

Helix purred. He could see I was sad about something, but what it was didn't seem to bother him any. He was looking at me as if my being a madman didn't make him like me any the less. But I think he found it interesting. He had a sort of quizzical look in his glowing eyes. As if he'd rather I stuck around. Well, if he wouldn't phone the law, I wouldn't. I wasn't responsible for myself any more.

"Now, *will* you shut up?" said the bottle. "I don't want to give you any trouble. You may not realize it, but you saved my life. Don't be scared. Look. I'm a soul, see? I was a man called Gregory—Wallace Gregory. I was killed in an automobile accident two hours ago—"

"You were killed two hours ago. And I just saved your life. You know, Gregory, that's just dandy. On my head you will find a jewelled turban. I am now the Maharajah of Mysore. Goo. Da. And flub. I—"

"You are perfectly sane. That is, you are right now. Get hold of yourself and you'll be all right," said the bottle. "Yes, I was killed. My body was killed. I'm a soul. The automobile couldn't kill that. But They could."

"They?"

"Yeah. The Ones who were chasing me when I got into your bottle."

"Who are They?"

"We have no name for Them. They eat souls. There are swarms of Them. Any time They find a soul running around loose, They track it down."

"You mean—any time anyone dies, his soul wanders around, running away from Them? And that sooner or later, They catch it?"

"Oh, no. Only some souls. You see, when a man realizes he is going to die, something happens to his soul. There are some people alive today who knew, at one time, that they were about to die. Then, by some accident, they didn't. Those people are never quite the same afterward, because that something has happened. With the realization of impending death, a soul gets what might be called a protective covering, though it's more like a change of form. From then on, the soul is inedible and undesirable to Them."

"What happens to a protected soul, then?"

"That I don't know. It's funny ... people have been saying for millennia that if only someone could come back from death, what strange things he could relate ... well, I did it, thanks to you. And yet I know very little more about it than you. True, I died, and my soul left my body. But then, I only went a very little way. A protected soul probably goes through stage after stage ... I don't know. Now, I'm just guessing."

"Why wasn't your soul 'protected'?"

"Because I had no warning—no realization that I was to die. It happened so quickly. And I haven't been particularly religious. Religious people, and freethinkers if they think deeply, and philosophers in general, and people whose work brings them in touch with deep and great things—these may all be immune from Them, years before they die."

"Why?"

"That should be obvious. You can't think deeply without running up against a realization of the power of death. 'Realization' is a loose term, I know. If your mind is brilliant, and you don't pursue your subject—*any* subject—deeply enough, you will never reach that realization. It's a sort of dead end to a questioning mind—a *ne plus ultra*. Batter yourself against it, and it hurts. And that pain is the realization. Stupid people reach it far easier than others—it hurts more, and they are made immune easier. But at any rate, a man can live his life without it, and still have a few seconds just before he dies for his soul to undergo the immunizing change. I didn't have those few seconds."

I fumbled for my handkerchief and mopped my face. This was a little steep. "Look," I said, " this is—well, I'm more or less of a beginner. Just what *is* a soul?"

"Elementally," said the bottle, "it is matter, just like everything else in the universe. It has weight and mass, though it can't be measured by earthly standards. In the present stage of the sciences, we haven't run up against anything like it. It usually centers around the pineal gland, although it can move at will throughout the body, if there is sufficient stimulus. For example—"

He gave me the example, and it was very good. I saw his point.

"And anger, too," the bottle went on. "In a fit of fury, one's soul settles momentarily around the adrenals, and does what is necessary. See?"

I turned to Helix. "Helix," I said, "we're really learning things today." Helix extended his claws and studied them carefully. I suddenly came to my senses, realizing that I was sitting on the floor of my laboratory, holding a conversation with an empty glass bottle; that Helix was sitting in my lap, preening himself, listening without interest to my words, and *not hearing* those from the bottle. My mind reeled again. I *had* to have an answer to that.

"Bottle," I said hoarsely, "why can't Helix hear you?"

"Oh. That," said the bottle. "Because there is no sound."

"How can I hear you?"

"Direct telepathic contact. I am not speaking to you, specifically, but to your soul. Your soul transmits my messages to you. It is functioning now on the nerve centers controlling your hearing—hence, you interpret it as sound. That is the most understandable way of communication."

"Then—why doesn't Helix get the same messages?"

"Because he is on a different—er—wavelength. That's one way of putting it, though thoughtwaves are not electrical. I can—that is, I believe I can—direct thoughts to him. Haven't tried. It's a matter of degree of development."

I breathed much easier. Astonishing, what a difference a rational explanation will make. But there were one or two more things—

"Bottle," I said, "what's this about my saving your life? And what has my flexible glass to do with it?"

"I don't quite know," said the bottle. "But purely by accident, I'm sure, you have stumbled on the only conceivable external substance which seems to exclude—Them. Sort of an insulator. I sensed what it was—so did They. I can tell you, it was nip and tuck for a while. They can really move, when They want to. I won, as you know. Close. Oh, yes, I was responsible for snatching the stopper out of your hand. I did it by creating a vacuum in the bottle. The stopper was the nearest thing to the mouth, and you weren't holding it very tightly."

"Vacuum?" I asked. "What became of the air?"

"That was easy. I separated the molecular structure of the glass, and passed the air out that way."

"What about Them?"

"Oh, They would have followed. But if you'll look closely, you'll see that the stopper is now fused to the bottle. That's what saved me. Whew! —Oh, by the way, if you're wondering what cooled the bottle so quickly, it was the vacuum formation. Expanding air, you know, loses heat. Vacuum creation, of course, would create intense cold. That glass is good stuff. Practically no thermal expansion."

"I'm beginning to be glad, now, that it happened. Would have been bad for you.... I suppose you'll live out the rest of your life in my bottle."

"The rest of my life, friend, is—eternity."

I blinked at that. "That's not going to be much fun," I said. "I mean—don't you ever get hungry, or—or anything?"

"No. I'm fed—I know that. From outside, somehow. There seems to be a source somewhere that radiates energy on which I feed. I wouldn't know about that. But it's going to be a bit boring. I don't know—maybe someday I'll find a way to get another body."

"What's to prevent your just going in and appropriating someone else's?"

"Can't," said the bottle. "As long as a soul is in possession of a body, it is invulnerable. The only way would be to convince some soul that it would be to its advantage to leave its body and make room for me."

"Hmm ... say, Bottle. Seems to me that by this time you must have experienced that death-realization you spoke about a while back. Why aren't you immune from Them now?"

"That's the point. A soul must draw its immunity from a body which it possesses at the time. If I could get into a body and possess it for just one split second, I could immunize myself and be on my way. Or I could stay in the body and enjoy myself until it died. By the way, stop calling me Bottle. My name's Gregory—Wallace Gregory."

"Oh. Okay. I'm Pete Tronti. Er—glad to have met you."

"Same here." The bottle hopped a couple of times. "That can be considered a handshake."

"How did you do that?" I asked, grinning.

"Easy. The tiniest molecular expansion, well distributed, makes the bottle bounce."

"Neat. Well—I've got to go out and get some grub. Anything I can get for you?"

"Thanks, no, Tronti. Shove along. Be seeing you."

Thus began my association with Wally Gregory, disembodied soul. I found him a very intelligent person; and though he had cramped my style in regard to the new glass—I didn't fancy collecting souls in bottles as a hobby—we became real friends. Not many people get a break like that—having a boarder who is so delightful and so little trouble. Though the initial cost had been high—after all, I'd almost gone nuts!—the upkeep was negligible. Wally never came in drunk, robbed the cash drawer, or brought his friends in. He was never late for meals, nor did he leave dirty socks around. As a roommate he was ideal, and as a friend, he just about had Helix topped.

One evening about eight months later I was batting the wind with Wally while I worked. He'd been a great help to me—I was fooling around with artificial rubber synthesis at the time, and Wally had an uncanny ability for knowing exactly what was what in a chemical reaction—and because of that, I began to think of his present state.

"Say, Wally—don't you think it's about time that we began thinking about getting a body for you?"

Wally snorted. "That's about all we can do—think about it. How in blazes do you think we could ever get a soul's consent for that kind of a transfer?"

"I don't know—we might try kidding one of them along. You know—put one over on him."

"What—kid one along when he has the power of reading every single thought that goes through a mind? Couldn't be done."

"Now, don't tell me that every soul in the universe is incapable of being fooled. After all, a soul is a part of a human being."

"It's not that a soul is phenomenally intelligent, Pete. But a soul reasons without emotional drawbacks—he deals in elementals. Any moron is something of a genius if he can see clearly to the root of a problem. And any soul can do just that. That is, if it's a soul as highly developed as that of a human being."

"Well, suppose that the soul isn't that highly developed? That's an idea. Couldn't you possess the body of a dog, say, or—"

"Or a cat...?"

I stopped stirring the beakerful of milkweed latex and came around the table, stopping in front of the bottle. "Wally—not Helix. Not that cat! Why, he's—he's a friend of mine. He trusts me. We *couldn't* do anything like that. My gosh, man—"

"You're being emotional," said Wally scornfully. "If you've got any sense of values at all, there'll be no choice. You can save my immortal soul by sacrificing the life of a cat. Not many men have that sort of an opportunity, especially at that price. It'll be a gamble. I haven't told you, but in the last couple of months I've been looking into Helix's mentality. He's got a brilliant mind for a cat. And it wouldn't do anything to him. He'd cease to exist—you can see that. But his soul is primitive, and has been protected since he was a kitten, as must be the case with any primitive mentality. Man needs some powerful impetus to protect his soul, because he has evolved away from the fear of death to a large degree—but a cat has not. His basic philosophy is little different from that of his wild forebears. He'll be okay. I'd just step in and he'd step out, and go wherever it is that good cats go when they die. You'd have him, in body, the same as you have now; but he'd be motivated by my soul instead of his own. Pete, you've *got* to do it."

"Gosh, Wally . . . look, I'll get you another cat. Or . . . say! How's about a monkey?"

"I've thought about all that. In the first place, a monkey would be too noticeable, walking around by himself. You see, my idea is to get into some sort of a body in which I can go where I please, when I please. In the second place, I have a headstart with Helix. It's going to be a long job, reconditioning that cat to my needs, but it can be done. I've been exploring his mind, and by now I know it pretty well. In the third place, you know him, and you know me— and he knows me a little now. He is the logical subject for something which, you must allow, is going to be a most engrossing experiment."

I had to admire the way Wally was putting it over. Being disso- ciated from emotionalism like that must be a great boon. He had caused me to start the conversation, and probably to put forward the very objections to which he had prepared answers. I began to resent him a little—but only a little. That last point of his told. It *would* be a most engrossing experiment—preparing a feline body and mind to bear a human soul, in such a way that the soul could live an almost normal life. . . "I won't say yes or no, Wally," I said. "I want to talk it over a little. . . Just how would we go about it, in case I said yes?"

"Well—" Wally was quiet a minute. "First we'd have to make some minor changes in his physique, so that I could do things that are impossible for a cat—read, write, speak and memorize. His brain would have to be altered so that it could comprehend an abstrac- tion, and his paws would have to be made a little more manageable so that I could hold a pencil."

"Might as well forget the whole thing, then," I told him. "I'm a chemist, not a veterinary surgeon. There isn't a man alive who could do a job like that. Why—"

"Don't worry about that. I've learned a lot recently about myself, too. If I can once get into Helix's brain, I can mess around with his metabolism. I can stimulate growth in any part of his body, in any ways, to any degree. I can, for instance, atrophy the skin between his toes, form flesh and joints in his claws. Presto—hands. I can—"

"Sounds swell. But how are you going to get in there? I thought you couldn't displace his soul without his consent. And—what about Them?"

"Oh, that will be all right. I can get in there and work, and his soul will protect me. You see, I've been in contact with it. As long as I am working to increase the cat's mental and physical powers, his soul won't object. As for getting in there, I can do it if I move fast. There are times when none of Them are around. If I pick one of those times, slide out of the bottle and into the cat, I'll be perfectly safe. My one big danger is from his soul. If it wants me out of there, it can bring a tremendous psychic force into play—throw me from here to the moon, or farther. If that happened—that will finish me. They wouldn't miss a chance like that."

"Golly ... listen, friend, you'd better not take the chance. It's a swell idea, but I don't think it's worth it. As you are now, you're safe for the rest of time. If something goes wrong—"

"Not worth it? Do you realize what you're saying, man? I have my choice between staying here in the bottle forever—and that's an awful long time, if you can't die—or fixing up Helix so that he can let me live a reasonable human existence until he dies. Then I can go, protected, into wherever it is I should go. Give me a break, Pete. I can't do it without you."

"Why not?"

"Don't you see? The cat has to be educated. Yes, and civilized. You can do it, partly because he knows you, partly because that is the best way. When we can get him speaking, you can teach him orally. That way we can keep up our mental communication, but he'll never know about it. More important, neither will his soul. Pete, can't you see what this means to me?"

"Yeah. Wally, it's a shabby trick on Helix. It's downright dirty. I don't like it—anything about it. But you've got something there ... all right. You're a rat, Wally. So am I. But I'll do it. I'd never sleep again if I didn't. How do we start?"

"Thanks, Pete. I'll never be able to thank you enough... First, I've got to get into his brain. Here's what you do. Think you can get him to lick the side of the bottle?"

I thought a minute. "Yes. I can put a little catnip extract—I have some around here somewhere—on the bottle. He'll lick it off... Why?"

"That'll be fine. See, it will minimize the distance. I can slip through the glass and be into his brain before one of Them has a chance at me."

I got the little bottle of extract and poured some of it on a cloth. Helix came running when he smelled it. I felt like a heel—almost tried to talk Wally out of it. But then I shrugged it off. Fond as I was of the big black cat, Wally's immortal soul was more important.

"Hold it a minute," said Wally. "One of Them is smelling around."

I waited tensely. Helix was straining toward the cloth I held in my right hand. I held him with the other, feeling smaller and smaller. He *trusted* me!

"Let 'er go!" snapped Wally. I slapped the cloth onto the side of the bottle, smeared it. Helix shot out of my grip, began licking the bottle frantically. I almost cried. I said, "May God have mercy on his soul..." Don't know why...

"Good lad!" said Wally. "I made it!" After a long moment, "Pete! Give him some more catnip. I've got to find out what part of his brain registers pleasure. That's where I'll start. He's going to enjoy every minute of this."

I dished up the catnip. Helix, forgive me!

Another long pause, then, "Pete! Pinch him, will you? Or stick a pin in him."

I chose the pinch, and it was a gentle one. It didn't fool Wally. "Make him holler, Pete! I want a real reaction."

I gritted my teeth and twisted the spiral tail. Helix yowled. I think his feelings were hurt more than his caudal appendage.

And so it went. I applied every possible physical and mental stimulus to Helix—hunger, sorrow, fright, anger (that was a hard one. Old Helix just wouldn't get sore!), heat, cold, joy, disappointment, thirst and insult. Hate was impossible. And Wally, somewhere deep in the cat's mind, checked and rechecked; located, reasoned, tried and erred. Because he was tireless, and because he had no sidetracking temptations to swerve him from his purpose, he made a perfect investigator. When he finally was ready to emerge, Helix and I were half dead from fatigue. Wally was, to hear him talk, just ready to begin. I got him back into his bottle without mishap, using the same method; and so ended the first day's work, for I absolutely refused to go on until the cat and I had had some sleep. Wally grumbled a bit and then quieted down.

Thus began the most amazing experiment in the history of physiology and psychology. We made my cat over. And we made him into a—well, guess for yourself.

Inside of a week he was talking. I waited with all the impatience of an anxious father for his first word, which was, incidentally, not "Da-da" but "Catnip." I was so tickled that I fed him catnip until he was roaring drunk.

After that it was easy; nouns first, then verbs. Three hours after saying "Catnip" he was saying "How's about some more catnip?"

Wally somehow stumbled onto a "tone control" in Helix's vocal cords. We found that we could give him a loud and raucous voice, but that by sacrificing quantity to quality, something approximating Wally's voice (as I "heard" it) could be achieved. It was quiet, mellow and very expressive.

After a great deal of work in the anterior part of Helix's brain, we developed a practically perfect memory. That's one thing that the lower orders are a little short on. The average cat lives almost entirely in the present; perhaps ten minutes of the past are clear to him; and he has no conception of the future. What he learns is retained more by muscular or neural memory than by aural, oral or visual memory, as is the case with a schoolchild. We fixed that. Helix needed no drills or exercises; to be told once was enough.

We hit one snag. I'd been talking to Wally the way I'd talk to anyone. But as Helix came to understand what was said aloud, my long talks with no one began to puzzle and confuse him. I tried hard to keep my mouth shut while I talked with Wally, but it wasn't until I thought of taping my mouth that I succeeded. Helix was a little surprised at that, but he got used to it.

And we got him reading. To prove what a prodigy he was, I can say that not one month after he started on his ABC's he had read and absorbed the Bible, Frazer's *Golden Bough* in the abridged edition, *Alice in Wonderland* and four geography texts. In two months he had learned solid geometry, differential calculus, the fourteen basic theories of metempsychosis, and every song on this week's Hit Parade. Oh, yes; he had a profound sense of tone and rhythm. He used to sprawl for hours in front of the radio on Sunday afternoons, listening to the symphony broadcasts; and after a while he could identify not only the selection being played and its composer, but the conductor as well.

I began to realize that we had overdone it a bit. Being a cat, which is the most independent creature on earth, Helix was an aristocrat. He had little, if any, consideration for my comparative ignorance — yes, ignorance; for though I had given him, more or less, my own education, he had the double advantage of recent education and that perfect memory. He would openly sneer at me when I made a sweeping statement — a bad habit I have always had — and then proceed to straighten me out in snide words of one syllable. He meant me no harm; but when he would look over his whiskers and say to me, "You don't really know very much, do you?" in that condescending manner, I burned. Once I had to go so far as to threaten to put him on short rations; that was one thing that would always bring him around.

Wally would spring things on me at times. He went and gave the cat a craving for tobacco, the so-and-so. The result was that Helix smoked up every cigarette in the house. I had a brainstorm, though, and taught him to roll his own. It wasn't so bad after that. But he hadn't much conception of the difference between "mine" and "thine." My cigarettes were safe with Helix — as long as he didn't feel like smoking.

That started me thinking. Why, with his mental faculties, couldn't he learn not to smoke my last cigarette? Or, as happened once, eat everything that was on the table — my dinner as well as his — while I was phoning? I'd told him not to; he couldn't explain it himself. He simply said, "It was there, wasn't it?"

I asked Wally about it, and I think that he hit the right answer.

"I believe," he told me, "that it's because Helix has no conception of generosity. Or mercy. Or any of those qualities. He is completely without conscience."

"You mean that he's got no feeling toward me? That bringing him up, feeding him, educating him, has done nothing to—"

Wally sounded amused. "Sure, sure. He likes you—you're easy to get along with. Besides, as you just said, you're the meal ticket. You mustn't forget, Tronti, that Helix is a cat, and until I take possession, always will be. You don't get implicit obedience from any cat, no matter how erudite he may be, unless he damn well pleases to give it to you. Otherwise, he'll follow his own sweet way. This whole process has interested him—and I told you he'd enjoy it. But that's all."

"Can't we give him some of those qualities?"

"No. That's been bothering me a little. You know, Helix has a clever and devious way of his own for going about things. I'm not quite sure how he—his soul—stands on this replacement business. He might be holding out on us. I can't do much more than I've done. Every attribute we have developed in him was, at the beginning, either embryonic or vestigial. If he were a female, now, we might get an element of mercy, for instance. But there's none in this little tiger here! I have nothing to work on." He paused for a moment.

"Pete, I might as well confess to you that I'm a little worried. We've done plenty, but I don't know that it's enough. In a little while now he'll be ready for the final stage—my entrance into his psyche. As I told you, if his soul objects, he can sling mine out of the solar system. And I haven't a chance of getting back. And here's another thing. I can't be sure that he doesn't know just why we are doing this. If he does—Pete, I hate to say this, but are you on the level? Have you told Helix anything?"

"Me?" I shouted. "Why, you—you ingrate! How could I? You've heard every single word that I've said to that cat. You never sleep. You never go out. Why, you dirty—"

"All right—all right," he said soothingly. "I just asked, that's all. Take it easy. I'm sorry. But—if only I could be sure! There's something in his mind that I can't get to... Oh, well. We'll hope for the best. I've got a lot to lose, but plenty to gain—everything to gain.

And for heaven's sake don't shout like that. You're not taped up, you know."

"Oh—sorry. I didn't give anything away, I guess," I said silently. "But watch yourself, Gregory. Don't get me roiled. Another crack like that and I throw you and your bottle into the ocean, and you can spend the rest of eternity educating the three little fishies. *Deve essere cosi.*"

"In other words, no monkey business. I took Italian in high school," sneered the voice from the bottle. "Okay, Pete. Sorry I brought it up. But put yourself in my place, and you'll see what's what."

The whole affair was making me increasingly nervous. Occasionally I'd wake up to the fact that it was a little out of the ordinary to be spending my life with a talking bottle and a feline cum laude. And now this friction between me and Wally, and the growing superciliousness of Helix—I didn't know whose side to take. Wally's, Helix's, or, by golly, my own. After all, I was in this up to my ears and over. Those days were by no means happy ones.

One evening I was sitting morosely in my easy chair, trying to inject a little rationality into my existence by means of the evening paper. Wally was sulking in his bottle, and Helix was spread out on the rug in front of the radio, in that hyperperfect condition that only a cat can achieve. He was smoking sullenly and making passes at an occasional fly. There was a definite tension in the air, and I didn't like it.

"Helix," I said suddenly, hurling my paper across the room, "what ails you, old feller?"

"Nothing," he lied. "And stop calling me 'old feller.' It's undignified."

"Ohh! So we have a snob in our midst! Helix, I'm getting damn sick of your attitude. Sometimes I'm sorry I ever taught you anything. You used to show me a little respect, before you had any brains."

"That remark," drawled the cat, "is typical of a human being. What does it matter where I got anything I have? As long as any talents of mine belong to me, I have every right to be proud of them, and to look down on anyone who does not possess them in such a degree. Who are you to talk? You think you're pretty good yourself, don't you? And just because you're a member of the cocky tribe of"—and here his words dripped the bitterest scorn—"Homo sapiens."

I knew it would be best to ignore him. He was indulging in the age-old pastime of the cat family—making a human being feel like a fool. Every inferiority complex is allergic to felinity. Show me a man who does not like cats and I'll show you one who is not sure of himself. The cat is a symbol of aloneness superb. And with man, he is not impressed.

"That won't do you any good, Helix," I said coldly. "Do you realize how easy it would be for me to get rid of you? I used to think I had a reason for feeding you and sheltering you. You were good company. You certainly are not now."

"You know," he said, stretching out and crushing his cigarette in the rug because he knew it annoyed me, "I have only one deep regret in my life. And that is that you knew me before my little renaissance. I remember little about it, but I have read considerably on the subject. It appears that the cat family has long misled your foolish race. And yet the whole thing is summed up in a little human doggerel:

> I love my dear pussy, his coat is so warm,
> And if I don't hurt him, he'll do me no harm.

"There, my friend and"—he sniffed—"benefactor, you have our basic philosophy. I find that my actions previous to your fortuitous intervention in my mental development, led you to exhibit a sad lack of the respect which I deserve. If it were not for that stupidity on my part, during those blind years—and I take no responsibility on myself for that stupidity; it was unavoidable—you would now treat me more as I should be treated, as the most talented member of a superlative race.

"Don't be any more of a fool than you have to be, Pete. You think I've changed. I haven't. The sooner you realize that, the better for you. And for heaven's sake stop being emotional about me. It bores me."

"Emotional?" I yelled. "Damn it, what's the matter with a little emotion now and then? What's happening around here, anyway? Who's the boss around here? Who pays the bills?"

"You do," said Helix gently, "which makes you all the more a fool. You wouldn't catch me doing anything unless I thoroughly enjoyed it. Go away, Pete. You're being childish."

I picked up a heavy ashtray and hurled it at the cat. He ducked it gracefully. "Tsk tsk! *What* an exhibition!"

I grabbed my hat and stormed out, followed by the cat's satiric chuckle.

Never in my life have I been so completely filled with helpless anger. I start to do someone a favor, and what happens? I begin taking dictation from him. In return for that I do him an even greater favor, and what happens? He corrupts my cat. So I start taking dictation from the cat too.

It wouldn't matter so much, but I had loved that cat. Snicker if you want to, but for a man like me, who spends nine-tenths of his life tied up in test tubes and electrochemical reactions, the cat had filled a great gap. I realized that I had kidded myself—Helix was a conscienceless parasite, and always had been. But I had loved him. My error. Nothing in this world is quite as devastating as the realization of one's mistaken judgment of character. I could have loved Helix until the day he died, and then cherished his memory. The fact that I would have credited him with qualities he did not possess wouldn't have mattered.

Well, and whose fault was it? Mine? In a way; I'd given in to Wally in his plan to remake the cat for his use. But it was more Wally's fault. Damn it, had I asked him to come into my house and bottle? Who did he think he was, messing up my easy, uncomplicated life like that? ... I had someone to hate for it all, then. Wallace Gregory, the rat.

Lord, what I would have given for some way to change everything back to where it was before Gregory came into my life! I had nothing to look forward to now. If Wally succeeded in making the change, I'd still have that insufferable cat around. In his colossal ego there was no means of expressing any of the gentler human attributes which Wally might possess. As soon as he fused himself with the cat, Helix would disappear into the cosmos, taking nothing but his life force, and leaving every detestable characteristic that he had—and he had plenty. If Wally couldn't make it, They would get him, and I'd be left with that insufferable beast. What a spot!

Suppose I killed Helix? That would be one way ... but then what about Wally? I knew he had immense potentialities; and though that threat of mine about throwing him into the ocean had stopped him once, I wasn't so sure of myself. He had a brilliant mind, and if I incurred his hatred, there's no telling what he might do. For the first time I realized that Wally Gregory's soul was something of a menace. Imagine having to live with the idea that as soon as you died, another man's soul would be laying for you, somewhere Beyond.

I walked miles and hours that night, simmering, before I hit on the perfect solution. It meant killing my beloved Helix; but, now, that would be a small loss. And it would free Wallace Gregory. Let the man's soul take possession of the cat, and then kill the cat. They would both be protected then; and I would be left alone. And, by golly, at peace.

I stumbled home at four, and slept like a dead man. I was utterly exhausted and would have slept the clock around. But that would not have suited Helix. At seven-thirty that morning he threw a glass of ice water over me. I swore violently.

"Get up, you lazy pig," he said politely. "I want my breakfast."

Blind with fury, I rolled out and stood over him. He stood quite still, grinning up at me. He was perfectly unafraid, though I saw him brace his legs, ready to move forward or back or to either side if I made a pass at him. I couldn't have touched him, and he knew it, damn him.

And then I remembered that I was going to kill him, and my throat closed up. I turned away with my eyes stinging. "Okay, Helix," I said when I could speak. "Comin' up."

He followed me into the kitchen and sat watching me while I boiled us some eggs. I watched them carefully—Helix wouldn't eat them unless they were boiled exactly two minutes and forty-five seconds—and then took his out and cut them carefully into cubes, the way he liked them. And then I put a little dash of catnip extract over them and dished them up. Helix raised his eyebrows at that. I hadn't given him any catnip for weeks. I'd only used it as a reward when he had done especially well. Recently I hadn't felt like rewarding him.

"Well," he said as he wiped his mouth delicately. "I see that little session of ambulating introspection in which you indulged after your outbreak last night did you good. There never need be any friction between us, Pete, if you continue to behave this way. I can overlook almost anything but familiarity."

I choked on a piece of toast. Of all the colossal gall! He thought he had taught me a lesson! For a moment I was tempted to rub him out right then and there, but managed to keep my hands off him. I didn't want him to be suspicious.

Suddenly he swept his cup off the table. "Call this coffee?" he said sharply. "Make some more immediately, and this time be a little careful."

"You better be careful yourself," I said. "I taught you to say 'please' when you asked for anything."

"'Please' be damned," said my darling pet. "You ought to know by this time how I like my coffee. I shouldn't have to tell you about things like that." He reached across the table and sent my cup to the floor too. "Now you'll have to make more. I tell you, I won't stand for any more of your nonsense. From now on this detestable democracy is at an end. You're going to do things *my* way. I've taken too much from you. You offend me. You eat sloppily, and I never did care particularly for your odor. Hereafter keep away from me unless I call. And don't speak unless you are spoken to."

I drew a deep breath and counted to ten very, very slowly. Then I got two more cups out of the closet, made more coffee, and poured it. And while Helix was finishing his breakfast, I went out and bought a revolver.

When I got back I found Helix sleeping. I tiptoed into the kitchen to wash the dishes, but found them all broken. His idea of a final whimsical touch. I ground my teeth and cleaned up the mess. Then I went into the laboratory and locked the door. "Wally!" I called.

"Well?"

"Listen, fella, we've got to finish this up now—today. Helix has gotten it into his head that he owns the place, me included. I won't stand for it, I tell you! I almost killed him this morning, and I will yet if this nonsense keeps up. Wally, is everything ready?"

Wally sounded a little strained. "Yes . . . Pete, it's going to be good! Oh, God, to be able to walk around again! Just to be able to read a comic strip, or go to a movie, or see a ball game! Well—let's get it over with. What was that about Helix? Did you say he's a little—er—intractable?"

I snorted. "That's not the word for it. He has decided that he is a big shot. Me, I only work here."

"Pete, did he say anything about—about me? Don't get sore now, but—do you think it's safe? If what you say is true, he's asserting his individuality; I wouldn't like that to go too far. You know, They have a hunch that something's up. The last time you got me into Helix's mind, there were swarms of Them around. When They sensed that I was making a change, They all drew back as if to let me get away with it. Pete, They have something up Their sleeve, too."

"What do you mean, 'too'?" I asked quickly.

"Why, nothing. Helix is one, They are another. Too. What's the matter with that?"

It didn't relieve me much. Wally probably knew I was planning to kill the cat as soon as he made the change, thus doing him out of several years of fleshly enjoyment before he went on his way. He wasn't saying anything, though. He had too much to lose.

I took the bottle out of the laboratory into the kitchen and washed it, just by way of stalling for a minute. Then I set it down on the sink and went and got my gun, loaded it and dropped it into a drawer in the bench. Next I set the bottle back on the bench—I was pretty sure Wally hadn't known about the gun, and I didn't want him to—and went for Helix.

I couldn't find him.

The cushion where he had been sleeping was still warm; what was he up to now?

I hunted feverishly all through the apartment, without success.

This was a fine time for him to do a blackout! With an exasperated sigh I went back into the laboratory to tell Wally.

Helix was sitting on the bench beside the bottle, twirling his whiskers with his made-over right paw and looking very amused. "Well, my good man," he greeted me, "what seems to be the trouble?"

"Damn it, cat," I said irritably, "where have you been?"

"Around," he said laconically. "You are as blind as you are stupid. And mind your tone."

I swallowed that. I had something more important to think about. How was I going to persuade him to lick the bottle? Mere catnip wouldn't do it, not in his present frame of mind. So—

"I suppose," Helix said, "that you want me to go through the old ritual of bottle-cataglottism again. Pardon the pun."

"Why, yes," I said, surprised but trying not to show it. "It's to your benefit, you know."

"Of course," said the cat. "I've always known that. If I didn't get something out of it, I'd have stopped doing it long ago."

That was logical, but I didn't like it. "All right," I said. "Let's go!"

"Pete!" Wally called. "This time, I want you to hold him very firmly, with both hands. Spread your fingers out as far as possible, and if you can get your forearms on him too, do it. I think you'll learn something—interesting."

A little puzzled, I complied. Helix didn't object, as I thought he might. Wally said, "Okay. They're drawing away now. Get him to lick the bottle."

"All right, Helix," I whispered tightly.

The pink tongue flashed out and back. The bottle tipped the tiniest bit. Then there was a tense silence.

"I ... think ... I'll ... make it..."

We waited, Helix and I.

Suddenly something deep within me wrenched sickeningly. I almost dropped with the shock of it. And there was a piercing shriek deep within my brain—Wally's shriek, dwindling off into the distance. And faintly, then, there was a rending, tearing sound. It was horrible.

I staggered back and leaned against the lathe, gasping. Helix lay unmoving where I had left him. His sides were pumping in and out violently.

Helix shook himself and came over to me. "Well," he said, looking me straight in the eye, "they got your friend."

"Helix! How did you know about that?"

"Why must you be so consistently stupid, Pete? I've known about that all along. I'll give you a little explanation, if you like. It might prove to you that a human being is really a very, very dull creature."

"Go ahead," I gulped.

"You and I have just been a part of a most elaborately amusing compound double cross." He chuckled complacently. "Gregory was right in his assumption that I could not overhear his conversations with you—and a very annoying thing it was, too. I knew there was something off-color somewhere, because I didn't think you were improving me so vastly just out of the goodness of your heart. But— someone else was listening in, and knew everything."

"Someone else?"

"Certainly. Have you forgotten Them? They were very much interested as to the possibilities of getting hold of our mutual friend Mr. Gregory. Being a lower order of spirit, They found it a simple matter to communicate with me. They asked me to toss Mr. Gregory's soul out to Them." He laughed nastily.

"But I was getting too much out of it. See what a superior creature I am! I told Them to stand by; that They would have a chance at Gregory when I was through using him, and not before. They did as I said, because it was up to me to give what They wanted. That's why They did not interfere during the transfers."

"Why, you heel!" I burst out. "After all Wally did for you, you were going to do that?"

"I wouldn't defend him, if I were you," the cat said precisely. "He was double-crossing you too. I know all about this soul-replacement business; needn't try to hide that from me. He was sincere, at first, about using my body, but he couldn't help thinking that yours would suit his purpose far better. Though why he'd prefer it to mine—oh, well. No matter. However, his idea was to transfer himself from the bottle to me, and then to you. That's why he told you to hold me firmly—he wanted a good contact."

"How—how the devil do you know that?"

"He told me himself. After I had reached a satisfactory stage of development, I told him that I was wise. Oh, yes, I fooled him into developing a communication basis in me! He thought it was a taste for alcohol he was building up! However, he caught wise in time to arrest it, but not before it was good enough to communicate with him. If he'd gone a little farther, I'd have been able to talk with you that way too. At any rate, he was a little dampened by my attitude; knew he'd never get a chance to occupy me. I suggested to him, though, that we join forces in having him possess *you*."

"*Me!*" I edged toward the drawer in the bench. "Go on, Helix."

"You can see why I did this, can't you?" he asked distantly. "It would have been embarrassing to have him, a free soul, around where he might conceivably undo some of the work he had done on me. If he possessed you, you would be out of the way—They would take care of that—and he would have what he wanted. An ideal arrangement. You had no suspicion of the plan, and he had a good chance of catching your soul off-guard and ousting it. He knew how to go about it. Unfortunately for him, your soul was a little too quick. It was *you* who finally killed Wallace Gregory, not I. Neat, eh?"

"Yes," I said slowly, pulling the gun out of the drawer and sighting down the barrel, right between his eyes. "Very neat. For a while I thought I'd be sorry to do this. Now, I'm not." I drew a deep breath; Helix did not move. I pulled the trigger four times, and then sagged back against the bench. The strain was too much.

Helix stretched himself and yawned. "I knew you'd try something like that," he said. "I took the trouble of removing the bullets from your gun before the experiment. Nice to have known you!"

I hurled the gun at him but I was too slow. In a flash he was out of the laboratory, streaking for the door. He reached for the knob, opened the door, and was gone before I could take two steps.

There was a worrisome time after that, once I had done all the hysterical things anyone might do—pound out, run left, run right, look up and back and around. But this was a *cat* I was chasing, and you don't catch even an ordinary cat that does not in some way want to be caught.

I wonder why he decided to crack a safe.

No, I don't. I know how his head works. Worked. He had plans for himself—you can be sure of that, and unless I'm completely wrong, he had plans for all of us, ultimately. There have been, in human history, a few people who had the cold, live-in-the-present, me-first attitude of a cat, and humanity has learned a lot of hard lessons from them. But none of them was a cat.

Helix may have made a try or two to get someone to front for him—I wouldn't know. But he was smart enough to know that there was one tool he could use that would work—money. Once he had that, who knows how he would have operated? He could write, he could use a telephone. He would have run a lethal and efficient organization more frightening that anything you or I could imagine.

Well—he won't do it now. As for me, I'll disappear into research again. Flexible glass would be a nice patent to own and enjoy, but thank you, I'm glad to pass on that one.

But Helix . . . damn him, I miss him.

To Shorten Sail

WHEN WE ROUNDED the last buoy and headed home, the *Barnacle* of Port Elizabeth seemed to embrace the breeze in her canvas grip, haul herself along hand over hand. But for her heavy keel, she was drawing mere inches. She was careened, lee rail under. She had a bone in her teeth and her lover at her helm. She was fast, and she was beautiful. From the lift and pull of her, a shift of a couple of inches would capsize her; you knew it, and you didn't care. It was glorious.

Percy lay on the slanting deck, his spindly arms wrapped around the tiller, his head thrown back, and he laughed from the sheer joy of it. Day after day, Percy was a pen pusher in an insurance office. But on weekends, he was master of the tiny sloop *Barnacle,* a little white-hulled dream of a craft. And this was the regatta; today Percy and I were living in fact that of which we had dreamed each night for a year, and of which we would dream for the year following.

We had never won the regatta. But this year we had everything with us. The wind was blowing half a gale, and we could barely run safely with every stitch aloft. The great new balloon jib flew tautly ahead of us, gave us wings. It was what we needed to show our heels to anything on the sound—except Granger's sable-sailed racing sloop, the *Black Flame*

It was nip and tuck between us and the *Flame.* She stood about twenty yards to starboard, booming along on exactly our course, at exactly our speed. We hadn't a knot's advantage, either of us. The wind whipped a prayer from my lips. Granger, with his steel mast and his electric winches, had won three years straight. I begged old King Neptune to give us a break.

And then the wind's howl in the rigging rose an octave. I saw that squall on the way. A vicious little slate gray williwaw bunching its muscles for a rush at us. I edged toward Percy, screamed at him, "Squall coming up—we'll have to shorten sail!" Topsails were tumbling down aboard most of the boats.

"If the Lord wants me to shorten sail," Percy squealed, "He'll blow some off!" He was quoting the great old clipper captains of the days when American ships were the finest on the seven seas. It was throwing the race and the craft into the laps of the gods; it was foolhardiness supreme; but it was more than a little magnificent.

I saw the *Black Flame*'s topsail sag and belly; Granger was frightened, for all his chrome and stainless steel. And then the sail lifted again and began to draw. He had seen that we were going to run with every stitch aloft; he was calling our bluff. I screamed to Percy, "The squall will yank the mast out of us! We'll have to shorten!"

"Go ahead and shorten then," said Percy.

I crawled over to the pinrail, tugged at the peak halyard (the line that holds the sail up). It was jammed—Percy had made it fast with a back hitch; the more the sail pulled, the tighter the line squeezed around the pin. I'd never be able to cast it off. The crazy fool! If he couldn't have this regatta, he didn't want his beloved sloop. It would be the end of the *Barnacle* if that blow struck us with our sail drawing.

Then everything happened at once. The halyard parted, and the mainsail came booming and flopping down. And as it struck the deck, the squall reached and blinded us. The *Barnacle* yawed violently, took the pull of the thrashing balloon jib, and steadied. A great green white-headed comber took the after end of the craft in its teeth, yanked the rudder out of her. And the wind shifted amazingly, so that it stood dead aft. The rain and fury of it passed, and there we were, rudderless, hauled by the jib as if we were hitched to Pegasus himself.

And the others? The sound was speckled with the flotsam that had been a regatta. Fourteen boats—fourteen, no less!—were dismasted or overturned, or both. Only the *Flame* was under weigh, crippled by a split topsail, but moving fast. There was nothing that Percy and I could do but throw ourselves on the billowing mass of canvas on the deck, to keep it from being carried away. No rudder, and one wild sail flying full and free, and—

And we won the regatta.

We won because the *Flame,* bless the mechanics that built her, couldn't run dead before a wind. She had to tack a mere three points, just once, mind you, but it cost her the race. Our balloon jib brought us frothing in over the line, not two lengths ahead of Granger. And when we had cut the jib adrift and thrown a line to a power boat, Percy lay in the tumbled mainsail and rolled gleefully. "She knows her way," he chortled. "Oh, the beauty of it! If she hadn't broken that halyard and lowered her own sail, she'd have broken up. She has a brain. She even knows when to shorten sail!"

"She does," I said. Why should I tell him that I had cut the halyard just before the squall struck us? Who am I to destroy a man's faith in the thing he loves?

Thanksgiving Again

"VACATIONS," SAID PEGGY suddenly, "are dangerous."

She was perched on the top step of the Lodge porch, and Rad Walsh had poured his lean body gracefully over the steps below her. He cocked a quizzical eyebrow in her direction. "Interestin'" he drawled. "May I ask what prompted the remark?"

"Oh, it's just what we were talking about—this great country, and the freedom of thought and action it allows us. . ." She glanced across the compound at the men folding the great red, white and blue flag that had just been taken in for the night. "Those things depend on circumstances, Rad."

"Little rebel," he said gently, "what do you mean by that? A citizen is a citizen, and enjoys a citizen's privileges."

She laughed. "I'm being a little foggy, I know. I was thinking about freedom, and what a—a comparative thing it is. Down South, you know, I have my daily job. I have set ideas, routines, environments. I see people I know all the time. I have my little sets of defenses, my varied suits of armor for each of them. I can't be hurt easily."

He came up beside her. "What are you driving at, Peg o' my heart?"

"Vacations. . . You see, Rad, when a person gets his vacation, he lets his hair down. He hasn't time to learn about people he meets. He throws himself into a new world, very brief, very beautiful. Everything happens so fast that it's distorted. He tries to dislike nothing, and when he likes something—or somebody—he does it violently, and with little regard for—for afterward."

Rad clasped his knee in long brown hands, stared pensively off across the valley. It was getting late, and the distant stretch of North woods was darkening green, blue-shadowed. The moon, deep behind a far ridge, was attempting with faint promise to silhouette the hills.

Peggy, staring at his rugged profile, felt her heart dip and turn like a wheeling hawk. She saw the corner of his mouth twitch, but before she could beg him to be serious, he had started.

> There was a young girl on vacation
> Who indulged in a harmless flirtation.
> When her fingers got burned
> She very soon learned
> It was quite an unpleasant sensation!

Peggy laughed in spite of herself. Oh, he was shrewd! And that trick of his, of bringing little gems of ad-libbed doggerel out of his hat—could she ever forget it? Could she ever forget *him?* She'd have to, after tomorrow.

"What you're leading up to," he said almost brutally, "is the fact that you're leaving tomorrow, that you've had a wonderful time here, and that you hope we can keep up a pretense of—" here his voice was a little ironic, putting quotes on his words—"nothing more than friendship. You fear that the combined stimuli of Thanksgiving Day and your pending departure will lead you—us—to make certain admissions relative to the high mutual regard—"

"Stop talking like a text in rhetoric!" Peggy snapped, breathless and more than a little indignant. "Yes, that's the general idea. Only you don't have to—to revel in it." She sniffed angrily, and Rad considerately handed her a clean handkerchief, over his shoulder, looking away. She snatched it, and when Rad looked at her again a moment later she was apparently trying to hide under it.

Because he was that kind of man, Rad knew just what to do. He slid an arm around her, let her bury her face in his shoulder. She cried unashamed, because he had forced her to tell him what was in her heart . . . she tried to be angry at him for it, but could not. Oh, why did this have to happen to her . . . now? Confound the man's unerring perception . . . and yet, maybe it was better this way.

He began talking, his voice rough and tender. "Peg . . . Peg—little old mumbly-Peg—there's nothing to cry about. Really. You're going away tomorrow—don't think about that, and the little seven hundred miles between us. Tomorrow's Thanksgiving, Peg, and we have lots to be thankful for. These ten days together—think of them often. Think of me, and of the fun we had, and of tonight, and be thankful—Peg! Please stop crying!" He tilted her chin up, took the handkerchief, dried her eyes. Through the mist that surrounded her she saw that telltale twitching of his mouth; and as ever, he was off before she could stop him:

> I ask you for a kiss
> I'm sure you won't say no;
> Oh prithee, pretty miss—

"I think we'd better go," finished Peggy hurriedly, quite eclipsing what might easily have been a brilliant gagline.

She tried to get up and move away, but couldn't, partly because he would not let her go, and partly because she didn't try very hard ... and their kiss was long and very, very sweet.

"Rad!" she said when she could speak again, "That—that wasn't fair." She was so annoyed that she almost took her arms from around his neck. He kissed her again.

"You don't have to go tomorrow," he said softly. "You won't ever have to go away from me."

"Rad," she said in a small, tight voice, "Please let me go."

More than a little surprised, he did. "It might have been a little sudden," he grinned, "But you've just been proposed to, my fran'." He thought she didn't understand.

"Yes—I know." Her voice was still strained, frightened.

"Peg! I want to make you happy—I thought I could start that way. You—you are happy, aren't you? And, oh darling, you will marry me?"

"No, Rad!"

"Is that an answer to the first question or the second?"

"The first... Rad, stop badgering me!"

He drew back, really perplexed; and it was a new experience for him. He took her by the shoulders, forced her to look at him. "Come on, child; give. What's the trouble? I love you; you know that, don't you? Don't you?" There was something approaching desperation in his tone.

"Oh, yes, Rad—yes! But Rad, don't ask me to marry you! How long have I known you? Nine, no, ten days. You don't know me—you couldn't; not in ten days; any more than I know you. Oh, Rad, I'm afraid! I have you here with me now; and when I go away tomorrow I'll have you, the way you are now, forever. I'll never forget you, and you'll always be fine and strong and tender. And if I married you—" (she was actually trembling) "—and it didn't work out, I couldn't bear it!" Peggy would have cried, but she was past it now, too deeply moved for tears.

Rad started to speak, but she interrupted him. "No, Rad. Don't try to persuade me. You might be able to; please don't try. Rad, I knew two people like you and me. They met the way we did, and they got married. And it didn't work. It was—awful. Neither of them are happy. They had known each other for two weeks before they married; it wasn't enough."

"It's enough for me," Rad said glumly. "Peg, there would be something in what you say if we could see each other constantly, every day. But not now—not with your leaving." His voice was still tender and patient, but just a little angry. "Can't you say yes or— or no?"

"I can't— I can't!" she said brokenly.

And Rad, a man in love and paradoxically still with his good sense, asked, "Just what can be done about this?"

Peggy, a girl in love, yet equally paradoxical, said, "We'll have to wait until we know each other better." And as she said it, she knew that it might mean losing him, that it was unfair, and perhaps foolish and—the right thing to do.

After a long silence Peggy said, "Rad, I'll come back here next year..."

He laughed hollowly. "It'll be Thanksgiving again."

"Rad, will you write to me, every week? Will you write and tell me all the thousand and one little things that are *you*? The things that don't matter, and the things that seem small and—"

"You mean, whether I always put the cap back on the toothpaste tube, and whether or not I insist on keeping pet snakes, and if I am picky about my food?" He looked at her. "Peg, that's not going to be much fun, when all I can think of is you and the funny way your hair streamlines your head, and the way your eyes twinkle when you're trying so hard to be serious..."

"You can write about those things too, if you like," she said; and the twinkle was there, all right.

He stared off into the twilight again, searching his mind for something to say, to make her stay. A whole year, and a letter each week ... fifty-two letters, and then Thanksgiving again ... suddenly he slapped his thigh, burst out laughing.

"It's a bargain!" he said when he could catch his breath. "I'll write you regularly; and when it's Thanksgiving again, I'll come to you—if you still want me. There'll be no nonsense about it, now, will there?"

"Oh, Rad..."

And they spent the rest of that long, long evening in finding out more and more about each other ... a year spent that way would be sure to teach two people all they would ever need to know about their "high mutual regard" ... it would be hard to do on paper, though. One of the things that has plagued lovers since the dawn of time is that you can't kiss by mail!

The next day was a bright, cool Monday. Early as it was when Peggy came out of the Lodge, Rad had been earlier. He was there on the steps to take her bag in one hand, her hand in the other. They both tried pitifully to be cheerful.

"Morning, early bird!" he said. She grinned.

"Consider yourself caught then," she returned.

"*Touché!* I asked for that. I hope your taxi breaks down."

"It won't. Papa Guichet's Model T is past that stage. The spirits of misfortune gave it up as a bad job, lo, these twenty years!"

They walked across the wide compound. Suddenly he stopped her, pointing to the newly risen flag.

"If," he said, "You should ever forget about me—such impossible things do happen—and you see that flag, let it remind you, Peg. It stands for something great, something solid and mighty and invincible—something greater than my love for you. It is the only thing I can think of that is worthy of comparison, and worthy of being a reminder."

She looked up at the floating tri-colored folds, and as she watched through stinging eyes, the colors misted out. "I'll have to b-borrow your handkerchief again, Rad..."

Then she was in the asthmatic old pre-war relic, and had time for one brief blushing kiss before Papa Guichet frightened all the wild life within a square mile by the clanking cacophony of his starting. He was a wise and understanding old man, and he knew that it was best to do these things quickly. The prosaic racket of his engine had knifed through many such partings, making them mercifully swift, if not gentle.

Peggy sobbed openly, straining to get a last glimpse from the cracked rear window; and when, all too soon, she got it, she huddled in the corner, crushing Radcliffe Walsh's last clean handkerchief to her face.

All her life she was to remember that seven-mile ride to the junction; the clatter of the ancient car, the smell of hot oil and raw gasoline mingled with the cool sweetness of the virgin forest; and over and through it all, Papa Guichet's sweet old voice singing an old French song about a little shepherdess. It had a hauntingly sweet tune, light and cheerful, and a meaningless, recurrent chorus line, *Fait ron, fait ron, petit patapon,* which ran through her head for weeks and weeks afterward.

She got her train, hardly knowing what she was doing, and hours later, when it was time to change trains, she went into a hotel and wrote the first letter to him...

"When I crossed the river," the letter said, "The first thing I saw was a flag. And it made me think of things—

"The flag stands for something great, something solid and mighty and invincible—something greater than my love for you. It is the only thing I can think of that is worthy of comparison, and worthy of being a reminder."

She was quoting him directly, and as his heartfelt, colorful words flowed from her pen, she was conscious of being a part of a great power, that was Rad, and Rad's love, and the flag she had just seen, and the flag that Rad had pointed to when he said those words.

Two days later she arrived back at the city; and the first thing she did was to burst impulsively in on her employer and thank him for the late vacation she had had that year. Then—back to the job; back to the weary hours of typing and interviewing and the million and one things that make up the life of a private secretary. It was the same as last year, and the year before, with but one difference—the knowledge that Rad had loved her, that he was thinking constantly of her. How did she know?

The day she had arrived—and she had been travelling for more than forty-eight hours—there were two airmail special delivery letters for her. One was dated on Thanksgiving Day—he had begun writing it five minutes after she left—and the other was dated the day after. And each and every day after that, there had been a letter from him. And they were letters, not notes. Eight, nine closely written pages. Each of them was a bit of him—his strength, his ruggedness, and the infinite tenderness that only a strong man can extend. There was a laugh on every page, and a little ache of desire, too. And he told her about himself; each letter was an engrossing chapter in a suave autobiography. Ah, he was a *man!*

Peggy answered them, too, all of them. In one of them she said, "Rad, you must be careful, or you'll overreach yourself. Remember, you must write me until next Thanksgiving. You are setting yourself a task of three hundred and sixty-five letters to me. I love them, darling, but you only 'contracted' for fifty-two!"

And in answer he said, "My contract was with you, not with myself, oh light o' my life. Fifty-two or three hundred and sixty-five—what does it matter? Thanksgiving is Thanksgiving; and oh! am I going to be thankful when it comes!"

> When you gave me your heart, you gave me the world,
> You gave me the night and the day,
> And thunder, and roses, and sweet green grass,
> The sea, and soft wet clay.
>
> I quaffed the dawn from a golden cup,
> From a silver one the night.
> And the steed I rode was the wild west wind,
> And the world was mine to fight.

With thunder I smote the evil of the earth
With roses I won the right
With the sea I washed, and with clay I built,
And the world was a place of light...

That's what he wrote; and more than anything else in the world it was a picture of him, and of the strong clean way he thought and acted. Sometimes Peggy hated herself for putting him off, and sometimes she was afraid of the power of the man, and sometimes there was no room for anything in her crowded heart but blind worship of him.

She kept all of his letters, and numbered them too. When she had ten of them, she felt that she had known him all her life: and when she had thirty, he seemed more than someone she knew; he was a part of her. When the letters drew into the upper forties, she caught herself wishing that he had written only once a week, because if he had, then the forty-sixth and forty-eighth and fiftieth letters would be near—oh, so near—to the time when he would be at her side again. She began pretending about it, looking forward to that fifty-second letter. If he *had* written only once a week, now, that letter would bring him ... she tried to think of what it would be like. She would get up, on the morning she got the Thanksgiving Day letter, and she would dress hurriedly, because it would be her wedding day—oh yes! In his own words, there would be no nonsense!—and she would open the door and slip out, and there at the top of the stairs would be Rad, his arms hungry for her, his eyes bright in his dark face.

The more she thought of this little game of make-believe, the more real it became to her, until she found herself looking forward to that letter as if it would really be that way. Try it, anyone. Live with a vivid expectation, and see how real it will become. And how hard it hits when it doesn't come as expected...

The fifty-first letter said:

"Peggy, I want you to think hard for the next couple of days about your name, and your title of Miss. You know, you won't have them forever! Not if I can help it. I can help it, can't I?"

And a little farther on:

"Peggy, I have a surprise for you. I hadn't meant to tell you any-thing about it, but I must; I'm bursting with it. Oh, I love you—I'm going to prove it to you. And so—I have a surprise! And that, adorable child, is all I'm going to tell you!"

Now what on earth was the man hinting at?

The fifty-second day dawned cold and clear, the clean brisk sort of day that was Rad Walsh if he were weather. Peggy woke very, very early, which was silly, because today was a holiday, and she did-n't have to work. She lay there half asleep for a moment, feeling that she should remember something and not knowing quite what it was. When it dawned on her, the force of remembrance bounced her right up out of bed to the middle of the floor. She dressed hurriedly, because this was going to be her wedding day. Her mirror told her blatantly that she was being very silly, and she told it crossly, "Why shouldn't I pretend?"

She should feel sad, she realized, but somehow she couldn't. Today—she ran over to the window—today, nothing could go wrong. Today was a day for people to be happy—happy and thankful...

A light knock sounded. And that would be his letter, first thing in the morning, by special delivery. She laughed for joy, flung the door open—and stood there, aghast.

"Rad!" she screamed, and would have fallen if his strong arms had not swept her close to him. They stood there in the doorway for a long time; and then she lifted her face twice to him; once for a kiss, and once to ask questions. Thus things were done in their order of importance!

"Rad, Rad, you darling! You promised to wait a year; you know you did! Oh, I'm glad you didn't, but..."

"Now, wait a minute," he said laughingly. "I said—but here... Read for yourself. I'm the mailman—here's the fifty-second letter."

Shaking, she took it from him, tore it open. It was short and very much to the point. It said,

"I promised you to write *regularly,* fifty-two letters, and then it would be Thanksgiving again. I saw you last on Thanksgiving Day, in Canada. And in Canada it falls on the first Monday in October.

And you live in the States, where it's the last Thursday in November. There are exactly fifty-two days between them..."

"Kiss me, Peggy. I've got the license."

Peggy kissed him. And then she married him. And when they came out of the little church around the corner, a parade was passing. Rad leaned down and whispered to her. "Look, Peggy, a band. It's for us!"

And then came the Stars and Stripes and the Union Jack; Peggy and Rad stopped, and Rad took off his hat. When they had passed, Peggy said breathlessly,

"Did you see them, Rad? Side by side, like us. Strong, and solid, and mighty and invincible, like us... I'm thankful, Rad, that they are just a little greater than our love could ever be..."

Bianca's Hands

BIANCA'S MOTHER WAS leading her when Ran saw her first. Bianca was squat and small, with dank hair and rotten teeth. Her mouth was crooked and it drooled. Either she was blind or she just didn't care about bumping into things. It didn't really matter because Bianca was an imbecile. Her hands...

They were lovely hands, graceful hands, hands as soft and smooth and white as snowflakes, hands whose color was lightly tinged with pink like the glow of Mars on snow. They lay on the counter side by side, looking at Ran. They lay there half closed and crouching, each pulsing with a movement like the panting of a field creature, and they looked. Not watched. Later, they watched him. Now they looked. They did, because Ran felt their united gaze, and his heart beat strongly.

Bianca's mother demanded cheese stridently. Ran brought it to her in his own time while she berated him. She was a bitter woman, as any woman has a right to be who is wife of no man and mother to a monster. Ran gave her the cheese and took her money and never noticed that it was not enough, because of Bianca's hands. When Bianca's mother tried to take one of the hands, it scuttled away from the unwanted touch. It did not lift from the counter, but ran on its fingertips to the edge and leaped into a fold of Bianca's dress. The mother took the unresisting elbow and led Bianca out.

Ran stayed there at the counter unmoving, thinking of Bianca's hands. Ran was strong and bronze and not very clever. He had never been taught about beauty and strangeness, but he did not need that teaching. His shoulders were wide and his arms were heavy and thick, but he had great soft eyes and thick lashes. They curtained his eyes now. He was seeing Bianca's hands again dreamily. He found it hard to breathe...

Harding came back. Harding owned the store. He was a large man whose features barely kept his cheeks apart. He said, "Sweep up, Ran. We're closing early today." Then he went behind the counter, squeezing past Ran.

Ran got the broom and swept slowly.

"A woman bought cheese," he said suddenly. "A poor woman, with very old clothes. She was leading a girl. I can't remember what the girl looked like, except—who was she?"

"I saw them go out," said Harding. "The woman is Bianca's mother, and the girl is Bianca. I don't know their other name. They don't talk to people much. I wish they wouldn't come in here. Hurry up, Ran."

Ran did what was necessary and put away his broom. Before he left he asked, "Where do they live, Bianca and her mother?"

"On the other side. A house on no road, away from people. Good night, Ran."

Ran went from the shop directly over to the other side, not waiting for his supper. He found the house easily, for it was indeed away from the road, and stood rudely by itself. The townspeople had cauterized the house by wrapping it in empty fields.

Harshly, "What do you want?" Bianca's mother asked as she opened the door.

"May I come in?"

"What do you want?"

"May I come in?" he asked again. She made as if to slam the door, and then stood aside. "Come."

Ran went in and stood still. Bianca's mother crossed the room and sat under an old lamp, in the shadow. Ran sat opposite her, on a three-legged stool. Bianca was not in the room.

The woman tried to speak, but embarrassment clutched at her voice. She withdrew into her bitterness, saying nothing. She kept peeping at Ran, who sat quietly with his arms folded and the uncertain light in his eyes. He knew she would speak soon, and he could wait.

"Ah, well..." She was silent after that, for a time, but now she had forgiven him his intrusion. Then, "It's a great while since anyone came to see me; a great while . . . it was different before. I was a pretty girl—"

She bit her words off and her face popped out of the shadows, shrivelled and sagging as she leaned forward. Ran saw that she was beaten and cowed and did not want to be laughed at.

"Yes," he said gently. She sighed and leaned back so that her face disappeared again. She said nothing for a moment, sitting looking at Ran, liking him.

"We were happy, the two of us," she mused, "until Bianca came. He didn't like her, poor thing, he didn't, no more than I do now. He went away. I stayed by her because I was her mother. I'd go away myself, I would, but people know me, and I haven't a penny—not a penny. . . They'd bring me back to her, they would, to care for her. It doesn't matter much now, though, because people don't want me any more than they want her, they don't. . ."

Ran shifted his feet uneasily, because the woman was crying. "Have you room for me here?" he asked.

Her head crept out into the light. Ran said swiftly, "I'll give you money each week, and I'll bring my own bed and things." He was afraid she would refuse.

She merged with the shadows again. "If you like," she said, trembling at her good fortune. "Though why you'd want to . . . still, I guess if I had a little something to cook up nice, and a good reason for it, I could make someone real cosy here. But—*why?*" She rose. Ran crossed the room and pushed her back into the chair. He stood over her, tall.

"I never want you to ask me that," he said, speaking very slowly. "Hear?"

She swallowed and nodded. "I'll come back tomorrow with the bed and things," he said.

He left her there under the lamp, blinking out of the dimness, folded round and about with her misery and her wonder.

People talked about it. People said, "Ran has moved to the house of Bianca's mother." "It must be because—" "Ah," said some, "Ran was always a strange boy. It must be because—" "Oh, *no!*" cried others, appalled. "Ran is such a good boy. He wouldn't—"

Harding was told. He frightened the busy little woman who told him. He said, "Ran is very quiet, but he is honest and he does his work. As long as he comes here in the morning and earns his wage, he can do what he wants, where he wants, and it is not my business to stop him." He said this so very sharply that the little woman dared not say anything more.

Ran was very happy, living there. Saying little, he began to learn about Bianca's hands.

He watched Bianca being fed. Her hands would not feed her, the lovely aristocrats. Beautiful parasites they were, taking their animal life from the heavy squat body that carried them, and giving nothing in return. They would lie one on each side of her plate, pulsing, while Bianca's mother put food into the disinterested drooling mouth. They were shy, those hands, of Ran's bewitched gaze. Caught out there naked in the light and open of the table-top, they would creep to the edge and drop out of sight—all but four rosy fingertips clutching the cloth.

They never lifted from a surface. When Bianca walked, her hands did not swing free, but twisted in the fabric of her dress. And when she approached a table or the mantelpiece and stood, her hands would run lightly up and leap, landing together, resting silently, watchfully, with that pulsing peculiar to them.

They cared for each other. They would not touch Bianca herself, but each hand groomed the other. It was the only labor to which they would bend themselves.

Three evenings after he came, Ran tried to take one of the hands in his. Bianca was alone in the room, and Ran went to her and sat beside her. She did not move, nor did her hands. They rested on a small table before her, preening themselves. This, then, was when they really began watching him. He felt it, right down to the depths of his enchanted heart. The hands kept stroking each other, and yet they knew he was there, they knew of his desire. They stretched themselves before him, archly, languorously, and his blood pounded hot. Before he could stay himself he reached and tried to grasp them. He was strong, and his move was sudden and clumsy. One of the hands seemed to disappear, so swiftly did it drop into Bianca's lap. But the other—

Ran's thick fingers closed on it and held it captive. It writhed, all but tore itself free. It took no power from the arm on which it lived, for Bianca's arms were flabby and weak. Its strength, like its beauty, was intrinsic, and it was only by shifting his grip to the puffy forearm that Ran succeeded in capturing it. So intent was he on touching it, holding it, that he did not see the other hand leap from the idiot girl's lap, land crouching at the table's edge. It reared back, fingers curling spiderlike, and sprang at him, fastening on his wrist. It clamped down agonizingly, and Ran felt bones give and crackle. With a cry he released the girl's arm. Her hands fell together and ran over each other, feeling for any small scratch, any tiny damage he might have done them in his passion. And as he sat there clutching his wrist, he saw the hands run to the far side of the little table, hook themselves over the edge and, contracting, draw her out of her place. She had no volition of her own—ah, but her hands had! Creeping over the walls, catching obscure and precarious holds in the wainscoting, they dragged the girl from the room.

And Ran sat there and sobbed, not so much from the pain in his swelling arm, but in shame for what he had done. They might have been won to him in another, gentler way. . .

His head was bowed, yet suddenly he felt the gaze of those hands. He looked up swiftly enough to see one of them whisk round the doorpost. It had come back, then, to see. . . Ran rose heavily and took himself and his shame away. Yet he was compelled to stop in the doorway, even as had Bianca's hands. He watched covertly and saw them come into the room dragging the unprotesting idiot girl. They brought her to the long bench where Ran had sat with her. They pushed her on to it, flung themselves to the table, and began rolling and flattening themselves most curiously about. Ran suddenly realized that there was something of his there, and he was comforted, a little. They were rejoicing, drinking thirstily, revelling in his tears.

Afterwards for nineteen days, the hands made Ran do penance. He knew them as inviolate and unforgiving; they would not show themselves to him, remaining always hidden in Bianca's dress or under the supper table. For those nineteen days Ran's passion and desire grew. More—his love became true love, for only true love knows reverence—and the possession of the hands became his reason for living, his goal in the life which that reason had given him.

Ultimately they forgave him. They kissed him coyly when he was not looking, touched him on the wrist, caught and held him for one sweet moment. It was at table ... a great power surged through him, and he gazed down at the hands, now returned to Bianca's lap. A strong muscle in his jaw twitched and twitched, swelled and fell. Happiness like a golden light flooded him; passion spurred him, love imprisoned him, reverence was the gold of the golden light. The room wheeled and whirled about him and forces unimaginable flickered through him. Battling with himself, yet lax in the glory of it, Ran sat unmoving, beyond the world, enslaved and yet possessor of all. Bianca's hands flushed pink, and if ever hands smiled to each other, then they did.

He rose abruptly, flinging his chair from him, feeling the strength of his back and shoulders. Bianca's mother, by now beyond surprise, looked at him and away. There was that in his eyes which she did not like, for to fathom it would disturb her, and she wanted no trouble. Ran strode from the room and outdoors, to be by himself that he might learn more of this new thing that had possessed him.

It was evening. The crooked-bending skyline drank the buoyancy of the sun, dragged it down, sucking greedily. Ran stood on a knoll, his nostrils flaring, feeling the depth of his lungs. He sucked in the crisp air and it smelled new to him, as though the sunset shades were truly in it. He knotted the muscles of his thighs and stared at his smooth, solid fists. He raised his hands high over his head and, stretching, sent out such a great shout that the sun sank. He watched it, knowing how great and tall he was, how strong he was, knowing the meaning of longing and belonging. And then he lay down on the clean earth and he wept.

When the sky grew cold enough for the moon to follow the sun beyond the hills, and still an hour after that, Ran returned to the house. He struck a light in the room of Bianca's mother, where she slept on a pile of old cloths. Ran sat beside her and let the light wake her. She rolled over to him and moaned, opened her eyes and shrank from him. "Ran ... what do you want?"

"Bianca. I want to marry Bianca."

Her breath hissed between her gums. "No!" It was not a refusal, but astonishment. Ran touched her arm impatiently. Then she laughed.

"To—marry—Bianca. It's late, boy. Go back to bed, and in the morning you'll have forgotten this thing, this dream."

"I've not been to bed," he said patiently, but growing angry. "Will you give me Bianca, or not?"

She sat up and rested her chin on her withered knees. "You're right to ask me, for I'm her mother. Still and all—Ran, you've been good to us, Bianca and me. You're—you are a good boy but—forgive me, lad, but you're something of a fool. Bianca's a monster. I say it though I am what I am to her. Do what you like, and never a word will I say. You should have known. I'm sorry you asked me, for you have given me the memory of speaking so to you. I don't understand you; but do what you like, boy."

It was to have been a glance, but it became a stare as she saw his face. He put his hands carefully behind his back, and she knew he would have killed her else.

"I'll—marry her, then?" he whispered.

She nodded, terrified. "As you like, boy."

He blew out the light and left her.

Ran worked hard and saved his wage, and made one room beautiful for Bianca and himself. He built a soft chair, and a table that was like an altar for Bianca's sacred hands. There was a great bed, and heavy cloth to hide and soften the walls, and a rug.

They were married, though marrying took time. Ran had to go far afield before he could find one who would do what was necessary. The man came far and went again afterwards, so that none knew of it, and Ran and his wife were left alone. The mother spoke for Bianca, and Bianca's hand trembled frighteningly at the touch of the ring, writhed and struggled and then lay passive, blushing and beautiful. But it was done. Bianca's mother did not protest, for she didn't dare. Ran was happy, and Bianca—well, nobody cared about Bianca.

After they were married Bianca followed Ran and his two brides into the beautiful room. He washed Bianca and used rich lotions. He washed and combed her hair, and brushed it many times until it shone, to make her more fit to be with the hands he had married. He never touched the hands, though he gave them soaps and creams and tools with which they could groom themselves. They were pleased. Once one of them ran up his coat and touched his cheek and made him exultant.

He left them and returned to the shop with his heart full of music. He worked harder than ever, so that Harding was pleased and let him go home early. He wandered the hours away by the bank of a brook, watching the sun on the face of the chuckling water. A bird came to circle him, flew unafraid through the aura of gladness about him. The delicate tip of a wing brushed his wrist with the touch of the first secret kiss from the hands of Bianca. The singing that filled him was part of the nature of laughing, the running of water, the sound of the wind in the reeds by the edge of the stream. He yearned for the hands, and he knew he could go now and clasp them and own them; instead he stretched out on the bank and lay smiling, all lost in the sweetness and poignance of waiting, denying desire. He laughed for pure joy in a world without hatred, held in the stainless palms of Bianca's hands.

As it grew dark he went home. All during that nuptial meal Bianca's hands twisted about one of his while he ate with the other, and Bianca's mother fed the girl. The fingers twined about each other and about his own, so that three hands seemed to be wrought of one flesh, to become a thing of lovely weight at his arm's end. When it was quite dark they went to the beautiful room and lay where he and the hands could watch, through the window, the clean, bright stars swim up out of the forest. The house and the room were dark and silent. Ran was so happy that he hardly dared to breathe.

A hand fluttered up over his hair, down his cheek, and crawled into the hollow of his throat. Its pulsing matched the beat of his heart. He opened his own hands wide and clenched his fingers, as though to catch and hold this moment.

Soon the other hand crept up and joined the first. For perhaps an hour they lay there passive with their coolness against Ran's warm neck. He felt them with his throat, each smooth convolution, each firm small expanse. He concentrated, with his mind and his heart on his throat, on each part of the hands that touched him, feeling with all his being first one touch and then another, though the contact was there unmoving. And he knew it would be soon now, soon.

As if at a command, he turned on his back and dug his head into the pillow. Staring up at the vague dark hangings on the wall, he began to realize what it was for which he had been working and dreaming so long. He put his head back yet farther and smiled, waiting. This would be possession, completion. He breathed deeply, twice, and the hands began to move.

The thumbs crossed over his throat and the fingertips settled one by one under his ears. For a long moment they lay there, gathering strength. Together, then, in perfect harmony, each co-operating with the other, they became rigid, rock-hard. Their touch was still light upon him, still light . . . no, now they were passing their rigidity to him, turning it to a contraction. They settled to it slowly, their pressure measured and equal. Ran lay silent. He could not breathe now, and did not want to. His great arms were crossed on his chest, his knotted fists under his armpits, his mind knowing a great peace. Soon, now. . .

Wave after wave of engulfing, glorious pain spread and receded. He saw color impossible, without light. He arched his back, up, up . . . the hands bore down with all their hidden strength, and Ran's body bent like a bow, resting on feet and shoulders. Up, up. . .

Something burst within him—his lungs, his heart—no matter. It was complete.

There was blood on the hands of Bianca's mother when they found her in the morning in the beautiful room, trying to soothe Ran's neck. They took Bianca away, and they buried Ran, but they hanged Bianca's mother because she tried to make them believe Bianca had done it, Bianca whose hands were quite dead, drooping like brown leaves from her wrists.

Derm Fool

I AM NOT generally a fussy man. A bit of litter around my two-and-a-half-room dugout on the West Side seldom bothers me. What trash that isn't big enough to be pushed out in the hallway can be kicked around till it gets lost. But today was different. Myra was coming, and I couldn't have Myra see the place this way.

Not that she cared particularly. She knew me well enough by this time not to mind. But the particular *kind* of litter might be a bit—disturbing.

After I had swept the floor I began looking in odd corners. I didn't want any vagrant breeze to send unexplainable evidence fluttering out into the midst of the room—not while Myra was there. Thinking about her, I was almost tempted to leave one of the things where she could see it. She was generally so imperturbable—it might be amusing to see her hysterical.

I put the unchivalrous thought from me. Myra had always been very decent to me. I was a bit annoyed at her for making me like her so much when she was definitely not my type. Crawling under the bed, I found my slippers. My feet were still in them. I set one on top of the mantel and went into the other room, where I could sit down and wrench the foot out of the other slipper. They were odd slippers; the left was much bigger than the right. I swore and tugged at that right foot. It came out with a rustle; I rolled it up in a ball and tossed it into the wastepaper basket. Now let's see—oh, yes, there was a hand still clutching the handle of one of the bureau drawers. I went and pried it off. Why the deuce hadn't Myra called me up instead of wiring? No chance to head her off now. She'd just drift in, as usual. And me with all this on my mind—

I got the index finger off the piano and threw it and the left foot away, too. I wondered if I should get rid of the torso hanging in the hall closet, but decided against it. That was a fine piece. I might be able to make something good out of it; a suitcase, perhaps, or a rain-proof sports jacket. Now that I had all this raw material, I might as well turn it to my advantage.

I checked carefully. My feet were gone, so I wouldn't have to worry about them until the morning. My right hand, too; that was good. It would be awful to shake hands with Myra and have her find herself clinging to a disembodied hand. I pulled at the left. It seemed a little loose, but I didn't want to force it. This wasn't a painful disease as long as you let it have its own way. My face would come off any minute now. I'd try not to laugh too much; maybe I could keep it on until she had gone.

I put both hands around my throat and squeezed a little. My neck popped and the skin sloughed dryly off. Now that was all right. If I wore a necktie, Myra wouldn't be able to see the crinkling edges of skin just above my collarbone.

The doorbell buzzed and I started violently. As I stood up, the skin of my calf parted and fell off like a cellophane gaiter. I snatched it up and stuffed it under a sofa pillow and ran for the door. As I reached it, one of my ears gave a warning crackle; I tore it off and put it in my pocket and swung the door wide.

"David!" She said that, and it meant that she was glad to see me, and that it had been eight months since the last time, and she was feeling fine, and she was sorry she hadn't written, but then she never wrote letters—not to anybody.

She swooped past me into the room, paused as if she were folding wings, shrugged out of her coat without looking to see if I were there behind her to take it, because she knew I was, crossed her long legs and three-pointed gently on the rug. I put a cigarette into one extended hand and a kiss in the palm of the other, and it wasn't until then that she looked at me.

"Why—David! You're looking splendid! Come here. What have you done to your face? It's all crinkly. It looks sweet. You've been working too hard. Do I look nice? I feel nice. Look, new shoes. Snake-skin. Speaking of snakes, how are you, anyway?"

"Speaking of snakes, Myra, I'm going to pieces. Little pieces, that detach themselves from me and flutter in the gusts of my furious laboring. Something has gotten under my skin."

"How awful," she said, not really hearing me. She was looking at her nails, which were perfect. "It isn't because of me, is it? Have you been pining away for me, David? David, you still can't marry me, in case you were going to ask."

"I wasn't going to ask, but it's nice to know, anyway," I said. My face fell, and I grabbed it and hid it under my coat. She hadn't seen, thank heavens! There remained only my left hand. If I could get rid of it—good heavens! It was already gone!

It might be on the doorknob. Oh, she mustn't see it! I went to the foyer and searched hurriedly. I couldn't find it anywhere. Suppose it had caught in her wraps? Suppose it were on the floor somewhere near where she was sitting? Now that I was faced with it, I knew I couldn't bear to see her hysterical. She was such a—a *happy* person to have around. For the millionth time since that skinning knife had slipped, I muttered, "Now, why did this have to happen to *me?*"

I went back into the living room. Myra was still on the floor, though she had moved over under the light. She was toying curiously with the hand, and the smile on her face was something to see. I stood there speechless, waiting for the storm. I was used to it by this time, but Myra—

She looked up at me swiftly, in the birdlike way she had. She threw her glances so quickly that you never knew just how much she had seen—under all her chatter and her glittering idiosyncrasies was as calm and astute a brain as ever hid behind glamour.

The hand—it was not really a hand, but just the skin of one—was like a cellophane glove. Myra slipped it on her own and peeped through the fingers at me. "Hiya, fellow reptile," she giggled; and suddenly the giggles changed into frightened little squeaks, and she was holding out her arms to me, and her lovely face was distorted by tears so that it wasn't lovely any more, but sweet—oh, so darned sweet! She clung close to me and cried pitifully, "David, what are we going to *do?*"

I held her tight and just didn't know what to say. She began talking brokenly: "Did it bite you, too, David? It bit m-me, the little beast. The Indians worship it. Th-they say its bite will ch-change you into a snake... I was afraid... Next morning I began shedding my skin every twenty-four hours—and I have ever since." She snuggled even closer, and her voice calmed a little. It was a lovely voice, even now. "I could have killed the snake, but I didn't because I had never seen anything like it, and I thought you might like to have it—so I sent it, and now it's bitten you, and you're losing your skin all the time, too, and—oh-h-h!"

"Myra, don't. Please, don't. It didn't bite me. I was skinning it, and my knife slipped. I cut myself. The snake was dead when I got it. So—*you're* the one who sent it! I might have known. It came with no card or letter; of *course* it was you! How ... how long have you been this way?"

"F-four months." She sniffed, and blew her pink nose on my lapel because I had forgotten to put a handkerchief in my breast pocket. "I didn't care after ... after I found out that it didn't hurt, and that I could count on when parts of my skin would come off. I—thought it would go away after a while. And then I saw your hand in a store window in Albuquerque. It was a belt buckle—a hand holding a stick, with the wrist fastened to one end of the belt and the stick to the other; and I bought it and saw what it was, because the hand was stuffed with the perfumed moulage you always use for your hummingbird brooches and things—and anyway, you were the only one who *could* have designed such a fascinating belt, or who *would* have thought to use your own skin just because ... because you happened to have it around—and I hated myself then and l-loved you for it—" She twisted out of my arms and stared into my eyes, amazement written on her face, and joy. "And I do love you for it, right *now*, David, *now*, and I never loved anyone else before and I don't care"—she plucked my other ear, and the skin rustled away in her hand—"if you *are* all dilapidated!"

I saw it all now. Myra's crazy desire to climb a mesa, one of those island tableaux of the desert, where flora and fauna have gone their own ways these thousand thousand years; her discovering the snake, and catching it for me because I was a combination taxidermist and jeweler, and she had never seen anything like it and thought I might want it. Crazy, brave thing; she had been bitten and had said nothing to anybody because "it didn't hurt"; and then, when she found out that I had the same trouble, she had come streaking to New York to tell me it was her fault!

"If you feel that way about it, Myra," I said gently, "then I don't care at all about this . . . this dry rot . . . little snake in the grass—" I kissed her.

Amazing stuff, this cast-off skin. Regularly as clockwork, every twenty-four hours, the epidermis would toughen, loosen and slip off. It was astonishingly cohesive. My feet would leave their skin inside my slippers, keeping the exact shape of the limb on which it had grown. Flex the dead skin a couple of times, and it would wrinkle in a million places, become limp and flexible. The nails would come off, too, but only the topmost layer of cells. Treated with tannic acid and afterward with wool oil, it was strong, translucent and soft. It took shellac nicely, and a finish of Vandyke-brown oil paint mixed with bronze powder gave a beautiful old-gold effect. I didn't know whether I had an affliction or a commodity.

That snake— It was about four feet long, thicker at head and tail than it was in the middle. It was a lusterless orange, darker underneath than it was on top, but it was highly fluorescent. It smelled strongly of honey and formic acid, if you can imagine that for yourself. It had two fangs, but one was on top of its mouth and the other on the lower jaw. Its tongue was forked, but at the roots only; it had an epiglottis, seven sets of rudimentary limbs and no scales. I call it a snake because it was more nearly a snake than anything else. I think that's fair. Myra is mostly a Puckish angel, but you can still call her a woman. See? The snake was a little of this and a little of that, but I'll swear its origin was not of *this* earth. We stood there hand in hand, Myra and I, staring at the beast, and wondering what to do about it all.

"We might get rich by renting it to side shows," said Myra.

"Nobody would believe it. How about renting ourselves to the A.M.A.?" I asked.

She wrinkled her nose and that was out. Tough on the A.M.A.

"What are we going to do about it, David?" She asked me as if she thought I knew and trusted me because of it, which is a trick that altogether too many women know.

"Why, we'll—" And just then came the heavy pounding on the door.

Now, there is only one animal stupid enough to bang on a door when there is a bell to ring, and that is a policeman. I told Myra to stay there in the lab and wait, so she followed me into the foyer.

"You David Worth?" asked the man. He was in plain clothes, and he had a very plain face.

"Come in," I said.

He did, and sat down without being asked, eyeing the whiskey decanter with little but evident hope. "M'-name's Brett. H. Brett."

"H. for Halitosis?" asked Myra gently.

"Naw, Horace. What do I look like, a Greek? Hey, headquarters's checkin' on them ornaments o' y'rs, Mr. Worth." The man had an astonishing ability to masticate his syllables. "They look like they're made of human skin. Y'r a taxidoimist, ain'tcha?"

"I am. So?"

"So where'dja get th' ror material? Pleece analysis says it's human skin. What do you say?"

I exchanged a glance with Myra. "It is," I said.

It was evidently not the answer Brett expected. "Ha!" he said triumphantly. "Where'd you get it, then?"

"Grew it."

Myra began to skip about the room because she was enjoying herself. Brett picked up his hat from the floor and clung to it as if it were the only thing he could trust. I began to take pity on him.

"What did they do down there, Brett? Microscopic cross-section? Acid and base analyses?"

"Yeah."

"Tell me; what have they got down there—hands?"

"Yeah, and a pair o' feet. Bookends."

"You always did have beautiful feet, darling," caroled Myra.

"Tell you what I'll do, Brett," I said. I got a sheet of paper, poured some ink onto a blotter, and used it as a stamp pad. I carefully put each fingertip in the ink and pressed it to the paper. "Take that down to headquarters and give it to your suspicious savants. Tell them to compare these prints with those from the ornaments. Write up your reports and turn them in with a recommendation that the whole business be forgotten; for if it isn't I shall most certainly sue the city, and you, and anyone else who gets in my way, for defamation of character. I wouldn't consider it impolite, Mr. Brett, if you got out of here right away, without saying good night." I crossed the room and held the door open for him.

His eyes were slightly glazed. He rose and walked carefully around Myra, who was jumping up and down and clapping her hands, and scuttled out. Before I could close the door again he whirled and stuck his foot in it.

"Lissen. I don't know what's goin' on here, see? Don't you or that lady try to leave here, see? I'm havin' the place watched from now on, see? You'll hear from me soon's I get to headquarters, see?"

"You're a big seesee," said Myra over my shoulder; and before I could stop her she plucked off her nose and threw it in the detective's face. He moved away, so fast that he left his hat hanging in midair; seconds later we heard the violence of his attempted passage down four flights of stairs when there were only three.

Myra danced three times around the room and wound up at the top of the piano—no mean feat, for it was a bulky old upright. She sat there laughing and busily peeling off the rest of her face.

"A certain something tells me," I said when I could talk, which was after quite a while, "that you shouldn't have done that. But I'm glad you did. I don't think Detective Inspector Horace Halitosis Brett will be around any more."

Myra gestured vaguely toward her bag. I tossed it to her, and she began dabbing at nose and lips in the skillful, absent way women have. "There," she said when she had finished. "Off with the old— on with the new."

"You're the first woman in creation who gets beauty treatments in spite of herself. Pretty neat."

"Not bad," she said impersonally to her mirror. "Not bad, Myra!"

Thinking of her, watching her, made me suddenly acutely conscious of her. It happens that way sometimes. You know you love the gal, and then suddenly you *realize* it. "Myra—"

I think she had a gag coming, but when she looked at me she didn't say anything. She hopped down off the piano and came over to me. We stood there for a long time.

"You sleep in there," I said, nodding toward the bedroom. "I'll—"

She put her arms around me. "David—"

"Mm-m-m?"

"I'll—have a nice torso for you at 12:48—"

So we stuck around and talked until 12:48.

It must have been about two weeks later, after we were married, that she started breaking bottles in my laboratory. She came into the laboratory one afternoon and caught me cold. I was stirring a thick mass in a beaker and sniffing at it, and was so intent on my work that I never heard her come in. She moved like thistledown when she wanted to.

"What are you cooking, darling?" she asked as she put away a beautiful pair of arms she had just "manufactured."

I put the beaker on the bench and stood in front of it. "Just some ... sort of ... er ... stickum I'm mixing up for— Myra, beat it, will you? I'm busy as—"

She slid past me and picked up the beaker. "Hm-m-m. Pretty. *Snff.* Honey and—formic acid. Using the smell of that beast as a lead, are you? Dr. David Worth, trying to find a cure for a gold mine. It's a cure, isn't it? Or trying to be?" Her tone was very sweet. Boy, was she sore!

"Well ... yes," I admitted. I drew a deep breath. "Myra, we can't go on like this. For myself I don't care, but to have you spending the rest of your life shedding your epidermis like a ... blasted cork oak—it's too much. You've been swell about it, but I can't take it. You're too swell, and it's too much for my conscience. Every time I come in here and start stuffing something of yours, I begin worrying about you. It hasn't been bad, so far—but, woman, think of it! The rest of your life, sloughing off your hide, worrying about whether or not you can find somewhere to take your face off when you're not home; trying to remember where you dropped a hand or a leg. You—Myra, you're not listening."

"Of course I'm not. I never listen to you when you're talking nonsense."

"It isn't nonsense!" I was getting sore.

"I wonder," she said dreamily, sloshing the mess around in the beaker, "whether this thing will bounce." She dropped it on the floor and looked curiously. It didn't bounce. I stood there fumbling for a cuss word strong enough, and wondering whether or not I could move fast enough to poke her one.

"David, listen to me. How long have you been a taxidermist?"

"Oh—eleven years. What's that got—"

"Never mind. And how much money have you saved in eleven years?"

"Well, none, until recently. But lately—"

"Quiet. And you have eight hundred-odd in the bank now. Those stuffed-skin gadgets sell faster than we can make them. And just because you have some funny idea that I don't like to give you my— by-products, you want to cut the water off, go back to stuffing squirrels and hummingbirds for buttons. David, you're a fool—a derm fool."

"That's not very punny."

She winced. "But here's the main thing, David. You've got this trouble, and so have I. We've been cashing in on it, and will, if only you'll stop being stupid about it. The thing I like about it is that we're partners—I'm *helping* you. I love you. Helping you means more to me than— Oh, David, can't you see? Can't you?"

I kissed her. "And I thought you were just a good sport," I whispered. "And I thought some of it was mock heroics. Myra—" Oh, well. She won. I lost. Women are funny that way. But I still had an idea or two about a cure—

I'd been wrong about the indefatigable Inspector Brett. It was Myra who found out that he was tailing us everywhere, parking for hours in a doorway across the street, and sometimes listening at the door.

I'd never have known it; but, as I've pointed out before, Myra has superhuman qualities. When she told me about it, I was inclined to shrug it off. He didn't have anything on us. I had to laugh every time I thought of what must have gone on at police headquarters when they checked up on my fingerprints and those of the hands they had bought in the stores.

The fact that it was human skin, and that the prints were identical in dozens of specimens, must have given them a nasty couple of days. Prove that the axiom about two points and a straight line is false, and where's your whole science of geometry? And prove that there can be not only identical fingerprints, but *dozens* of identical ones, and you have a lot of experts walking around in circles and talking to themselves.

Brett must have appointed himself to crack this case. I was quite willing to let him bang his head against a wall. It would feel nice when he stopped. I should have known Myra better. She had a glint in her eye when she talked about that gang buster.

In the meantime I kept working on that cure. I felt like a heel to skulk around behind Myra's back that way. You see, she trusted me. We'd had that one row about it, and I'd given in. That was enough for her. She wouldn't spy on me when I was working alone in the lab; and I knew that if she did realize it, suddenly, she would be deeply hurt. But this thing was too big. I *had* to do what I was doing, or go nuts.

I had a lead. The formic-honey idea was out, as a cure, though certain ingredients in them, I was sure, had something to do with the cause. That cause was amazingly simple. I could put it down here in three words. But do you think I would? *Heh.* I've got a corner on this market—

But this was my lead: My *hair* never came off! And I wear a minuscule mustache; every time my face came off it left the mustache. I have very little body hair; now, with this trouble, I had none. It came off, for the follicles were comparatively widely separated. First, I thought that this phenomenon was due to a purely physical anchorage of the skin by the hair roots. But, I reasoned, if that had been the case, layer after layer of skin would have formed under my mustache. But that did not happen. Evidently, then, this amazing separative and regenerative process was nullified by something at the hair roots. I could tell you what it was, too, but—I should knife myself in the back!

I worked like a one-armed pianist playing Mendelssohn's "Spinning Song." It took months, but by repeated catalysis and refinement, I finally had a test tube full of clear golden liquid. And—know what it was? Look: I hate to be repetitious, but I'm not saying. Let it suffice that it can be bought by the gallon at your corner drugstore. Nobody knew about it as a cure for my peculiar disease—if you want to call it that—because as far as I know no one had ever seen the disease before. *Bueno.*

Then I went to work on the cause. It didn't take long. As I have said, the most baffling thing about the trouble was its simplicity.

In the windup, I had it. An injection to cause the trouble, a lotion to cure or isolate it. I got ten gallons of each fluid—no trouble, once I knew what to get—and then began worrying about how to break the news to Myra.

"Kirro," I said to her one day, "I want a good face from you tonight. I want to make a life mask of you. Have to get all set first, though. You lose your face at 8:45, don't you? Well, come into the lab at 8:30. We'll plaster you with clay, let it dry so that it draws the face off evenly, back it with moulage, and wash the clay off after the moulage has hardened. Am I brilliant?"

"You scintillate," she said. "It's a date."

I started mixing the clay, though I knew I wouldn't use it. Not to take her face off, anyway. I felt like a louse.

She came in on time as if she hadn't even looked at a clock—how I envy her that trick!—and sat down. I dipped a cloth in my lotion and swabbed her well with it. It dried immediately, penetrating deeply. She sniffed.

"What's that?"

"Sizing," I said glibly.

"Oh. Smells like—"

"*Shh.* Someone might be listening." That for you, dear reader!

I went behind her with a short length of clothesline. She lay back in the chair with her eyes closed, looking very lovely. I leaned over and kissed her on the lips, drawing her hands behind her. Then I moved fast. There was a noose at each end of the line; I whipped one around her wrists, drew it tight, threw it under the back rung of the chair, and dropped the other end over her head. "Don't move, darling," I whispered. "You'll be all right if you keep still. Thrash around and you'll throttle yourself." I put the clock where she could see it and went out of there. I don't want to hear my very best beloved using that kind of language.

She quieted down after about ten minutes. "David!"

I tried not to listen.

"David—please!"

I came to the door. "Oh, David, I don't know what you're up to, but I guess it's all right. Please come here where I can look at you. I . . . I'm afraid!"

I should have known better. Myra was never afraid of anything in her life. I walked over and stood in front of her. She smiled at me. I came closer. She kicked me in the stomach. "That's for tying me up, you . . . you heel. Now, what goes on?"

After I got up off the floor and got my gasping done, I said, "What time is it, bl—er, light of my life?"

"Ten minutes to ni— David! David, what have you done? Oh, you fool! You utter dope! I told you— Oh, *David!*" And for the second and last time in my life, I saw her cry. Ten minutes to nine and her face was still on. Cured!—at least, her face. I went behind her where she couldn't reach me.

"Myra, I'm sorry I had to do it this way. But—well, I know how you felt about a cure. I'd never have been able to talk you into taking it. This was the only way. What do you think of me now, stubborn creature?"

"I think you're a pig. Terribly clever, but still a pig. Untie me. I want to make an exit."

I grinned. "Oh, no. Not until the second-act curtain. Don't go away!" I went over to the bench and got my hypodermic. "Don't move, now. I don't want to break this mosquito needle off in your jaw." I swabbed her gently around the sides of the face with the lotion, to localize the shot.

"I ... hope your intentions are honorable," she said through clenched teeth as the needle sank into the soft flesh under her jawbone. "I—Oh! Oh! It ... itches. David—"

Her face went suddenly crinkly. I caught her skin at the forehead and gently peeled it off. She stared wide-eyed, then said softly:

"I can't kiss you, marvelous man, unless you untie me—"

So I did, and she did, and we went into the living room where Myra could rejoice without breaking anything of value.

In the middle of a nip-up she stopped dead, brain wave written all over her face. "David, we're going to do some entertaining." She sat there in the middle of the floor and began to scream. And I mean she could scream.

In thirty seconds flat, heavy footsteps—also flat—pounded on the stairs, and Brett's voice bellowed: "Op'n up in th' name o' th' law!" He's the only man I ever met who could mumble at the top of his voice.

Myra got up and ran to the door. "Oh—Mr. Brett. How nice," she said in her best hostess voice. "Do come in."

He glowered at her. "What's goin' *on* here?"

She looked at him innocently. "Why, Mr. Brett—"

"Was you screamin'?"

She nodded brightly. "I like to scream. Don't you?"

"Naw. What'a idear?"

"Oh, sit down and I'll tell you about it. Here. Have a drink." She poured him a tumbler of whiskey so strong I could almost see it raise its dukes. She pushed him into a chair and handed it to him. "Drink up. I've missed you."

He goggled up at her uncertainly. "Well—I dunno. Gee, t'anks. Here's how, Miz Worth." And he threw it down the hatch. It was good stuff. Each of his eyes independently scanned his nose. He blinked twice and regretfully set the glass down. She refilled it, signaling behind her back for me to shut up. I did. When Myra acts this way there is nothing to do but stand by and wonder what's going to happen next.

Well, she got Brett started on the history of his life. Every two hundred words he'd empty that glass. Then she started mixing them. I was afraid that would happen. Her pet—for other's consumption; she wouldn't touch it—was what she called a "Three-two-one." Three fingers of whiskey, two of gin, one of soda. Only in Brett's case she substituted rum for the soda. Poor fellow.

In just an hour and a half he spread out his arms, said, "Mammy!" and folded up.

Myra looked down at him and shook her head. "*Tsk, tsk*. Pity I didn't have any knockout drops."

"Now what?" I breathed.

"Get your hypo. We're going to infect John Law here."

"Now Myra—wait a minute. We can't—"

"Who says? Come on, David—he won't know a thing. Look—here's what we'll do with him."

She told me. It was a beautiful idea. I got my mosquito, and we went to work. We gave him a good case; shots of the stuff all over his body. He slept peacefully through it all, even the gales of merriment. The more we thought of it— Ah, poor fellow!

After we had what we wanted from him I undressed him and swabbed him down with the lotion. He'd be good as new when he came to. I put him to bed in the living room, and Myra and I spent the rest of the night working in the lab.

When we finished, we took the thing and set it in the living room. Brett's breathing was no longer stertorous; he was a very strong man. Myra tiptoed in and put the alarm clock beside him. Then we watched from the crack of the laboratory door.

The first rays of the sun were streaming through the windows, lighting up our masterpiece. The alarm went off explosively; Brett started, groaned, clutched his head. He felt around for the clock, knocked it off the chair. It fell shouting under the daybed. Brett groaned again, blinked his eyes open. He stared at the window first, trying vaguely to find out what was wrong with it. I could almost hear him thinking that, somehow, he didn't know where he was. The clock petered out. Brett began to stare dazedly about the room. The ceiling, the walls, and—

There in the geometric center of the room stood Detective Inspector Horace Brett, fully clothed. His shield glittered in the sun. On his face was a murderous leer, and in his hand was a regulation police hogleg, trained right between the eyes of the man on the bed. They stared at each other for ten long seconds, the man with the hangover and the man's skin with the gun. Then Brett moved.

Like a streak of light he hurtled past the effigy. My best corduroy bedspread streaming behind him, clad only in underwear and a wrist watch, he shot through the door—and I mean *through,* because he didn't stop to open it—and wavered shrieking down the stairs. I'd never have caught him if he hadn't forgotten again that there were only three flights of stairs there. He brought up sharp against the wall; I was right behind him. I caught him up and toted him back up to the apartment before the neighbors had a chance to come rubbering around. Myra was rolling around on the floor. As I came in with Brett, she jumped up and kissed his gun-toting image, calling it fondly a name that should have been reserved for me.

We coddled poor Brett and soothed him; healed his wounds and sobered him up. He was sore at first and then grateful; and, to give him due credit, he was a good sport. We explained everything. We didn't have to swear him to secrecy. We had the goods on him. If I hadn't caught up with him, he'd have run all the way to headquarters in his snuggies.

It was not an affliction, then; it was a commodity. The business spread astonishingly. We didn't let it get too big; but what with a little false front and a bit more ballyhoo, we are really going places. For instance, in Myra's exclusive beauty shop is a booth reserved for the wealthiest patrons. Myra will use creams and lotions galore on her customer by way of getting her into the mood; then, after isolating the skin on her face, will infect it with a small needle. In a few minutes the skin comes off; a mud pack hides it. The lady has a lovely smooth new face; Myra ships the old one over to my place where my experts mount it. Then, through Myra's ballyhoo, the old lady generally will come around wanting a life mask. I give her a couple of appointments—they amount to séances—sling a lot of hocus pocus, and in due time deliver the mask—life-size, neatly tinted.

They never know, poor old dears, that they have contracted and been cured of the damnedest thing that ever skipped inclusion in "Materia Medica." It's a big business now; we're coining money.

Like all big business, of course, it has its little graft. A certain detective comes around three times a week for a thirty-second shave, free of charge. He's good people. His effigy still menaces our living room, with a toy gun now. Poor fellow.

He Shuttles

"Why are you sitting here alone in this little room?" asked the man.

"I am not alone any more, because you have come," I told him. He had not been there an hour ago, or a minute ago either, but I was not surprised. That was because it was this man, and no other.

"Why are you sitting here, looking at a white sheet of paper in your typewriter, pulling your ear with one hand and that fuzzy hair with the other?" he asked.

"I am doing it because I am a person who writes stories for other people to read," I said. "But I am not writing now because I can't think of anything to write about. That makes me unhappy, so I pull my ear and my hair. It isn't fuzzy."

"It is fuzzy." The man looked at me for a little while. "Are the stories you write true?"

"No," I said. "I have never written a story that was true. People don't like to read things that are true. They only like things that might be true. One must be very clever to write a story that is true and make it seem as if it might be true. And I am not very clever, so I must rely on my imagination."

"Oh," he said, as if he understood me, which was surprising because I'm sure I didn't know what I was talking about.

"I will tell you a story," he said. "But it is a true story, and must be believed. If I tell you the story, will you believe it?"

"If it is a good story, I don't care whether it is true or not," I said. "If credence is the price I must pay, I pay it gladly." I set my margin, lit a cigarette and looked at him.

He said again, "The story is true." And he began to speak. This is what he said:

I was going about the world doing my duty, when my attention was called to a man named MacIlhainy Tobin, whose conceit was phenomenal. It was unfortunate and incurable, because it was quite justified. He was indeed a superior person. He did not need my help, because his wits were so very sharp; but when I offered it he took advantage of it, for he was one of those who never miss an opportunity for gain. I did not offer him gain, but neither had those of whom he had taken advantage in the past. He felt that he could twist whatever circumstance crossed his path into something of value for him. And in this instance he was misled purely because he had no precedent to follow that involved failure.

He was alone in his great study, thinking of the things he had done and been which proved his superiority. "I am a man," he said, "who has never made a mistake."

"That is not true," I said to him. "Perfection is an unnatural thing, and against laws that cannot be broken. You exist, and you are perfect. That is your mistake."

He looked over his plainlike desk at me.

"I have never seen you before, sir," he said cordially. "I did not see you come into my room or sit opposite me, but I am not startled. You are welcome."

"Thank you," I said. "I startle nobody. You are proud of yourself?"

"Yes," he said, and smiled. He was a magnificent man, with a great square jaw and large gray eyes. His hair was like burnished platinum, and the lamplight delighted in leaping from it. "I have everything I want, including the desire for things which I may not have. I am complete, and in flux, and therefore greatly contented with myself."

"You have been ruthless," I said.

He smiled and spread his hands. "I have been logical."

"You have paid the penalties for all you have done?"

"Yes. One must. That, too, is logical."

"Are you proud of that, then?"

No one may be angry toward me, but if it had been possible, he would have been furious. "That is my one shame," he said softly. "That in the reasonable course of events, even such as I must bow to circumstance. I regret that there are powers beyond my control. My ego is as well-ordered and methodical as it can possibly be, and yet I am forced to turn aside from the creations of fools whose stupidity has led them to believe that their lives are for purposes which cannot benefit me."

"You are ashamed of being human, then. No human can achieve divinity and stay human—without my help."

He raised his silver eyebrows. "What is divinity?"

"Complete satisfaction. I ask you, then: Granting that, what is divinity?"

He stared at his hands. "For me, it would be . . . it would be power. Complete control over all the Universe. If I could receive the homage from all things, past, present and future, living and unliving and dead, that I get now from my own ego, then I would be completely satisfied."

"Do you want that, then?"

He was silent for a long while, thinking. "No!" he said suddenly. "It would be *ne plus ultra*. Could I not fight fools, I could no longer be contented with myself, for my successes. I have more powers now than those you offer me; for if everything were possible to me, I would lose all urges. That loss I cannot afford. What powers have you?"

"I have none," I told him, "except the ability to give powers. These must be of your choice."

"Wishes, then?"

I nodded. "Three wishes—and they will be true to the letter."

"I have heard of the things you have done," he said. "You are a legend in many lands. Why have you invariably given three wishes to fools?"

"I have never met any others."

He laughed uproariously. "Even for such as you," he said, wiping his eyes, "there must be new experiences. You are about to have one. You will grant me three wishes, and find out that I am not a fool. You may even find out a thing or two about yourself."

"I am not a personality, but an instrument," I told MacIlhainy Tobin. "I can no more find out anything about myself than can that beautiful paper knife discover that it was stolen from the British Museum. I have my function and I perform it."

"What is your source, then? For whom do you do your work?"

"That is beyond my ability to question. Perhaps I, too, am a stolen instrument—and perhaps again I am that source. You are fumbling with the unknowable. It is not like you to fumble."

"*Touché.* Will you give me time to consider my wishes?"

"The wishes are yours, to use as you please, when you please. I will be ready when you are." I left him then. He sat for a long while looking at the empty chair across that great desk. Then he laughed and went to bed.

MacIlhainy Tobin was an extremely well-disciplined man. He did not let my visit interfere with his daily life. He ran his great corporations and held his conferences and played his excellent golf, just as usual. But all the while he thought. He thought of the power that was his for the asking, and the homage. Often he thought of himself, and of what a power he was in the world. Sometimes he thought of me, and wondered frankly if my coming was a reward, or a test, or a punishment.

He spent long hours over his books, and he bought more and more books. He read legends and histories and fairy tales, and learned what others had done with my three wishes. Sometimes he laughed richly, and sometimes he frowned and bit his lip.

There were those who did not seem to be fools, and yet they were all made unhappy by the wishes, ultimately. They were returned, by their impulsiveness, to their original states, or they asked for things that were too great for them to handle, and went mad. There were a few who were philosophic, and said that now they would be happy to cultivate their own gardens. There did not seem to be any malice in the fulfillment of my three wishes. Each was given exactly the things for which he asked. And yet, without exception, each had been hurt, usually quite terribly, by the power I had given.

When MacIlhainy Tobin thought of this, he would pull his lip and scowl. And he made up his mind to outwit me. That was hardly just, I thought; for it was his power, not mine. He would have to outwit himself, then, not me. It would be interesting to see if his wits were sharp enough for that task. No one had ever done it before. I bore him no malice, I think because I can bear none toward anyone.

It was two years before MacIlhainy Tobin was ready for me, and in that time he had formulated thousands of wishes, and rejected thousands. I knew he was ready because he had begun to suffer.

"May I talk with you before I state my wishes?" he asked me when he saw me again.

"Certainly."

"When you grant me a wish, is it a complete thing? For example, should I wish to be a bird, would I be a bird exactly like other birds, or would I differ?"

I smiled. "MacIlhainy Tobin, you are the first man who has ever asked me that question. No, you would differ, for there is that about you, and about all men, which is beyond us, you and I. There is a small part of you that which is completely you, and yet different. It can observe, and feel, but only in terms of you as you are now. It has no will; it cannot control you or any part of you. It is something that you have built yourself, something that neither of us can touch or change or destroy. That, no matter what you wish to be, you must carry with you."

"I expected that. A soul, eh?"

"I don't know. I know nothing of that. I can grant your wishes. If one of them is that you know—"

He shook his head. "I'd rather not."

"You are indeed an amazing man, MacIlhainy Tobin."

"Yes. Tell me, may I postpone one, or two, or all, of these wishes?"

"Of course; they belong to you."

"And may I have them consecutively, the fulfillment of the second to begin after the completion of the first?"

"Yes." A cautious man, this.

He sat silent for a moment, his eyes glittering. "How can a man avoid paying the penalties for his acts?" he asked me suddenly.

"By dying—"

"Ah," he said. "Very well, I am ready to state my wishes."

I waited.

"First, from the time I awake tomorrow morning until the time I go to sleep tomorrow night, I want complete obedience from my fellow men, complete dominance of my will over theirs."

"Granted."

"Second, I want complete freedom from penalties of any and all kinds for my acts during that time."

"You are indeed an extraordinary man, MacIlhainy Tobin. You want death, then?"

"By no means," he chuckled. "You see, tomorrow I shall be careful to do something that carries a penalty of death." He laughed softly.

"You consider that a master stroke. You have exhausted only two wishes, and yet have what others would have required dozens to cover. You may have riches, authority, worship, invulnerability, revenge—anything you desire. Remarkable. Why do you limit yourself to one day?"

"Because I can plan one day. To plan more than that in minute detail would leave me open to a possible shift in circumstances. With what I can do in one day, I'll have all I can ever want, in every way."

"But suppose you live only a week or two after tomorrow; have you thought of that?"

"Yes. Is my second wish granted?"

"Granted. The third?"

"Postponement of the third."

"Ah—you wish to be deprived of the power to make that third wish? Until when?"

"Until I begin the day after tomorrow."

"Perfect. If you find it advantageous to return to your present state, or to continue your powers, or your life indefinitely, you will be able to. May I congratulate you?"

The slight inclination of his massive head was acceptance. "May I ask one more question?"

"Of course."

"I know that I shall be free of penalties tomorrow. But how will this be done?"

"If you do something to include death as one of your penalties,

247

then your freedom must be arranged in the only other way possible."

"And that is—"

"I do not know. All I can do is give you your wishes."

"Very well. Good-bye," MacIlhainy Tobin said to the empty room.

Tobin awoke vastly refreshed. It had been a pleasant evening, he thought, and he rather admired himself for sleeping so well after it. Today, then, was his day.

Landis was stepping softly about, opening the drapes to the early morning sun. He picked up a tray and brought it to Tobin's huge bed.

"Six o'clock, sir." Landis stood and moved as if the ramrod up his back were woven of barbed wire. The only detectable line of demarcation between his chin and his neck was his faultless little tie, all of which by no means detracted from his excellence as a butler-valet.

"Ah—Landis. Good." Tobin watched the man's deft hands blend three coffees in the silver-bound eggshell cup. "Has Synthetic Rubber moved?"

"According to the wire service, sir, it will advance one and seven-eighths at opening this morning. Mr. Krill, of Schambers Brokerage, gave the wrong information."

"Splendid. I shall deal with Mr. Krill." Tobin brooked no interference on the part of any of the string of brokers who were forced to report all overnight orders to him. "Anything else?"

"The German army opened a new offensive during the night. Three more ships have been sunk. The president has suggested, off the record, another special session of Congress. In Tokyo—"

"Never mind all that. Today I shall be occupied with more personal matters. How's the Groot situation?"

"Mr. Groot was found dead an hour ago, sir. Suicide."

Tobin clucked happily. "What a pity. I shall have to take over his holdings. Anything else?"

"That is all, sir."

"Er—Landis—you hate my guts, don't you?"

The butler recoiled. "Why, sir—"

248

"Tell the truth." Tobin's voice was very soft.

"I do. You're the most cold-blooded scoundrel in creation. I've met many sharks since I have worked for you, but you're the grand-daddy of them all."

Tobin laughed easily. "That will do, Landis. You will forget this incident. Is my bath ready?"

"Your bath is ready, sir," said Landis, as if no one had previously mentioned a bath.

"Good. Get out of here."

"Very good, sir."

Tobin lay back on the pillow and chuckled. It worked, then. Had he not the power to demand the truth and get it, Landis could never have brought himself to such an admission. Nor could he have forgotten it that way. He would have taken his dignity and his morning coat away forever; Tobin knew him. Still smiling, he went and luxuriated in his tub.

He chose a soft gray suit of radical cut—he could wear those seamless shoulders and still look broad and powerful. A light gray shirt. And as he remembered that he had some murdering to do today, he chose a deep purple tie, which somehow suited the occasion—crepe soles, of course; they would come in handy. Homburg; the stained bamboo cane; a ring to match his tie; ah, splendid.

"The town car, sir?" asked Landis.

"I'll walk." He strode out of the house, leaving his butler shocked and shaken at such a radical departure from habit. He must remember to have Landis recall his pretty speech of the morning; the fool would probably drop dead.

He walked to the corner and stood there waiting for the light to change, enjoying the morning air. A round-shouldered youth touched his arm.

"Mister, you look like Wall Street to me—"

Tobin regarded him frigidly.

"As a fellow investor, I want to tell you that Bowery Flophouse is up five points, McGinnis' hash joint is up two blocks, an' I'm up a tree. Situation shaky. How's about a couple dimes? You won't feel it, an' it'll make me feel richer'n you look."

Tobin laughed and clapped him on the shoulder. "As I live and breathe, a panhandler with originality!" He looked the threadbare creature over curiously. Might as well get it over with; this trash would be as good as any. "You can do something for me."

"Sure, boss. Sure. Name it an' it's yours."

Tobin knew that. "Look! See that big tractor-trailer job that just pulled up for the light? Get underneath it; lie down with your chest up against a tire. Go ahead; now."

The youth's eyes glazed a little, and he went off to do what he was told. Tobin walked on casually, glad to have the killing off his mind. "His life for mine; it's rather a pity. I might have found some-one more worthy."

A shrill scream behind him did nothing to his steady pace. Hor-ror and shame were penalties—and today he paid none.

Curiosity, though, did what shame could not. It would be a con-founded nuisance if the boy bungled the job. He stopped and turned. The crowd he expected was milling around the truck; and then he saw a policeman, supporting the reeling panhandler. The boy was fighting to go back to the truck; strong hands kept him away. Of course! Some idiot had seen him, pulled him out in time. Rage surged through Tobin; rage, and hatred of anyone foolish enough to inter-fere with MacIlhainy Tobin. He snapped himself into line quickly, though. He had all day. He turned and went again toward his offices.

"Good heavens!" I said, letting my fingers slip off the keys. "Must you go about the world making it possible for people to do that sort of thing?"

"Must you write stories?" asked the man.

"Well—to keep on living. But you—"

"Just," he nodded, "to remain extant."

"But what's the differ— Oh, I—see. Will you have some wine?"

"Thank you."

He extended a small crystal cup and it touched my arm and was full. There was a . . . a pale spot on my arm—

"Please go on," I said.

"Sykes!" Tobin boomed as he strode into his office suite.

"Yes, sir."

Sykes would be a little annoying, Tobin realized, for he would be precisely the same under stress of Tobin's new and absolute command as he was at any other time.

"Get in touch with every available holder of a seat in the Stock Exchange. Have them all here at ten o'clock. Miss Twigg! Have papers drawn up for each of the men that Sykes brings in, signing over to me complete ownership of ninety percent of their properties, holdings, and interests, corporative or private. Miss Allen, I want Krill here immediately. Farrel! Sykes, where the devil is Farrel? Three minutes late? When he comes in, fire him. After seven years with me he should know better. Miss Betteredge, read my mail, except the personals. Miss Willis, read the personals. Philip, drop the profits on 227, 89 and 812, and put them all in Synthetic Rubber. It's good for two points today. I'm riding it. Give it a number. Sykes! Damn it, where's— Oh. I don't want to see anyone but Krill. If Thurston and Greenblatt phone, tell them no. Farrel! Where— That's right, Sykes. Thanks. Promote Goober, but give him ten dollars a week less than Farrel was getting. Get out of the way." And, smoothly as ever, the day was begun.

Once in his office, Tobin shrugged out of his coat and threw off his hat. Both were caught expertly before they reached the nub-piled carpet, by the omnipresent Sykes. "Anything else, sir?"

"Yes. Go to hell. Wait a minute! Don't take me so seriously, man! Get busy on those property transfers. You're about to be working for the richest man in creation. *Move,* now!"

The communicator gave its discreet whisper.

"Well?"

"There are seven hundred and twelve members of the Stock Exchange on the way to the auditorium. The rest are either unavailable or refuse to come unless they have more information."

"Refuse? Refuse? Tell them that if they don't get here immediately, the whole financial world is going to smash—really smash, this time. Tell them I will give all the details when they get here. That'll scare them. They know me."

"Yes, Mr. Tobin. Mr. Krill is waiting."

"Krill, eh? Send him right in."

The broker was a slender man with a wide forehead and a little pointed chin. He was pale—his face, his eyes, his hands. He came straight across the room and put his hands on Tobin's desk.

"All right, Tobin. I can take it. You have too many noses scattered around. I knew you'd smell me out."

"Why did you quote the wrong price on Synthetic, then?"

"I'd tell you, and it would make some difference to you if you were human."

"Unfortunately, Krill, I'm not particularly human today," Tobin said, and smiled. "Tell me, anyway."

"I've had my eye on Synthetic Rubber for quite a while. I didn't know you controlled it, or I wouldn't have touched it. I got a tip and put every cent of capital of the United Charities into it. Dozens of organizations whose business is caring for poor, sick and old people. I've done wonders for United in the time I've handled their investments. I didn't think your man would be interested in the stock, or the fact that I would jump it. I thought I could get out with a decent profit this morning before you were interested. I quoted a lower price on it on the slim chance that you'd have the information from no one else. I lost. If I try to sell now, I'll be delayed until you dump; I know that. And you can afford to keep the price down until I must let those shares go. What are you going to do?"

"You had no business giving me false information." Tobin flicked a switch.

"Yes, sir?" said the communicator.

"Dump Synthetic."

"Yes, sir."

Krill stood quite still. "Eighty thousand people—sick people, Tobin, and kids—are going to suffer because you did that. My mistake for hoping."

"Are you going to kill yourself now, Krill?" Tobin asked conversationally.

"Wh—"

"Tell me!"

"What else can I do?"

"Krill, there's something I tried to do this morning that didn't work out. I'll have to try again. It might as well be you. Never let it be said I wouldn't help out a man in a jam. Krill, I don't want you cluttering up my office. Go out into the waiting room and die. Go on!"

Krill looked at him strangely and his lips writhed. He closed the door very gently behind him.

Tobin drew interlocking circles on his scratch pad for a few minutes. The communicator buzzed.

"Yes?"

"Mr. Tobin! Mr. Krill just collapsed in the waiting room!"

"*Tsk, tsk!* Will he be all right?"

"He's—dead, Mr. Tobin."

He snapped off the instrument and laughed to himself. Ah, well. He was not the first man who had cheated death by giving the old fellow another customer.

"Sykes!"

The secretary popped up like a neat little jack-in-the-box.

"Mr. Tobin. I . . . I couldn't help hearing what you said to Mr. Krill. It . . . it's uncanny—" He mopped his rabbit-face. "You told him, and . . . and he— My goodness!"

This was annoying. "Sykes, you heard nothing, remember, nothing of this affair. Understand?"

Sykes said blankly: "You called me, Mr. Tobin?"

Tobin nodded, more to himself than to Sykes. "How many of the Exchange members are here?"

"Eleven hundred odd, sir. That's about all we can expect, I'm afraid. The rest are out of reach or willing to chance not coming."

"Hm-m-m. Get whoever is drawing up those property transfers and change 'ninety percent' to 'one hundred percent' on all those to be signed by holdouts. The fools— In the meantime, get all of them on the phone—a conference line. I'll talk to them all at once."

"Yes, sir."

"Then go down to the auditorium and tell those who have come to take it easy and keep quiet until I get there."

Left alone again, Tobin beamed upon himself. Things were going fine. He'd have everything finished by two this afternoon at this rate, and then he'd have the whole evening to himself. There ought to be a great many amusing things to do. The phone rang.

"Conference call, sir."

"How many are on the line?"

"Six hundred and twenty-four, sir."

"Good. That will be enough. Put 'em on."

The connection was made. "Hello—MacIlhainy Tobin, New York. I want each of you to give me absolute attention. Do not hang up.

"Each and every one of you will have drawn up a document signing over to me all your holdings, private possessions, interests and enterprises. Everything you own, in whole or in part. No loopholes; I want ironclad documents. I want them signed, witnessed, and in the mail before twenty-four hours from the present time. There is no need for me to persuade or threaten you; you will do as I say because you want to and because you must. You will let no one stop you, or change your documents in any way. Those of you who wish may apply for positions in my organization. Remuneration will be on a merit basis. That is all. Drop everything and attend to this immediately."

He hung up and signaled the switchboard. "Put me on the annunciator in the auditorium."

Over the loudspeaker Tobin repeated his message. More than a thousand men left quietly and went back to their offices and homes— to figure, to phone, to dispossess themselves.

"I'd no idea it would be as easy as that," Tobin muttered happily. "Let's see—there are about one hundred and thirty men who did not get my message. That means I have well over seventeen hundred seats in the Exchange. Enough, I think, to whittle down the objectors. Sykes!"

"Mr. Tobin?"

"We are about to be swamped with highly valuable mail. Double the office force and have a plan prepared for unifying the industries that have been signed over to me. Get it ready as soon as possible.

Two weeks should be sufficient. Sykes, this firm is going places— See that those papers are delivered."

Well, that was that. Tobin had an organization strong enough to beat down any resistance, and had the best business minds obtainable working for him. He owned the financial structure of the United States and had a stranglehold on the world. That should be enough to keep him pleasantly occupied for the next ten thousand years or so. That third wish— tomorrow he would wish for a lifetime that could be ended only by his own hand. That ought to do it. It still left him an out— He had time for a final decision on that, too. He must phrase it to exclude illness; he was not a young man any longer. Never mind; it could be slept on.

He called it a day at three o'clock and left Sykes to clean up the details.

Again MacIlhainy Tobin refused a car and left Sykes even more surprised than Landis had been. He wandered about casually, peering around, looking for something really amusing to do. A cafeteria seemed a good place; he went in and had a cup of coffee. He hated cafeteria coffee, but today—everything was different. Even his sense of taste could not be penalized by the bellywash.

He spread a late paper out and turned the pages restlessly. A small item on an inside page caught his eye. "Rudolph Krill, broker— Tobin Building—heart failure—" Tobin chuckled. That wouldn't be on the inside pages tomorrow. Not when United Charities got wind of the facts. Quite a joke, that. Heart failure. Why, Krill—

The smile froze on his broad face. Heart failure? Since when was that a punishable offense—for a second party? It was, of course, suicide. Krill had willed himself to death. But—that wasn't murder.

Tobin stood up and sent his cup crashing to the floor. He stalked past the startled cashier, who managed to enunciate: "Ch-check, please—"

"Be quiet!" Tobin said, without turning his head, and kept on moving. This wouldn't do at all. He had to murder someone, or pay the price of his freedom from punishment.

Whose idea was this death penalty for murder, anyway? Blessed civilization. Tobin snorted. If you killed a man cleverly enough to outwit society, there was no penalty. Society killed without penalty. Armies—Tobin was furious. He thought he had freed himself from the stupidity of mankind for good and all. And now, even with his superhuman power, he had to stoop to the level of man—kowtow to idiocy. He must murder someone so clumsily that it must be detected and traced to him, immediately. He walked a little faster. Time was short. He'd wasted hours—

Opportunity, from force of habit, presented itself to him. A busy street corner, a taxi cutting across traffic to make a turn, a man standing just off the curb—

Tobin pushed him. This was not like the morning. This time the tires were moving, and moving fast. This time they drew blood, chewed on bones and bits of cloth. In the split second of horror before the crowd began to chatter, Tobin saw that he had done it this time. The man was dead. You couldn't cut an angleworm up that way and expect it to live.

A policeman had his notebook out, was taking names, details. Tobin stepped up and touched him on the shoulder. "I did it, officer. I pushed him."

The policeman pushed his hat back on his head and stared at him. "Yeah. Me, too. Fifty people see him try to run across and get hit, an' you pushed him. Better go home and sleep it off, buddy. Move on; I got things to do." He turned away.

A little dazed, Tobin was three blocks away before he realized he could have forced that policeman to believe him. He was halfway back to the crowded corner before he realized that then the policeman would have to take him in for questioning. An arrest was a penalty; something would happen to stop it! He was—invulnerable.

Tobin leaned wearily against a lamppost and tried to think. Every murderer made fatal mistakes; evidently he was no exception. He knew it now. No matter what he did, who he killed or how, something would happen to save him from blame. There must be a way out!

He'd try again. He had to keep trying until he managed to commit an indisputable murder.

At the next corner another policeman was directing traffic. Tobin walked over to him and took the man's gun. The officer never missed it because of a rending crash at the far corner. A sedan and a coupé— The man ran away and left Tobin with the gun. He wouldn't miss it until Tobin was well out of sight; that was certain. Tobin followed him and helped himself to bullets. No one noticed—

He picked a busy corner and a likely-looking victim, a young man with a briefcase. Tobin fired four times at twenty feet. The man screamed and fell, clawing at his chest. People ran toward him, gabbling. Some idiot collided violently with Tobin, sent the gun flying yards away. Another man picked it up— Why go into details? The police came and took the man away. No one had seen Tobin fire. The murdered man had screamed, and people had seen him fall. Tobin was left in the crowd while the Black Maria and the ambulance wailed away with their unoffending cargoes.

It was a new and different Tobin who found his way into a small park and sat heavily on a bench. The cocky air was gone, and the breezy smile, and the lift from the shoulders. MacIlhainy Tobin could not know fear today, but his was bewilderment.

For the first time he noticed the shabby figure beside him. They recognized each other at the same time. The boy sprang to his feet.

"You! Who—what are you, anyway? You're the guy made me lie down under that truck this mornin'. I oughta—" He clutched the bench and weaved a little on his feet. Pickings apparently had not been so good. "Joke, I guess— Hell of a price you tried to make me pay to save yourself a couple nickels—" He walked off, trying to keep his head up.

Tobin watched him go. It never occurred to him that a dollar now would save a life. "Hell of a price—" The words said themselves over and over in his tired brain. The price of lying down under that truck was—death.

Tobin sat there and laughed. He roared. Murder wasn't the only thing carrying a death penalty. There was—suicide!

Where, then? When? Some place where no one would bother

him, and some means that couldn't fail. Poison? He'd throw it off. Ropes broke; guns missed fire. Gas wasn't certain. Knives broke or missed vital spots.

He finally faced it like the man he was. He couldn't kill himself because he couldn't be killed. He'd keep fighting until he won, or lost—he had never lost before— Ah, well. He hailed a cab and went home.

MacIlhainy Tobin dined in his usual lonely splendor. He was a little more himself, now. He felt a little rueful, but once he knew what he had to face, he could stand it. He'd die tonight, then. The richest, most powerful man in the history of the world, and he was going to die. It was grimly humorous. Why hadn't he taken a chance on boredom? He could have had his power indefinitely. He had stipulated that his power would last until he slept. As soon as he slept he would pay the penalty for paying no penalties—death. There *must* be a way! One more try—

"Landis!"

"Sir?"

"I want the whole household in the library in fifteen minutes—maids, gardeners, chauffeur, everyone. You, too."

"Very good, sir."

They were all there—twenty-six, including Landis. Tobin got them settled and then locked the door and put the key in his pocket.

"I've called you here as witnesses," he began. "I want your complete attention. All of you are to watch everything I do, hear every word I say, and remember your stories when the police come and question you. You are not to be surprised. There is to be no screaming, fainting, or interference. Riggs, Cramp, come here. And Landis."

The gardener and the chauffeur towered over the butler as they stood together. Tobin folded his arms and leaned back against the desk.

"Landis, you are not to resist or be frightened. Riggs, Cramp, hold him firmly." This ought to do the trick, thought Tobin. Pity he hadn't thought of it in the first place.

He went to the wall and lifted down a heavy scimitar. It was Damascus steel, and Tobin knew that it would pass the time-honored test of slicing a feather floating in midair.

"Hold your head to one side, Landis. That's it. Can everyone see? Very good."

He swung the blade high over his head and brought it down with all his strength. It seemed to melt into Landis' neck; Tobin thought it would never stop. He saw terror on the faces about him, but no one made a move. He had no idea there was so much blood in that scrawny body.

"Let him go." The dead man fell with a squashy *thump*.

"Now," said Tobin, "you are all to wait here quietly for one hour. Then call the police and tell them what has happened."

"Yes, Mr. Tobin," they chorused.

"Good night, everyone."

A few minutes later he lay comfortably in bed and went over it all in his mind. The subtlety of it pleased him. Those murders this afternoon—they had failed because he had relied on coincidence to damn him. Coincidence had worked the other way. But, by merely setting his stage, he had nullified coincidence. He could not be blamed for the other murders, therefore he had done nothing to deserve a death penalty. He *must* be blamed for this one.

It had happened in his day of power, so he would not be penalized. A signed statement lay on the bureau, a carbon copy with an original signature was now in the mail. The fact that the penalty would, in the natural course of events, be brought to bear weeks or months from the time of the murder, did not matter. The fact remained that he had *done something to deserve a death penalty*. That was enough, and he was content with himself and the world.

He lay for a long while watching the butt of his cigarette burn to a white ash in the bedside tray. When it had gone out he yawned, stretched lazily and turned out the light. The last thing that he remembered was the faint tinkle of the doorbell. That would be the police. He smiled and went to sleep.

"He did it then. Got away with it. I must say I'm sorry," I said to the man.

"Wait. I haven't finished."

"But—"

"He hadn't finished with his day of power—quite. Listen."

MacIlhainy Tobin awoke gently. He smiled. That would be the police. He heard the faint tinkling of the doorbell. He reached up and turned on the light, stretched lazily and yawned. His eyes fell on the bedside tray. A wisp of smoke began curling from the dead ash there; a tiny sliver of paper appeared and grew into a cigarette butt. He was quite content with himself and the world— The smoke was curling *downward* toward the butt, not from it, something deep inside his mind told him. Thoughts of the penalty, of the statements, of the afternoon's murders slipped through his mind. After a while he gripped the edge of the sheet, pressed it from him. He arose, pushed his pajamas off. His trunks sailed from a nearby chair into his hand; he bent and laid them on the floor, stepped into them. They flowed up his legs after he was standing straight up; he caught the waist, pulled it together. A button flung itself from the floor, placed itself over the buttonhole, the threads held it intact again. He finished dressing like a man in a movie film run backward—it *was* running backward.

Backward, he went to the door, down the stairs, into the library. Backward he did the murder, saw Landis' corpse lift limply into the grip of the two servants, pulled the scimitar out of the wound while blood flowed into it, lifted it high over his head, hung it on the wall— and all the while he was talking gibberish, a horrible language, spoken with inhalations. He went back to the table and ate, and eating was revolting. He went backward out of the house, the cab driver handed him money, backed swiftly up to the park. He saw the boy again, the murders—everything. Until finally he got back home, disgorged his breakfast neatly, went upstairs, pressed his clothes off, wet himself with a towel, got into the tub and climbed out dry; went to bed. Landis moved about softly, backward, closing the curtains— Tobin drifted off to sleep, and as soon as it enveloped him—

"Six o'clock, sir."

"Ah—Landis. Good. Has Synthetic Rubber moved?"

And so he began again his day of power. Again he ordered a shabby youth to kill himself, and swept into his office to start the day, and arranged for the transfers, and ordered Krill to die, and went through all those senseless murders, and went home, and killed Landis, and went to bed. And again, just after he closed his eyes, he heard the doorbell. That would be the police. Again he smiled, and watched the cigarette grow in the ashtray, and again he killed Landis, and again, and again, and again, he lived through his day, backward and forward, backward and forward. His body did as it had done the first time, and so did his mind, but there was something deep inside him, something that neither he nor I could touch nor destroy, that wept and wailed and had no will, that suffered and cried, and knew utmost horror, and had not strength enough even to go mad— It was the only way. He could not die, for he deserved death and denied himself death.

Tobin has another wish coming when he wakes in the morning.

"That story is true," said the man.

"I—believe it. Er—when did it happen?" I said.

"When? When? You speak of time, and MacIlhainy Tobin?"

"Oh—why did you tell me this story?"

"Because after MacIlhainy Tobin had two wishes, he—stopped. If I grant a man wishes, I must grant him three. So you see, my work here is finished. I want you to tell people. I can do no more here." And he left me.

Perhaps he was never here at all. But this is the story I wrote last night.

Turkish Delight

IT WAS DURHAM'S fault, though when it happened he was as scared as the rest of us. The whole crew clustered on the poop deck, staring off into that ghostly fog, listening to our hearts beat boomingly, great waves of sound that rolled and tumbled about on the unseen waste of water. It was that way, and we were horror-struck even before the screaming started.

We had dropped the hook off the Dodecanese Islands, to wait the lifting of the fog. That in itself was unusual, but then everything about this trip was unusual. We trusted our skipper, a rocky old squarehead who could sail two sticks and a rag around the world, or navigate a rowboat from here to the moon. We'd have followed him, too; and if he'd wanted to send the *Willowtree* butting full ahead, why, there would never have been a murmur from us. But this fog was—different ... anyway, we'd dropped the anchor, and were standing by.

There wasn't much to do. There was a lookout forward, and one on the wing of the bridge, and there was a fireman down below keeping steam up. The rest of us were on deck. It was too quiet to sleep, and too hot. Even with the heavy crude oil we were carrying from Constanta, the *Willowtree* vibrated like a Model T when she was running, and now the stillness was disturbing. We lolled about, and talked quietly—a typical sailor's bull session. With a difference. We were all disembodied voices. I didn't know who the man next to me at the rail was, save that he was a living bulk whose breath stirred the fog about his head, making the dim light from the anchor lamp flicker.

And Durham's voice came from somewhere, quietly, talking about Haiti. Some wild adventure of his—the details don't matter. The gist of it was that once he had jumped ship there and headed for the hills.

He'd bedded up in the lianas, and had been awakened by drums. "Thought they was in me head, first," he said. "Quiet like, more as if I was feelin' 'em 'stead o' hearin'. I got up and followed the sound. Dark? It was black as—" (Durham's simile was vivid) "—an' after a bit I saw firelight, just like it was comin' up out of th' ground. An' the moanin' an' groanin'—gawsh! Give me th' creeps. I flopped, and crawled over to see. There was a pit dug in th' ground, deep, an' maybe a hundred feet around. Fire was down there, an' some kind of altar." Durham's voice shook, and we began to *feel* the scene, just as if the fog were a medium for carrying his emotion, carrying it the way a clear cold night carries the sound of bells. There was nothing lost in the telling.

His voice went on and on, and through it came the almost sound-less beat of drums—or hearts? The voodoo sacrament, ever weird and compelling to white men in spite of skepticism, took on real meaning now ... we felt the power of it, and the nameless evil ... perhaps it was the fog. I don't know.

Couldn't he talk of something else? A great impatience surged through us, and someone said shakily, "S-shut up, will ya, Bull?" And he did, and the thread of his story ceased, with the pictures it had conjured up, of the moaning and the firelight and the drums...

The drums? But what was that, in the deathly silence that followed? It was just my heart, that steady pluh-boom! pluh-boom! The beat continued, unhurried, barely audible, its rhythm speaking in a language we dared not understand, in terms inevitable. And now it was louder. No, not louder. There was just—more of it. It *was* my heartbeat, for my heart was beating with it—and yet it was more, for against my suddenly cold flesh I could feel my rough clothes vibrating too. The beat of it was looming over the dark ship, shaking the air so that we could feel it on our cheeks, and *something* was coming to us through the fog.

And then we heard the moan. Almost as inaudible as the first drumming, it was far more terrifying. It was inhuman, and yet ... it was something in pain, and yet crooning joyfully. It had panic in it, but shook with terrible control. It rose slowly and died away, and caught at its dwindling echoes and gathered them and built them into something greater and yet more horrible. None of us made a sound.

The drumming, heartlike, devastating, was so intense that we could all but see it, and the moaning died away only to grow again into a great shuddering scream—something tangible, something to fear. We fell back before it as if it were a blast of heat, and I for one knew that I had reached the limit of my endurance. Stumbling, falling, cursing, I ran forward to the fire-room hatch, groped along the bulkhead until I caught the cable that controlled the whistle. I caught it and pulled, and it bit deeply into my hands, but I did not care. The sounds rose together; that awful, mysterious mouthing from the fog, and the friendly hissing gurgle of the ship's whistle clearing its brazen throat. The sound we knew and the one we feared battled for supremacy in the vibrant mist.

The ship shook from stem to stern as live steam burst through the whistle vents, and with a shattering roar gave tongue to our fear and our defiance. And as the cable slipped upward through my bleeding fingers and the whistle stilled, the frightful ululation from the fog dwindled and fell to nothing, and the drums ceased and the crew—cheered.

I staggered to the rail and peered out there. Daylight was coming and, as I watched, the curtain began to lift. The ship heeled slightly, partly from the press of the dawn wind, partly—yes, I could see it now—partly from the wash thrown up by some vessel that must have run close under our counter. And now I could see her— and though it was funny now, I was too weak to laugh. She was Turkish—*Turkish!* On her stern floated the white star and crescent on a red field, and on her bridge was an old type, cracked, crankturned foghorn, and on her well deck was a great drum. It's written there in your *Rules of the Road at Sea,* if you'll look; a Turkish vessel under way uses a *drum* for a fog signal!

We had been frightened, then, of nothing. But fear is enough in itself. Sailors are an odd, impressionable lot!

Niobe

AT HER INSISTENCE we rode together, though I knew what was to happen. She was very beautiful—more beautiful than Iris, though it was Iris I loved. Her name was Niobe, and her hair was such a great and glorious mass that when the light was from above, her strong face was in shadow. Her hair was dark as the color of embers is dark compared with flame, and a countrywoman was once heard to mumble that Niobe carried her soul in her hair. I was Harald then, and I believed that Niobe had no soul. And I believe it now.

We rode out on the moors, the foothills of Carn Englyn, in "Little-England-Beyond-Wales." I came with her, for she was armed and I was not. I stayed by her, for she rode as well as I and could shoot better than any man. I was not afraid, for fear is an emotion based on hope—hope of escape; and there was no hope in me. I did not speak except at the end of the ride, and then only briefly. But she talked as we travelled, in her voice like somber music, and she reveled in her coolth and hatred of me.

"I grew up alone," she murmured, "All alone but for my own world, which is dead these three centuries, and but for you. As Harald the poet you came to me from the moors, wild as the hairy gorse and filled with laughter that unnerved me. I mistrusted your unplanned thoughts and sudden movements, and I despised you because you were something I could not understand."

She was silent for a time, and the heather whispered to our horses' hoofs. She was a strange creature, Niobe. She regarded the world and its folk and its modern sun and sky and dwellings and atmospheres as dreams she dreamed by daylight. I do believe that the crest of the Pembrokes was engraved on her unearthly heart. Easily it might be, for her thoughts were of the Pembrokes and her books and her dress and her ways were those of the Pembrokes. And her loves, all but her one great love. Ah, could I be blamed for that? . . . Her mind was born three hundred years ago, as the mind of Mary Sidney, sister of Sir Philip and dowager Countess of Pembroke. Her brother was a poet, and at his death the seventeenth century countess turned to poetry and—poets. Spenser knew, and told of her. What became of the mind of Mary Sidney, none know; but I know that after three hundred years Mary Sidney was Niobe Pembroke. Yes, I know that.

"You were a fool who danced in the sun and dared to love a degraded world, while I stood in dark places about the manse and watched you. You dared to love the trees about you, and the smell of heath-born wind. I stood apart and saw you, and heard you chant your poetry in strange keys, and I hated and despised you. I found your scrawlings on tattered papers about the house and grounds, and I saved them and wept over them secretly. You dared to love and let me stay alone. You dared to love," Niobe coldly crooned, "to love Iris. Unseen I saw you with her, and I read and heard your songs after she came. Your songs were finely written and possessed of delicacy and laughter, those qualities I hate."

Niobe's eyes were ice-green or they were gray. Like Northern Lights they were, that change while you watch, so that you see that they are perceptibly different without having seen the change. Her eyes touched me gently, as gently as her strong hand touched her weapon, and I knew it would be soon now.

"Oh, you were obedient," she said. "I ordered you to stay by me, and you did. I ordered you to speak to me, to read to me, and you did. I despised you for it. You spoke well, you read well, when I put words on your lips or a book in your hands. But when I asked you to speak to me from your mind and heart, you stuttered and stammered like a peat-digger, saving your ready word-magic for your pen and for—Iris. You could parrot my words and the words of the poets while I was by you, but otherwise my presence struck you impatiently dumb. I hate you for making me a traitor to myself, by tempting me away from my life in the past to the degenerated life of the so-called present. I hate you for choosing an inferior woman to me— to *me!* But most of all I hate you for making me envy her—she who is but a dust-mote whirling in the waning sunlight of an unreal world."

I still said nothing, for I knew Niobe and I knew of hate, and therefore I knew the power of Niobe's hate. I gazed at the craggy shoulder of Carn Englyn, rearing up out of Pembrokeshire, and I thought of Iris. Iris was a slender thing, and swayed with the wind like a stalk of golden wheat. The wind of my laughter and of my passion brought laughing and passionate response in Iris. I loved Iris. I gazed for a moment at Niobe, staid and inscrutable. I might have loved Niobe, I thought, watching a sunbeam trying to escape the ordered depth of her hair. But a man with a body and a soul cannot love a woman who is gifted with utter and eternal composure. Even now, as she spoke of her love and her torture and her hate, there was no passion in it. None, none at all, even when she met my eyes and gripped them with her own and whispered,

"I killed Iris this morning, Harald."

I stopped my horse and slid off its back and leaned on the warm withers, looking again deep into Niobe's eyes. No passion there— great God, there was not even satisfaction! At last I spoke:

"I have made you suffer, Niobe. I have taken your pride from you. I know what you will do now, Niobe, and when you have done it you may reflect that you have done exactly what I want you to do, and have given me what I most desire. Kill me now, Niobe."

My horse reared and fled at the sound of the shots; hers stood still and trembled, for it feared her, as did all living things. She put a bullet into each of my eyes and one in my heart, and rode away. I lay there with my torn dead eyes staring at a gush of blood dripping slowly from a heather-blossom.

After the flesh was quite cold I was no longer Harald, and so I rose from it and drifted away toward the manse and Niobe. It was dark then, and cold; but then I knew it would be cold. The moor was lovely as I saw it now, without light.

I floated to the manse and puffed through the window of Niobe's great chamber. Niobe sat before her mirror, and her hair was down, pouring, cascading down to pile up lightly on itself beneath her chair. Never a woman had such hair... She sat with her chin in her hands, and she was trying to smile at herself and could not. I settled over her like a pall and my voice cried deep in her brain, "To the tomb, Niobe!"

She did not start, and for a full minute did not move. Then she turned slowly and looked behind her. One eyebrow lifted—her one concession to facial mobility—and slowly she turned back to the mirror. I let her watch herself for a moment and then spoke to her mind again.

"Dress, Niobe, and go to the tomb!"

Niobe rose and dressed.

It was a long way to the tomb, and all that way Niobe's face was still and her heart beat slowly and evenly. I was with her—she carried me!—and I knew she was frightened. She knew where the tomb was, but she had never been there. I knew why. It was the one Pembroke property which she shunned—and oh, I knew why!

A wind wailed about the tomb, and it spoke to Niobe in Harald's voice.

"To the tomb, Niobe!" Like a somnambulist she approached it, and her cloak streamed behind her and whipped upward and then close to her, and the wind plucked at her hair and smothered the cloak. "Read, Niobe."

She screamed suddenly, again and again, but none heard. The scream left her lips as laughter—Harald's gay, triumphant laughter, as it was when he first kissed Iris. And over and above it shouted the wind—"Read, Niobe! Read, Niobe!"

I was an aura, a steady and directionless light about her, and as she leaned closer to the stone, fighting the wind, fighting me, fighting herself, the light grew bright and the weathered words leapt out to her.

"*Read, Niobe!*" cried the wind, cried Harald, cried the aura about Niobe, cried—Niobe herself.

She read it, then, the epitaph she dreaded. Her voice was clear and carried well over the wind; she was shaken beyond trembling; she had known fear and had plumbed the depths even beyond fear, as had Harald on the moor. The old, stilted verses were lovely from her lips:

> Underneath this marble hearse
> Lies the subject of all verse;
> Sidney's sister, Pembroke's mother;
> Death, ere thou hast slain another
> Fair and learn'd and good as she,
> Time will throw his dart at thee.

Niobe was a woman, in spite of all, and the laudatory phrases elated her; enough, at least, so that she rose from utter hopelessness to the level of fear again, and stopped.

"Read on!" wailed the wind and I, and laughed gustily. "The prophecy! Read on, Niobe!"

Faltering at first, then with increasing clarity, she read—

> Marble piles let no man raise
> To her name for after days;
> Some kind woman, born as she,
> Reading this, like Niobe,
> Shall turn marble, and become
> Both her mourner and her tomb!

And with a wild shriek of laughter—*my* laughter—Niobe fulfilled the prophecy.

And I love Niobe now. A man with a body and with a soul might not, but I may. We are almost happy together, as, riding the chill wind, I wail about the tomb . . .

[*Note:* This, the tomb of Mary, Countess of Pembroke, who died in 1621, still exists, epitaph (by William Browne) and all. About the monument, the "mourner and her tomb," one cannot be so certain! All other facts authenticated.]

Mahout

"MAKE WAY FOR the mahout!" bellowed the crew's messman. Everybody stood up but me. I'd never seen anything like this on a ship before. I watched the door. A spindly little Cajun shuffled in, looked around at the solemn crew, giggled, blushed, went to his seat. Everyone sat down with him, went on as if nothing had happened.

"Now what the devil kind of high jinx might that be?" I asked Wacky Robinson. Wacky and I had shipped together before, on another ship. This was my first trip, first day out, first meal on this tub.

Wacky washed down an improbable amount of rice and gravy with an impossible amount of iced tea. "That," he said, using the hair on his wrist as a napkin, "is Jacques the Giant Killer. That's Luchaire, the 4 to 8 fireman. That high jinx? Ah, we're kidding him. That is ... well, maybe it's kidding. He—he rates it."

"Him? That swamp runner? Don't look to me as if he could even punch carbon."

Wacky laughed. "That's what Muggsy thought."

"Muggsy? You don't mean—"

"Yeah, I mean. All 240 pounds of Muggsy Trent, the terror of Proctor, the muscle of Mobile, the horror of Houston, the Galveston Gorilla, the—"

"O.K., O.K., Wacky," I said. Wacky could keep this up for two trips; I knew him. "So what's that got to do with the scrawny little crawfish?"

"Le'me tell you. Just listen at this." Wacky lit a Denobill to frighten away the mosquitoes, and leaned back against the bulkhead. "Muggsy was quartergasket on here, couple of trips back. You know Muggsy. Six foot two, more muscle than brains. Big enough so he didn't need brains. Nice guy, if you keep out of his way when he's feeling good and leave him alone when he ain't.

"One night a bunch of us is playin' knock rummy here in the messroom. Muggsy is sitting over there and the Cajun is perched on the other table back of him, kibitzing. Minding his own business, mouth shut. One hand, Muggsy gets three queens, three 9s, an' a 4. He knocks right away; if no one can count less than four, he gets two bits from each man. Everyone is caught cold but the first assistant; he grins an' turns up as nice a rummy as you ever saw, 2 to 8 in clubs. Which means Muggsy has to fork over four bits.

"No one ever saw Muggsy lose an' grin yet. He turns purple, looks around him and sees Luchaire behind him. 'Jinx!' he roars, and hauls off and lets the little guy have a terrific backhand. Luchaire takes off like a flying fish and I'll never forget the noise his head makes when it hits this bulkhead here. Muggsy would have jumped on him again but the first assistant catches his arm and says, 'Your deal, Muggsy.' Muggsy cools off a little and everybody sits down again, except for a couple who carry the Cajun out.

"Five minutes later he is back. He is considerably messed up. But he is the maddest little guy I ever saw. 'Moggsy,' he says, 'you treat me like a rat, no? So. I am a rat now. I keel you like a rat. You mus' sleep sometime, no?' An' he beat it. Funny; that breaks up the game when the other thing don't.

"Muggsy goes into the fireman's foc's'le an hour later, and there is the Cajun sitting on his bunk, sharpening an eleven-inch knife on a whetstone. He looks up at the big guy and grins and keeps on working. Muggsy leaves. When he comes off watch that night he sticks his head into the fireman's ventilator. He hears that whht! whht! He doesn't turn in. He is walking the poop deck trying to keep awake when he turns around and sees Luchaire sitting on one of the bitts sharpening his knife. Muggsy goes back to the wheel, watch or no watch. Eleven hours he steers that night.

"The second night it is the same story. Muggsy is getting groggy, and scared. Once he runs up behind the Frenchman; Luchaire turns around real slow and he has his knife in his hand. Doesn't look at Muggsy; just at the knife. Muggsy goes below.

"Third night, one in the morning, we make the Mississippi. A bunch of 8 to 12 men are on the poop, looking at the riverbank.

Muggsy is trying to be cheerful, but he is half dead from not sleeping, and from fear. He is one scared son-of-a-gun. All of a sudden he jumps sky high. Luchaire is right beside him, that hog sticker shining in the moonlight. Muggsy breaks down. Never saw anything like it. Cries. Asks Luchaire what he wants. Says he'll do anything—anything... Luchaire grins and puts his knife away. 'Jomp ovair de side,' he whispers, 'or go down below an' shine my shoes.'

"That big mass o' muscle shines shoes. Yeah. Leaves the ship when we dock, and hasn't been heard from since. Can't face us."

I looked over at the little Frenchman again. "I'll—think twice before I call anyone tough guy... Wacky, why did the messman call him 'ma-hout'?"

"Ever see one of those guys from Ceylon with a little bull hook? They can make elephants sit up and beg."

At the next meal, I stood up, too.

The Long Arm

HE WAS SHORT and stocky and on his square face was a hunted look. He flattened himself against the brick wall in the dimness of the alley, and tried to stop his shrill panting. He had been running hard, and though he would not admit it to himself, he was frightened. Through his small brain curled ugly thoughts of vengeance and violence; as in the hunted the world over, his fear transmuted itself into anger.

It was all Alice's fault, he thought bitterly. A man would do a lot because of a nagging woman—a lot. Some things that wouldn't occur to him otherwise... What kick had she, anyway? He'd been good to her, after his fashion. And what did it get him? Just the same old song, over and over— "Where were you last night? Where are you going? Where have you been? How much money did you spend?" Arrgh. Well, he'd left—run out. Alice and everything she stood for—they were part of his past. They would be, that is, if that flat-foot didn't catch up with him...

He listened intently. A truck somewhere—a towboat's whistle from the river—a muffled honk from a taxi—footsteps—the bull's footsteps? He tried to squeeze closer to the wall. The steps passed the mouth of the alley, and the release of pent-up emotion was a sob ... but the footsteps stopped, silenced for the space of two heartbeats, and then began again—returning now. "It's him!" he breathed, looking wildly about for some way of escape, some plan... "Goin' to be a close thing, Deuce," he addressed himself hysterically. "Just like Alice to put the bulls on a guy ... she must know about the money, then." For the first time he really regretted his act in taking the pittance that Alice had so painstakingly saved up, so carefully hidden.

Conscience had little to do with his fear; the penalty he faced had plenty. Locked up, he guessed, for the rest of his life in the big house.

For a lot of it, anyway. Why couldn't they leave him alone? There was no harm in him. He was a right guy ... the footsteps turned into the alley, and Deuce dived into the friendly shelter offered by a couple of ash cans.

Peeping out, he saw the detective. Yeah, it was the flat-foot all right. Detective Sergeant McGonigle and Deuce were acquaintances from 'way back. Deuce had seen far too much of him before the bull got his transfer into another department. And now Deuce had committed just the crime that would set his old nemesis on his trail again. Just like old times...

McGonigle moved carefully, carrying his huge bulk with astonishing lightness. In his hand was a flashlight, and in the gleam of it his face was stern and duty-bound. No hope of mercy from him, Deuce knew that. Once caught, no amount of pleading, bribing, defiance would do any good. Once let that huge hand close on his shoulder, and it was all up. Deuce knew.

McGonigle came abreast of him, and things happened too fast, almost, to think about. The relentlessly probing beam swept around the cans, vividly pointed up Deuce's ruddy face and frantic, button eyes. For a frozen split second they stared at each other, hunter and hunted, and then McGonigle grunted and dove. Deuce shot his compact body sidewise; the ham-sized paw missed by very little more than nothing. Deuce found the wall against his feet; he shoved violently, launched himself like a torpedo at the detective's legs. Caught off balance, McGonigle fell in a mighty chaos of massive limbs. Deuce rolled once, bounced to his feet, and was off down the alley like a scared squirrel. He had a wicked but short-lived hope that the flat-foot had fallen against something, but the pounding of heavy feet behind him was proof enough that, though damaged, the mighty frame was still under control.

After that it wasn't much of a chase—half a block, maybe. McGonigle flung his arms around the fugitive and they slid to a halt. Deuce kicked and squalled, but not for long. He was through. He knew it.

A few minutes later, in a neighboring ice cream parlor, they sat together on stools confronted by huge elaborations in the way of sodas. And McGonigle held forth:

"Five hours I've been after ye, lad. Ye've tore me trousers an' ye've busted me flashlight, but I don't hold it agin' ye. Now be sinsible. Ye've a foine big house to live in, an' yer sister Alice told me herself that she won't say a word about the eighty-five cents ye took offen her. An' she'll stop tellin' yer mother on ye all the time, too. I thought I'd seen the last of ye whin they took me out of the truant force, always dodgin' school the way ye were. Now I'm in Missing Persons." He looked at Deuce and shook his great head. "Ye've a lot o' th' divil in ye for a ten-year-old. Goin' to go home an' stay out o' trouble now?"

Deuce grinned and nodded and began sucking greedily at a straw.

The Man on the Steps

JOSEPH BERX IS a man we all admire. He is a leader of men and a master of machines, a power in our country and one of those who make our country a power in the world. But it was not always so. Something strange happened to Joseph Berx, master industrialist, years ago when he was just Joe Berx, master mechanic.

He was young then, and uncertain, and more than a little unhappy, for he had reached a crisis in his life. It was one of those crossroads we all come to sooner or later, when to go one way may mean starvation, the other, stasis... Joe was walking along a downtown street one blustery February evening mulling over his problem, when a sharp blast of wind sent him scurrying into the friendly shelter offered by the pillars of an old federal building. He stood there in the shadows, acutely uncomfortable all through, when he heard a voice: "In trouble, son?"

Joe started and saw a man standing on the steps. The voice was deep and kindly and sounded as if it came a long way to get to him. A strange thing indeed, but not to Joe, who answered the man. "Yes, sir, I am. I don't know what to do."

Joe could not see very clearly, but he thought the man smiled. "I've a long life behind me, young man, and perhaps I've hurdled your problem, or one like it. Tell me about it."

Joe did. He said, "I've worked a long while for one man, sir, and now a group of us want to break away and form our own company because the boss mistreats us. And though we are enthusiastic, we are poorly organized and with little capital, and I am afraid that many of us have differing ideas about the best way to run the new organization. They have unanimously voted me the head and frankly, sir, I don't think I am big enough for the job. I feel I should take it, but I am afraid..."

Joe knew the man was smiling now. He had a weary, proud, noble face, sternly cut, but warm. He said, "I had the same problem. I too felt it was my right to break an allegiance because of oppression. I too found my fellows enthusiastic but disorganized; and unanimously they asked me to lead them. Like you—" the deep voice mellowed "—I felt myself unfit. It was a big job—too big for one man, I thought, especially if I were that man."

"What did you do?" asked Joe.

"I took the job."

"Why?"

"It was my duty."

"Duty? Who made it your duty?"

The man looked piercingly at Joe. "Those who had faith in me, and those who needed me. When I realized that, I acceded, for I knew, as you will, that their trust and necessity would make me great enough to succeed, if I lacked greatness at the beginning."

"I—see. And what happened?"

He was silent for a while, and then sighed. "It was hard, boy, hard. There were times when I was ready to give up, and times when in my heart I did give up only to be recalled by those who depended on me. It took years... I had a wife and a home, and I loved my land and wanted to return to it, and could not. I—I told them that when they appointed me. I told them I had other interests; that I would cooperate but truly did not think I could lead. But—I consented."

"Did you—" Joe's voice trailed off.

"Fail, lad? No. No, I won my fight. The cost was great, but I won independence. To have freedom is to have youth and strength—to fight a hard fight for it is to grow old early. I did—but it was worth it, for those about me had independence, and their children had it, and theirs, and theirs... I have faith in those children and the children to come. They will and must keep that liberty. As long as they have it and keep it alive, I too live. It was worth anything I gave, more than I ever could give; and it will be so as long as they also live for it. That is the kind of struggle you face. The price of success is high, young man, for a good fight must be a clean fight, if the victory is to be a permanent one. What are you going to do with your problem? Have I helped you?"

"You have helped, sir," said Joe Berx steadily. "I will do as they ask. But—who are you, sir?"

The man smiled. "You have known me all your life, lad. Remember me, and help me by carrying on my work, and perhaps—perhaps you'll know me better."

And Joe Berx went his way, thinking, "That man—who was that man?" He went his way, and he acted upon his decision. Now he is Joseph Berx, power in the land, and a great American

Once, on a blustery February afternoon, he passed the Sub-Treasury Building in lower New York. He looked up at the great statue on the steps, and the thought came to him, "That man, years ago—that was George Washington—or his spirit!"

He was quite right. It *was* George Washington—or his spirit.

Punctuational Advice

SO WE GOT chatting, as neighbors will. She was living in the cozy little three room flat—third floor front. I had a comfortable little cubbyhole down the hall. It was a nice rooming house.

"Have you met Mrs. Katz?" she asked.

"The landlady? Of course," I said.

"She's a very wonderful woman," she said, and smiled all over her charming face.

"I think she's nice," I said, "but I'm against landladies on principle."

She laughed. "I say she's wonderful. She's responsible for the most wonderful thing that ever happened to me."

"Do tell," I said, intrigued.

"You asked for it," she said. She was such a happy little thing!

"About two months ago," she began, "I went down to pay my rent. You know Mrs. Katz—well, you will, if you stay here a couple of weeks. I defy you to go near her looking down in the mouth without her asking you your trouble, and if she can help. She's that sort of a person. Anyway, she asked me; and I was feeling terrible. The one thing in the world that would have made me burst into tears was to have someone put a hand on my shoulder and look sympathetic. And she put a hand on my shoulder and looked sympathetic. And I burst into tears. Silly, isn't it?"

"No," I said.

"It is," she laughed. "But it was horrible at the time. Well, Mrs. Katz soothed me and gave me a clean hanky and generally restored me to normal, and as soon as I had control of myself I felt I really ought to tell her what it was all about. So I did; she had to calm me down again twice while I told her, but I got it out. I was in a state!"

"Seems as though. What was the trouble?"

"It was the young man who used to have the room you're in now. I was furious at him. He'd take me out. He'd give me little things. He'd do things for me. He'd do anything in the world but propose! I tried everything. Hints were no good; the right atmosphere was no good; even the suggestions of his friends would not turn the trick."

"How'd you know about that last item?" I asked pointedly.

"Never mind," she said in mock sternness. "Where was I? Oh, yes! Well, Mrs. Katz was very understanding. She didn't even smile. I asked her despairingly what on earth I could do. She considered it carefully, patting that lovely white hair of hers, and finally she said, 'Tell you what—I'll send your rent receipt up to you and maybe a note with it, telling you what to do. I'll have to think this out.' I thanked her and went back to my room."

"Did she?" I asked when the girl had been silent, smiling, so long that I thought she'd forgotten her story.

She nodded. "She did. She's a very clever woman. She did it in a way that gave me the satisfaction of having thought it out for myself. A—a sort of hint."

"What was it?"

"Just a piece of paper tucked around the rent receipt. On it she'd drawn a big question mark. That was all. I sat on my bed after the boy brought it up to me, and I wondered and puzzled and thought— silly, but it was better than mooning over my misery. I was almost frantic with curiosity over what she might have meant by it."

"If anything," I said.

"Now don't sneer! She knew what she was doing. You know, for nearly a week I went to work every day in a fog. Question mark; question mark... I doodled question marks on my scratch pads at the office and even on tablecloths in restaurants. How could a question mark help me make that hesitant young hero of mine propose? I even put on a poker face and handed him a piece of paper with a question mark on it, to see if by some remote chance that was the thing to do. He just looked blankly at me."

"It didn't occur to you, did it, that Mrs. Katz found the matter beyond her and took that brief and effective way of telling you so?"

"Will you stop interrupting? Come to think of it, I did wonder

280

a bit if that was what she meant ... but I wouldn't ask her. It was the nearest thing I had to an answer; I had to know."

"O.K.," I said. "What happened? The suspense is terrible."

She smiled. "I knew I'd wear you down. Well, I just kept thinking 'question mark ... question mark' over and over until one afternoon it dawned on me that this is leap year; and then of course I knew what to do!"

"What," I asked in something like exasperation, "did you do?"

"Just as Mrs. Katz suggested. Her note said, 'question mark,' so I—" she giggled, "—questioned Mark... Here he comes now. Mark, this is our new neighbor."

He was a nice young man. As I shook hands with him I reflected that Mrs. Katz was indeed a very clever woman.

Place of Honor

THE KIND OF understanding that existed between Matty and Grover Cleveland MacDonald was something rare and wonderful ... each knew what the other wanted; to each, the attainment of the other's desire was desire itself. They were not demonstrative, but they were used to each other. They knew each other's habits and silently bore with each other's bad ones.

Reasonably enough, MacDonald was more than a little inter-ested in the great man for whom he had been named. His birthday and President Cleveland's coincided, and so did their wedding anniver-sary. He had met her through her father; he had met her father through the latter's splendid biography of Grover Cleveland.

MacDonald was a quiet little man, the personification of patience. He was a telegraph clerk, and for years had been working Sundays, Tuesday being his day off. He and Matty had nearly everything they wanted, which wasn't very much. They had an annuity to add to Grover's pension for their old age; they had a house of their own, a couple of thousand in the bank which they didn't quite know what to do with, and they had—each other.

One bright Tuesday in March they went for a walk, looking very neat and very much as if there were no one else in the world. From the noisy, hurrying shopping section they walked up the avenue, a region of sedate shops with astronomical rents and the ability to subsist with almost frightening permanence on one sale every two weeks. Art shops, antique shops, fur shops, each with its discreet magnificence, its tony exclusion of all but the initiated.

They both saw it at once, staring out at them from a beautiful subdued in velvet display window: a print of Grover Cleveland—a beautiful, vaguely yellowed, microscopically perfect one. It was quite large, evidently quite old. With one accord, silent, Matty and Grover went into the shop, where the clerk, in his own good time, greeted them.

He was tired without being worn. "Yes, sir, it is an 1872 print. Yes, it is by—" Matty and Grover fell silent in true awe at the name of the engraver. "No, madam, there are only three copies exactly like this. One is in the capitol, the other at the Metropolitan. Truly a rare piece. The price? One thousand dollars, sir."

They nodded and thanked him and went outside to look again. Was that a half smile on the noble, sensitive face? Matty and Grover looked at each other. He knew she wanted it, and she knew he wanted it, and each made a firm and silent resolution. Next Monday was Grover Cleveland's birthday, and Grover MacDonald's, and Matty and Grover's anniversary.

The next day, Wednesday, Grover came home from work ten minutes later than usual, with a small flat package. While Matty was in the kitchen, Grover went into the living room, took down Uncle Howard's shaggy portrait from the place of honor over the mantel, and instead hung a tiny engraving of Grover Cleveland. It was much smaller than the one they had seen in the window, but it was every bit as precise. The aristocratic face looked out from a small oval in white cardboard, about an inch and a half high, an inch and a quarter wide. A tiny, perfect little thing... Grover MacDonald had a quiet but powerful dramatic sense.

"Oh!" cried Matty when she saw it later. "It's lovely, but it's so little." It was, too, in that great expanse of creamy wall.

"It'll do," said Grover gravely, "until we can get a better one." And he smiled.

All too slowly the great day came. Grover couldn't wait to get home; Matty couldn't wait until he did. She was standing by the door when he came in. He kissed her, and she took his arm and half dragged him into the living room. There it was, over the mantel—the print from the shop on the avenue.

They stood speechless, staring at it; Matty in the same delighted amazement she had felt when she hung it there, amazement that it was so perfectly fitted to the room; Grover in amazement even greater.

"Oh, Matty ... Matty it's— I can't tell you!" After another

moment, "Darling, what did you do with the little one?"

She sniffed. "After seeing the big one hanging there I knew there was no place in this house for the other. I threw it in the furnace."

"You" Grover sat down heavily and gazed at the exquisite print. Should he tell her? Should he tell her that he had determined to buy the big print—that he had drawn a thousand dollars out of the bank, never suspecting that she would draw out her own money for this? And should he tell her that, because of his hours, he couldn't get to the shop, and so had put the—the small print up until Tuesday? No, he couldn't tell her. He had wanted to pay a thousand for this print; well, he had. The one she'd thrown away—the little one—was a folded piece of paper with Grover Cleveland's head showing through the oval hole ... Grover Cleveland's head, engraved on a thousand dollar bill!

The Ultimate Egoist

So I WAS holding forth as usual, finding highly audible reasons for my opinion of myself. I could do that with Judith. She was in love with me, and women in love are funny that way. You can tell them anything about yourself, and as long as it's a buildup they'll believe it. If they can't they'll try.

We were walking down to the lake for a swim. What got me started in this vein—should I say "vain"?—was the fact that Judith looked so wonderful. She was a brunette who was a redhead when she was close by, which she usually was, and turned blonde when the sun hit her. Lovely. Her transparent skin seemed proof that her flesh was rose-ivory all the way through, and she had long green eyes. She moved like a hawk tilting against the wind and she loved me. Wonderful. Since I was thinking about wonderful things I just naturally began talking about myself, and Judith held my hand and skipped along beside me and agreed with everything I said, which was as it should be.

"Let me put it this way," I declaimed. "The world and the universe are strictly as I see them. I see no fallacy in the supposition that if I disbelieve in any given object, theory, or principle, it does not exist."

"You've never seen Siam, darling," said Judith. "Does that mean that Siam does not exist?" She was not disagreeing with me, but she knew how to keep me talking. That was all right because we enjoyed hearing me talk.

"Oh, Siam can exist if it wants," I said generously, "providing I have no reason to doubt its existence."

"Ah," she said. She hadn't exactly heard all this before because I expressed myself with a high degree of originality. There were so many ins and outs to my faceted personality that I found my ego quite inexhaustible. Judith giggled.

"Suppose you really and truly doubted Siam, Woodie."

"That would be tough on the Siamese."

She laughed outright, and I joined her, because if I had not she would have been laughing *at* me, and that would have been unthinkable.

"Darling," she said, pulling my head down so she could bite my ear, "you're marvelous. Do you mean to tell me in so many words that you created all this—these old trees, that sprouted so many years before you were born; the stars and that nice, warm old sun, and the flow of sap, and life itself—wasn't that quite a job, honey?"

I looked at her blankly. "Not at all. Truly, darling. I have never seen nor heard nor read anything to disprove my conviction that this universe is my product, and mine alone. Look—I exist. I can take that as a basic fact. I observe that I have a particular form; hence there must be a physical environment to suit it."

"How about the possibility that your exquisite form might be the *result* of your physical environment?"

"Don't interrupt," I said patiently. "Don't be sarcastic and above all don't be heretical. Now.

"Since my existence requires a certain set of circumstances, those circumstances must necessarily exist to care for me. The fact that part of these circumstances are century-old trees and ageless heavenly bodies is a matter of little importance except insofar as it is a credit to the powers of my fertile imagination."

"*Whew!*" She let go of my hand. "You're strong."

"Thank you, darling. Do you see my point?"

"In theory, O best beloved. My, my, how you do go on. But— what's to prevent my thinking that the universe is a figment of *my* imagination?"

"Nothing. It would be a bit fantastic, of course, in the face of my certain knowledge that it's my creation."

"I'll be damned," she said. She could say things like that—and worse—because she looked so young and sweet that most people simply wouldn't believe it was she who spoke. "I'll be *very* bedamned," she said, and added under her breath a sentence containing the word "insufferable." I imagine she was talking about the weather.

We walked along, and she plucked a leaf of sassafras and chewed on it. The leaf was the kind of green against her lips that showed how red her lips were against her cheeks. "Wouldn't it be funny," she said after a bit, "if all that nonsense you drool were true, and things just stopped *being* when you doubted them?"

"Please!" I said sharply, changing my bathing trunks from my right hand to my left so I could raise a more admonitory forefinger at her. "Nonsense? Drool? Explain yourself, Judith!"

"Oh, stop it!" she shouted, quite taking me aback. "I love you, Woodie," she went on more quietly, "but I think you're a conceited ass. Also, you talk too much. Let's sing songs or something."

"I do not feel like singing songs or something," I said coldly, "while you are so hysterically unfair. You can't disprove a thing I've said."

"And you can't prove it. Please. Woodie—I don't want to fight. This is a summer vacation and we're going swimming today and I love you and I agree with everything you say. I think you're marvelous. Now for Heaven's sake *will* you talk about something else for a change?"

"I can't prove it, hm-m-m?" I said darkly.

She clapped two slim hands to her head and said in a monotone, "The moon is made of green cheese. It isn't but if it did happen to be and you found out, it certainly would be. I am going out of my mind. I am going to gnash my teeth and paw the air and froth at the mouth and you make me SICK!"

"Your reasoning is typically feminine," I told her, "spectacular but highly inaccurate. My point is this." I ignored her moans. "Since I am the creator of all things"—I made an inclusive gesture—"I can also be their destroyer. A case in point—we'll take that noble old spruce over there. I don't believe in it. It does not exist. It is but another figment of my imagination, one without a rational explanation. I do not see it any more because it is not there. It could not be there: it's a physical and psychic impossibility. It—" At last I yielded to her persistent yanking on my elbow.

"Woodie! Oh— Woodie ... it's gone! Th-that tree; it's ... oh, Woodie! I'm scared! What happened?"

She pointed wordlessly at the new clearing in the copse.

"I dunno. I—" I wet my lips and tried again. "My God," I said quietly. "Oh, my God." I was shaking and stone-cold, there in the sun, and my throat was tight. Judith had bruised my arm with her nails; I felt it sharply when she let me go and stood back from me. It wasn't the disappearance of a thousand board feet of good spruce that bothered me particularly. After all, it wasn't my tree. But—oh, my God!

I looked at Judith and was suddenly conscious that she was about to run away from me. I put out my arms, and she ran into them instead. She cried then. We both knew then who—what—I was; neither of us could admit it. But anyway, she cried ... you know, I was quite a fellow. The miracle of growth was my invention, and the air was warm and the sky blue for me, and the moon was silver and the sun golden, all for me alone. The earth would quake beneath my feet if I so chose, and a supernova was but a flash in my brainpan. And yet when Judith cried in my arms I just did not know what to do. We sat together on a rock beside the road and she cried because she was scared and I patted her shoulder and felt perfectly rotten. I was scared too.

What was real? I dropped my fingers to the stone and stroked its mossy coolth. Something that was all legs scuttled out from under my fingertips. I glanced down at it. It was red-brown and shiny and rather horrible. What peculiar ideas I did have at times!

The stone, for instance. It didn't *have* to be there. It wasn't necessary to me, save as a minor element in a pretty bit of scenery that I appreciated. I might just as well not—

"Uff," said Judith, and bit her lip as she plumped down on the bare earth where that stone had been.

"Judith," I said weakly as I climbed to my feet and helped her up. "That was a—a trick."

"I didn't like it," she said furiously. "Ooooh."

"I didn't do anything," I said plaintively. "I just... It just..."

She rubbed her lip. "I know, I know. Let's see you put it back, smart man. Go ahead! Don't look so helpless! Go *on!*"

I tried. I tried with everything I had, and you know, I couldn't put it back? Truly. It wasn't there, that's all. You've got to have some belief in a thing before you can so much as imagine it; you have to allow for its possibility. That stone was gone, and gone for good. It was terrifying. It was something more inevitable, more completely final, than death.

Afterward we walked along together. Judith clung to my hand all the way down to the lake. She was considerably shaken. Oddly, I wasn't. This thing was like a birthmark with me. I hadn't quite realized I was this way until that day; and then I just had the feeling, "I'll be damned, it's true after all."

It was true, and as time went on I realized more and more what was going to happen because of it. I was so certain that I couldn't even worry about it. For your own peace of mind, I'd try not to get into the same frame of mind, if I were you. I know what I am talking about, because I am you, being as to how you are all figments of my imagination...

So there we were down at the lake, and as long as I was with Judith I was all right. She kept me from thinking about anything but her own magnificent self, and that was what was required to maintain the status quo. Anything I doubted had no chance to exist. I couldn't doubt Judith. Not then I couldn't. Ah, what a beauty she was! ... too bad about Judith.

I stood there watching her dive. She was a wonder. Only girl I ever knew personally who could do a two-and-a-half off a twelve-foot board. Maybe she could fly like that because she was half-angel. I noticed Monte Carleau looking at her too, through his expensive polarized sunglasses. I went over to him and took the glasses away from him.

I didn't like Monte. I guess I envied him that long brown chassis of his, and his blue-black hair. I can admit things like that now.

"Hey!" he barked, grabbing for the specs. "What's the huge idea?"

I put on the glasses and watched Judith, who was poised for a cutaway, up there on the twelve-foot, and I talked to Monte over my shoulder. "I don't like you," I told him. "I don't like your staring at Judith. And I don't like to see you wearing glasses on account of I feel like poking you every time I see you and I'd hate to hit a guy with glasses on."

Judith did her cutaway and it was perfect. Then Monte grabbed me and twisted me around. He was thirty pounds heavier than I and one of those guys who takes credit to himself for being what he was born. "Gettin' big, hey?" he barked. "Little ol' Woodie, a tough guy after all these years! What's that twist see in you anyway? She sure shows bad taste."

"—and I don't like a guy that fights with his mouth," I said as if I hadn't been interrupted. I could just see Monte Carleau lying flat on his back with a busted jaw.

As a matter of fact I did see Monte Carleau lying flat on his back with a busted jaw. I shrugged and walked over to where Judith was climbing out of the water.

"What happened to the glamour-boy?" she asked, seeing the crowd gathering around the writhing figure on the bank.

"Oh—he just overlooked a possibility."

"Woodie—you didn't hit him?"

"Nup."

"Another—trick, Woodie?"

I didn't answer. She watched me for a moment, standing near, smelling of wet wool and wonder. She looked down at her nails, drew a deep breath and shrugged. She saw the glasses and reached for them.

She put them on and looked out across the lake, and gasped at the way the polarized glass killed the glare. "That *is* something. How does it work?" she asked in the tone that women in love use, and which signifies, "You know this as well as everything else, you great, big, clever brute, you."

I said vaguely, "Oh, it's something about making the lightwaves all vibrate in one plane. I dunno."

"It hardly seems possible."

"No," I said. I'm pretty simple about things like that, anyway.

As far as I was concerned it wasn't possible...

"Ouch!" she said. "Ouch. I was looking at that patch on the lake where all that sun glare is, and the glasses killed it, and all of a sudden it was there, just as if I hadn't had the glasses on at all ... Woodie! Did you—?" She snatched off the glasses and stared at me with her eyes very wide.

I didn't say anything. Just tried to think about something else.

"You've ruined a good pair of sunglasses," she said.

"I've ruined an industry, I'm afraid."

She twitched the glasses into the lake and crinkled up the smoothness over her eyes. "Woodie—this was funny for a while. I—think ... oh darling, I'm so scared."

I spread my hands. "I can't—*help* it, honey. Honestly. It's just that—uh—since I figured something out up the trail there, anything I don't believe just ... isn't. Just *can't be!*"

She looked at me while she shook her head, so that her long green eyes slid back and forth. "I don't like it. I don't like it at all, Woodie."

"Can't be helped."

"Let's go back," she said suddenly, and went to the dressing cabins.

I didn't worry much about Judith for a while after that. There were too many other things to worry about.

I was looking at some pictures in a magazine one day, and ran across the picture of an albino catfish which had a profile like a shrimp and a complexion like a four-color cosmetic ad. Weirdest thing I ever saw, and I couldn't be expected to believe it. A week later I read in the paper that the genus Clariidae had disappeared from the earth, simultaneously and with no apparent explanation— not only from its natural habitat, but from aquaria all over the world. I got quite a shock from that. You can imagine.

Good thing I've got a matter-of-fact sort of mind. Suppose I had been highly imaginative, now, like those characters who write for magazines. I might have believed in any old thing! "Ghosties and ghoulies and lang-leggedy beasties, and things that go boomp i' th' nicht—" as they put it in Scotland. People who believe in those things do see them, come to think of it. Maybe everybody's like me, only they don't realize it. I hoped, at the time, that nobody ever would. Another like me could certainly complicate things. I've made enough of a hash of it. A nice, churned-up, illimitably negative hash.

It didn't matter what the circumstances were in those next days, I drove a hard bargain with the fates. I could accept things—anything—unless something gave me cause to doubt. For quite a while I didn't realize where this was leading me; then I saw that every recognized fact must wind up in incredulity. Take a fact; reason from it; sooner or later you'll run up against something a little hard to take. My particular egocentricity led me to disbelieve, completely, anything I could not fully understand. For a lightweight like me that made my skepticism pretty inclusive after a while!

What I did was to get away from that summer resort—and Judith. She was the sort to stick to a man, no matter what. I wanted to find out "what."

She didn't want me to go. She was definite about it. "Something's happened to you, Woodie," she said quietly as she systematically threw out all the clothes I put in my suitcase, just as systematically as I put them in. "I told you before I don't like it. Isn't that enough to make you stop it?"

"I'm not doing anything I can stop," I said.

"I would stop," she said illogically, "if you asked *me* to."

"I told you, darling—I'm not doing anything. Things happen, that's all."

"Matter," she said suddenly, planting herself in front of me, "can be neither created nor destroyed."

I sighed and sat down on the edge of the bed. She immediately sat beside, on, and around me. "You been reading books," I said.

"Well, what about it? You're worried because things happen. You made a rock vanish. But you can't destroy matter. It has to turn into energy or something. So you just couldn't have done it."

"But I did."

"That doesn't matter. It isn't logic," she said, in a *quod erat demonstrandum* tone.

"You're overlooking one thing, irresistible creature," I said, pushing her away from me, "and that is the fact that I don't believe that

precept about the indestructibility of matter, and never did. Therefore matter can be destroyed. Matter's just a figment of my imagination, anyway."

She opened and closed her lovely mouth twice and then said,
"But in school—"

"*Damn* school!" I snapped. "Do I have to prove it to you?" I
looked about the room for demonstration material, but couldn't see
anything offhand I could do without. I was travelling light. My eyes
fell on her low-heeled pumps. "Look—you've lost your shoes some-
place, I'll wager."

"I have not. I—*eek!*"

"—and your socks—"

"Woodie!"

"And that cute little blue beret—"

"Woodie, if you—"

"—what! No sunsuit?"

I suppose I went too far. As far as that was concerned, I should
have realized that she didn't need one. As for those—well, how was
I supposed to know she didn't use 'em? . . . I think that this was the
only time I ever consciously did anything constructive with my cre-
ative imagination. Once somebody gave me a shapeless, hooded,
scratchy burnoose from North Africa. It wasn't pretty, and it wasn't
comfortable, but it was the most all-fired enveloping garment ever
devised by the mind of man. But she didn't deserve this kind of treatment. When I thought "Cover up" I thought "Burnoose" automatically . . .

She clutched it around her. Now, get this. She didn't say, "You're
a beast." Or "heel." Or "Schlemiel." She said, "I think you're wonderful, Woodie." And she ran out, crying.

I sat there for a long time and then I finished my packing.

When I got back to the city and into my room I felt much better.
The way I was now, I had to have things around me that I knew and
was used to. They lent solidity to a quivering old universe. As long
as they stood firm, the universe was safe.

My room was pretty nice. If you came to see me, we could drink
coffee, if you didn't mind getting up every time I reached for the

sugar. Small. The carpet was on the wall and there was a Navajo rug on the floor. Couple of pastels and a nice charcoal of Judith. Indirect lighting, which meant a disk of black cardboard hanging by rubber bands from the otherwise unshaded bulb. Books. Bed. A radio that was going twenty-four hours a day.

Why should there be only twenty-four hours in a day?

I throttled the thought before it got anywhere.

I switched on both lights, the radio, and the hotplate under my coffee brewer. That humming noise was the meter turning like a phonograph playing the "Landlord's Blues" (the utilities were included in the three fifty a week).

While I was hanging up my coat, Drip burst in, bellowing "Hiyah, Woodie? Hiyah, pal, back huh. What happened, huh?"

I closed the closet, spun around and gave him the old one-two on the mouth and chin, planted a foot in his stomach, and kicked him out in the hall. Opposite my door is what was first a crack, then a dent, now a hollow, where the Drip had continually hit it. I didn't have anything against him, but I'd asked him, I'd asked him time and time again, to knock before he came in.

As soon as I had the door closed he bumped timidly upon it.

"Who is it?"

"Me?"

I opened up. "Oh. Hello, Drip."

He came in and started his greetings and salutations all over again. Poor old Drip. He'd been pushed around by half the population from Eastport to Sandy Hook, and if he minded it, it never showed. He had a voice which was squeaky without being high, a curving stance that was apprehensive rather than round-shouldered, a complexion which was more pink than healthy, shoulders which were much broader than they were strong, and an untruthful aggressive chin. The guy was whacked but harmless.

He once asked me what I thought of him and I said, "You're the Creator's transition between a hypothesis and a theory." He's still trying to figure it out ... if he's where he can figure anything.

Drip was useful, though. I don't care who you are, if you are with the Drip, you feel superior. So he was useful. The fact that he felt correspondingly inferior was his hard luck. It was no one's fault that he pushed an eight-ball ahead of him through life. Certainly not his.

He talked like this:

"Gee? Woodie? It's good to see you again? What are you going to do. Go back to work. Without? Finishing your vacation. Gee? Something must have. Did you fight. With Judith? Gosh ... everything happens to you?"

"Do you want some coffee and stop crossquestioning me," I said.

"I'm sorry." The phrase was a reflex with him.

"What've you been doing with yourself, Drip?"

"Nothing? Nothing? Why are you. *Back,* Woodie?"

"Well, I'll tell you." I scratched my head. "Oh, hell. Never mind. Drip, I'm going to grab an oil can."

"Sh-ship out. On a tanker again? Oh, Woodie, you can't. *Do* that? I thought you'd quit going to sea."

"I can do anything," I said with conviction. "I'm—jittery around here, thassall."

He looked at the Arabian prayer-rug on the wall and the way it was reflected in the big mirror across the room. "If you go, could I have your room," he whispered as if he were asking me to die for him.

"No, boy. I want you to come with me."

"What?" he screamed. "Me. On a ship. Oh? No! Nono*no!*"

Looking at Drip, putting sugar in his coffee, I felt suddenly sorry for him. I wanted to help him. I wanted him to share the exultance I had known in the days before I met Judith and had dropped the anchor.

"Sure. Why not, Drip? I hit my first ship when I was sixteen, and I got treated all right."

"Oh, yes," he said without sarcasm, "you can do all sorts of things. Not me? I could never do the things you've done?"

"Nuts," I said. Being with Drip always did one of two things: made me think how wonderful I was, or how pathetic he was. This was the latter case. In trying to help him out a little, I completely forgot my new potentialities. That's where I made my mistake.

"Look," I said, "why is it that you're afraid of the ghost of your own shadow? I think it's because you refuse to make the effort to over-come your fear. If you're afraid of the dark, turn the light out. If you're afraid of falling, jump off a roof—just a little garage roof some place. If you're afraid of women, stick around them. And if you're afraid to ship out, for gosh sakes come along with me. I'll get a quartermaster's job and you can be ordinary seaman on my watch. I'll show you the ropes. But on any account, face your fear."

"That's the way you do things, isn't it?" he said almost adoringly.

"Well, sure. And you could if you tried. Come on, Drip. Make an effort."

His forehead wrinkled up and he said, "You don't know the kind of things I'm afraid of."

"Name 'em!"

"You'd laugh."

"No!"

"Well, like now, there's a—a— right outside the door. Oh, it's horrible!"

I got up and opened the door. "There's nothing there but some dirt that should have been swept up three days ago."

"You see?" he said. "You want me to see things your way and you can't begin to see the things I see." And he began to cry.

I put my hand on his shoulder. "Drip. Cut it out. I can see every-thing you can. I can—" Why—of *course* I could! Drip was a part of—of everything. His ideas, his way of thought were a part of every-thing. Why not see what he saw? "Drip, I'll see things the way you do. I *will!* I'll see everything with your eyes. I'll show you!"

And immediately the room began to shake itself; things wavered uncomfortably; then I realized that Drip was astigmatic. I also real-ized with a powerful shock that I had been nearly colorblind, com-pared with the vividness with which he saw things. *Whew!*

Then I became conscious of the terrors—the million unidentifi-able fears with which the poor dope had been living, day and night.

The ceiling was going to crush me. The floor was going to rise up and strike me. There was something in the closet, and it would jump out at me any second. I was going to swell inside my clothes and choke to death—I was going to go blind any day now—I was going to be run over if I went outside, suffocate if I stayed in. My appendix was going to burst some night when I was alone and I would die in agony. I was going to catch some terrible disease. People hated me. And laughed ... I was alone. I was on the outside looking in. I was on the inside looking on. I hated myself.

Gradually the impact of the thing faded while the horror grew. I glanced at Drip; he was still crying into his coffee, but at least he was not trembling. I was trembling ... poor, scared, morbid, dismal Drip was, in that moment, a tower of strength.

I must have stood there for quite a while, pulling out of it. I had to *do* something! I couldn't shrink against Drip! I had my self-respect to think of. I—

"Wh-what was that you said about ... outside the door?"

He started, looked up at me, pointed wordlessly at the door. I reached out and opened it.

It was out there, crunched in a corner in the dimness, waiting for someone to come along. I slammed the door and leaned against it, mopping my forehead with my sleeve.

"Is it out there?" whispered Drip.

I nodded. "It's ... covered with mouths," I gasped. "It's all *wet!*"

He got up and peeked out. Then he laughed. "Oh, that's just the little one. He won't hurt you. Wait till you see the others. Gee? Woodie. You're the first one who ever saw them, besides me. Come on? I'll show you more."

He got up and went out, waiting just outside for me. I realized now why he had always refused to precede me through a door. When he went out he trod on a writhing thing and killed it so it would not creep up my legs. I realized that I must have done it for him many times in the past without realizing it.

We came to the top of the stairs. They wound away from under my feet. They looked fragile. They looked dangerous. But it seemed all right as long as he led the way. He had a certain control over the thousands of creeping, crawling, fluttering things around us. He passed the little landing and something tentacular melted into the wall. Little slimy things slid out from under his feet and reappeared just behind mine. I pressed very close to him, crushed by the power of hate which oozed from them.

When we reached his room, which was just above mine, he put his hand on the doorknob and turned to me. "We have to burst in," he whispered, "there's a big one that hides here. We can frighten him away if we come suddenly. Otherwise he might not know we were inside. And if he found us in there he would. Eat us?"

Drip turned the knob silently and hurled the door open. A livid mass of blood and blackness that filled the whole room shrank into itself, melting down like ice in a furnace. When it was in midair, and about the size of a plum, it dropped squashily to the floor and rolled under the bed. "You see," said Drip with conviction. "If we went in quietly we would shrink down. With it?"

"My God!" I said hoarsely. "Let's get out of here!"

"Oh, it's all right," he said almost casually. "As long as we know exactly what time it is, he can't come back until we go." I understood now why Drip had his wall covered with clocks.

I was going to sink down on a chair because I felt a little weak, but I noticed that the seat of the straight-back he had—it was red plush—was quivering. I pointed to it.

"What? Oh, don't mind that," said Drip. "I think it's stuffed with spiders. They haven't bitten anyone yet, but soon they will. Burst the seat. And swarm all over the room?"

I looked at him. "This is hor—Drip! What are you grinning about?"

"Grinning. I'm sorry? You see, I never saw anyone frightened before by my things?"

"*Your* things?"

"Certainly. I made them up."

I have never been so furious. That he should terrify me—*me*—with figments of his phobiacal imagination; make me envy him for knowing his way about his terrifying world; put me in an inferior position—it was unthinkable! It was—impossible!

"Why did you make them up?" I asked him with frozen intensity.

His answer, of all things in the fluid universe, was the most rational. I have thought of it since. He said:

"I made them up because I was afraid of things. Ever since I could remember. So I didn't know what it was I was afraid of, and I had to make up something to fear. If I didn't do that I *would go crazy...* "

I backed away from him, mouthing curses, and the lines of the room straightened out as I regained my own point of view. The colors dulled to my old familiar tones, and Drip, that improbable person, that hypothesis, faded out, lingering a moment like a double exposure, and then vanished.

I went downstairs. Drip was better off nonexistent, I thought as I tuned out a jam session. He was a subversive influence in this—my universe. He was as horrible a figment of imagination as was that thing in the hall of his. And just as unbelievable ... I got me Tchaikovsky's B minor concerto on the radio because that's the way I felt, and I lay down on the bed. Jive would have driven me morbid, because Drip had been a hep-cat, and I didn't want to think of him somehow.

Footsteps came soft-shoeing up the corridor and stopped outside my door. "Woodie—"

"Oh, damn," I said. "Come in, Judith."

She passed the knob from one hand to the other as she entered, looking at me.

"I must be quite a guy to have such a lovely shadow."

"Every man in the world seems to be after me," she said, "and I'm stupid enough to follow you. I came back to say goodbye."

"Where are you going?"

"No place."

"Where am I going?"

"You've already gone."

"I... Where?"

"Here. From the camp. You forgot to kiss me before you left. You can't get away with that."

"Oh." I got up and kissed her. "Now why did you follow me?"

"I was afraid."

"What; that I'd jump a ship?"

She nodded. "That and ... I dunno. I was afraid, thassall."

"I promised you I'd stay ashore, didn't I?"

"You're such an awful liar," she reminded me without malice.

"Heh!" I said. "Always?"

"As long as I've known you—"

"I love you."

"—except when you say that. Woodie, that's one thing I *have* to be sure of."

"I know how it is, insect." I let her go and reached for my hat. "Let's eat."

I remember that meal. It was the last meal I ate on earth. Minestrone, chicken cacciatore and black coffee at a little Italian kitchen. And over the coffee I explained it to her again, the thing that had happened to me.

"Woodie, you're impossible!"

"Could be. Could be. I've found a lot of things impossible in the last couple of days. They don't exist any more. Drip, for instance."

"Drip? What happened?"

I told her. She began putting on her hat.

"Wait," I said. "I haven't finished my coffee."

"Do you realize what you're telling me? Woodie, if you're wrong about all this, you don't know it—you believe it—and you're insane. If you're right—you *murdered* that boy!"

"I did nothing of the kind. I did nothing of any kind. Damn it, darling, I know this is a little hard to take. But the universe is my dream, and that's ... all. Drip couldn't have existed—you told me that yourself when you first met him."

"That was strictly a gag," she said, and stood up.

"Where are you going?"

"I don't know." She sounded tired. "Anywhere ... away from you, Woodie. Let me know when you've got all this out of your head. I've never heard anything so... Oh, well. And anyway, there's a natural explanation for everything that's happened."

"Sure. I've given you one and you won't believe it."

She threw up her hands in what I saw was very real disgust. I caught her hand as she turned away. "Judith!" She stood there not looking at me, not trying to get away, simply not *caring*. "You don't mean this, Judy kid. You can't. You're the only thing I can believe in now."

"When you 'dreamed' me up, Woodie, you let me have too much discernment to stay in love with a . . . a lunatic," she said quietly. She slipped her hand out of mine and went away from there.

I sat still for a long time watching tomato sauce seep into a piece of Italian bread. "When it gets to that pore in the bread," I told myself, "she'll come back." A little later, "When it gets to the crust—" It took quite a while, and she still didn't come back. I tried to laugh it off, but laughing hurt my face. I paid my way out and drifted down the street. I found me a ginmill and I got good . . . and . . . plastered.

Listen, winged things. Listen, things that delight in liveness and greenness. I am sorry I created you, I am sorry I dreamed of you, watched you grow, watched you die and die and live again to see your ultimate death. You were made of laughter and of the warmth in my heart. You were made of the light of the sun I made. You and shy creatures, and strong and beautiful things and people, and music, and richness, and magic, and the beat of hearts; you are gone because I was awakened. Forgive me, my glorious phantasms!

I knew what to start on. It's called Habañera Seco and they brew it in Guatemala and it's smooth like scotch and strong like vodka and worse all around than absinthe. If you can't stand to mix these— and who can?—you can't drink Habañera. . .

One drink and I felt better. Two, much better. Three, and I was back where I started from. Four, I started getting dismal. Seven, I was definitely morbid. Great stuff. Far as I was concerned, the woes of the world were in a bottomless bottle, and it was my duty and desire to empty the bottle and buy another. Judith was gone, and without Judith there was no sun anymore, and nothing for it to shine on. Everything was over, I said dramatically to myself; and, by God, I'd see that a good job was done of it. I staggered out and leaned against the doorpost, looking up the street.

"Wake up, Woodie," I quavered. "It's all over now. It's all done. There's nothing left any more, anywhere, anywhere. A life is an improbable louse on a sterile sphere. A man is a monster and a woman is a wraith! I am not a man but a consciousness asleep, and now I wake! Now I wake!" I pushed away from the doorpost and began screaming, "Wake! Wake!"

Just how it happened I can't say. Things slipped and slid out of existence. There was no violence, nothing fell; everything went out of focus and left me alone in an element which was deep and thick and the essence of solitude. What struck coldly into me was something I saw just before I ... went. It was Judith. She was running down the street toward me with her arms out, and a smile keeping tears from running all the way down her face. She had come back after all, but the thing couldn't be stopped now. My dream was gone!

I and that thick element expanded soundlessly to the limits of my dream, the universe, and where we passed, mighty suns and nebulae joined the nothingness of us. I rode again in a place where there is no time, where I had been before I dreamed up a universe. I thought about it then, how birds and rocks and wars and loveliness and choking exultance had been figments of my proud imagination.

Only now can I dare to face that ultimate question, that last, deep, inclusive conception ...

... for if all things in a universe were but peopling a dream, and if they could not exist when their existence was doubted, then it is possible that I myself am a mere figment of my imagi

It

It walked in the woods.

It was never born. It existed. Under the pine needles the fires burn, deep and smokeless in the mold. In heat and in darkness and decay there is growth. There is life and there is growth. It grew, but it was not alive. It walked unbreathing through the woods, and thought and saw and was hideous and strong, and it was not born and it did not live. It grew and moved about without living.

It crawled out of the darkness and hot damp mold into the cool of a morning. It was huge. It was lumped and crusted with its own hateful substances, and pieces of it dropped off as it went its way, dropped off and lay writhing, and stilled, and sank putrescent into the forest loam.

It had no mercy, no laughter, no beauty. It had strength and great intelligence. And—perhaps it could not be destroyed. It crawled out of its mound in the wood and lay pulsing in the sunlight for a long moment. Patches of it shone wetly in the golden glow, parts of it were nubbled and flaked. And whose dead bones had given it the form of a man?

It scrabbled painfully with its half-formed hands, beating the ground and the bole of a tree. It rolled and lifted itself up on its crumbling elbows, and it tore up a great handful of herbs and shredded them against its chest, and it paused and gazed at the gray-green juices with intelligent calm. It wavered to its feet, and seized a young sapling and destroyed it, folding the slender trunk back on itself again and again, watching attentively the useless, fibered splinters. And it snatched up a fear-frozen field creature, crushing it slowly, letting blood and pulpy flesh and fur ooze from between its fingers, run down and rot on the forearms.

It began searching.

303

Kimbo drifted through the tall grasses like a puff of dust, his bushy tail curled tightly over his back and his long jaws agape. He ran with an easy lope, loving his freedom and the power of his flanks and furry shoulders. His tongue lolled listlessly over his lips. His lips were black and serrated, and each tiny pointed liplet swayed with his doggy gallop. Kimbo was all dog, all healthy animal.

He leaped high over a boulder and landed with a startled yelp as a longeared cony shot from its hiding place under the rock. Kimbo hurtled after it, grunting with each great thrust of his legs. The rabbit bounced just ahead of him, keeping its distance, its ears flattened on its curving back and its little legs nibbling away at distance hungrily. It stopped, and Kimbo pounced, and the rabbit shot away at a tangent and popped into a hollow log. Kimbo yelped again and rushed snuffling at the log, and knowing his failure, curvetted but once around the stump and ran on into the forest. The thing that watched from the wood raised its crusted arms and waited for Kimbo.

Kimbo sensed it there, standing dead-still by the path. To him it was a bulk which smelled of carrion not fit to roll in, and he snuffled distastefully and ran to pass it.

The thing let him come abreast and dropped a heavy twisted fist on him. Kimbo saw it coming and curled up tight as he ran, and the hand clipped stunningly on his rump, sending him rolling and yipping down the slope. Kimbo straddled to his feet, shook his head, shook his body with a deep growl, came back to the silent thing with green murder in his eyes. He walked stiffly, straight-legged, his tail as low as his lowered head and a ruff of fury round his neck. The thing raised its arms again, waited.

Kimbo slowed, then flipped himself through the air at the monster's throat. His jaws closed on it; his teeth clicked together through a mass of filth, and he fell choking and snarling at its feet. The thing leaned down and struck twice, and after the dog's back was broken, it sat beside him and began to tear him apart.

"Be back in an hour or so," said Alton Drew, picking up his rifle from the corner behind the wood box. His brother laughed.

"Old Kimbo 'bout runs your life, Alton," he said.

"Ah, I know the ol' devil," said Alton. "When I whistle for him for half an hour and he don't show up, he's in a jam or he's treed something wuth shootin' at. The ol' son of a gun calls me by not answerin'."

Cory Drew shoved a full glass of milk over to his nine-year-old daughter and smiled. "You think as much o' that houn'-dog o' yours as I do of Babe here."

Babe slid off her chair and ran to her uncle. "Gonna catch me the bad fella, Uncle Alton?" she shrilled. The "bad fella" was Cory's invention—the one who lurked in corners ready to pounce on little girls who chased the chickens and played around mowing machines and hurled green apples with a powerful young arm at the sides of the hogs, to hear the synchronized thud and grunt; little girls who swore with an Austrian accent like an ex-hired man they had had; who dug caves in haystacks till they tipped over, and kept pet crawfish in tomorrow's milk cans, and rode work horses to a lather in the night pasture.

"Get back here and keep away from Uncle Alton's gun!" said Cory. "If you see the bad fella, Alton, chase him back here. He has a date with Babe here for that stunt of hers last night." The preceding evening, Babe had kindheartedly poured pepper on the cows' salt block.

"Don't worry, kiddo," grinned her uncle, "I'll bring you the bad fella's hide if he don't get me first."

Alton Drew walked up the path toward the wood, thinking about Babe. She was a phenomenon—a pampered farm child. Ah well— she had to be. They'd both loved Clissa Drew, and she'd married Cory, and they had to love Clissa's child. Funny thing, love. Alton was a man's man, and thought things out that way; and his reaction to love was a strong and frightened one. He knew what love was because he felt it still for his brother's wife and would feel it as long as he lived for Babe. It led him through his life, and yet he embarrassed himself by thinking of it. Loving a dog was an easy thing, because you and the old devil could love one another completely without talking about it. The smell of gun smoke and wet fur in the rain were perfume enough for Alton Drew, a grunt of satisfaction and the scream of something hunted and hit were poetry enough. They weren't like love for a human, that choked his throat so he could not say words he could not have thought of anyway. So Alton loved his dog Kimbo and his Winchester for all to see, and let his love for his brother's women, Clissa and Babe, eat at him quietly and unmentioned.

His quick eyes saw the fresh indentations in the soft earth behind the boulder, which showed where Kimbo had turned and leaped with a single surge, chasing the rabbit. Ignoring the tracks, he looked for the nearest place where a rabbit might hide, and strolled over to the stump. Kimbo had been there, he saw, and had been there too late. "You're an ol' fool," muttered Alton. "Y' can't catch a cony by chasin' it. You want to cross him up some way." He gave a peculiar trilling whistle, sure that Kimbo was digging frantically under some nearby stump for a rabbit that was three counties away by now. No answer. A little puzzled, Alton went back to the path. "He never done this before," he said softly.

He cocked his .32–40 and cradled it. At the county fair someone had once said of Alton Drew that he could shoot at a handful of corn and peas thrown in the air and hit only the corn. Once he split a bullet on the blade of a knife and put two candles out. He had no need to fear anything that could be shot at. That's what he believed.

The thing in the woods looked curiously down at what it had done to Kimbo, and tried to moan the way Kimbo had before he died. It stood a minute storing away facts in its foul, unemotional mind. Blood was warm. The sunlight was warm. Things that moved and bore fur had a muscle to force the thick liquid through tiny tubes in their bodies. The liquid coagulated after a time. The liquid on rooted green things was thinner and the loss of a limb did not mean loss of life. It was very interesting, but the thing, the mold with a mind, was not pleased. Neither was it displeased. Its accidental urge was a thirst for knowledge, and it was only—interested.

It was growing late, and the sun reddened and rested awhile on the hilly horizon, teaching the clouds to be inverted flames. The thing threw up its head suddenly, noticing the dusk. Night was ever a strange thing, even for those of us who have known it in life. It would have been frightening for the monster had it been capable of fright, but it could only be curious; it could only reason from what it had observed.

What was happening? It was getting harder to see. Why? It threw its shapeless head from side to side. It was true—things were dim, and growing dimmer. Things were changing shape, taking on a new and darker color. What did the creatures it had crushed and torn apart see? How did they see? The larger one, the one that had attacked, had used two organs in its head. That must have been it, because after the thing had torn off two of the dog's legs it had struck at the hairy muzzle; and the dog, seeing the blow coming, had dropped folds of skin over the organs—closed its eyes. Ergo, the dog saw with its eyes. But then after the dog was dead, and its body still, repeated blows had had no effect on the eyes. They remained open and staring. The logical conclusion was, then, that a being that had ceased to live and breathe and move about lost the use of its eyes. It must be that to lose sight was, conversely, to die. Dead things did not walk about. They lay down and did not move. Therefore the thing in the wood concluded that it must be dead, and so it lay down by the path, not far away from Kimbo's scattered body, lay down and believed itself dead.

Alton Drew came up through the dusk to the wood. He was frankly worried. He whistled again, and then called, and there was still no response, and he said again, "The ol' fleabus never done this before," and shook his heavy head. It was past milking time, and Cory would need him. "Kimbo!" he roared. The cry echoed through the shadows, and Alton flipped on the safety catch of his rifle and put the butt on the ground beside the path. Leaning on it, he took off his cap and scratched the back of his head, wondering. The rifle butt sank into what he thought was soft earth; he staggered and stepped into the chest of the thing that lay beside the path. His foot went up to the ankle in its yielding rottenness, and he swore and jumped back.

"*Whew!* Somp'n sure dead as hell there! Ugh!" He swabbed at his boot with a handful of leaves while the monster lay in the growing blackness with the edges of the deep footprint in its chest sliding into it, filling it up. It lay there regarding him dimly out of its muddy eyes, thinking it was dead because of the darkness, watching the articulation of Alton Drew's joints, wondering at this new uncautious creature.

Alton cleaned the butt of his gun with more leaves and went on up the path, whistling anxiously for Kimbo.

Clissa Drew stood in the door of the milk shed, very lovely in redchecked gingham and a blue apron. Her hair was clean yellow, parted in the middle and stretched tautly back to a heavy braided knot. "Cory! Alton!" she called a little sharply.

"Well?" Cory responded gruffly from the barn, where he was stripping off the Ayrshire. The dwindling streams of milk plopped pleasantly into the froth of a full pail.

"I've called and called," said Clissa. "Supper's cold, and Babe won't eat until you come. Why—where's Alton?"

Cory grunted, heaved the stool out of the way, threw over the stanchion lock and slapped the Ayrshire on the rump. The cow backed and filled like a towboat, clattered down the line and out into the barnyard. "Ain't back yet."

"Not back?" Clissa came in and stood beside him as he sat by the next cow, put his forehead against the warm flank. "But, Cory, he said he'd—"

"Yeh, yeh, I know. He said he'd be back fer the milkin'. I heard him. Well, he ain't."

"And you have to— Oh, Cory, I'll help you finish up. Alton would be back if he could. Maybe he's—"

"Maybe he's treed a blue jay," snapped her husband. "Him an' that damn dog." He gestured hugely with one hand while the other went on milking. "I got twenty-six head o' cows to milk. I got pigs to feed an' chickens to put to bed. I got to toss hay for the mare and turn the team out. I got harness to mend and a wire down in the night pasture. I got wood to split an' carry." He milked for a moment in silence, chewing on his lip. Clissa stood twisting her hands together, trying to think of something to stem the tide. It wasn't the first time Alton's hunting had interfered with the chores. "So I got to go ahead with it. I can't interfere with Alton's spoorin'. Every damn time that hound o' his smells out a squirrel I go without my supper. I'm gettin' sick and—"

"Oh, I'll help you!" said Clissa. She was thinking of the spring, when Kimbo had held four hundred pounds of raging black bear at bay until Alton could put a bullet in its brain, the time Babe had found a bearcub and started to carry it home, and had fallen into a freshet, cutting her head. You can't hate a dog that has saved your child for you, she thought.

"You'll do nothin' of the kind!" Cory growled. "Get back to the house. You'll find work enough there. I'll be along when I can. Dammit, Clissa, don't cry! I didn't mean to— Oh, shucks!" He got up and put his arms around her. "I'm wrought up," he said. "Go on now. I'd no call to speak that way to you. I'm sorry. Go back to Babe. I'll put a stop to this for good tonight. I've had enough. There's work here for four farmers an' all we've got is me an' that ... that huntsman.

"Go on now, Clissa."

"All right," she said into his shoulder. "But, Cory, hear him out first when he comes back. He might be unable to come back. He might be unable to come back this time. Maybe he ... he—"

"Ain't nothin' kin hurt my brother that a bullet will hit. He can take care of himself. He's got no excuse good enough this time. Go on, now. Make the kid eat."

Clissa went back to the house, her young face furrowed. If Cory quarreled with Alton now and drove him away, what with the drought and the creamery about to close and all, they just couldn't manage. Hiring a man was out of the question. Cory'd have to work himself to death, and he just wouldn't be able to make it. No one man could. She sighed and went into the house. It was seven o'clock, and the milking not done yet. Oh, why did Alton have to—

Babe was in bed at nine when Clissa heard Cory in the shed, slinging the wire cutters into a corner. "Alton back yet?" they both said at once as Cory stepped into the kitchen; and as she shook her head he clumped over to the stove, and lifting a lid, spat into the coals. "Come to bed," he said.

She laid down her stitching and looked at his broad back. He was twenty-eight, and he walked and acted like a man ten years older, and looked like a man five years younger. "I'll be up in a while," Clissa said.

Cory glanced at the corner behind the wood box where Alton's rifle usually stood, then made an unspellable, disgusted sound and sat down to take off his heavy muddy shoes.

"It's after nine," Clissa volunteered timidly. Cory said nothing, reaching for house slippers.

"Cory, you're not going to—"

"Not going to what?"

"Oh, nothing. I just thought that maybe Alton—"

"Alton!" Cory flared. "The dog goes hunting field mice. Alton goes hunting the dog. Now you want me to go hunting Alton. That's what you want?"

"I just— He was never this late before."

"I won't do it! Go out lookin' for him at nine o'clock in the night? I'll be damned! He has no call to use us so, Clissa."

Clissa said nothing. She went to the stove, peered into the wash boiler, set it aside at the back of the range. When she turned around, Cory had his shoes and coat on again.

"I knew you'd go," she said. Her voice smiled though she did not.

"I'll be back durned soon," said Cory. "I don't reckon he's strayed far. It is late. I ain't feared for him, but—" He broke his 12-gauge shotgun, looked through the barrels, slipped two shells in the breech and a box of them into his pocket. "Don't wait up," he said over his shoulder as he went out.

"I won't," Clissa replied to the closed door, and went back to her stitching by the lamp.

The path up the slope to the wood was very dark when Cory went up it, peering and calling. The air was chill and quiet, and a fetid odor of mold hung in it. Cory blew the taste of it out through impatient nostrils, drew it in again with the next breath, and swore. "Nonsense," he muttered. "Houn' dawg. Huntin', at ten in th' night, too. Alton!" he bellowed. "Alton Drew!" Echoes answered him, and he entered the wood. The huddled thing he passed in the dark heard him and felt the vibrations of his footsteps and did not move because it thought it was dead.

Cory strode on, looking around and ahead and not down since his feet knew the path.

"Alton!"

"That you, Cory?"

Cory Drew froze. That corner of the wood was thickly set and as dark as a burial vault. The voice he heard was choked, quiet, penetrating.

"Alton?"

"I found Kimbo, Cory."

"Where the hell have you been?" shouted Cory furiously. He disliked this pitch-darkness; he was afraid at the tense hopelessness of Alton's voice, and he mistrusted his ability to stay angry at his brother.

"I called him, Cory. I whistled at him, an' the ol' devil didn't answer."

"I can say the same for you, you ... you louse. Why weren't you to milkin'? Where are you? You caught in a trap?"

"The houn' never missed answerin' me before, you know," said the tight, monotonous voice from the darkness.

"Alton! What the devil's the matter with you? What do I care if your mutt didn't answer? Where—"

"I guess because he ain't never died before," said Alton, refusing to be interrupted.

"You *what?*" Cory clicked his lips together twice and then said, "Alton, you turned crazy? What's that you say?"

"Kimbo's dead."

"Kim ... oh! Oh!" Cory was seeing that picture again in his mind—Babe sprawled unconscious in the freshet, and Kimbo raging and snapping against a monster bear, holding her back until Alton could get there. "What happened, Alton?" he asked more quietly.

"I aim to find out. Someone tore him up."

"Tore him up?"

"There ain't a bit of him left tacked together, Cory. Every damn joint in his body tore apart. Guts out of him."

"Good God! Bear, you reckon?"

"No bear, nor nothin' on four legs. He's all here. None of him's been et. Whoever done it just killed him an'—tore him up."

"Good God!" Cory said again. "Who could've—" There was a long silence, then. "Come 'long home," he said almost gently. "There's no call for you to set up by him all night."

"I'll set. I aim to be here at sunup, an' I'm goin' to start trackin', an' I'm goin' to keep trackin' till I find the one done this job on Kimbo."

"You're drunk or crazy, Alton."

"I ain't drunk. You can think what you like about the rest of it. I'm stickin' here."

"We got a farm back yonder. Remember? I ain't going to milk twenty-six head o' cows again in the mornin' like I did jest now, Alton."

"Somebody's got to. I can't be there. I guess you'll just have to, Cory."

"You dirty scum!" Cory screamed. "You'll come back with me now or I'll know why!"

Alton's voice was still tight, half-sleepy. "Don't you come no nearer, bud."

Cory kept moving toward Alton's voice.

"I said"—the voice was very quiet now—"*stop where you are.*" Cory kept coming. A sharp click told of the release of the .32-40's safety. Cory stopped.

"You got your gun on me, Alton?" Cory whispered.

"Thass right, bud. You ain't a-trompin' up these tracks for me. I need 'em at sunup."

A full minute passed, and the only sound in the blackness was that of Cory's pained breathing. Finally:

"I got my gun, too, Alton. Come home."

"You can't see to shoot me."

"We're even on that."

"We ain't. I know just where you stand, Cory. I been here four hours."

"My gun scatters."

"My gun kills."

Without another word Cory Drew turned on his heel and stamped back to the farm.

Black and liquidescent it lay in the blackness, not alive, not under-standing death, believing itself dead. Things that were alive saw and moved about. Things that were not alive could do neither. It rested its muddy gaze on the line of trees at the crest of the rise, and deep within it thoughts trickled wetly. It lay huddled, dividing its new-found facts, dissecting them as it had dissected live things when there was light, comparing, concluding, pigeonholing.

The trees at the top of the slope could just be seen, as their trunks were a fraction of a shade lighter than the dark sky behind them. At length they, too, disappeared, and for a moment sky and trees were a monotone. The thing knew it was dead now, and like many a being before it, it wondered how long it must stay like this. And then the sky beyond the trees grew a little lighter. That was a manifestly impos-sible occurrence, thought the thing, but it could see it and it must be so. Did dead things live again? That was curious. What about dis-membered dead things? It would wait and see.

The sun came hand over hand up a beam of light. A bird some-where made a high yawning peep, and as an owl killed a shrew, a skunk pounced on another, so that the night shift deaths and those of the day could go on without cessation. Two flowers nodded archly to each other, comparing their pretty clothes. A dragonfly nymph decided it was tired of looking serious and cracked its back open, to crawl out and dry gauzily. The first golden ray sheared down between the trees, through the grasses, passed over the mass in the shadowed bushes. "I am alive again," thought the thing that could not possi-bly live. "I am alive, for I see clearly." It stood up on its thick legs, up into the golden glow. In a little while the wet flakes that had grown during the night dried in the sun, and when it took its first steps, they cracked off and a small shower of them fell away. It walked up the slope to find Kimbo, to see if he, too, were alive again.

Babe let the sun come into her room by opening her eyes. Uncle Alton was gone—that was the first thing that ran through her head. Dad had come home last night and had shouted at mother for an hour. Alton was plumb crazy. He'd turned a gun on his own brother. If Alton ever came ten feet into Cory's land, Cory would fill him so full of holes he'd look like a tumbleweed. Alton was lazy, shiftless, selfish, and one or two other things of questionable taste but undoubted vividness. Babe knew her father. Uncle Alton would never be safe in this county.

She bounced out of bed in the enviable way of the very young, and ran to the window. Cory was trudging down to the night pasture with two bridles over his arm, to get the team. There were kitchen noises from downstairs.

Babe ducked her head in the washbowl and shook off the water like a terrier before she toweled. Trailing clean shirt and dungarees, she went to the head of the stairs, slid into the shirt, and began her morning ritual with the trousers. One step down was a step through the right leg. One more, and she was into the left. Then, bouncing step by step on both feet, buttoning one button per step, she reached the bottom fully dressed and ran into the kitchen.

"Didn't Uncle Alton come back a-tall, Mum?"

"Morning, Babe. No, dear." Clissa was too quiet, smiling too much, Babe thought shrewdly. Wasn't happy.

"Where'd he go, Mum?"

"We don't know, Babe. Sit down and eat your breakfast."

"What's a misbegotten, Mum?" the Babe asked suddenly. Her mother nearly dropped the dish she was drying. "Babe! You must never say that again!"

"Oh. Well, why is Uncle Alton, then?"

"Why is he what?"

Babe's mouth muscled around an outsize spoonful of oatmeal. "A misbe—"

"Babe!"

"All right, Mum," said Babe with her mouth full. "Well, why?"

"I told Cory not to shout last night," Clissa said half to herself.

"Well, whatever it means, he isn't," said Babe with finality. "Did he go hunting again?"

"He went to look for Kimbo, darling."

"Kimbo? Oh Mummy, is Kimbo gone, too? Didn't he come back either?"

"No dear. Oh, please, Babe, stop asking questions!"

"All right. Where do you think they went?"

"Into the north woods. Be quiet."

Babe gulped away at her breakfast. An idea struck her; and as she thought of it she ate slower and slower, and cast more and more glances at her mother from under the lashes of her tilted eyes. It would be awful if Daddy did anything to Uncle Alton. Someone ought to warn him.

Babe was halfway to the woods when Alton's .32–40 sent echoes giggling up and down the valley.

Cory was in the south thirty, riding a cultivator and cussing at the team of grays when he heard the gun. "Hoa," he called to the horses, and sat a moment to listen to the sound. "One-two-three. Four," he counted. "Saw someone, blasted away at him. Had a chance to take aim and give him another, careful. My God!" He threw up the cultivator points and steered the team into the shade of three oaks. He hobbled the gelding with swift tosses of a spare strap, and headed for the woods. "Alton a killer," he murmured, and doubled back to the house for his gun. Clissa was standing just outside the door.

"Get shells!" he snapped and flung into the house. Clissa followed him. He was strapping his hunting knife on before she could get a box off the shelf. "Cory—"

"Hear that gun, did you? Alton's off his nut. He don't waste lead. He shot at someone just then, and he wasn't fixin' to shoot pa'tridges when I saw him last. He was out to get a man. Gimme my gun."

"Cory, Babe—"

"You keep her here. Oh, God, this is a helluva mess. I can't stand much more." Cory ran out the door.

Clissa caught his arm: "Cory I'm trying to tell you. Babe isn't here. I've called, and she isn't here."

Cory's heavy, young-old face tautened. "Babe— Where did you last see her?"

"Breakfast." Clissa was crying now.

"She say where she was going?"

"No. She asked a lot of questions about Alton and where he'd gone."

"Did you say?"

Clissa's eyes widened, and she nodded, biting the back of her hand.

"You shouldn't ha' done that, Clissa," he gritted, and ran toward the woods. Clissa stood looking after him, and in that moment she could have killed herself.

Cory ran with his head up, straining with his legs and lungs and eyes at the long path. He puffed up the slope to the woods, agonized for breath after the forty-five minutes' heavy going. He couldn't even notice the damp smell of mold in the air.

He caught a movement in a thicket to his right, and dropped. Struggling to keep his breath, he crept forward until he could see clearly. There was something in there, all right. Something black, keeping still. Cory relaxed his legs and torso completely to make it easier for his heart to pump some strength back into them, and slowly raised the 12-gauge until it bore on the thing hidden in the thicket.

"Come out!" Cory said when he could speak.

Nothing happened.

"Come out or by God I'll shoot!" rasped Cory.

There was a long moment of silence, and his finger tightened on the trigger.

"You asked for it," he said, and as he fired the thing leaped sideways into the open, screaming.

It was a thin little man dressed in sepulchral black, and bearing the rosiest baby-face Cory had ever seen. The face was twisted with fright and pain. The man scrambled to his feet and hopped up and down saying over and over, "Oh, my hand. Don't shoot again! Oh, my hand. Don't shoot again!" He stopped after a bit, when Cory had climbed to his feet, and he regarded the farmer out of sad china-blue eyes. "You shot me," he said reproachfully, holding up a little bloody hand. "Oh, my goodness."

Cory said, "Now, who the hell are you?"

The man immediately became hysterical, mouthing such a flood of broken sentences that Cory stepped back a pace and half raised his gun in self-defense. It seemed to consist mostly of "I lost my papers," and "I didn't do it," and "It was horrible. Horrible. Horrible," and "The dead man," and "Oh, don't shoot again."

Cory tried twice to ask him a question, and then he stepped over and knocked the man down. He lay on the ground writhing and moaning and blubbering and putting his bloody hand to his mouth where Cory had hit him.

"Now what's going on around here?"

The man rolled over and sat up. "I didn't do it!" he sobbed. "I didn't I was walking along and I heard the gun and I heard some swearing and an awful scream and I went over there and peeped and I saw the dead man and I ran away and you came and I hid and you shot me and—"

"*Shut up!*" The man did, as if a switch had been thrown. "Now," said Cory, pointing along the path, "you say there's a dead man up there?"

The man nodded and began crying in earnest. Cory helped him up. "Follow this path back to my farmhouse," he said. "Tell my wife to fix up your hand. *Don't* tell her anything else. And wait there until I come. Hear?"

"Yes. Thank you. Oh, thank you. *Snff.*"

"Go on now." Cory gave him a gentle shove in the right direction and went alone, in cold fear, up the path to the spot where he had found Alton the night before.

He found him here now, too, and Kimbo. Kimbo and Alton had spent several years together in the deepest friendship; they had hunted and fought and slept together, and the lives they owed each other were finished now. They were dead together.

It was terrible that they died the same way. Cory Drew was a strong man, but he gasped and fainted dead away when he saw what the thing of the mold had done to his brother and his brother's dog.

The little man in black hurried down the path, whimpering and holding his injured hand as if he rather wished he could limp with it. After a while the whimper faded away, and the hurried stride changed to a walk as the gibbering terror of the last hour receded. He drew two deep breaths, said: "My goodness!" and felt almost normal. He bound a linen handkerchief around his wrist, but the hand kept bleeding. He tried the elbow, and that made it hurt. So he stuffed the handkerchief back in his pocket and simply waved the hand stupidly in the air until the blood clotted. He did not see the great moist horror that clumped along behind him, although his nostrils crinkled with its foulness.

The monster had three holes close together on its chest, and one hole in the middle of its slimy forehead. It had three close-set pits in its back and one on the back of its head. These marks were where Alton Drew's bullets had struck and passed through. Half of the monster's shapeless face was sloughed away, and there was a deep indentation on its shoulder. This was what Alton Drew's gun butt had done after he clubbed it and struck at the thing that would not lie down after he put his four bullets through it. When these things happened the monster was not hurt or angry. It only wondered why Alton Drew acted that way. Now it followed the little man without hurrying at all, matching his stride step by step and dropping little particles of muck behind it.

The little man went on out of the wood and stood with his back against a big tree at the forest's edge, and he thought. Enough had happened to him here. What good would it do to stay and face a horrible murder inquest, just to continue this silly, vague search? There was supposed to the ruin of an old, old hunting lodge deep in this wood somewhere, and perhaps it would hold the evidence he wanted. But it was a vague report—vague enough to be forgotten without regret. It would be the height of foolishness to stay for all the hick-town red tape that would follow that ghastly affair back in the wood. Ergo, it would be ridiculous to follow that farmer's advice, to go to his house and wait for him. He would go back to town.

The monster was leaning against the other side of the big tree.

The little man snuffled disgustedly at a sudden overpowering odor of rot. He reached for his handkerchief, fumbled and dropped it. As he bent to pick it up, the monster's arm *whuffed* heavily in the air where his head had been — a blow that would certainly have removed that baby-faced protuberance. The man stood up and would have put the handkerchief to his nose had it not been so bloody. The creature behind the tree lifted its arm again just as the little man tossed the handkerchief away and stepped out into the field, heading across country to the distant highway that would take him back to town. The monster pounced on the handkerchief, picked it up, studied it, tore it across several times and inspected the tattered edges. Then it gazed vacantly at the disappearing figure of the little man, and finding him no longer interesting, turned back into the woods.

Babe broke into a trot at the sound of the shots. It was important to warn Uncle Alton about what her father had said, but it was more interesting to find out what he had bagged. Oh, he'd bagged it, all right. Uncle Alton never fired without killing. This was about the first time she had ever heard him blast away like that. Must be a bear, she thought excitedly, tripping over a root, sprawling, rolling to her feet again, without noticing the tumble. She'd love to have another bearskin in her room. Where would she put it? Maybe they could line it and she could have it for a blanket. Uncle Alton could sit on it and read to her in the evening — Oh, no. No. Not with this trouble between him and Dad. Oh, if she could only do something! She tried to run faster, worried and anticipating, but she was out of breath and went more slowly instead.

At the top of the rise by the edge of the woods she stopped and looked back. Far down in the valley lay the south thirty. She scanned it carefully, looking for her father. The new furrows and the old were sharply defined, and her keen eyes saw immediately that Cory had left the line with the cultivator and had angled the team over to the shade trees without finishing his row. That wasn't like him. She could see the team now, and Cory's pale-blue denim was nowhere in sight.

She giggled lightly to herself as she thought of the way she would fool her father. And the little sound of laughter drowned out, for her, the sound of Alton's hoarse dying scream.

She reached and crossed the path and slid through the brush beside it. The shots came from up around here somewhere. She stopped and listened several times, and then suddenly heard something coming toward her, fast. She ducked under cover, terrified, and a little baby-faced man in black, his blue eyes wide with horror, crashed blindly past her, the leather case he carried catching on the branches. It spun a moment and then fell right in front of her. The man never missed it.

Babe lay there for a long moment and then picked up the case and faded into the woods. Things were happening too fast for her. She wanted Uncle Alton, but she dared not call. She stopped again and strained her ears. Back toward the edge of the wood she heard her father's voice, and another's—probably the man who had dropped the briefcase. She dared not go over there. Filled with enjoyable terror, she thought hard, then snapped her fingers in triumph. She and Alton had played Injun many times up here; they had a whole repertoire of secret signals. She had practiced birdcalls until she knew them better than the birds themselves. What would it be? Ah—blue jay. She threw back her head and by some youthful alchemy produced a nerve-shattering screech that would have done justice to any jay that ever flew. She repeated it, and then twice more.

The response was immediate—the call of a blue jay, four times, spaced two and two. Babe nodded to herself happily. That was the signal that they were to meet immediately at The Place. The Place was a hide-out that he had discovered and shared with her, and not another soul knew of it; an angle of rock beside a stream not far away. It wasn't exactly a cave, but almost. Enough so to be entrancing. Babe trotted happily away toward the brook. She had just known that Uncle Alton would remember the call of the blue jay, and what it meant.

In the tree that arched over Alton's scattered body perched a large jay bird, preening itself and shining in the sun. Quite unconscious of the presence of death, hardly noticing the Babe's realistic cry, it screamed again four times, two and two.

It took Cory more than a moment to recover himself from what he had seen. He turned away from it and leaned weakly against a pine, panting. Alton. That was Alton lying there, in—parts.

"God! God, God, God—"

Gradually his strength returned, and he forced himself to turn again. Stepping carefully, he bent and picked up the .32–40. Its barrel was bright and clean, but the butt and stock were smeared with some kind of stinking rottenness. Where had he seen the stuff before? Somewhere—no matter. He cleaned it off absently, throwing the befouled bandanna away afterward. Through his mind ran Alton's words—was that only last night?—"*I'm goin' to start trackin'. An' I'm goin' to keep trackin' till I find the one done this job on Kimbo.*"

Cory searched shrinkingly until he found Alton's box of shells. The box was wet and sticky. That made it—better, somehow. A bullet wet with Alton's blood was the right thing to use. He went away a short distance, circled around till he found heavy footprints, then came back.

"I'm a-trackin' for you, bud," he whispered thickly, and began. Through the brush he followed its wavering spoor, amazed at the amount of filthy mold about, gradually associating it with the thing that had killed his brother. There was nothing in the world for him any more but hate and doggedness. Cursing himself for not getting Alton home last night, he followed the tracks to the edge of the woods. They led him to a big tree there, and there he saw something else—the footprints of the little city man. Nearby lay some tattered scraps of linen, and—what was that?

Another set of prints—small ones. Small, stub-toed ones.

"Babe!"

No answer. The wind sighed. Somewhere a blue jay called.

Babe stopped and turned when she heard her father's voice, faint with distance, piercing.

"Listen at him holler," she crooned delightedly. "Gee, he sounds mad." She sent a jay bird's call disrespectfully back to him and hurried to The Place.

It consisted of a mammoth boulder beside the brook. Some

upheaval in the glacial age had cleft it, cutting out a huge V-shaped chunk. The widest part of the cleft was at the water's edge, and the narrowest was hidden by bushes. It made a little ceilingless room, rough and uneven and full of pot-holes and cavelets inside, and yet with quite a level floor. The open end was at the water's edge.

Babe parted the bushes and peered down the cleft.

"Uncle Alton!" she called softly. There was no answer. Oh, well, he'd be along. She scrambled in and slid down to the floor.

She loved it here. It was shaded and cool, and the chattering stream filled it with shifting golden lights and laughing gurgles. She called again, on principle, and then perched on an outcropping to wait. It was only then she realized that she still carried the little man's briefcase.

She turned it over a couple of times and then opened it. It was divided in the middle by a leather wall. On one side were a few papers in a large yellow envelope, and on the other some sandwiches, a candy bar, and an apple. With a youngster's complacent acceptance of manna from heaven, Babe fell to. She saved one sandwich for Alton, mainly because she didn't like its highly spiced bologna. The rest made quite a feast.

She was a little worried when Alton hadn't arrived, even after she had consumed the apple core. She got up and tried to skim some flat pebbles across the roiling brook, and she stood on her hands, and she tried to think of a story to tell herself, and she tried just waiting. Finally, in desperation, she turned again to the briefcase, took out the papers, curled up by the rocky wall and began to read them. It was something to do, anyway.

There was an old newspaper clipping that told about strange wills that people had left. An old lady had once left a lot of money to whoever would make the trip from the Earth to the Moon and back. Another had financed a home for cats whose masters and mistresses had died. A man left thousands of dollars to the first man who could solve a certain mathematical problem and prove his solution. But one item was blue-penciled. It was:

One of the strangest of wills still in force is that of Thaddeus M. Kirk, who died in 1920. It appears that he built an elaborate mausoleum with burial vaults for all the remains of his family. He collected and removed caskets from all over the country to fill the designated niches. Kirk was the last of his line; there were no relatives when he died. His will stated that the mausoleum was to be kept in repair permanently, and that a certain sum was to be set aside as a reward for whoever who could produce the body of his grandfather, Roger Kirk, whose niche is still empty. Anyone finding this body is eligible to receive a substantial fortune.

Babe yawned vaguely over this, but kept on reading because there was nothing else to do. Next was a thick sheet of business correspondence, bearing the letterhead of a firm of lawyers. The body of it ran:

In regard to your query regarding the will of Thaddeus Kirk, we are authorized to state that his grandfather was a man about five feet, five inches, whose left arm had been broken and who had a triangular silver plate set into his skull. There is no information as to the whereabouts of his death. He disappeared and was declared legally dead after the lapse of fourteen years.

The amount of the reward as stated in the will, plus accrued interest, now amounts to a fraction over sixty-two thousand dollars. This will be paid to anyone who produces the remains, providing that said remains answer descriptions kept in our private files.

There was more, but Babe was bored. She went on to the little black notebook. There was nothing in it but penciled and highly abbreviated records of visits to libraries; quotations from books with titles like "History of Angelina and Tyler Counties" and "Kirk Family History." Babe threw that aside, too. Where could Uncle Alton be?

She began to sing tunelessly, "Tumalumalum tum, ta ta ta," pretending to dance a minuet with flowing skirts like a girl she had seen in the movies. A rustle of the bushes at the entrance to The Place stopped her. She peeped upward, saw them being thrust aside. Quickly she ran to a tiny cul-de-sac in the rock wall, just big enough for her to hide in. She giggled at the thought of how surprised Uncle Alton would be when she jumped out at him.

She heard the newcomer come shuffling down the steep slope of the crevice and land heavily on the floor. There was something about the sound— What was it? It occurred to her that though it was a hard job for a big man like Uncle Alton to get through the little opening in the bushes, she could hear no heavy breathing. She heard no breathing at all!

Babe peeped out into the main cave and squealed in utmost horror. Standing there was, not Uncle Alton, but a massive caricature of a man: a huge thing like an irregular mud doll, clumsily made. It quivered and parts of it glistened and parts of it were dried and crumbly. Half of the lower left part of its face was gone, giving it a lopsided look. It had no perceptible mouth or nose, and its eyes were crooked, one higher than the other, both a dingy brown with no whites at all. It stood quite still looking at her, its only movement a steady unalive quivering.

It wondered about the queer little noise Babe had made.

Babe crept far back against a little pocket of stone, her brain running round and round in tiny circles of agony. She opened her mouth to cry out, and could not. Her eyes bulged and her face flamed with the strangling effort, and the two golden ropes of her braided hair twitched and twitched as she hunted hopelessly for a way out. If only she were out in the open—or in the wedge-shaped half-cave where the thing was—or home in bed!

The thing clumped toward her, expressionless, moving with a slow inevitability that was the sheer crux of horror. Babe lay wide-eyed and frozen, mounting pressure of terror stilling her lungs, making her heart shake the whole world. The monster came to the mouth of the little pocket, tried to walk to her and was stopped by the sides. It was such a narrow little fissure, and it was all Babe could do to get in. The thing from the wood stood straining against the rock at its shoulders, pressing harder and harder to get to Babe. She sat up slowly, so near to the thing that its odor was almost thick enough to see, and a wild hope burst through her voiceless fear. It couldn't get in! It couldn't get in because it was too big!

The substance of its feet spread slowly under the tremendous strain and at its shoulder appeared a slight crack. It widened as the monster unfeelingly crushed itself against the rock, and suddenly a large piece of the shoulder came away and the being twisted slushily three feet farther in. It lay quietly with its muddy eyes fixed on her, and then brought one thick arm up over its head and reached.

Babe scrambled in the inch farther she had believed impossible, and the filthy clubbed hand stroked down her back, leaving a trail of muck on the blue denim of the shirt she wore. The monster surged suddenly and, lying full length now, gained that last precious inch. A black hand seized one of her braids, and for Babe the lights went out.

When she came to, she was dangling by her hair from that same crusted paw. The thing held her high, so that her face and its featureless head were not more than a foot apart. It gazed at her with a mild curiosity in its eyes, and it swung her slowly back and forth. The agony of her pulled hair did what fear could not do—gave her a voice. She screamed. She opened her mouth and puffed up her powerful young lungs, and she sounded off. She held her throat in the position of the first scream, and her chest labored and pumped more air through the frozen throat. Shrill and monotonous and infinitely piercing, her screams.

The thing did not mind. It held her as she was, and watched. When it had learned all it could from this phenomenon, it dropped her jarringly, and looked around the half-cave, ignoring the stunned and huddled Babe. It reached over and picked up the leather briefcase and tore it twice across as if it were tissue. It saw the sandwich Babe had left, picked it up, crushed it, dropped it.

Babe opened her eyes, saw that she was free, and just as the thing turned back to her she dove between its legs and out into the shallow pool in front of the rock, paddled across and hit the other bank screaming. A vicious little light of fury burned in her; she picked up a grapefruit-sized stone and hurled it with all her frenzied might. It flew low and fast, and struck squashily on the monster's ankle. The thing was just taking a step toward the water; the stone caught it off balance, and its unpracticed equilibrium could not save it. It tottered for a long, silent moment at the edge and then splashed into the stream. Without a second look Babe ran shrieking away.

Cory Drew was following the little gobs of mold that somehow indicated the path of the murderer, and he was nearby when he first heard her scream. He broke into a run, dropping his shotgun and holding the .32–40 ready to fire. He ran with such deadly panic in his heart that he ran right past the huge cleft rock and was a hundred yards past it before she burst out through the pool and ran up the bank. He had to run hard and fast to catch her, because anything behind her was that faceless horror in the cave, and she was living for the one idea of getting away from there. He caught her in his arms and swung her to him, and she screamed on and on and on.

Babe didn't see Cory at all, even when he held her and quieted her.

The monster lay in the water. It neither liked nor disliked this new element. It rested on the bottom, its massive head a foot beneath the surface, and it curiously considered the facts it had garnered. There was the little humming noise of Babe's voice that sent the monster questing into the cave. There was the black material of the briefcase that resisted so much more than green things when he tore it. There was the little two-legged one who sang and brought him near, and who screamed when he came. There was this new cold moving thing he had fallen into. It was washing his body away. That had never happened before. That was interesting. The monster decided to stay and observe this new thing. It felt no urge to save itself; it could only be curious.

The brook came laughing down out of its spring, ran down from its source beckoning to the sunbeams and embracing freshets and helpful brooklets. It shouted and played with streaming little roots, and nudged the minnows and pollywogs about in its tiny backwaters. It was a happy brook. When it came to the pool by the cloven rock it found the monster there, and plucked at it. It soaked the foul substances and smoothed and melted the molds, and the waters below

326

the thing eddied darkly with its diluted matter. It was a thorough brook. It washed all it touched, persistently. Where it found filth, it removed filth; if there were layer on layer of foulness, then layer by foul layer it was removed. It was a good brook. It did not mind the poison of the monster, but took it up and thinned it and spread it in little rings round rocks downstream, and let it drift to the rootlets of water plants, that they might grow greener and lovelier. And the monster melted.

"I am smaller," the thing thought. "That is interesting. I could not move now. And now this part of me which thinks is going, too. It will stop in just a moment, and drift away with the rest of the body. It will stop thinking and I will stop being, and that, too, is a very interesting thing."

So the monster melted and dirtied the water, and water was clean again, washing and washing the skeleton that the monster had left. It was not very big, and there was a badly healed knot on the left arm. The sunlight flickered on the triangular silver plate set into the pale skull, and the skeleton was very clean now. The brook laughed about it for an age.

They found the skeleton, six grimlipped men who came to find a killer. No one had believed Babe, when she told her story days later. It had to be days later because Babe had screamed for seven hours without stopping, and had lain like a dead child for a day. No one believed her at all, because her story was all about the bad fella, and they knew that the bad fella was simply a thing that her father had made up to frighten her with. But it was through her that the skeleton was found, and so the men at the bank sent a check to the Drews for more money than they had ever dreamed about. It was old Roger Kirk, sure enough, that skeleton, though it was found five miles from where he had died and sank into the forest floor where the hot molds builded around his skeleton and emerged—a monster.

So the Drews had a new barn and fine new livestock and they hired four men. But they didn't have Alton. And they didn't have Kimbo. And Babe screams at night and has grown very thin.

Butyl and the Breather

I WAS STILL melancholic about chasing the Ether Breather out of the ken of man, the day I got that bright idea of bringing the Breather back. I should have let it stay in idea form. I should not have gone to see Berbelot about it. I also should have stayed in bed. I've got brains, but no sense. I went to see Berbelot.

He wasn't glad to see me, which he did through the televisor in his foyer. Quite a gadget, that foyer. I knew that it was an elevator to take guests up to his quarters in the mansion, the "House that Perfume Built." I hadn't known till now that it was also a highly efficient bouncing mechanism. I had no sooner passed my hand over the sensitized plate that served as a doorbell when his face appeared on the screen. He said "Hmph! Hamilton!" and next thing I knew the foyer's walls had extended and pinned me tight. I was turned upside down, shaken twice, and then dropped on my ear outside the house. I think he designed that bouncer just for me. He was a nice old boy, but, man, how he could hang on to a grouch. A whole year, this one had lasted. Just because I had been tactless with the Breather.

I got up and dusted myself off and swore I'd never bother the irascible old heel again. And then I hunted a drugstore to call him up. That's the way it was. Berbelot was a peculiar duck. His respect for me meant more than anger against him could make up for. He was the only man I ever met that ever made me sorry for anything.

I went into the visiphone booth and pressed my identification tab against the resilient panel on the phone. That made a record of the call so I could be billed for it. Then I dialed Berbelot. I got his bun-faced valet.

"I want to speak to Mr. Berbelot, Cogan."

"Mr. Berbelot is out, Mr. Hamilton."

"So!" I snapped, my voice rising. "You're the one who tossed me

out just now with that salesman mangler on your doorstep! I'll macer-
ate you, you subatomic idiot!"

"Oh ... I ... I didn't, Mr. Hamilton, really. I—"

"Then if you didn't Berbelot did. If he did, he's home. Incidentally, I saw him in the viewplate. Enough of the chitchat, doughface.
Tell him I want to speak to him."

"B-but he won't speak to you, Mr. Hamilton. He gave strict orders
a year ago."

"Tell him I've thought of a way to get in touch with the Ether
Breather again. Go on. He won't fire you, you crumb from the bread-
line. He'll kiss you on both cheeks. Snap into it!"

The screen went vacant as he moved away, and I heard Berbelot's voice—"I thought I told you"—and then the bumble of Cogan's,
and then "WHAT!" from the old man, and another short bumble
that was interrupted by Berbelot's sliding to a stop in front of the
transmitter. "Hamilton," he said sternly into the visiplate, "if this is
a joke of yours ... if you think you can worm your way into my
confidence with ... if you dare to lead me on some wild-goose cha ...
if you—"

"If you'll give me a chance, King of Stink," I said, knowing that
if I got him really mad he'd listen to me, being the type that got
speechless with rage, "I'll give you the dope. I have an idea that I
think will bring the Breather back, but it's up to you to carry it out.
You have the apparatus."

"Come up," he whispered, his wattles quivering. "But I warn
you, if you dare to take this liberty on a bluff, I shall most certainly
have you pried loose from your esophagus."

"Comin' up!" I said. "By the way, when I get into that foyer
again, please be sure which button you push."

"Don't worry," he growled, "I have a dingus up here that is quite
as efficient. It throws people from the sixtieth floor. Do come up."
The screen darkened. I sighed and started for the "House that Perfume Built."

The elevator glided to a stop that made my stomach feel puffy,
and I stepped out. Berbelot was standing in front of it looking suspicious as a pawnbroker. I held out my hand with some remark about

how swell it was to see him again, and he just stared at it. When I thought he was going to forego the honor of shaking it, he put his hand into mine, withdrew it quickly, looked at it, and wiped it carefully on his jacket. Without his saying a word I gathered that he wasn't glad to see me, that he thought I was an undesirable and unsanitary character, and that he didn't trust me.

"Did I ever tell you," I said as calmly as I could, "that I am terribly sorry about what happened?"

Berbelot said, "I knew a man who said that after he murdered somebody. They burned him anyway."

I thought that was very nice. "Do you want to find out about my idea or not?" I gritted. "I don't have to stay here to be insulted."

"I realize that. You're insulted everywhere, I imagine. Well, what's your idea?"

I saw Cogan hovering over the old man's shoulder and threw my hat at him. Since Berbelot apparently found it difficult to be hospitable, I saved him the trouble of inviting me to sit down by sitting down.

"Berbelot," I said, when I had one of his best cigarettes fuming as nicely as he was, "you're being unreasonable. But I have you interested, and as long as that lasts you'll be sociable. Sit down. I am about to be Socratic. It may take a little while."

"I suffer." He sat down. "I suffer exceedingly." He paused, and then added pensively, "I never thought I could be so irritated by anyone who bored me. Go ahead, Hamilton."

I closed my eyes and counted ten. Berbelot could manufacture more printable invective than anyone I ever met.

"Question one," I said. "What is the nature of the creature you dubbed Ether Breather?"

"Why, it's a . . . well, apparently a combination of etheric forces, living in and around us. It's as if the air in this room were a thinking animal. What are you—"

"I'll ask questions. Now, will you grant it intelligence?"

"Of course. A peculiar kind, though. It seems to be motivated by a childish desire to have fun—mostly at some poor human's expense."

"But its reactions were reasonable, weren't they?"

"Yes, although exaggerated. It reached us through color television; that was its only medium of expression. And it raised particular hell with the programs—a cosmic practical joker, quite uninhibited, altogether unafraid of any consequences to itself. And then when you, you blockhead, told it that it had hurt someone's feelings and that it ought to get off the air, it apologized and was never heard from again. Again an exaggerated reaction. But what has that got to do with—"

"Everything. Look; you made it laugh easily. You made it ashamed of itself easily. It cried easily. If you really want to get in touch with it again, you just have to go on from there."

Berbelot pressed a concealed button and the lights took on a greenish cast. He always claimed a man thought more clearly under a green light. "I'll admit that that particular thought sequence has escaped me," he nodded, "since I do not have a mind which is led astray by illogical obscurities. But in all justice to you—not that you deserve anything approaching a compliment—I think you have something there. I suppose that is as far as you have gone, though. I've spent hours on the problem. I've called that creature for days on end on a directional polychrome wave. I've apologized to it and pleaded with it and begged it and told it funny stories and practically asked it to put its invisible feet out of my television receiver so I could kiss them. And never a whisper have I had. No, Hamilton; the Ether Breather is definitely miffed, peeved, and not at home. And it's all your fault."

"Once," I said dreamily, "I knew a woman whose husband went astray. She knew where he was, and sent him message after message. She begged and she pleaded and she wept into visiphones. It didn't get her anywhere. Then she got a bright idea. She sent him a telefacsimile letter, written on her very best stationery. It described in great detail the nineteen different kinds of heel she thought he was."

"I don't know what this has to do with the Breather, but what happened?" asked Berbelot.

"Why, he got sore. He got so sore he dropped everything and ran home to take a poke at her!"

"Ah," said Berbelot. "And the Breather laughs easily, and you think it would—"

"It would," I nodded, "get angry easily, if we could find the right way to do it."

Berbelot rubbed his long hands together and beamed. "You're a hot-headed fool, Hamilton, and I'm convinced that your genius is a happy accident quite unattached to your hypothetical mind. But I must congratulate you for the idea. In other words, you think if we get the Breather sore enough, it will try to get even, and contact us some way or other? I'll be darned!"

"Thought you'd like it," I said.

"Well, come on," he said testily. "What are we waiting for? Let's go down to the laboratory!" Suddenly he stopped. "Er ... Hamilton ... this story of yours. Did that man poke his wife after he got home?"

"I dunno," I said blankly. "I just made up the story to illustrate my point. Could be."

"Hm-m-m. If the Breather decided to ... I mean, it's a big creature, you know, and we have no idea—"

"Oh, never mind that," I laughed, "the Breather can't get past a television screen!"

Which only goes to show you how little I knew about the Ether Breather.

I was amazed by Berbelot's laboratory museum. Did you know that in the old days more than two hundred years ago, they used electrically powered sets with a ground glass, fluorescent screen built right into the end of huge cathode tubes? Imagine. And before that, they used a revolving disk with holes punctured spirally, as a scanning mechanism! They had the beginnings of frequency modulation, though. But their sets were so crude, incredible as it may seem, that atmospheric disturbances caused interference in reception! Berbelot had copies of all these old and laughable attempts at broadcasting and receiving devices.

"All right, all right," he snapped, elbow-deep in one of the first polychrome transmitters, "you've been here before. Come over here and give me a hand. You're gawking like a castor bean farmer."

I went over and followed his directions as he spot-welded, relayed, and wound a coil or two of hair-fine wire. "My gosh," I marveled, "how did you ever learn so much about television, Berbelot? I imagine it must have used up a little of your spare time to make a fortune in the perfume business."

He laughed. "I'll tell you, Hamilton," he said. "Television and perfumery are very much alike. You know yourself that no such lovely women ever walk the Earth as you see every day in the news broadcasts. For the last eighty years, since the Duval shade selector was introduced, television has given flawless complexions to all the ladies that come over the air, and bull-shoulders to all the men. It's all very phony, but it's nice to look at. Perfumery is the same proposition. A woman who smelled like a rose petal naturally would undoubtedly have something the matter with her. But science gets to work on what has been termed, through the ages, as 'B.O.' My interest in aesthetically deluding the masses led me to both sciences."

"Very ingenious," I said, "but it isn't going to help you to make the Breather sore."

"My dear boy," he said, "don't be obtuse. Oh, turn down the nitrogen jets a trifle—that's it." He skillfully spotted seven leads into the video-circuit of the polychrome wave generator. "You see," he went on, running the leads over to a box control with five push buttons and a rheostat set into it, "the Breather requires very special handling. It knows us and how our minds work, or it could never have thought, for instance, of having our secretary of state recite risqué verse over the air, the first time that official used color television. Now, you are noteworthy for your spontaneity. How would you go about angering this puff of etheric wind?"

"Well, I'd ... I'd tell it it was a dirty so-and-so. I'd insult it. I'd say it was a sissy and dare it to fight. I ... I'd—"

"That's what I thought," said Berbelot unkindly. "You'd cuss it out in your own foul idiom, forgetting that it has no pride to take down, and, as far as we know, no colleagues, community, inamoratae, or fellows to gossip to. No, Hamilton, we can't insult it. It can insult us because it knows what we are and how we think, but we know nothing of it."

"How else can you get a being sore, then, when you can't hold it up to ridicule or censure before itself or its fellow creatures?"

"By doing something to it personally that it won't like."

"Yeah—take a poke at it. Kick it in its vibrations. Stick a knife into its multiple personality."

Berbelot laughed. "To change the subject, for no apparent reason," he said, "have you ever run across my *Vierge Folle?*"

"A new perfume? Why, no."

Berbelot crossed the room and came back with a handful of tiny vials. "Here."

I sniffed. It was a marvelously delicate scent. It was subtle, smooth, calling up a mental picture of the veins in fine ivory. "Mmm. Nice."

"Try this one," he said. I did. It was fainter than the other; I had to draw in a lot of it before I detected the sweet, faint odor. "It's called *Casuiste,*" said Berbelot. "Now try this one. It's much fainter, you'll have to really stretch to get it at all."

"Nice business," I grinned. "Making the poor unsuspecting male get inside the circle of the vixen's arms before he's under her spell." I'd been reading some of his ad proofs. He chuckled. "That's about the idea. Here."

Berbelot handed me the vial and I expelled all the air in my lungs, hung my nose over the lip of the tube and let the air in with a roar. Next thing I knew I was strangling, staggering, swearing and letting go murderous rights and lefts at empty air. I thought I was going to die and I wished I could. When I blinked the tears out of my eyes, Berbelot was nowhere to be seen. I raged around the laboratory and finally saw him whisk around behind a massive old photoelectric transmitter. With a shriek I rushed him. He got practically inside the machine and I began taking it apart, with the firm conviction that I would keep on taking things apart long after I reached him. Luckily for him there were four thick busbars between us. He crouched behind them giggling until I reached a red-eyed state of wheezing impotence.

"Come out!" I gasped. "You ape-faced arthritic, come out of there and I'll hit you so hard you'll throttle on your shoelaces!"

"That," he said instructively, "was a quadruple quintessence of musk." He grinned. "Skunk." He looked at me and laughed outright. "Super-skunk."

I wrenched ineffectually at the bars. "A poor thing, but your very own, I'll bet," I said. "I am going to stick your arm so far down your neck you'll digest your fingernails."

"Mad, aren't you?"

"Huh?"

"I said, you're sore. I didn't cuss you out, or hold you up to ridicule, or anything, and look how mad you are!"

I began to see the light. Make the Breather angry by—"What are you gibbering about?"

He took out a white handkerchief and waved it as he unwrapped his own body from the viscera of the old-fashioned transmitter. I had to grin. What can you do with a man like that?

"O.K.," I said. "Peace, brother. But I'd suggest you treat the Breather better than you just treated me. And how in blazes you expect to get a smell like that through a polychrome transmitter is a little beyond me."

"It isn't simple," he said, "but I think it can be done. Do you know anything about the wave theory of perception?"

"Not a helluva lot," I said. "Something about a sort of spectrum arrangement of the vibrations of sensory perception, isn't it?"

"Mmm ... yes. Thought waves are of high-frequency, and although ether-borne, not of an electromagnetic character. So also are the allied vibrations, taste and smell. Sound, too."

"Wait a minute! Sound is a purely physical vibration of air particles against our auditory apparatus."

"Of course—from the source of the sound *to* that apparatus. But from the inner ear to the hearing center in the brain, it is translated into a wave of the spectrum group I'm talking about. So with touch and sight."

"I begin to see what you're driving at. But how can you reach the Breather with these waves—providing you can produce and transmit them?"

"Oh, I can do that. Simply a matter of stepping up high-frequency emanations."

"You seem pretty confident that the Breather will be affected by the same waves that influence our senses."

"I wouldn't use the same waves. That's why I brought up the spectrum theory. Now look; we'll take thought waves of the purely internal psyche ... the messages that relay brain impulses to different brain centers. Pure thought, with no action; pure imagery. These are of a certain wave length. We'll call it 1,000. Now, take the frequencies of smell, touch and sight waves. They're 780, 850, and 960 respectively. Now, how did we contact the Ether Breather?"

"By the polychrome wave."

"That's right."

"And you mean that the ratio—"

Berbelot nodded. "The ratio between the Breather's thought waves and its sensory vibrations must be the same as that between ours."

"Why must it be?"

"Because its mental reactions are the same, as I told you before— only exaggerated. It reasons as we do, more or less. Its mental set-up corresponds with ours."

"Doggone," I said admiringly, "it's all so simple when you're told how to do it. You mean, then, to discover the ratio between what is to me a pain the neck, and what it would be to the Breather."

"That's it. But it won't be a pain in the neck."

"Where will it be, then?"

"You're tuning in the wrong frequency," he chuckled. "I'm going to make him suffer the best way I know how, and—my business is perfumery."

"Ah," I breathed.

"Now, I'm going to cook up something really pretty. I'm going to turn out a stench that will make the Breather's illimitable edges curl!"

"From the smell of that essence of ancient egg you just gassed me with," I said, "it ought to be pretty."

"It will be. Let's see; for a base we'll use butyl mercaptan. Something sweet, and something sour—"

"—something borrowed and something blue."

"Don't be a silly romanticist." He was busy at his chemical bench. "I'll scorch a little pork fat and ... ah. Attar of roses."

For a moment he was quiet, carefully measuring drops of liquid into a sealed exciter. Then he flipped the switch and came over to me. "It'll be ready in a jiffy. Let's rig up the transmitter."

We did as we had done before, a year ago. We maneuvered the transmitting cells of the polychrome transmitter over and above a receiver. It would send to Berbelot's country place eight hundred miles away by a directional beam, and return the signal by wire. If the Breather interfered, it would show up on the receiver. When we had done it before, we had had the odd experience of holding a conversation with our own images on the screen.

"Now I'll distill my *odeur d'ordure*," he said, "and when it's run through, you can be my guinea pig."

"Not on your life, Berbelot," I said, backing away. He grinned and went about fixing his still. It was a beautiful little glass affair, and he worked entirely under a huge bell jar in transferring it from the exciter. Butyl and burned meat and attar of roses. My gosh.

In half an hour it was ready—a dusty brown colloid, just a few drops in the retort. "Come on, Hamilton," said Berbelot, "just a little sniff. I want to give you a preview."

"Uh-uh!" I snorted. "Here—wait."

I gave a buzz on the buzzer, and in a couple of seconds Cogan, Berbelot's valet, popped in. Cogan's face always reminded me, for some reason, of a smorgasbord tray.

"Did you bring your nose?" I asked, leading him over to the chemical bench.

"Yessir."

"Well"—I slid back the little panel in the neck of the retort, standing at arm's length—"stick it in there."

"Oh, but I—" He looked plaintively toward Berbelot, who smiled.

""Well . . . oh!" The "Well" was diffidence, and the "Oh" was when I grabbed him by the collar and stuck his face in the warm fumes.

Cogan went limp and stiffened so fast that he didn't move. He rose slowly, as if the power of that mighty stench was lifting him by the jawbone, turned around twice with his eyes streaming, and headed for the door. He walked lightly and slowly on the balls of his feet, with his arms bent and half raised, like a somnambulist. He walked smack into the doorpost, squeaked, said, "Oh ... my ... goodness—" faintly, and disappeared into the corridor.

"Well," said Berbelot pensively. "I really think that that stuff smells bad."

"Seems as though," I grinned. "I ... oh, boy!" I ran to the retort and closed the slide. "Good gosh! Did we give him a concentrated shot of *that?*"

"*You* did."

It permeated the room, and of all malodorous effluvia, it was the most noisome. It was rotten celery, than which there is no more sickening smell in nature. It was rancid butter. It was bread-mold. It was garlic garnishing fermented Limburger. It was decay. It was things running around on six legs, mashed. It was awful.

"Berbelot," I gasped, "you don't want to kill the Breather."

"It won't kill him. He just won't like it."

"Check. *Whew!*" I mopped my face. "Now how are you going to get it up to the Ether Breather?"

"Well, we'll use the olfactometer on it," he said.

"What's that?"

"Trade gadget. I knocked it together years ago. Without it I wouldn't have made a cent in this business." He led me over to a stand on which was an enormously complicated machine, all glittering relays and electratomic bridges. "Good heavens!" I said. "What does it do—play music?"

"Maybe you wondered why I could reel off so much about the wave theory of sensory perception," he said. "Look—see these dials? And this sensitized knob?"

"Yeah?"

"That fist-sized, faceted knob has each of its twelve hundred and two sides coated with a different chemical reagent, very sensitive. I drop it into a smell—"

"You *what?*"

"You heard me. An odor is an emanation of gases from the smellable specimen, constituting a loss of mass of about one fifty-billionth in a year, more or less, depending on the strength of the odor and the consistency of the emanating body. Now, I expose this knob to our Cogan-crusher"—he walked over to the retort with the knob in his hand, trailing its cable, and slid the panel back a bit— "and the gas touches every surface. Each reacts if it can. The results are collected, returned to the olfactometer, translated into a number on the big dial."

"And that is—"

"The ratio I spoke to you about. See . . . the dial reads just 786. With the frequency of abstract thought set arbitrarily, at 1,000, we have a ratio between this smell and thought."

"Take it easy, Berbelot. I'm a layman."

He smiled. "That gives us an equation to work with. 786 is to 1,000 as x is to our polychrome wave."

"Isn't that a little like mixing liquor?" I said. "One set of figures is in thought vibrations, the other in radio waves."

"Ratios are like that," he reminded me. "I can have one third as many apples as you have oranges, no matter how many or how few oranges you have."

"I consider myself stood in the corner," I said. "By golly, with that gadget, no wonder your perfumes are practically a monopoly nowadays. Would it be giving away a trade secret to tell me what went into that *Doux Rêves* of yours? How on Earth did you figure out that odor? It'll make a ninety-year-old woman put on lipstick and a centenarian buy spats."

He laughed. "Sure, I'll tell you. *Doux Rêves* is 789.783 on that dial, which happens to be the smell of a rich juicy steak! But they don't associate it with steak when they buy it—at three hundred an ounce. It just smells like something desirable."

"Berbelot, you're chiseling the public."

"Mmmm-hm. That's why I pay half a billion in income tax every year. Get over on that bench."

"In front of the receiver? What are you going to do?"

"Oh, I'll have to be over here by the transmitter. I've got to adjust a carrier wave that will have the right ratio to the polychrome wave. Don't turn on the receiver yet."

I sat down. This amazing man was about to pull something unheard of. I didn't feel comfortable about it, either. How could he be so confident? He didn't know much about the Breather, any more than I did. He was acting like a man in perfect control of everything—which he was—who didn't have to worry about taking a rap for what he was about to do. Well, he built that smell, didn't he? I didn't. I could always blame him for it, even if I was the instigator. I remember wondering if I'd be able to convince the Ether Breather of that, in case the Breather got tough. Oh, well.

"O.K., Hamilton. Turn her on!"

I did so, and a few seconds later the transmitting floods clicked on. From the suspended bank of cells came a hum as soft as their soft glow. The screen flickered and cleared, and I saw myself in it, almost as if I were looking into a mirror, except that my image was not reversed. "O.K., Berbelot."

"Right. Here goes a shot of Berbelot's *Essence of Evil!*"

I heard a switch click and then the faint grate of a rheostat. I stared at my image and my image stared back, and Berbelot came and stood where he could see me. It was only later that I remembered noticing that he was careful to stand out of range of the transmitter. The image didn't change—each tiny movement was mine, each facial twist, each—

"Look!" snapped Berbelot, and faded back to his switchboard again.

For a moment I didn't notice anything in particular, and then I saw it, too. The smallest possible twitching of the nostrils. A sudden little movement of the head. And then a just audible sniffing through the speaker. As suddenly the movement stopped.

"You got something that time, Berbelot," I yelped, "but it seems to have gone away again. The image is true."

"Splendid!" said the old man. He clicked off the transmitter and the receiving screen glowed blankly. "Now listen. I only gave it about as much as we got a few moments ago when you left the slide open. This time I'm going to give it what you gave poor Cogan!"

"My gosh! What am I supposed to do?"

"Sit tight! If and when the Breather starts kicking, give it right back to him. Don't admit that we did it to coax him back, or, being what he . . . it. . . is, he'll just get coy and disappear again."

"I think you're right. Want me to get him real mad, then?"

"For a while. Then we'll sign off and go to work on him tomorrow. After a bit we'll tell him the whole story; he'll think it's funny. Having fun seems to be his reason for living—if you can call that supercosmic existence living. Then he'll be appeased. Y'know, Hamilton, if we get him running errands for us he might make us a nice piece of change. We could buy up an advertising agency and have him blank out all competition with his typically wise-guy sort of interference, for instance."

"You think of everything! All right, let's go!"

The floods and cells lit up again, and in a few seconds I was staring at myself in the screen. It made me feel a little queasy. There I was looking at myself, looking at myself, looking at myself, as it were. It dizzied me.

The rheostat twirled over, and an auxiliary somewhere deep in the complicated transmitter moaned quietly. For about five minutes I strained my eyes, but not by the slightest sign did my image show that it sensed anything off-color.

"Are you sure your gadgets are working all right?" I asked Berbelot.

"Absolutely. Nothing yet? I'll be darned. Wait. A little more juice here, and I think I can build that smell up a—"

"What goes on here?" roared the speaker.

I stared. I was still seated, but my image was rising slowly. One odd thing about it—when it had been my true image, it showed me from the waist up. As it rose from the bench in the picture, it had no legs. Apparently the Breather could only distort just those waves that were transmitted. A weird sight.

I'd never have known that as my face. It was twisted, and furious, and altogether unpleasant.

"Are you doing that, punk?" it asked me.

"Wh-what?"

"Don't be like that," whispered Berbelot. He was off to one side, staring entranced and exultant into the receiver. "Give'm hell, Ham!"

I drew a deep breath. "Am I doing what, and who's a punk?" I asked the receiver pugnaciously.

"That stink, and you are."

"Yeah, I'm doing it, and who are you to call me one?"

"Well, cut it out, and who do I look like?"

"I wish you boys would have one conversation at a time," said Berbelot.

"None of your lip, pantywaist," I told the Breather, "or I'll come out there and plaster your shadow with substance."

"Wise guy, huh? Why, you insignificant nematode!"

"You etheric regurgitation!"

"You little quadridimensional stinkpot!"

"You faceless, formless, fightless phantasm!" I was beginning to enjoy this.

"Listen, mug, if you don't stop that business of smelling up my environment I'll strain you through a sheet of plate glass."

"Try it and I'll knock you so flat you'll call a plane a convex hemisphere."

"If you had the guts that God gave a goose, you'd come up here and fight me."

"If you weren't about as dangerous as a moth on a battle cruiser, you'd come down here and fight."

"Touché," said Berbelot.

"Oh, yeah?" said the Breather.

"Yeah!"

"Cliché," said Berbelot.

"I don't like your face," said the Breather.

"Take it off then."

"Not as long as I can insult you by making you look at it."

"It's more of a face to brag about than you got."

"Why, you hair-mantled, flint-hurling, aboriginal anthropophagus!"

Berbelot clicked off both transmitter and receiver. It was only then that I realized that the Breather had made me see red. I was in the laboratory, on my feet, all set to take a swing at a thousand-dollar television set.

"What'd you do that for?" I snapped, turning on Berbelot.

"Easy, lad, easy!" he laughed. "The Breather's had enough, in the first place. In the second place, he was quoting Carlyle, an ancient seventeenth or eighteenth century author. You ran him plumb out of originality. You did fine!"

"Thanks," I said, wiping my fevered brow. "Think he was sore?"

"I gathered as much. We'll work on him in the morning. I'm going to leave the smell on—just a suggestion of it, so he won't forget us."

"Don't you think he'll start messing up commercial programs again?"

"No. He knows where the trouble is coming from. He's too sore just now to think of anything but that source. He might think of the commercials later on, but if there's any danger of that we'll wise him up and laugh the whole thing off."

"Darned if you don't get me into the doggonedest things," I said wonderingly.

He chuckled, and slapped me on the back. "Go on upstairs and get Cogan to feed you. I'll be along soon; I have some work to do. You're spending the night here, my boy."

I thanked him and went upstairs. I should have gone home.

I was dog tired, but before I thought of going to bed I had some figuring to do. It had been a delicious meal, though from the way Cogan acted I thought dark thoughts about arsenic in the coffee and/or a knife in the back. But the room he had shown me to was a beauty. Berbelot, as I should have expected, was as good at decorating as he was at anything else. The place was finished in chrome and gray and black, the whole thing centering around a huge mirror at one end. Building a room around a mirror is the most complimentary thing a host can do in a guest room.

It was a fascinating mirror, too. It wasn't exactly silvered—it was of a dull gray sheen, like rough-finished stainless steel. And whether it was metal or glass I couldn't tell. It gave a beautiful image—deep and true, and accentuating natural color. Probably something he "knocked together" himself.

I walked up and down absently, thinking about Berbelot and the Breather. They had a lot in common. No one could tell exactly what they were, or how great, or how powerful. Thinking about the

Breather's series of cracks at me, I realized that he, or it, had spoken exactly in my idiom. Berbelot did that, too. And yet I knew that both of them could have completely swamped me with dialectical trickery.

My shadow caught my eye and I amused myself for a moment by making shadows on the wall opposite the mirror. A bird—a cat—a funny face. I'd done it ever since I was a kid and the thing fascinated me. I was pretty good at it. I wandered around the room making shadow pictures on the wall and thinking about the Breather and Berbelot, and then found myself looking into that deep mirror.

"Hi!" I said to my reflection.

It looked out at me placidly. Not a bad-looking guy, in a pair of Berbelot's cellusilk pajamas and that cocky expression. That was quite a mirror. What was it that made a guy look different? The color trick? Not entirely. Let's see. I stuck out my tongue and so did my reflection. I thumbed my nose, and turned cold inside. I knew now what it was.

The image was—not reversed.

I stood there with my right arm up, my right thumb to my nose. The reflection's right arm—the one toward my left, since it was facing me—was raised, and it thumbed its nose. I was white as a sheet.

Was I bats? Did I have a mental hangover from seeing that unreversed image in the television set downstairs?

"This is awful," I said.

It couldn't be a mirror. Not even Berbelot could build a—or was it a mirror? A—a television screen? Couldn't be—not with the depth it had. It was almost as if I were standing in front of a glass cabinet, looking at me inside. The image was three-dimensional. I suddenly decided I had been thumbing my nose long enough. This must be some trick of that old devil's, I thought. No wonder he didn't have dinner with me. He was rigging up this gadget while I was eating. If it *was* a television screen—and I'd never heard of one like this—then that thing in there wasn't me—it was the Ether Breather. I listened carefully, and sure enough, heard the hum of transmitting cells. What a gag! There were cells somewhere hidden in this room sending my image away and returning it by wire! But that screen—

My reflection suddenly set its legs apart and put its hands on its hips. "What are you looking at?" it asked me.

"N-nothing," I said as sarcastically as I could while my teeth were chattering. "The Breather again, huh?"

"That's right. My, but you're ugly."

"Mind your tongue!" I said sharply. "I can switch you off, you know."

"Heh!" he jeered. "I don't have to be afraid of that any more, thanks to a trick you just showed me."

"Yeah? You can't kid me, bud. You're just some amoral cosmic ray's little accident."

"I warn you, don't get tough with me."

"I'll do what I please. You couldn't pull your finger out of a tub of lard," I euphemized.

He sighed. "O.K. You asked for it."

And then I had to live through the worst thing that any poor mortal in the history of the world ever experienced. It's one thing to have an argument with yourself in the mirror. It's something entirely different to have your reflection reach out a leg, kick down the mirror with a shattering crash, walk up to you and belt you in the mouth a couple of times before it smears you on the carpet with a terrific right hook. That's what happened to me. Just that, so help me, Hannah.

I lay there on the rug looking up at me, which had just socked I, and I said "Whooie!" and went to sleep.

I've no idea how long I lay there. When light glimmered into my jarred brain again, Berbelot was kneeling beside me chafing my wrists. The beautiful mirror—or whatever the devil it was—was in some thousand-odd pieces on the floor, and I had gone to about as many pieces psychically. I finally realized that Berbelot was saying something.

"Hamilton! What happened? What happened? Do you realize you just busted thirty thousand dollars' worth of apparatus? What's the matter with you ... are you sick?"

I rolled over and sat up, then went hand over hand up Berbelot until I was standing beside him. My head felt like a fur-lined ball of fire and every time my heart beat it blinded me.

"What did you wreck that receiver for?" Berbelot said irascibly.

"Me wreck it? Me didn't wreck it . . . I wrecked it," I said groggily. "I was standing in front of the mirror when who should kick it down and poke me but myself"—I shook my head and let the pain of it shake my carcass—"Ow! *Whew.* I was just—"

"Stop it!" Berbelot snapped.

Almost as suddenly I recovered. "Receiver . . . what do you mean receiver?"

Berbelot was hopping mad. "The new job," he shouted, pointing at the debris. "My first three-dimensional television receiver!"

"Three . . . what are you talking about, man?"

He calmed down the way he invariably did when he was asked a question about television. "It's a box of tiny projectors," he said. "They're set . . . studded . . . inside that closet affair behind the screen you just broke. The combined beams from them give a three-dimensional, or stereoscopic, effect. And now you've gone and wrecked my screen," he wailed. "Why were you ever born? Why must I suffer so because of you? Why—"

"Wait a minute, Pop—hold on there. I didn't bust your precious screen."

"You just said you did."

"Mmm-mm. So help me. It was the Breather. I had a little argument with him and he kicked down the screen and came out and beat the stern off me."

"What?" Berbelot was really shocked this time. "You're a gibbering maniac! That was your own image! You were broadcast and your image reproduced there!"

"You're a muddy-headed old stink-merchant!" I bellowed. "I suppose I kicked down your mirror, put three teeth on hinges, and then knocked myself colder'n a cake of carbon ice just for a chance to lie to you!"

"This is what comes of getting an overgrown cretin to help out in an experiment," moaned Berbelot. "Don't try my patience any more, Hamilton!"

"*Your* patience? What the hell was that new-fangled set doing in this room anyway?"

He grinned weakly. "Oh—that. Well, I just wanted to have some fun with you. After you left I tuned in on the Breather and told him to stand by; I'd put him in touch with ... with the guy that was smelling up his world."

"You old crumb! Fun! You wanted me to argue with that misplaced gamma-particle all night, hey? Why I ought to ... I think I will at that!" And I grabbed him by the neck.

"Allow *me*," said a voice behind us, and we were seized, each by a shoulder. Then our heads were cracked violently together and we found ourselves groveling at the feet of my spittin' image. Berbelot looked up at my erstwhile reflection in silent awe.

"Where were you?" I growled.

"In the corner," he said, throwing a thumb over his shoulder. "You're a pretty-looking pair, I must say."

"Berbelot," I said, "meet your Ether Breather. Now I'm going to stand on your face until you eat the shoes off my feet, because you called me a liar."

Berbelot said, "Well, I'm damned!"

The Breather remarked quietly, "You two better explain yourselves in a hysterical hurry. Otherwise I shall most certainly take you apart and put you together again, alternating the pieces."

"Oh, we were just trying to get in contact with you again."

"What for?"

"We were interested in you. We talked to you a year or so ago and then you disappeared. We wanted to talk to you again." In spite of my anger at him I found something else to admire Berbelot for. He had remembered the Breather's peculiar childishness and was using it just when somebody had to do something, quickly.

"But you told me to stop interfering!" Presto—the creature was already plaintive, on the amicable defensive. Its mutability was amazing.

"He told you," Berbelot snorted, indicating me, where I rolled and moaned over my twice-bruised sconce. "I didn't."

"Don't you speak for each other, then? We do."

"You—singular and plural—are a homogeneous being. All humanity is not blessed with my particularly affable nature."

347

"Why you old narcissist!" I snorted, and lunged at him. For every inch of my lunge the Breather calmly kicked me back a foot. I did some more moaning.

"You mean you are my friend and he is not?" said the Breather, staring at me coldly as one does at a roach which is going to be stepped on if and when it moves out from the wall.

"Oh, I wouldn't go so far as to say that," said Berbelot kindly.

I had an inspiration which, for all I know, saved my life. "You said you learned from me how to come out of the television set!" I blurted.

"True. I should be grateful for that, I suppose. I shall not tear you in little pieces." He turned to Berbelot. "I heard your call, of course, but being told once was enough for me. I did not understand. When I say something I generally mean it. Humans are not understandable, but they are very funny."

The scientist in Berbelot popped up. "What was that you said about Hamilton showing you how to come out of the set?"

"Oh, I was watching him from the screen over there. I am sorry I broke it. He was walking around the room making pictures on the walls with shadows. That's what I am doing now."

"Shadow pictures?"

"Certainly. I am a creature living in five dimensions and aware of four, just as you live in four dimensions and are aware of three. He made three-dimensional shadows that were projected on a two-dimensional surface. I am making four-dimensional pictures that are being projected in three dimensions."

Berbelot frowned. "On what surface?"

"On that of your fourth dimension, of course."

"Our fourth. Hm-m-m . . . with what light source?"

"A five-dimensional one just as your Sun, for instance, has four."

"How many dimensions are there altogether?"

"How high is up?" twinkled the Breather.

"Could I project myself into your world?"

"I don't know. Maybe . . . maybe not. Are you going to stop making that awful smell?" he said suddenly.

"Of course! We only made it to get you angry enough to come to us for a talk. We didn't mean anything by it."

"Oh!" squealed the Ether Breather delightedly. "A joke! Fun!"

"Told you he'd take it well," murmured Berbelot.

"Yeah ... suppose he hadn't? You're a rat, Berbelot. You made darn sure that if someone had to take a rap from this aeration here, it wouldn't be you. Nice guy." There was a strained silence for a while, and then I grinned. "Aw, hell, you had it doped out, Berbelot. Shake. I'd have done the same if I had the brains."

"He isn't bad at all, is he?" asked the Breather in surprise, staring at me.

"Well, is everything all right now, Breather? Do you feel that you're welcome to come any time you wish?"

"Yes ... yes, I think so. But I won't come this way again. I can only take form in that lovely new three-dimensional machine of yours, and I have to break a screen to get out. I am sorry. I'll talk to you any time, though. And may I do something for you sometime?"

"Why should you?" I piped up glumly.

"Oh, think of the *fun* we'll have!"

"Would you really like to do something for us?"

"Oh, yes. Please."

"Can you direct that interference of yours into any radio frequency at any time?"

"Sure."

"Now look. We are going to start a company to advertise certain products. There are other companies in the same business. Will you leave our programs strictly alone and have all the fun you want with our competitors?"

"I'd love that!"

"That will be splendid!"

"Berbelot, we're rich!"

"You're rich," he corrected gleefully, "I'm richer!"

BACK WORDS

Story Notes by Paul Williams

"Heavy Insurance": released for newspaper syndication July 16, 1938 by the McClure Newspaper Syndicate; published in the *Milwaukee Journal* July 16, 1938; believed to be Theodore Sturgeon's first sale as a professional writer and his first published story.

Comments by Theodore Sturgeon:
I was in the merchant marine. I began to write while I was doing that, while I was at sea. And finally, one magical day, I got a letter when I got back north that said I'd sold a story. I sold one to a newspaper syndicate, and I was so excited I quit my job, I went ashore and I was going to be a writer.

Well, I sold the story for five dollars. On publication. It had taken me three months to research it. And they were willing to buy one story, sometimes two, a week. No more. So for almost six months, I lived on five dollars and sometimes ten a week. I lived on West 63rd Street, where Lincoln Center now is, and it cost me seven and a half dollars a week for the room; and I ate on whatever was left. [interview with Paul Williams, December 1975]

I worked out a way to rob the American Express Company out of several hundred thousand dollars. And I did my homework, I wrote to the company and I found out precisely how they shipped this and that and the other thing, and I got it all worked in, and I wrote it as a story because I didn't have quite the guts to do it myself. [interview with David Hartwell, September 1972]

... I was certain that it was a "perfect crime" which would net me a fortune. When the time came to pull the caper, I lacked the immoral courage to try it, so wrote it as a story instead. The research fell down in the matter of "carbon ice"—dry ice—which was a curiosity at the time, and I couldn't find data on the actual weight; I don't think I had ever seen any. All I knew for sure was that it deliquesces—changes from

a solid to a gas without going through a liquid stage. [from TS's notes accompanying republication of the story in the *Program Guide,* Colorado Mountain College, 1984 (in connection with a TS speaking appearance)]

Editor's notes:

It is not known what newspapers other than the *Milwaukee Journal* published the McClure short-short story series, which appeared in the *Journal* under the heading "Daily Short Story." Sturgeon was only one of many free-lance writers contributing to the series.

"Heavy Insurance," on the evidence of Sturgeon's letters to his mother in the spring of 1938, was titled by him "—So They Put Me in Here," and was purchased by McClure in the last week of May, 1938. His often-repeated tale about quitting the merchant marine when he stopped in New York and found that the story had sold was not strictly true, although there's no lack of romance in what did happen. Sturgeon graduated from high school in 1936 (though in correspondence and interviews he sometimes claimed with pride not to have graduated), and later that year enrolled in the Pennsylvania State Nautical Schoolship Annapolis ("the Annie"). He quit the nautical school in the spring of 1937, got Ordinary Seaman's papers, and shipped out on a merchant marine ship. Over the course of the next year he served on various ships, all coastwise freighters or oil tankers making calls on the Atlantic coast between Providence, Rhode Island and Port Arthur, Texas (with some trips further south, including stops in Guatemala and Panama).

In April of 1938 Sturgeon got in an argument with the mate of the ship he'd been on, the California, and told him off and quit. When he went to get his bags, he was confronted by a fellow crewman who'd had TS's words ("I don't like this ship or the crew") repeated to him. A fight ensued, with a number of sailors involved, and Sturgeon, who'd employed a kind of judo trick that caused another seaman to break his jaw against the bulkhead, was arrested and offered a choice of 30 days in the Tombs (they were docked in New York, apparently) or a $30 fine. He paid the fine, and spent some time "beached" in New York, writing and submitting stories (as he had been doing already while at sea) and considering whether and when to ship out again.

About a month later, May 21, 1938, still in New York, he wrote his mother (she'd moved to Scotland): *The short on which I put my fondest hopes, a detective story and, if I may say so, a very unusual one, is always being kept for approval and then rejected.* Liberty *had it for 10 weeks,* Collier's *for two months; now it is out again and has been out for a month. Everything else I send is rejected within two weeks. But "—So They Put Me in Here" is driving me mad.* (We can deduce from this that he probably wrote the story at the end of 1937, at the age of 19.)

On May 31, he wrote her (rather casually, saving this news for the fourth page of his letter): *But my life is not unremunerative and pointless. The other day I sold my story "—So They Put Me in Here," and was so encouraged that I wrote a longer one called "Beauty Transplanted."* He goes on to talk about his agent-to-be's enthusiasm for the new story and her insistence that he should be writing for the slick magazines, not wasting himself on the pulps.

The week "Heavy Insurance" was published Sturgeon shipped out again, and he remained at sea for the rest of 1938. He did live in New York between January and July of 1939, selling short-short stories to McClure (and doing some contract work for them rewriting other people's stories) and struggling to sell stories to other and better-paying markets. Then he shipped out again in July, returning to New York in October. The apartment on West 63rd is one he lived in for a few months at the beginning of 1940.

"The Heart": first published in *Other Worlds*, May 1955. In his introduction to this story when it was included in the collection *Sturgeon in Orbit* (1964), Sturgeon describes it as *This odd little thing—actually one of the first stories I ever wrote in my life.* If this recollection is accurate, we can suppose that it was written in 1937-1938, or possibly earlier.

"Cellmate": first published in *Weird Tales*, January 1947. In a letter to his mother dated April 25, 1946, TS mentions: *Sold a story to* Weird Tales *last week, by the way—an old one I wrote when I was 19.* This could refer to either "Cellmate" or "Fluffy." In a conversation with Sam Moskowitz (circa 1961), Sturgeon apparently gave the impression that all of the stories he sold to *Weird Tales* in the late 1940s were early (pre-1942) stories that he'd been unable to sell when he wrote them. Moskowitz, in his book of biographical sketches *Seekers of Tomorrow* (1965), lists "Cellmate," "The Deadly Ratio" ("It Wasn't Syzygy"), "The Professor's Teddy Bear," "Abreaction," "The Perfect Host," and "The Martian and the Moron" as stories "resurrected from the trunk." A study of Sturgeon's correspondence from 1946–1948 indicates quite clearly that "Deadly Ratio," "Professor's Teddy Bear," "The Perfect Host," and "The Martian and the Moron" were not from the trunk but were written after the war. "Abreaction" is also not a prewar story; the indisputable evidence is the bulldozer, which TS learned to drive in 1942.

That leaves "Cellmate," and "Fluffy" (which is not on Moskowitz's list, although it appeared in *Weird Tales* in the issue after "Cellmate"). Sturgeon told me in 1975 that "Fluffy" was a prewar story. I don't consider that definite proof, memory being what it is, but for the purposes of this collection, which attempts to present stories in chronological order of composition, these two stories are being grouped with Sturgeon's earliest work.

"Fluffy": first published in *Weird Tales*, March 1947. Sturgeon himself had a fair amount of experience as a house guest after his parents moved to Scotland while he was at sea in 1937. On shore he stayed with various relatives, family friends, and new friends that he'd met on his travels.

The protagonist, Ransome, is a stock Sturgeon character: the glib, utterly self-absorbed male (he usually comes to a bad end). TS to his mother, October 31, 1938: *My best stories are those in which I play up and magnify my own weaknesses. Contrary to the psychology of, say, Burroughs, who was a frail tubercular and thus created the immortal Tarzan, my best pieces are those which deal with those parts of my own make-up which are highly undesirable and unlikeable and inadmirable, as you will see for yourself soon.*

"Alter Ego": unpublished (the unpublished manuscripts and fragments from this period are almost all from a trunk that was left in Staten Island, as described in the notes on "Helix the Cat"). This may have been written in fall 1938, after the invasion of Czechoslovakia, or any time in the following year.

"Mailed through a Porthole": unpublished. Written November 1938. While many of the early stories here are efforts at writing to formula that Sturgeon was embarrassed by even as he worked on them, this is one that he was proud of. He told his mother (May 13, 1939): *I went up to see the editor of* Unknown *which is a new Street and Smith book. He liked me. He told me what he wanted and I liked the idea of it because I thought he was right when he said he had no formula. I gave him a* *story without a plot called "Mailed through a Porthole" which was very beautiful. He rejected it. I wrote another story which he liked but said it had "Purely intellectual appeal" which was true. It was called "Sudden Death?" and had to do with a hypothetical acceleration of the perceptions when anyone is killed suddenly, so that the thing is slowed interminably to him. It was about a man getting run over by a subway train and dying slowly in horrible agony and someone on the platform says "He never knew what hit him." It was cold and scientific and very horrible and it was rejected.*

("Sudden Death?" is not included here because no manuscript for it has been found. Every Sturgeon story that the editor knows of and has been able to obtain a copy of is or will be included in these volumes.)

In the same letter Sturgeon describes going to see the editor of *Adventure* (which he calls *the oldest pulp magazine there is*), who rejected "Porthole," then asked to see it again, and eventually rejected it again.

The story derives from Sturgeon's experience on the tanker *W.W. Mills*, waiting out one hurricane and having a near miss with another. To his mother, August 26, 1938: *A hurricane considers no man's plans; that's what we're hove to for. I'm going to write this trip up some time—it's been quite an experience. Not that anything has happened; it's just the tension aboard, wondering whether we'll miss it or not.* To his mother, October 15, 1938, referring to the great September hurricane: *We met it when it was a baby down off the Bahamas; and a large-sized baby it was too. The engines broke down when we were directly in the path of it, off Miami; fortunately for us it took a freakish turn north and came near depopulating Connecticut... A hurricane may be exciting and mildly fictional; but it may strike anywhere, and if it comes around the one who scoffs, he scoffs no longer—if he's alive. No fun.*

"A Noose of Light": unpublished. This was rejected by A.P. Waldo (no relation to Sturgeon's father E. M. Waldo, as far as I know), fiction editor of the McClure Syndicate. There is also some indication that it was submitted to *Weird Tales* in 1940. The address on the first page of the manuscript dates it as a 1938 or 1939 story.

"Strangers on a Train": unpublished. The untitled manuscript has been given a title by the editor.

"Accidentally on Porpoise": unpublished. Written December 1938. Another story Sturgeon was fond of; he was frustrated by his agent's inability to sell it, and fired her. In a letter to his fiancee Dorothe Fillingame, January 10, 1939, he says, *Sure, it's got enough for a novel, and I'll do it that way some day.* In fact, there is a clear link between this story and "When You Care, When You Love" (1962), which was intended as the first section of a never-finished novel, *The Tulip Tree. The Unbegotten Man,* the title of a novel Sturgeon announced as forthcoming circa 1950 but never wrote, is another indication of his lifelong interest in writing a novel-length story about the re-creation of a human being.

"The Right Line": unpublished. The oil town honky-tonk setting is based on TS's days on the beach in Port Arthur, Texas, on the Gulf Coast, home port for the tankers he shipped on. He did work very briefly as a "sandwich man" there, in the summer of 1938.

"Golden Day": syndicated by McClure, March 4, 1939. Sturgeon cites this as an example of "unique short-story technique" (see notes on "One Sick Kid"). He wrote to Dorothe, March 6, 1939: *Prepare yourself and Co. for latest release, sent to your home very soon ... story was the kind of inspiration I'd be happy to get twice a year ... it's one of the reasons McClure is so picky with my stuff; they want them all to be as good ... you heard about the poor — that wrote "Pigs Is Pigs"; well, "Golden Day" is mine...* (ellipses and dashes in original)

The McClure Newspaper Syndicate short-shorts were sent out to newspapers on 8½" x 15" sheets of paper, with the slug "DAILY SHORT STORIES" and little subheads partway through the stories to break them into sections. (In this case the subheads are *Accident* after "an awful thing to carry around with you" and *Anniversary* after "she was terribly pleased.") The sheets are dated—evidently one story was provided for each day—and the author is credited.

"Permit Me My Gesture": syndicated by McClure, March 10, 1939. TS to Dorothe, April 22, 1939: *When you come to New York I want you to sit in on a plotting session and see how it goes. Doesn't matter who with; Boord* [sometime agent] *or Hatch* [roommate and fellow writer] *or both. What I'm desperate for, as I've told you, is short, uncomplicated young love notions with a gag or gadget. "Heavy Insurance," for instance, is a gag (fool the reader) idea. So is "Golden Day." "Permit Me My Ges-*

ture" and "Watch My Smoke" are gadgets. Three, possibly four, but in preference two characters. No crime, gangsters, rackets, or any suggestion of such. You begin to see now how rigid formula can be? TS to D, February 27, 1939: *Speaking of plotz, please send some ... don't mull over them so ... don't polish them ... when Hatch and I are tops we have turned out six plotz in two hours ... and they're always better than those we spend a day on ... 'struth, because they're so easily molded into formula ... not more than three main characters, and a gadget; telephones, by the way, and counterfeit money, and twins are rejected on sight as gadgets ... so that's the layout; please help, not so much because I need anyone's help but because I want yours...*

"Watch My Smoke": syndicated by McClure, March 13, 1939. This was also published in England, in the *Guide and Ideas* newspaper, May 13, 1939, Sturgeon's first UK publication.

The following letter, from a British literary agent to "Miss Baker," evidently one of Sturgeon's editors at McClure's New York office, understandably excited the young author and (temporarily) raised his hopes almost painfully:

CECIL BROOKS, LTD.
London, England

May 13, 1939
Dear Miss Baker

I am arranging to have a copy of the "Guide and Ideas" sent to you containing Theodore Sturgeon's story WATCH MY SMOKE.

My own opinion is that this boy can write and that his stuff will sell in this country.

You know as well as I do that the quality of your short stories, like the quality of everybody else's, varies considerably. Some are the type which would never sell in this country; others have possible sales, and others have strong sales potentialities, and I would say that Sturgeon's work comes into the last-named classification.

Now that we have sold one of his stories we are taking out of our files all material we have of his. Our next step will be to push his stuff as much as ever we can, and endeavor to build up, step by step, a reputation here for Theodore Sturgeon's short stories, so that as time goes on, each new one he writes will be regarded by editors as "worthy of immediate consideration."

What does he do apart from writing short shorts? Does he write any longer stories—three, four or five thousand word stuff? If so, get him to let you have it and pass it over to us and we will endeavor to sell it, through you, of course.

Sincerely,

June 6, 1939, TS wrote Dorothe: *Best news in the writing racket is that McClures is drawing me up a contract to begin middle of next month . . . I am to get 50% of McClure's profits on all my foreign sales . . . as I live and breathe, Dorothe—as I love you—that letter from Brooks Ltd. was straight stuff. It burned me up when I read that the Babe, Inc., [D's mother] doubted it. . . I don't know if you realize it, Toots, but that is without exception the biggest break and the finest build-up that we have had so far. Do you realize what it means? I know you don't bother much with short fiction; but if you ever read the full-page stories in the Sunday papers, you'll notice that a very large percentage of them are written by English authors—Belloc-Lowndes, for instance. Why? Certainly not because they are especially fine literature. But it seems that editors on both sides of the water are deeply impressed by the fact that they can print an overseas writer. The fact that I have sold American newspapers doesn't cut an awful lot of ice here. But it does in England—plenty. And—now get this—as soon as my stuff is pushed over there, it will be in increasingly great demand here. Remember how Orson Welles crashed the Abbey Theater? He claimed he was in the New York Group Theater, which was not true. But it got him in Abbey, and when he got back it got him in the Group.*

"Watch My Smoke" had its origins in a visit Sturgeon made to Canada in the summer of 1934, when he was 16. He was spending a month or more with his uncle and aunt (his mother's sister), "recuperating" from acute rheumatic fever while his parents and his brother went to Europe (he has written that in fact he exerted himself as excessively as possible, by way of protest). In an interview in April 1978, Sturgeon described the place to me, his voice still full of the wonder and awe he must have felt at 16 when he heard about the local "bush pilots":

This was up in northern Quebec. It was very wild at that time. The town had duck-board sidewalks and dirt streets, it was really going back, and there were virtually no roads up there at all. There was a railroad that went up there, but everything was flown in and out with these Balanca [?] monoplanes ... I've written some about those guys, those bush pilots. They are a breed of their own, they were really fantastic people, full of tricks. I remember coming in— They were all seaplanes, because there's nothing up there but lakes and there was no flat ground whatsoever.

Sometimes coming into those lakes at dusk, you couldn't see the surface of the water—it just started to flare out, it could have been 15 feet under you, five feet under you, 30 feet under you, you couldn't see. So they all used to carry a roll of toilet paper up there in the cockpit, and they'd come down just as close to the water as they could figure, and they'd stream out a whole length of toilet paper, and then they'd go around again and come in and land on that, because that would float on top of the water, they could see where the surface was. Otherwise they would stall out or fall in or dive in or whatnot.

They were full of tricks like that. One guy got out of a very very narrow lake, he flew some serum up to a guy who had a dangerous disease in a mining camp, and he had to land on this funny crooked little lake that was full of stumps and stuff. Well, he got in all right, but it looked like there was no way to get out. So he tied a rope to the tailskid of the plane and pulled it above the shore, and he tied it to a tree which was bent over a log. And he had an Indian standing by with an axe. He revved the thing up until it was screaming, you know, and then he waves his hand and the Indian hits the rope and bang! he takes off. He managed to get up over the treetops and skid out between the mountains and stuff and get up in the air again. They were certainly marvelous.

"**The Other Cheek**": syndicated by McClure, April 10, 1939. The *Milwaukee Journal*, the only U.S. newspaper from which Sturgeon had clippings of some of these stories (though certainly not the only paper they appeared in), did not use the subheads provided in the release, but did break up the stories at the same places, using a line space with three asterisks centered in it.

Sturgeon spent his adolescence in Philadelphia; when he wrote this story his fiancée was still living there. As a merchant seaman, he would stay in the waterfront district (at the Seamen's Institute) when he visited her.

"**Extraordinary Seaman**": syndicated by McClure, circa June 1939. Sold February 27, 1939; probably written that month. This is the only longer story Sturgeon sold to McClure, although he made many attempts. He was paid $25 for it.

TS to Dorothe, June 25, 1939: *Glad, and a little surprised, that you so liked "Extraordinary Seaman" ... the editor at McClure didn't think so much of it, and neither did I ... she bought it only because it was the first tanker story I had submitted and she is in favor of my using my various backgrounds ... the dialogue is A-1, and the plot is very stupid; but she liked it for exactly the opposite reasons, which only shows to go you ... at any rate, it sold, and bought me my new suit, so what the hell ... but if you liked it so well, then I'd better not send you "A God in a Garden," on account of because you might not be able to stand it, so superior is it to the "Seaman." "Ether Breather" is almost as good.*

The story was sent out by McClure on a galley sheet, 15" x 22", with a large illustration, designed to take up a full newspaper page.

"One Sick Kid": syndicated by McClure, April 29, 1939. Although he again got to use his tanker background and mention Tortugas (an occasional TS nickname, presumably because of its anagrammatic similarity to his surname), Sturgeon did not like this story. To Dorothe, March 30, 1939: *I sold McClures again, which means five bucks at the end of April ... I submitted three really brilliant stories to them, and one very mediocre one whose two selling points were its sickening flag-waving and its idea. The latter is as weak as my stomach just now (epsom, iron, quinine, strychnine) but I got it from a newspaper article and the clipping was attached to the MS. I have rarely been so discouraged; the sale contributed rather than cheered me. McClure's also rejected a story written on the editor's plot, in the editor's way; yet they bought, last month, a story which is against the policies they stated before I wrote it ["Permit Me My Gesture"?] ... damn them! To make you slog and slog for the miserable delayed pennies they pay? What right have they to be so _____ picky? ...*

Mom of course knew just what to say, when she finally commented on a batch of the McClure short-shorts. Sturgeon quotes her (she was a dedicated and productive, though not much published, story writer herself, and he respected her opinions tremendously) in his reply letter: "The newspaper things are decent quality for newspaper things. The one I liked best was the piece about the seasick lad and the coastguard cutter." And: "I'd love to see some of your good stuff." That provoked this outburst (TS to Christine Hamilton Sturgeon, February 2, 1940):

Naow mum: I appreciate your appreciation of me as a rising literary star. I mean that; I'm not being sarcastic. But you must realize that my philosophy of life is an egoistic (not ego̱tistic, n.b.) one. Self-advancement, self-development, self-gratification. I think I told you that it seems to me there are only two ways to achieve happiness in this our life, and one is to adjust the world to suit oneself, and the other, to adjust oneself to suit the world? And that I frankly consider myself not big enough for the former job? It is in that honest conviction that I avoid egotism ... I know just how much I have to be proud of, no matter what I tell other people. *And my writing adheres to that philosophy. I told you above that the new "comic" field has just saved my life and my hopes.* [TS had gotten an assignment writing continuity for a Street & Smith comic strip called *Iron Munro*, included in *Shadow Comics* magazine.] *Proof enough that for me there is no such thing as prostituting my art. I am a writer and I am a good one. I have an artistic approach toward things which afford me, personally, amusement, but I do not regard my writing as an art, but a craft. I will succeed faster and better in the only way which means anything to me just now, as a craftsman, than I ever could as an artist. I will never write a* Grapes of Wrath *or a* Gone With the Wind *or an* Appointment at Samarra *because I have no message, no ardor, no lessons to teach. I am a teller of tales, and in telling tales I find my delight. I tell the tales that people want to be told, and no others, because I am not egocentric but just egoistic. That is called writing formula. I write formula. I know you didn't mean the line about "good stuff" as such, but it was the deadliest of insults. Why? Because when I write I do the very best I know how! Good stuff? You have it. A story is good if it sells; it is of "great" material if it gets audience huzzas. All of those stories were stories the people asked me to tell them. That I sold them means I did my job capably. That "Ether Breather" was not only voted the best story in the issue but the most entertaining story of the* year *proves to my satisfaction that it was near-great. Now listen to me very, very carefully, oh most wonderful of mothers. I do not know if I will ever write novels. If I do, they probably will not be great. But if one or some are great, then it will be only because they are the most magnificent pieces of escapist hedonism ever to see print. And don't throw Bodenheim at me. I know him now; as a matter of fact I threw him out of this very room two nights ago because he was objectionably drunk. That is his trouble. You told me once that he was a fine poet, and that he degenerated by way of large checks,* Replenishing Jessica, *and* A Virtuous Girl.

You're wrong, Mum. Maxwell Bodenheim is a great poet. He is touched by a Power greater than men or Man. He is an instrument. He is a voice for a Great Thought. I know because I've seen that ordinary-looking sandy-haired little man be *that voice. He is a poet and he is an artist and he has gained, not lost, in his art. And I want no art like Bodenheim's. I have a life to live and a girl to marry and children to bring into the world—a life* of *me, outside of me. Let the Bodenheims and the Joe Goulds and the Linc Gillespies and the John Rose Gildeas live out their infernos of beauty. I'll feed what pap to fools I'm paid for, and live a clean life on their stupidity.*

But I don't *write down! I* can't, *and sell stories. Be proud of my doing the impossible. I have sold thirty-two stories and a poem in a year of writing—and five months of that year I was, for some reason or other, hors de combat. I have made a living out of writing. I have only done it by working like hell when I worked. Be proud of me, then, for that; but oh, mum, don't you know by this time that there is little lofty about young Ted? I'm no Wells or Welles; Shaw or Shakespeare. I give humor and originality and the utmost in refined horror (that's "He Shuttles," due out in 60 days—my novelette) to people who* need *it. I'm no uplifter. I repeat: I'm a craftsman ... what was it Pete* [his older brother] *once said— "I respect a good whore more than a lousy bishop"? There you have it. Literary snobbishness is for people who sell* Story *after twelve tears* [sic] *of trying, during which they lived on relief or off friends. Not for me.*

I mentioned the story you lauded—"One Sick Kid," it was called— because I was completely dumfounded that you should pick that, of all those releases, to like ... Mother, are you sure it's not because you're a little prejudiced in favor of the sea? That story was ding-dong stuff; it had a shot of supersuperpseudo-patriotism in it to make it sell, the way you put—well, you don't, but some do—a shot of baking-powder in flapjax. That story was a crime against literature—even my kind. It was surpassed only in sloppy sentimentalism by "Some People Forget," the Memorial Day number, for which I take no responsibility—it was an ordered story, as are all those having to do with specific dates. I can't excuse "One Sick Kid" on those or any other grounds. But there are, I think, some excellent stories there. Did you know that as short-story technique, "Golden Day" is unique? "Watch My Smoke" and "Cajun Providence" are good enough for any slick mag ... sold them to McClure when I needed five sure dollars quickly faster than $250 maybe some-

time. I never mind doing that on occasion because there're always more where they came from ... wonder if you'll like the next lot better? I'll send them over after "He Shuttles" is released. In the next lot will be what I think is the most powerful little short short I've yet done: "Turkish Delight" to McClure's. Also the most whimsical: "Derm Fool," Unknown. *And the novelette.*

(Note that at the time of writing, the author of this epistle was two weeks short of his 22nd birthday, and six weeks shy of marriage and the tremendous financial responsibilities he imagined—correctly—it would bring. Unfortunately, the issues stirred up here continued to swirl unresolved in him throughout his lifetime.)

"His Good Angel": syndicated by McClure, May 12, 1939. Also published in England, in *Guide and Ideas,* May 20, 1939, under the title "An Answer Has Been Arranged."

"Some People Forget": syndicated by McClure, May 30, 1939. As noted in the letter quoted under "One Sick Kid," "Some People Forget" is a story written (at the request of the syndicate) to be released on a particular day, in this case Memorial Day (for non-U.S. readers, it's a holiday on which soldiers who died for this country in past wars are to be honored and remembered).

TS to David Hartwell, 1972, regarding his childhood experience with bullies: *I was very underweight and undersized and a natural target for everybody around me. I was pretty well brutalized by that whole thing. I had to figure out different ways to go to school each day, because kids would lay for me on the way.*

"A God in a Garden": first published in *Unknown,* October 1939. Written April 1939. This was Sturgeon's first sale to John W. Campbell, Jr., editor of *Astounding Science-Fiction* and *Unknown.* It was his first story sale to anyone other than the McClure Syndicate (though there is some suggestion in his correspondence that he may have written or ghost-written "confession" stories in 1938 and/or 1939), and in fact he would not sell a new story to a market other than Campbell or McClure until 1946, though not for lack of trying. It was probably not the first fantasy story he wrote (we don't know for sure when "Fluffy" or "Cellmate" was written, but there is evidence that some of the early stories he wrote to try to sell in 1938 and the beginning of 1939 were horror fiction of some kind).

It is however the story whose sale marks his entrance into the science fiction and fantasy field, which would be his home as a writer for better or worse for the rest of his life. ("Ether Breather" was his first *published* story in the field, but not his first sale.)

TS to his mother, May 13, 1939: *I wrote another story called "A God in a Garden" which is a nice euphonious title, and he* [Campbell] *liked it very much and asked me to rewrite it. I did. He bought it last week. This morning I got a check for eighty dollars.*

TS to Dorothe, August 16, 1939 (at sea): *This letter has been stretched over a week. Know how I write to you? By the page. I hate to take a half-filled page out of the mill* [typewriter]; *I almost invariably write right down to the bottom before quitting. Sometimes that leaves me in the middle of a sentence, and two or three days may pass before I get to my predicate. But I can almost always recapture the mood just by rereading what has gone before, something I would like to be able to do with my work. If I don't finish a story at one sitting it is liable to be patchy. A notable exception was "A God in a Garden"; I was really in the groove then. I had such perfect control over it that each of twenty-eight pages began with a new paragraph—a godsend when I had to rewrite it, for I slipped many pages of old ms. into the new draft simply by changing the page numbers!*

"A God in a Garden" was also the first story of Sturgeon's to be anthologized. (He would in time become one of the most anthologized living story writers in the English language.) Phil Stong purchased it in August 1940 for an anthology entitled *The Other Worlds, An Omnibus of Imaginative Stories,* published by Wilfred Funk, Inc., in 1941. Sturgeon to Williams, 1975: *I remember I went around to the publisher, after I'd signed the agreement and everything else, and met receptionists and typists and people and said, "Where's Mr. Stong?" "Oh, he's not here, of course, he's in—" and I timidly asked for my ten dollars, and they said, "Oh well that you know has got to wait until the book is published..." And I recall I really needed that money, oh boy did I need that money.*

Between April of 1939 and June of 1941 Theodore Sturgeon sold 26 stories to John Campbell, 10 for *Astounding* and 16 for *Unknown.* Sturgeon had read *Astounding* as a high school student, and *Weird Tales,* and H. G. Wells and E. R. Eddison. He had a fondness for science fiction and fantasy, but there's no indication that he ever thought of himself as wanting to be a science fiction writer as such. Instead, he became one because that was the only market that welcomed him as a writer.

But he did have a special resonance with *Unknown,* a brand new magazine when Sturgeon beached himself in Brooklyn at the beginning of 1939 and threw himself full time into the writing racket. He told David Hartwell: *Somebody brought me a Volume I, Number 1 of* Unknown *and said, "Boy, this is what you ought to be writing." And I was absolutely thrilled with the magazine.* It appealed to him as a writer as well as as a reader. To Dorothe, February 10, 1939: *Have you seen Street and Smith's new sheet,* Unknown? *They have no policy except that the stories be of the Unknown in any aspect, and must be entertaining. As an escape from that bedevilling incubus, formula, it is a godsend. I'm submitting a story to them next Tuesday.*

Unknown is still regarded by those who read it during its brief five-year existence, and those who have discovered it since, as the quintessential fantasy magazine and one of the most memorable runs of any American fiction magazine. It is certainly possible that without it Theodore Sturgeon would not have had his career, and we would not have his stories, any of them. In a 1946 letter to his mother (March 25) he described it as *the most remarkable fantasy magazine ever published—pure Dunsany, Eddison, Wells and sometimes even Cabell-style stuff. Believe me: fifty years from now some bright young anthologist will unearth the files of* Unk., *and make the contemporary literary lights look to their laurels. There has never been a magazine quite like it. I hope I live to see its counterpart, but that's asking an awful lot.*

The original magazine blurb (run in large type under the title at the beginning of the story; presumably written by John Campbell) read as follows: HE WAS MOST EXCESSIVELY UGLY, AND HAD QUEER IDEAS AS TO HOW TO DEAL WITH TRUTH—BUT HE HAD POWER! There was also a blurb in the table of contents at the beginning of the magazine: IT ISN'T A GOOD IDEA TO TELL NOTHING BUT THE TRUTH—BUT A GOD MIGHT MAKE WHAT YOU TELL BE TRUE!

(The Joe Mancinelli character, with his broken English, is presumably a backhanded tribute to Achille Tronti, an Italian seaman whom Sturgeon lived with in Hell's Kitchen in New York City at various times in 1938 and 1939. TS to his mother, March 10, 1938: *He says that anytime I come ashore in New York, let him know and "To my amenies I give not wan cop water, bot to you who is my fran' to de 'eart is my 'ouse your 'ouse, my bread your bread, do you want it my pents your pents."*)

"Fit for a King": syndicated by McClure, June 10, 1939. Sturgeon did not know when he wrote this that he would be managing a hotel himself in two years. The paragraphs about what a man will endure (overwork, unjust treatment) when he's saving up to marry that special girl are a cute touch, not only a love note to Dorothe but a silent protest aimed at McClure and all the publishers rejecting his stuff.

"Ex-Bachelor Extract": syndicated by McClure, June 17, 1939. TS to David Hartwell, 1972, in response to a question about the syndicated short-short stories: *Some of them were kind of cute. A lot of them were boy-meets-girl type things, some of them were stories I wrote from . . . like, somebody once told me about the old sailing skipper, with this huge storm coming up, and his mate says to him, "Captain, you'd better shorten sail!" And the captain says, "If the Lord wants me to shorten sail, he'll blow some off!" And take off and write a story about that, that kind of situation. And about the girl who catches her man by, there's something so compelling about her and he never can figure out what it is, and the gimmick is that in the lobes of her ears and the crooks of her elbows and a little bit on her breastbone she's putting extract of vanilla instead of . . . and every time he gets near her he thinks about cookies and yellow curtains in the kitchen and so on. And she nails him that way. There's all kinds of gimmicks like that that I would use. Short-shorts are a very difficult form to write, and it always takes off from some little concept like that.* (This particular gimmick was apparently suggested by TS's mother, or perhaps borrowed from a story of hers.)

"East Is East": syndicated by McClure, June 24, 1939.

"Three People": unpublished. Written late May 1939, clearly aimed at McClure's Fourth of July slot, but rejected. An excerpt from a letter from TS's brother Peter to their mother, November 21, 1929 (Ted was 11, Peter 13) offers some background: "Ted and I went out Saturday last week with Romeo Wagner, alias Waggy, alias Bunky Hill, or just 'Bunky.' We went up back and rang doorbells, which we had done almost every week before. We went up to our favorite doorbell and as it was Wagner's turn he went up on the porch and—a man steps out of a dark corner and collars him! Ted and I did three blocks in five seconds in different directions. We met in an alley. So we march up and deliver ourselves to the man. 'I did it too, Sir,' I said, and he grabs me and Ted. 'You're going to the police station!' he said. Bunky starts crying, Ted halfway, and I was self-possessed (externally). He said 'You kids have been *terrorizing* the neighborhood for weeks, what's the idea?' Bunky bawled to let us go, Ted argued and I reasoned. Then he said, 'Well, since it's your first capture—but if you are ever in this neighborhood again I'll—' We have never been on that street since!"

"Eyes of Blue": syndicated by McClure, July 1, 1939. Do all these stories of slumming rich girls falling for forceful guys who turn out to be of the proper class after all tell us something about young TS's psyche, or his values, or just about his sense of what would sell?

"Ether Breather": first published in *Astounding Science-Fiction*, September 1939, as "The Ether Breather." The title was streamlined when the story appeared in Sturgeon's first book, the story collection *Without Sorcery* (Prime Press, 1948). Sturgeon's notes on the story in that book read as follows:

Science-fiction sneers at science: A television 'mirror,' non-reversing, was a great crowd-catcher at Radio City this year (1948). Science sneers at science-fiction: Color television is already a commercial reality!

"Ether Breather" was my first science-fiction story. It might be of interest to remark here that the scanning-disc set, mentioned here in sneering terms, was, at the time of writing, the only widely-used method of video-transmission, while the iconoscope was a laboratory locus for the wishful thinking of ambitious electronicians.

TS to Dorothe, May 31, 1939: *McClure's turned down "Three People." Bloomfield turned down "Salty Peanut." The News turned down "Police Escort." I had a fight with Hatch. He's been following me around and I got sick of it. Two days ago I tore off six thousand words and submitted it to Campbell. It's called "Ether Breather" and he may like it. Pray for it. Now I'm writing again, and well, but I don't know ... it's a kind of writing I haven't done before; it's writing because I have to write, because there are stories within me that have to be told but which cannot be slanted at any market, because they are as they are. I must write them before I can clear my mind for more pen-prostitution ... If Campbell doesn't take that story I'm going to get a ship. I'll stay on her three months and then I'll marry you and the hell with the consequences.*

TS to his mother, November 11, 1939: *Thanx for the plot; I might be able to use it, tho war stuff is definitely not selling over here; escape is in demand. The Austrian refugee makes it a war story, however, there are possibilities ... what I need in the way of plots just now is sheer fantasy. That and science-fiction seems to be my forte. "Ether Breather," which comes to you under separate cover, is truly a masterpiece, tho I do say so as shouldn't. It took first place in that issue's pop. poll, and was cited in an article on the subject by Henry Kuttner, one of the old-timers in stf., in his article in* Writer's Digest. *Read the copy of* Unknown *I'm sending; it'll give you an idea of the sort of stuff I write.*

The "pop. poll" was an *Astounding* feature called "The Analytical Laboratory": readers of the magazine would rank the stories in each issue and the compiled results were printed a few issues later. It was considered a strong indicator of reader preferences; often the longest stories or serials had the strong advantage, so it was all the more remarkable that Sturgeon's debut story received first place ... and then went on to be the readers' favorite story of the year in the year-end poll. "Ether Breather" was not a particularly well-remembered story in the science fiction field even a few years later—most readers and anthologists agreed that there were many far better stories in *Astounding* at that time—but something about it clearly made a huge impact on readers when it first appeared.

Note that there was no television industry when the story was written. The hack writer who narrates the story is named Ted Hamilton, TS's first and middle names; he has a friend he went to high school with named Dorothe. (TS's fiancee changed her name to Dorothe from Dorothy shortly after they met, in high school, because with the change the name becomes a near-anagram for "Theodore.")

The original story-blurbs: (table of contents) VERY FRIENDLY, SLIGHTLY CHILDLIKE—AND EASILY OFFENDED. BUT THEY PLAIN RAISED BLAZES WITH THE TELEVISION SYSTEM! And at the start of the story: THEY MERELY MEANT TO AMUSE—BUT THEY CONSTITUTED THE WEIRDEST STATIC IN HISTORY!

"Her Choice": syndicated by McClure, July 8, 1939. This was originally called "The Fourth," and was another attempt to write a Fourth of July story. TS to Dorothe, June 13, 1939. *"The Fourth," though superior as a plotted little story, lacked the patriotic motif preferred by the jelly-bellied flag-flappers. It was deferred, with minor changes fitting it for any ol' occasion, in favor of a juicy piece of lousiness by some woman who wrote a little number about a Bohemian mother who made a hideous sofa-cushion with the Stars & Stripes embroidered thereon. .. Do tell me what you thought of the stories* [clippings that he sent]. *I know that some of them are lousy; and I welcome any and all comments.*

"Cajun Providence": syndicated by McClure, July 15, 1939. For two very different TS assessments of this piece, see his comments under "One Sick Kid" and "Strike Three."

"Strike Three": unpublished. Written June 1939. TS to Dorothe, June 25, 1939: *The other gentle little kick in the teeth I got* [the first was rereading a story he'd had high hopes for and discovering it was worthless] *was from McClure's, by their giving me their first rejection in nine weeks— with vitriolic comments, by the way. Psychologically they are sound in doing it—it's a more or less disciplinary measure. They don't like any author selling them too often. They have the idea that if they buy too often from one source, then said source is probably going to dry up on them, or at least drop in quality. As far as the author's cockiness is concerned, they are right—one can't sell consistently without inserting, after a while, a slapdash element into one's work. But what burns me is that they count manuscripts to determine when an author's streak has lasted long enough, rather than consulting the mss themselves to determine whether the writer is suffering yet from literary declinitis, if I may coin a disease. Two weeks ago I sold them "Cajun Providence," which was as hackneyed a piece of tripe as ever passed through this mill. "Strike Three," which they rejected last week, was every bit as good as "Ex-Bachelor Extract" and "Her Choice." I never thought they'd take the "Cajun" number; and I never dreamed they'd reject "Strike Three." It only goes, again, to show you ... you know, the last time they disciplined me thataway (it was in February, right after I sold the "Seaman") I got seventeen consecutive rejects from them. It's a lousy outfit, and I'm sick of their pickiness and their low wordage rates, but what can I do? It's the one outfit on which I can count for a steady income. I've been getting five per from them alone for going on three months. But after July 15, due to this business, there'll be no more for at least three weeks unless I can sell some other market this week. Nice, hey?*

As far as McClure's is concerned, I can, I am sure, break their jinx. The contact lens notion is brilliant, and I had, as you know, planned to give it to Nannine Joseph [an agent] *for Collier's. But I will have to give them a minor masterpiece if I want to resume my steady sales—I found that out by previous experience. After I sold the "Seaman," you see, I*

considered myself well established, and began submitting inferior sto-
ries—coasting as far as that outlet was concerned, and saving my ener-
gies for longer work. You know what happened. This time I'm going to
break the jinx and break it well—I've got to. I hate to hand them a poten-
tial $250 worth of story for a lousy fin, but right now McClure's is eas-
ily worth it to me. Their best point is their speed—I can submit a story
any time and know about it within 24 hours. If I went ahead with that
plan I had for Joseph, it would be at least three months before I got my
check—if any. Impasse—almost. The only way out is to re-establish
myself with McClure's, and fast.

The comments from McClure are handwritten on a printed rejection
form, postmarked June 21, 1939: "How do you get that way? Where's
the action, reader interest, surprise ending, originality? Otherwise, it's
ok."

Sturgeon spent a lot of time in his high school days writing sonnets
and giving them to girls; it's possible this piece is directly autobiograph-
ical.

"Contact!": syndicated by McClure, August 5, 1939. See comment under
"Strike Three." The idea for this story was provided by Dorothe.

"The Call": syndicated by McClure, August 19, 1939.

"Helix the Cat": first published in *Astounding, the John W. Campbell*
Memorial Anthology, edited by Harry Harrison, Random House, 1973.
Written July 1939.

This is the text of TS's introduction to the story, from the Harrison
volume:

There are times when one wonders, about one's own life and affairs,
"Who writes this plot?"

Over here is your editor, assiduously trying to round up original sto-
ries for what amounts to being a final issue of the olden, golden Astound-
ing Stories. *Back in the dim past is a story I wrote called "Helix the Cat,"*
which John Campbell had seen and rejected, not because he didn't like
it, but because it fell too exactly between ASF *and his fantasy magazine*
Unknown. *I do not remember writing the story, but to reason from the*
return address on the manuscript (Seaman's Church Institute, New York)
it must have been written while I was at sea as a teen-aged ordinary sea-
man, in 1938 or 1939, picking up my mail there whenever I was in port.

In 1940 I got married and moved to Staten Island, renting the second floor of a little house in West New Brighton. The landlady was a nice quiet mind-her-own-business kind of person; I remember her particularly for the time when my wife was in the hospital for our first baby, and I proudly showed her the bassinet I had built. She went right to work with her sewing machine and covered it for me in pink sateen and dotted swiss, complete with a canopy; it was so beautiful my wife cried when she saw it.

We went off then to run a hotel in the West Indies, and the war broke out while we were there, and all our stuff was put in storage. But a few things remained in the attic, and life went on, and we all lost track of one another. Then, just about the time your editor was beginning to gig the "Golden Age" writers for originals, this same Mrs. Myers, from Staten Island and more than thirty years back, wrote to my agent that she had a box of old papers of mine and did I want them. Want them I did, and in the box was "Helix the Cat."

The temptation to edit and rewrite and undate and polish has been enormous, but after torturous consideration I have decided to give you what John Campbell read—and liked, and didn't buy—so you can share for a moment his eyes and his reaction. For me, it has brought him back for a moment. It may for you, too.

"Helix" was apparently written just before Sturgeon went to sea for the first time in almost seven months. (The "Seaman's Church" address was one he consistently used on his manuscripts when he was in New York as well as while he was at sea; it was a convenient maildrop.) On August 28, 1939, while at sea, he wrote his mother: *Sure my cat has a name. Monkeyface, not because of its originality, but because of the delightful way Achille* [his Italian roommate] *says it. My really pet cat is "Helix," the spiral-tail egocentric of my* Unknown *novelette, whose fate is still undecided. There's $110 in that, by the way.* In this letter to his mother, and in another to Dorothe August 16, he makes it clear that he has done no writing at all aboard ship, where he has been since late in July. However, Sam Moskowitz in his book *Seekers of Tomorrow,* working from his notes of a 1961 interview with Sturgeon, writes, "It was while trying to find a ship out of a Texas port that Sturgeon made a deal with a small-town politician who owned a general store to write his campaign speeches for him. In payment, Sturgeon received day-old cupcakes, literally all that stood between him and starvation at the time. The politician won the election. Sturgeon did write one science fiction story at this time, 'Helix the Cat,' about a scientist and his cat, but the story was never sold and the manuscript has been misplaced." (No doubt the speech-writing incident happened, but not in August 1939, and not in conjunction with the writing of "Helix.")

After selling Campbell "A God in a Garden" in late April and "Ether Breather" at the end of May, Sturgeon struck out with "Helix" and with another story, written in June, called "Guy's Eye." On June 25, he wrote Dorothe, *"Guy's Eye," although as good as anything I have written, is not as admirably suited for Campbell as the other two—not by a long shot. If he buys it, I'll be lucky as hell. If he doesn't, there is no other market—nobody else will. That's the main trouble in writing for that kind of a market.* Later in the letter he reports, *Owah! I'm in a terrific slump, darling ... the same kind I was in just before I wrote "Ether Breather" ... I fear the handwriting on the wall ... If "Guy's Eye" comes back it's a ship for mine ... dammit, I have a thousand and one swell ideas and no way of putting them over ... If I don't turn in something sensational by Tuesday to McClure I might as well forget to eat for the next month or so ... dammit again, why does this have to happen to me at a time like this? ... Oh for a break—just one teensy weensy break ... enough of this nonsense. Please do what you can in the various ways I've suggested—especially in prayer and concentration toward Campbell ... dammit dammit DAMMIT....*

June 30: *You were wrong; the prayers, tho appreciated, had little affect on Campbell. "Guy's Eye" came back. J.C. wrote a very nice little note, which doesn't put any money in my pocket. It'll go out again Monday to one of the Thrilling group. McClure's bought "Contact!" as I knew they would. I was sorry to see it go... My weekly releases and chex will continue, by the way, until July 15. After that—well, I'll most likely go in hock. If I'm still in New York.*

In his August 28 letter to his mother, TS says, *After making a very comfortable amount of cash in the writing racket I went into a slump—the first of any real consequence. I guess you know what it is; you can't get a decent plot to save your soul, and when you do you can't write it; it won't jell.*

The title "Helix the Cat" has a bit of personal significance: the creator of the very popular cartoon "Felix the Cat," Pat Sullivan, was a friend of Sturgeon's mother when she was doing public relations work in New York in the 1920s, and it was through that friendship that she acquired her nickname, "Felix."

"To Shorten Sail": syndicated by McClure, September 9, 1939. See comment under "Ex-Bachelor Extract." TS to Dorothe, July 18, 1939: *Wrote, delivered and sold a story to McClure's today, just like that ... a nice little number about a yacht race ... had a swell time doing it too ... the editor and the big boss were both out, and the secretary and the bookkeeper and I had a two-hour gabfest in the offices ... most hilarious, with the radio just a-jammin' away ... nice way to run a staid and conservative old newspaper syndicate ... found out, incidentally, what they get for my stories. A paper subscribes for six stories a week at about $2.50 ... you can see how many times they must sell them to make a profit, since it costs them nearly a hundred a week ... also why they can't pay any more than they do...*

"Thanksgiving Again": unpublished. Sturgeon received the following rejection letter from McClure, dated July 28, 1939:

> Dear Mr. Sturgeon:
>   We are glad to accept "... TO SHORTEN SAIL ..." but we are frightfully disappointed in THANKSGIVING AGAIN. To both of us, it seems to lack entirely any of the real Thanksgiving spirit and atmosphere. It is just another love story that might do for any ordinary day, and not a very good one at that.
>   Don't bother about it any more unless you think you can sell it to another market. It just is not our idea of a story for that particular holiday. No doubt you can sell it—and we hope so. Sorry you had to spend so much time on it.
>   THE CALL has been scheduled for August 19th.
>   With warm good wishes,
>   Sincerely,
>   A.P. Waldo, Fiction Editor

Sturgeon did apparently try other markets, unsuccessfully. In a letter to his mother, November 11, 1939, he complained that President Roosevelt had changed the date of Thanksgiving, spoiling the gimmick of the story, that there are 52 days between Canadian Thanksgiving and the U.S. holiday: *Brilliant notion, but Franky made it 45 days, so* Collier's *tossed the yarn, worth $650.*

Reading the story, I'm not surprised at Sturgeon's inability to sell to "the slicks" (the high-paying fiction markets) at this time. Like many another first-rate writer, when he tried to prostitute himself he ended up with flat, uninteresting (uninspired) material. The craftsmanship he sometimes boasted of in his letters to his mother is not in evidence here. The high literary quality of his later work makes one think that his rejection by mainstream publishers and his need to take refuge in the science fiction world must have been due to prejudice and ignorance on the part of those publishers; but perhaps it was also due to a tendency, for whatever reason (resentment of and discomfort with formula seems one likely factor), to put his worst foot forward.

The big surprise in the story is the early appearance of the poem "Thunder and Roses," which plays a central role in his well-known 1947 story of the same name.

"Bianca's Hands": First published in *Argosy* (U.K.), May 1947. Probably written between May and July, 1939.

This is Sturgeon's first major work, and the mystery of its vast stylistic superiority to almost everything else he wrote at the time makes it worthwhile to take a close look at the available evidence as to when it was written and how much revised. First, the basic history of the story. Sam Moskowitz gives this account (based on his 1961 interview with Sturgeon) in his book *Seekers of Tomorrow*:

"While trying to write more stories for Campbell [after "A God in A Garden"] Sturgeon found himself persistently distracted by a bizarre notion that kept creeping into his thoughts. Unable to continue with his regular work until he disposed of it, he interrupted the story he was working on and in four hours wrote 'Bianca's Hands.'

"... Through the years, Sturgeon had tried to sell the nightmarish 'Bianca's Hands,' which he had written compulsively when he was 21. Agents, editors, friends were horrified by the concept. An editor told him he would never buy from an author whose mind could conceive notions like that. An agent told him he didn't want to be associated with an author whose bent carried him in such directions. Every magazine it was submitted to rejected it.

"Impelled by his recent good fortune in selling to new markets, Sturgeon mailed the story to the British *Argosy*, through which a prize of $1,000 was being offered for the best short story submitted before a certain date.

"It won the prize—Graham Greene took second place—and was published in *Argosy* for May, 1947. More than just money was involved here.

The various ups and downs of his literary career had severely shaken Sturgeon's estimate of himself. One of the most accomplished stylists in the field, he still doubted whether he could actually write well enough to be a sustained success at writing. The bull's-eye scored by this story, written at a very early stage in his career, convinced him that he had always possessed the qualifications to be a good writer. His work immediately began to reflect his new confidence."

In a 1983 interview with the Science Fiction Radio Show, Sturgeon recalled: *When I first started to write I was in New York and I needed money badly and I went to see an editor. He gave me an assignment for a sports story, and I've never been a sports addict. It had to do with basketball; I didn't know basketball at all, but he had given me the assignment and I was going to get my forty dollars, which is what they paid in those days. I was hard at work at it and the idea for "Bianca's Hands" came in slant-wise and I said, in effect, "Go away, I'm busy." But the idea came back again. I finally said, "Oh, all right," and I wrote it in about three hours, that's all, just to get it out of my way. Then I finished the sports story, which I sold, eventually. I put that manuscript in my bottom drawer. I knew I had a very unusual story here and I kept it like one of the family jewels. In about three years I got hungry enough to say, "Well, I've got to sell the family jewels," but I found to my amazement I couldn't give the story away.*

Sturgeon repeated in this interview the story about an editor and an agent who reacted to the story with extreme revulsion. In the introduction to his 1964 collection *Sturgeon in Orbit*, he wrote, *Once I had an editor push a whole pile of manuscripts back at me: his lips were rage-white and he was trembling, and he said he would never buy a story from a man who wrote the likes of "Bianca's Hands."*

Moskowitz's account of the effect the *Argosy* prize had on Sturgeon is echoed in a letter TS wrote (but did not mail) to his ex-wife Dorothe on March 10, 1947, the day he got the cablegram from England saying he'd won the prize: *It's more than a thousand dollars. The curse is off me with it. My faith in its quality and in my own is restored, and I don't think that I shall ever again experience that mystic diffidence and childish astonishment when one of my stories sells or is anthologized. I know now why they do, and I'm proud of it, and I know how to use it.*

From the same letter: *I'll tell you about that story. I didn't want to write it because I knew it wouldn't sell. But I nearly starved because it kept getting between me and what else I tried to write. I set it down in sheer self defense. I kept it for a long time and finally submitted it because I was forced to—I needed money badly enough that I was willing to soil it by selling it. My preciosity took quite a blow by its definite rejection. It's bounced ever since.*

And then he tells a remarkable story of rewriting fifteen hundred words of "Bianca's Hands" from memory, in the West Indies where he was unable to write, on an evening (February 10, 1942) that was most traumatic to him for reasons he doesn't reveal, but that had to do with his relationship with his wife. He rewrote the story, without a copy of the manuscript, apparently to calm and distract himself. *I chose that because it was the story I loved the best. I got interested enough in it to forget the time ... After that, to try to write was to find myself all too vividly back in the verandah of HM-1. To try to write anything ... but to try to write "Bianca's Hands" was inconceivable.*

The first mention of "Bianca's Hands" that I have found in TS's surviving correspondence is in a June 16, 1939 letter to his mother: *Al Gellman was here night before last... In the course of the evening my unfinished symphony—"Bianca's Hands"—was brought out. It's a fragment, a mere beginning and a mood, which actually haunted me and wouldn't let me do anything else until I wrote it. It won't be finished for months, and I don't want it to be. I'm going to polish every syllable of it. I don't care how long it takes—it's mine, you see, and not for any market I ever heard of. Anyway, Al stopped his bluster long enough to read two or three paragraphs, suddenly began to read as if he was drinking a long draught of something strange, finished the six short pages and sat for ten minutes looking at me as if he had never seen me before. ... Never have I been so gratified, so sincerely complimented by anyone.*

June 25, 1939, to Dorothe: *As far as Joseph is concerned, I believe I have a solution which may get me farther along than any demonstration of my ability to "slant" my plots and change my style. It is "Bianca's Hands," still unfinished. That is really fine writing—the finest I have ever done—and when it's finished I am sure it will sell* Unknown. *But before it goes there I'm going to give it to Joseph. The story is really a magnificent work—the hell with false modesty. I know good writing when I see it. If Joseph can place it—if she does, it'll be somewhere where the editor is willing to depart completely from any known formula—I'll be in the money. If she can't, then Campbell will buy it. And Joseph will have found out that I really can write. But it'll take time. "Bianca's Hands" will* not *be rushed or forced. I don't care if it takes two years.*

July 18, 1939, to Dorothe: *That wasn't a bad suggestion about the "Hands" ... if it comes that way, I'll do it that way ... you must remember though that that yarn is the result of a haunt, and I must be haunted again to do any more ... and it has to be done the way the haunt dictates ... it may be days or years before it's finished, and who cares?*

In the summer of 1993 Noël Sturgeon and I found a cache of Theodore Sturgeon manuscripts and papers in the house where he once lived in Woodstock, New York. Among them was a manuscript of "Bianca's Hands." It is thirteen pages long, with a title page. The title page is on Sturgeon's 1946 letterhead, typed in a standard typeface. There is a typed notation, "(About 5000 words)", and the 5000 has been crossed out in pencil and 3500 written in, suggesting the manuscript was cut down after the page was typed.

The rest of the manuscript, except for the last three lines and an inserted replacement paragraph on page 11, is typed in the italic face Sturgeon used from 1937 to 1941. The first regular page has the notation "about 5000 words" in the upper left. In the upper right, below the name "Theodore Sturgeon," is a cut-out piece of paper with TS's 1946 address typed on it in standard type (it may date from 1945, since it includes the apartment number, which Sturgeon only used on correspondence when he was new to the apartment in fall 1945).

Behind the cut-out piece of paper are two addresses: the "Seamans Church Inst." which he used until the end of 1939, x-ed out, and below it a Staten Island address that was effective from August 1940 to June 1941. There is no evidence of editing on the manuscript except for the taped-on insert paragraph on page 11, which judging by the typeface is from 1945-46, and the ending—the last page is cut, two sheets taped together, and the bottom sheet has most of the last sentence of the story (beginning "but they hanged") in the new typeface. This and the pencilled-in "3500" suggest that the story was longer in its prewar form, perhaps quite a bit longer. An anomaly is that the last page is numbered "14" in italic, but there is no page 13, and no easy way a page 13 could have been cut out if the italic typewriter was not available, because we go from p. 12 to p. 14 in the middle of a sentence. My guess is that the last page was misnumbered by mistake—possibly in the process of retyping a new ending in 1939 or 1940.

This is not the manuscript of the finished story. There are minor (word choices, a few changed phrases, no actual changes of content) differences throughout between manuscript and published story. [I have not actually seen the May 1947 *Argosy*, but I believe the text of the story in the 1953 Sturgeon collection *E Pluribus Unicorn* is taken from the magazine version, possibly by way of the 1951 Groff Conklin anthology *In the Grip of Terror*, the story's first US publication.] Some of these may have been done by the copy editor at British *Argosy* (the store-owner's name was originally "Guttstardt"; the "man" who married them was a priest), but by the nature and quality of other changes it seems quite clear that Sturgeon retyped and improved the story himself before sending it to *Argosy*. (In the Science Fiction Radio Show interview he said: *A friend of mine wrote me from England and said there was a literary contest ... The deadline was New Year's Eve. Well, I got this letter Christmas Eve, so I dug this thing out of the trunk and ran it through the typewriter without changing anything and sent it off and it must have arrived within minutes of the deadline.* In the unsent letter to Dorothe he said: *I was in love last December—hurriedly, deeply in love, with an urgency that was new to me. I dragged out "Bianca's Hands" with a kind of defiance and sent it off. It must have arrived in London mere hours before that deadline. It did me good. I have written well since then—better than ever, notably in "Thunder and Roses" and "The Blue Letter," just because "Bianca's Hands" had been rewritten. I had no hopes for it, mind you. But I had achieved something great by rewriting it without flinching. Oddly enough, that love lasted just long enough for the purpose. And now, with no end of fine competition, in a high-quality market, it has walked off with the prize.*)

The manuscript with the multiple addresses and the 1939 letters quoted above suggest that "Bianca's Hands" was finished in its "5000 word" form after July 18, 1939 and before the end of that year, and that it was sent out, or more probably sent out again, in late 1940 or early 1941 in the same form. That the manuscript contains alterations in a new typeface suggests that some changes were made in 1945/1946, *after* the manuscript had been sent out at least once in that era (or the title page word count would have reflected the altered length to begin with). It may or may not have been sent out (again) in the altered form, but the cleanness of the alterations suggests it was.

We still don't know when the first part of the story was written (the reference to "six pages" in the June 16 letter gives support to the idea that the original burst of writing was incomplete, although they could well have been single-spaced pages—Sturgeon did use single-space on some of his first drafts from the period—containing most of the story as we know it). It could conceivably have been as early as spring 1938, when Sturgeon may have been doing some kind of writing-for-hire, although it's far more likely that it was during the first six months of 1939, quite possibly as late as May or even early June. The only reference in the 1939 correspondence to any kind of writing-for-hire is the February contract with McClure to rewrite other people's rejected short stories. But it is possible TS preferred not to talk about stray jobs like basketball articles or confession stories.

What seems more likely to me is that the "basketball story" is a red herring, and that much or most of "Bianca's Hands" was written on or about May 31, 1939, when TS wrote Dorothe the words quoted above under "Ether Breather": *Now I'm writing again, and well, but I don't know ... it's a kind of writing I haven't done before; it's writing because I have to write, because there are stories within me that have to be told but which cannot be slanted at any market, because they are as they are. I must write them before I can clear my mind for more pen-prostitution...*

Judith Merril, in an article entitled "Theodore Sturgeon" in *The Magazine of Fantasy and Science Fiction*, September 1962, recalls Sturgeon showing her the carbon copy of the "Bianca's Hands" manuscript at the beginning of 1947, while he was waiting to hear from *Argosy*. She didn't like it. "Ted, perhaps defensively, explained it had been written many years earlier, and that he had showed it to me for one section, just redone: several paragraphs of deliberately constructed poetry, highlighting an emotional crisis, but spelled out like prose, so that it did not appear to break into the narrative. And it was in pointing this out (I had missed it, as he expected) that he stopped, astonished, and said he had just realized how much he did know about how to write—that it was a skill, with him, not just a talent."

The replacement paragraph in the manuscript I've examined—the only part of the text that could really be described as "just redone"—is the paragraph that begins "He left them and returned to the shop," describing Ran's ecstatic afternoon in nature after his marriage and before the nuptial dinner. Apart from this, it seems reasonable to assume, on the evidence of the manuscript as well as Sturgeon's comments, that the entire story as we know it was written in 1939, with only slight changes afterward (and one possible major change: the discarding of a long section of text after the end of the story as we know it).

Theodore Sturgeon recorded "Bianca's Hands" on a 1976 album issued by Alternate World Recordings, entitled *STURGEON: Theodore Sturgeon Reads.* At one point he considered titling his first story collection *Bianca's Hands and Others,* but the story was left out of the collection because British *Argosy* wouldn't release U.K. rights.

"Derm Fool": First published in *Unknown,* March 1940. Written fall 1939. Sturgeon loved puns and verbal sight gags *(I found my slippers. My feet were still in them)* and clearly had a lot of fun with this story. The idea had come to him near the beginning of his summer dry spell, and apparently stayed around till he was ready to write it. June 30, 1939, to Dorothe: *I am teased by several notions for Campbell, who wants more whimsical stuff, like the "God," from me. Among them are: A man who sheds his skin like a snake; a man who captures a human soul in a little box; and an affliction whereby the face is turned into a pliable medium like putty. But none of them are crystallizing. I have been going over my rejects and by Wednesday of next week should have at least six stories out—among them, possibly, my grand oeuvre, "Bianca's Hands."*

The original blurbs: (table of contents) AFTER PEELING THE FINGERS OFF THE PIANO, AND THE HAND OFF THE BUREAU DRAWER, HE DECIDED TO LEAVE THE TORSO IN THE CLOSET ... And (start of story): IT WASN'T EXACTLY A DISEASE—BUT IT WAS ANNOYING TO HAVE TO COLLECT THE ARMS AND LEGS AND TORSOS EVERY DAY—

"He Shuttles": First published in *Unknown,* April 1940. Written fall 1939. In correspondence Sturgeon spoke with pride of having sold a "novelette," meaning a short story whose length qualified it to be thought of as something longer than a short story (but shorter than a novella, or short novel). He also identified "He Shuttles" as being a story of horror (as distinct from the whimsical stories he had previously sold to John Campbell).

Campbell thought enough of the story to herald it in "Of Things Beyond," a small column describing the lead stories for next month's magazine: "Theodore Sturgeon has a novelette in the April issue that is his own curious blend of the oppressive inevitableness of Greek tragedy and completely modern lightness. 'He Shuttles' is both an answer and a title. It's about a very, very clever man who had three wishes—just any three he wanted..."

"He Shuttles" is an early example of Sturgeon as author breaking the "fifth wall" to speak directly to the reader as writer rather than narrator. (Later, more striking examples are "The Perfect Host" and *Some of Your Blood*.)

Title page blurb: A VERY LOGICAL—AND VERY UNPLEASANT—LITTLE STORY BASED ON THE OLD FAIRY TALE. HE HAD THREE WISHES. HE WAS VERY CLEVER. HE WOULD ESCAPE ALL PENALTIES...

"Turkish Delight": syndicated by McClure, November 18, 1939. The Dodecanese are Greek islands in the Aegean Sea, off the southwest coast of Turkey, but Sturgeon's travels had not yet taken him outside the Western Hemisphere.

"Niobe": unpublished. This uncharacteristic piece is I believe the only unpublished work in this volume that is not from the trunk left behind in Staten Island. It was found among Sturgeon's papers in the house in Woodstock. (Clearly there were a number of unsold manuscripts that Sturgeon put in storage or brought with him when he left New York for the West Indies in June of 1941, including "Fluffy," "Cellmate," "The Heart," and "Bianca's Hands.") It can be dated by the original return address on the manuscript, "161 West 63rd St, New York, N. Y.", where Sturgeon lived from late December 1939 to mid-March 1940. It was his brother Peter's apartment, but there's no evidence TS used it as a mailing address except when he was living there. This address is crossed out on the manuscript and "209 Pelton Ave., West New Brighton, Staten Island, N.Y.C." typed below it, Sturgeon's address from approximately August 1940 to June 1941.

A hint of the origin of this story can be heard in Sturgeon's comment to David Hartwell in 1972, when asked what he was reading before he started to write: *I was reading H.G. Wells and Lord Dunsany, and the Pre-Raphaelites, whom I absolutely adored as a 13-, 14-year-old kid. I was so caught up in William Morris and the Rossettis, and Thomas De Quincey, and that was the whole area that I was most deeply soaked in. I loved that stuff, it was poetic and it was cadenced and it was full of color and it was—you know, the magic land of Somewhere Else.*

"Mahout": syndicated by McClure, January 22, 1940.

"The Long Arm": syndicated by McClure, February 5, 1940.

"The Man on the Steps": syndicated by McClure, February 22, 1940.

"Punctuational Advice": syndicated by McClure, February 29, 1940.

"Place of Honor": syndicated by McClure, March 18, 1940.

"The Ultimate Egoist": first published in *Unknown*, February 1941.
Probably written March 1940. Sturgeon wrote at least two introductions
to this story. The first accompanied its appearance in his first story collection, *Without Sorcery,* 1948:

The Messiah complex has been responsible for much unhappiness,
much friction, possibly a few great fortunes, and perhaps a messiah or
two...

This yarn sprang fully-armed from the rather low brow of a story by
a per se non-extant writer named Rene Lafayette. I hurled his story away
from me and leapt to the typewriter, finishing the opus in one sitting and
seven cups of coffee. Then I finished Rene's novelette. May it be immor-
tal. It was called "The Indigestible Triton."

It might be of interest to point out that even as "The Ultimate Ego-
ist" had its nascence in the work of a figmentary individual, its author is
also a figment. The original byline was E. Hunter Waldo.

This was indeed the first Sturgeon story to be published under a pseudonym. The impetus was that John Campbell, editor of *Astounding* and
Unknown, was buying Sturgeon stories faster than he could print them,
particularly when *Unknown* changed from a monthly to a bimonthly
format. With the help of the new pseudonym, two Sturgeon stories
appeared in the February 1941 *Unknown,* and two each in the June 1941
issues of *Astounding* and *Unknown.* Sturgeon was becoming a dominant
voice in the two most popular and influential magazines of (respectively)
science fiction and literary fantasy.

The pseudonym was partially based on Sturgeon's birth name, Edward
Hamilton Waldo. This name was legally changed when young Ted was
adopted by his stepfather William Sturgeon; unfortunately there was
some confusion about this when the publisher of *Without Sorcery* filled
out the copyright forms for that book, as a result of which (TS, 1972)
"Theodore Sturgeon" winds up as a pseudonym; and in libraries the
world over, if you look up Sturgeon you are referred to Waldo. And if
they don't happen to have that cross-filing then my books cannot be
found in library catalogs.

Ironically, "Rene Lafayette" was a pseudonym of a writer who was to become science fiction's most notorious example of the Messiah complex, L. Ron Hubbard. In a letter in the August 1941 issue of *Unknown*, Sturgeon says that "The Ultimate Egoist" was inspired by a line in "Lafayette"'s story *in which the hero, finding himself able to breathe underwater, wonders if he himself is a figment of his own imagination.*

The second Sturgeon introduction (or "rubric," a term he was fond of) to "The Ultimate Egoist" was written in 1979 for his collection *The Golden Helix:*

This is a very early one—one of the first I ever sold—and that must be very clear to the critical sophisticates among you. Yet there is a wonderful freshness about the ignorance of a beginning writer, who has yet to learn the fine points of plot and characterization, and the technicalities of "crisis" and "climax" and "denouement" and all that, and tumbles ahead, writing any damn thing that comes into his head.

This was fun to do. So much of what I have written may have been illuminating and instructive (especially to the author), but it wasn't joyful. This is.

On the assumption that Sturgeon read *Unknown* in those days almost as soon as the first copies arrived in Campbell's office, I'm dating the composition of "Egoist" as late February or early March. Sturgeon was about to be married. In a 1944 letter to his mother he describes his wife Dorothe as "a strawberry blonde, five two barefoot, with the proportions of a scant de Milo, green eyes which are really blue with a corona of yellow around the pupils..."

And in a 1947 letter (9/25) to his mother, he wrote, *A collection of my works is scheduled for next year. Tentative title:* Bianca's Hands and Others. *Any better suggestions? I'm willing to use any other of my titles but "The Ultimate Egoist." I think that's a little too close to home...*

Magazine blurb (title page): IT'S A BAD IDEA, PERHAPS, TO QUESTION TOO CLOSELY THE REALITY OF THE WORLD ABOUT YOU. MAYBE IT ISN'T—

"It": first published in *Unknown*, August 1940. Written March or April 1940. TS and Dorothe Fillingame were married March 17, 1940. Moskowitz reports, "In ten consecutive hours of inspiration, on their honeymoon, Sturgeon wrote the nightmarish masterpiece that created his first reputation, 'It'."

In the introduction to his collection *The Golden Helix* (1979), Sturgeon talks about his lifetime of writing stories:

Funny ones have been written with pressure and terror all around, strictly laugh-clown-laugh. Frightening ones have been written in peaks of joy. (The horridest horror story I ever wrote was done on my honeymoon. Catharsis works that way too.)

Sturgeon's introduction to "It" for *Without Sorcery* (1948):

I have been asked repeatedly how this story was written, or how one gets ideas like this, or what one has to be or go through to be able to write such a horror.

I can only answer that it wrote itself. It unfolded without any signal effort on my part from the first sentence. The names of the characters were taken off my ubiquitous coffee-maker. I was supremely happy as I wrote it—no twistings, no warpings, no depression. Possibly it was catharsis—in other words, I was feeling so good that I took what poisons were in me at the moment and got rid of them in one pure plash of putrescence. It was very easy to do and I wish I could do it again.

The note about the names of the characters explains why the name "Cory Drew" is also the name of the central character in a completely unrelated, untitled, unfinished story found in Sturgeon's papers that seems to date from earlier in 1940.

"It" was also included in the last Sturgeon collection published during his lifetime, *Alien Cargo* (1984). Sturgeon's introduction reads in part:

In 1975 I accepted an invitation to the San Diego Comic Convention, all expenses. I thought it was kind of them, but was mystified, for though I had written instructional comics just before this country entered WW II, and a couple of issues of something called Iron Monroe *[sic], derived from a John Campbell series back in the '30s, I had no track record in comics; nor was I a fan or collector. At the banquet, Ray Bradbury was giving out awards and uttering verbal bouquets about the recipients, in one case gracefully calling another writer 'teacher,' and I suddenly realized, with a sweet and shocking clutch of the gut, that he was talking about me. I rose to go up front and accept the award—it was the Convention's highest, the Golden Ink Pot, the same award they gave Siegel and Shuster for* Superman*—and for the first time in my life I faced an audience and couldn't think of anything to say beyond two words; one was 'thank' and the other was 'you.'*

Subsequently I learned for the very first time that my story "It" is seminal; that it is the great grandaddy of The Swamp Thing, The Hulk, The Man Thing, *and I don't know how many other celebrated graphics.*

(There was at least one comic book version of "It," published long after the original story had influenced comics writers and screenwriters of the 1950s and 1960s. It was adapted by Roy Thomas and drawn by Marie Severin and Frank Giacoia, and was published by Marvel Comics under the title *Supernatural Thrillers,* Vol. 1, No. 1, December 1972, "featuring IT! from the world-famous chiller by: Theodore Sturgeon.")

William F. Nolan in his 1968 anthology *3 to the Highest Power* quotes Sturgeon as saying to him, in a 1967 phone interview, *My first really successful story was "It," a horror tale set in the woods of my childhood.* Sturgeon lived on Staten Island for the first ten and a half years of his life, before moving to Philadelphia. There were certainly woods on Staten Island, and more of them in the 1920s than now, but probably the setting of the story also reflects Sturgeon's farm experiences, as described in his 1965 essay published (in 1993) as the pamphlet *Argyll:*

In 1931, '33, and '35 Mother and Argyll went to Europe for the summer. In '31 they boarded us on a farm in Vermont where they worked us like slaves. In '33 we worked on a farm in Bucks County [Pennsylvania]. Sturgeon speaks of the latter farm's owner as *an amazing guy, a White Russian prince, who could do anything with his hands. He rebuilt an absolutely ruined house and barn all by himself; I once watched him saw through a 12x12 with a handsaw without stopping; it took him an hour and forty minutes.*

Angelina and Tyler Counties are in eastern Texas, not far from Port Arthur, which Sturgeon frequented as a merchant seaman. I do not know where he and Dorothe went on their honeymoon.

The blurb on the title page of the story in *Unknown* read: IT WASN'T VICIOUS; IT WAS SIMPLY CURIOUS—AND VERY HORRIBLY DEADLY!

"Butyl and the Breather": first published in *Astounding Science-Fiction,* October 1940. Probably written spring 1940. This is one of the very few instances of Sturgeon writing a sequel to an earlier story, or a series. The only other example I can think of, other than the stories he wrote in order to expand "Baby Is Three" into *More than Human* (and the sequels he announced but never wrote, for "When You Care, When You Love" and "Tandy's Story"), is a pair of stories late in his career, "The Country of Afterward" (1979) and "The Trick" (1983). (In a December 1940 letter to his mother TS mentions that Campbell recently rejected a novelette he wrote, and says: *it was a sequel, and so can't be sold to any other rag.*

He doesn't say what story it was a sequel to.)

The blurb on the magazine title page read: THE ETHER BREATHERS RETIRED, AND THE PERFUME MAGNATE WANTED TO SMOKE 'EM OUT. HE DID. A REALLY GOOD PERFUMER OUT TO MAKE A FOUL ODOR CAN ACCOMPLISH MIRACLES!

Look About You!

A purple dog casts orange shade,
  A black moon hangs in a silver sky,
My arms bake white in the brown sunlight
  And I feel sounds with my eye.

Fish with feathers swarm the sea
  And convex caves build the liquid land;
Three great whales and a horse with scales
  Dance on the scarlet sand.

We each live in a wonderland;
  A blue to you is a red to me,
A shade is seen, and we call it green—
  I wonder what you see?

I know my world. It bores me so!
  And I must bear it until I die,
While your every day is a land of fey—
  And you're as bored as I!

Theodore Sturgeon

[First published in Unknown, *January 1940.]*

Books by Theodore Sturgeon

Without Sorcery (1948)
The Dreaming Jewels (1950)
More Than Human (1953)
E Pluribus Unicorn (1953)
Caviar (1955)
A Way Home (1955)
The King and Four Queens (1956)
I, Libertine (1956)
A Touch of Strange (1958)
The Cosmic Rape (1958)
Aliens 4 (1959)
Venus Plus X (1960)
Beyond (1960)
Some of Your Blood (1961)
Voyage to the Bottom of the Sea (1961)
The Player on the Other Side (1963)
Sturgeon in Orbit (1964)
Starshine (1966)
The Rare Breed (1966)
Sturgeon Is Alive and Well... (1971)
The Worlds of Theodore Sturgeon (1972)
Sturgeon's West (with Don Ward) (1973)
Case and the Dreamer (1974)
Visions and Venturers (1978)
Maturity (1979)
The Stars Are the Styx (1979)
The Golden Helix (1979)
Alien Cargo (1984)
Godbody (1986)
A Touch of Sturgeon (1987)
The [Widget], the [Wadget], and Boff (1989)
Argyll (1993)
The Ultimate Egoist (1994)